**Praise for the
Awakening Novels**

"A new voice in dark paranormal, Regan Hastings brings
sizzle and magic to the genre."
—*New York Times* bestselling author Christina Dodd

EVERYTHING

His touch opened up something inside her. The barest flicker of recognition deep within. The sense of familiarity was back and she knew, in her soul, that he was
telling her the truth. Maybe she would remember him,
eventually. But the question was, what exactly would she
recall? Was he to be trusted as he said? Or would her
memories tell her to stay as far away from the sexually
charged man as possible?

"No," she said softly, meeting that strange gray stare.
"I don't know you. I don't want to know you. I just want
to leave."

"And go where?" He slid his hands up until he was
cupping her cheeks in his big palms. She felt the overwhelming rush of heat slicing from his body into hers
and she nearly trembled at the force of it.

But she wasn't going to give in to something that made
zero sense to her. "That's none of your business."

"Everything about you is my business, Shea."

She sucked in a gulp of air and the fear she tasted was
dark and bitter. "What do you want from me?"

"Everything," he admitted, "and I will accept nothing
less."

VISIONS OF MAGIC

AN AWAKENING NOVEL

REGAN HASTINGS

A SIGNET ECLIPSE BOOK

SIGNET ECLIPSE
Published by New American Library, a division of
Penguin Group (USA) Inc., 375 Hudson Street,
New York, New York 10014, USA
Penguin Group (Canada), 90 Eglinton Avenue East, Suite 700, Toronto,
Ontario M4P 2Y3, Canada (a division of Pearson Penguin Canada Inc.)
Penguin Books Ltd., 80 Strand, London WC2R 0RL, England
Penguin Ireland, 25 St. Stephen's Green, Dublin 2,
Ireland (a division of Penguin Books Ltd.)
Penguin Group (Australia), 250 Camberwell Road, Camberwell, Victoria 3124,
Australia (a division of Pearson Australia Group Pty. Ltd.)
Penguin Books India Pvt. Ltd., 11 Community Centre, Panchsheel Park,
New Delhi - 110 017, India
Penguin Group (NZ), 67 Apollo Drive, Rosedale, North Shore 0632,
New Zealand (a division of Pearson New Zealand Ltd.)
Penguin Books (South Africa) (Pty.) Ltd., 24 Sturdee Avenue,
Rosebank, Johannesburg 2196, South Africa

Penguin Books Ltd., Registered Offices:
80 Strand, London WC2R 0RL, England

First published by Signet Eclipse, an imprint of New American Library,
a division of Penguin Group (USA) Inc.

First Printing, February 2011
10 9 8 7 6 5 4 3 2 1

Copyright © Maureen Child, 2011
All rights reserved

SIGNET ECLIPSE and logo are trademarks of Penguin Group (USA) Inc.

Printed in the United States of America

To Mark, because in one way or another, all of the books are for you.

ACKNOWLEDGMENTS

There are a lot of people I'd love to mention here, but then the acknowledgment page would be as long as the book....But some names must be named.

To my husband and family, a huge thank-you for putting up with me when I'm on deadline and for always believing.

Great friends Susan Mallery, Kate Carlisle, Christine Rimmer and Teresa Southwick—as a plot group, you're all amazing. As friends, you're all irreplaceable. Thanks so much for keeping me on track....

Thank you to the practicing Wiccans I spoke to during my research. I appreciate all of your time and advice. And thanks for understanding that a fiction writer takes the facts and then spins them the way she wants them to be for her story.

Many thanks to my agent, Donna Bagdasarian, who loved this story and pushed me to make it even bigger—then went out and fought for it.

And a big thank-you to Kerry Donovan, my editor, who helped make this book the best it could be, by asking all the right questions. To Claire Zion and everyone at NAL for all their hard work and their belief in this series. And to the art depertment for the amazing cover—thank you all.

Prologue

After she had waited for centuries, Torin's patience was long dead. The woman he craved was, at last, almost his. For hundreds of years, he'd wandered the far reaches of the globe, a shadow in his woman's life, always alert for signs of the magic stirring. Now that the long-anticipated moment had come, to have the Awakening strike on a tidy suburban street in Long Beach, California, seemed almost a joke. One he didn't find amusing.

Across the street from him, a bell rang and hundreds of schoolchildren spilled from a pale green stucco building like ants from a hill. Their bright laughter sounded sharp to a man already on a razor's edge. His gray eyes narrowed behind his dark glasses as he watched the kids scatter in the sunlight. The last barrier between him and his woman had fallen. His skin felt electrified with the rising of power in the air. His blood hummed and if he'd had a heartbeat, it would have been thundering in his chest.

A woman hurried past him to gather up her child and gave him a quick, appraising glance. Her steps quickened, her gaze shifted from him and she rushed her child away as if they were being chased by demons.

He knew what people saw when they looked at him. Taller than most men, he had long, dark hair that fell loose to his shoulders. He wore a black T-shirt that clung to the hard muscles of his chest and abs. His black jeans and scuffed shit-kicker boots finished off the dangerous image. His face was lean and hard, sculpted with sharp planes and angles and his pale gray eyes gave away none of his thoughts.

He looked exactly what he was.

A warrior.

A killer.

An Eternal whose second chance had finally arrived—and this time he would not be denied.

Chapter 1

"They took my mom away last night."

Shea Jameson wanted to lock her classroom door and walk away. It was the only sane thing to do. But the tremor in her student's voice pulled at her. The day was over at Lincoln Middle School and the hallways should have been emptied. Shea knew because she always waited until everyone else had left the building before she headed home. She made it a point to avoid crowds whenever she could. As a teacher, she was faced with classes filled with kids every day, but they didn't bother her. It was the parents of those children that worried her.

She looked down at Amanda Hall and sympathy rose up inside her. Shea had heard the rumors, the whispers. She'd watched as the teachers had reluctantly protected Amanda from those who only yesterday had been her friends. And she knew that the girl's situation was only going to get worse.

"Ms. Jameson, I don't know what to do."

Her heart broke for the petite blond girl leaning against a row of closed lockers in the empty, quiet school hallway. The child's face was streaked with tears, her blue eyes swimming with them. Her arms were crossed over her middle, as if she was trying to console herself, and when she looked up at Shea, stark misery and panic were stamped on her small features.

She wouldn't be able to turn her back on the girl, despite the risks, Shea thought with an inner sigh. How could she and still live with herself?

"I'm so sorry, Amanda." She glanced over her shoulder to be sure there was no one near. Not a soul was around, though, and the silence, but for Amanda's soft sniffling, was deafening. The beige walls were decorated with posters announcing the coming Fall Festival and Shea's gaze slid away from the drawings of cackling wart-encrusted witches burning at stakes.

The small hairs at the back of her neck stood straight up and she could have sworn that there was someone close by, watching her. A shiver of something icy slid along Shea's spine, but the halls were still empty. For now.

She shouldn't have stopped, a voice in her mind whispered. Shouldn't have spoken to the girl. No one knew better than Shea that there were spies everywhere. That no one was safe anymore. If someone should see her talking to this child now, her own personal nightmarish circus would begin again, and there was no guarantee that this time Shea would survive it.

But how could she walk away from a child in desperate need? Especially when she knew exactly what Amanda was going through? Shifting her books and papers in her arms, Shea dropped her free hand to the girl's shoulder and tried to think of something comforting to say. But lies wouldn't do her any good and the truth was far too terrifying.

If Amanda's mother had really been taken, she wouldn't be coming back. In fact, it was probably only a matter of time before the authorities came to snatch up Amanda as well. And that realization pushed her to speak.

"Amanda," Shea asked quietly, "do you have anyone you can stay with?"

The girl nodded. "My grandma. The police took me there last night. Grandma didn't want me to come to school today, but I did anyway and everyone's being so mean . . ." She shook her head and frowned in spite of her tears. A flash of anger dazzled her damp eyes. "My mom's not evil. I don't care what they say. She didn't do anything wrong. I would know."

Shea wasn't so sure of that. These days, secrets were all that kept some women alive. But even if Amanda was right and her mother was innocent, there was little chance she'd be released. Still, what was important now was Amanda's safety. The girl had already learned one harsh lesson today—*don't trust anyone.* Her friends had turned on her and soon everyone else would, too. Once word got out about her mother being taken, the girl would be in danger from so many different directions, she'd never find shelter.

"Amanda," Shea whispered fiercely, "don't come back to school tomorrow. Go to your grandmother's and stay there."

"But I have to help my mom," the girl argued. "I thought you could go with me to the principal and we could tell her that my mom's not what they think. Mom's the president of the PTA!"

Shea winced as the girl's voice rose. She couldn't afford for anyone to see them. Couldn't risk being seen helping the child of a detainee. Leaning down, she caught Amanda's eye and said, "Your mom would want you to be safe, wouldn't she?"

"Yeah . . ."

"Then that's the best thing you can do for her."

"I don't know . . ."

"Amanda, listen to me," Shea said, her words coming faster now as the creeping sensation of being watched flooded back into her system. "There's nothing we can do to help your mom right now. The best thing for everyone is for you to leave here and go straight to your grandmother's. Okay? No stops. No talking to anyone."

"But—"

A door opened down the hall and Shea glanced toward the sound. Her stomach pitched with nerves as she spotted the school principal coming out of her office. Lindsay Talbot's eyes narrowed as she noticed Amanda and Shea huddled together, speaking in whispers. Instantly Ms. Talbot darted back into her office.

"Just go, Amanda," she said, giving the girl's shoulder a quick squeeze. "Go now."

The girl picked up on the urgency in Shea's voice, nodded briefly, then turned and ran down the hall toward the back door. Once she was gone, Shea took a deep breath, steeled herself and walked in the opposite direction. Her heels clicked on the tile floor as she neared the glass wall of the school's office. The front door was only a few feet away and the sunlit afternoon shone like a beacon of safety. She was leaving, no matter what, she thought, but she had to know what Ms. Talbot was doing.

Shea glanced through the office windows in time to see the principal hang up the phone. Then the woman turned around, met Shea's gaze and gave her a cat-about-to-eat-a-canary smile.

Just like that, she knew it was over.

All of it.

Shea had been happy here. For a while. She enjoyed spending her days with the kids. She had convinced herself over the last year and a half that she'd finally found safety. That her normal behavior, her gift for teaching, was enough to prove to everyone that she was nothing more than she claimed to be. A sixth-grade science teacher.

But as she met Lindsay Talbot's harsh stare, she felt the old familiar stir of panic. Fear rushed through her, churning her stomach, making her hands damp and drying out her mouth. She had to run.

Again.

She let her papers fall to the floor in a soft rustle of sound, then tightened her grip on her shoulder bag and raced for the front door. As her hand pushed the cold steel bar, she heard Lindsay Talbot call out behind her, "You won't get away. They're coming."

"I know," Shea murmured, but she ran anyway. What else could she do? If she stayed, she would end up with Amanda's mother. Just one more woman locked away with no hope of ever getting out.

Outside, she squinted at the beam of sunlight that slanted into her eyes, and took the steps down to the sidewalk at a dead run. She dug into her purse as she turned toward the parking lot, blindly fumbling for her keys. Her only hope was to be gone before the MPs arrived. It would take them time to find her and in that time she would disappear. She'd done it before and she could do it again. Dye her hair, change her name, find a new identity and lose herself in some other city.

She wouldn't go back to her apartment. They'd be expecting her to, but she wasn't that stupid. Besides, she didn't need anything from her home. She traveled light these days. A woman constantly on the move couldn't afford to drag mementos from one place to the next. Instead, she kept a packed suitcase in her car trunk and a stash of emergency cash tucked into her bra at all times, on the off chance that she'd have to leave in a hurry.

A cold wind rushed at her, pulling her long hair free of the knot she kept it in. Slate gray clouds rolled in off the ocean and seagulls wheeled and dipped overhead. She hardly noticed. Parents were still milling around out front, picking up their kids, but Shea ran past them all, ignoring those who spoke to her.

Her car was at the far end of the parking lot, closest

to the back exit. She was always prepared to run—to slip away while her pursuers were coming in the front. She was sprinting now, her heart hammering in her chest, breath rattling in her lungs. She held her keys so tightly the jagged edges dug into her palm.

The soles of her shoes slid unsteadily on the gravel-laced asphalt, but she kept moving. One thought pulsed through her mind. *Run. Run and don't look back.*

Her gaze fixed on her nondescript beige two-door compact, she never saw the man who leapt out at her from behind another car. He pushed her down and her knees hit the asphalt with a grinding slide that tore open her skin and sent pain shooting along her legs.

His hands reached for her as a deep voice muttered, "Gimme the purse and you can go."

Absently, she heard voices rising in the distance as parents saw the man attacking her. *Oh, God, not now,* she thought as she turned over and stared up into the wild eyes of a junkie who desperately needed money. She couldn't deal with this now. There was too much attention on her.

He pulled a knife as if he sensed she was hesitating. "Give me the money *now*."

Shea shook her head, and when he reached for her again, she instinctively lifted both hands as if to push him off and away. But she never made contact with him. She didn't need to. A surge of energy suddenly pulsed through her and shot from her fingertips. As a *whoosh* of sound erupted, the man in front of her erupted into flames.

Shea stared up at him, horrified by what was happening. By what she'd *done*. His screams tore through the air as he tried to run from the fire. But it only fed the flames consuming him and as his shrieks rose higher and higher, Shea staggered to her feet, glanced down at her hands and shuddered.

That was when she heard it.

The chanting.

Over the sounds of the dying man's cries, voices roared together, getting louder and louder as she was surrounded. One word thundered out around her, hammering at her mind and soul, reducing her to a terror she hadn't known in ten years.

She looked up into the faces of her students' parents as they circled her. People she knew. People she liked. Now, though, she hardly recognized them. Their features were twisted into masks of hatred and panic and their voices joined together to shout their accusation.

"Witch! Witch! Witch!"

Shea fought for air as the mob tightened around her. There was no way out now. She was going to die. And if the crowd didn't kill her, then the MPs would take her away when they arrived and she would be as good as dead anyway. It was over. The years of terror and dread, the hiding, the praying, the constant worrying about survival.

"Stop!" she shouted, her voice raw with horror at what she'd done. At what they were about to do to her. "I didn't do anything!"

A useless argument, since they'd all seen what had happened. But how? How had she done it? She wasn't a witch. She was just . . . her. "If I had power, wouldn't I be using it now?"

Some of the people around her seemed to consider that and their expressions reflected worry. It was not what Shea had been after. If they were worried about their own safety, they'd be just that much more eager to kill her.

Her head whipped from side to side, desperately looking for a way out of this. But she couldn't find one. In the distance she heard the wail of sirens that signaled the MPs' imminent arrival. And the Magic Police

weren't going to let her get away. They might save her
from the mob. On the other hand, they might stand back
and let these everyday, ordinary people solve their problem for them.

Frantic, she stumbled back as the crowd pushed in
until she realized they were herding her closer to the
burning man stretched out on the asphalt. Heat from
the flames reached for her. The stench of burning flesh
stained the air. Shea looked from the dead man to the
crowd and back again and knew that whatever happened next, she deserved it.

The fire suddenly erupted, growing until hungry licks
of orange and red flames leapt and jumped more than
six feet high. Someone in the crowd screamed. Shea
jolted. Black cars with flashing yellow lights raced into
the driveway and then screeched to a stop. Men in black
uniforms piled out and pointed guns, but they were the
least of her problems now.

Flames reached for Shea. Engulfed her. The roar of
the quickening fire deafened her to her surroundings.
She screamed and looked up into a pair of pale gray
eyes reflecting the shifting colors of the flames. She felt
hard, strong arms wrap around her, as a deep voice whispered, "Close your eyes."

"Good idea," she answered, then fainted for the first
time in her life.

Chapter 2

When Shea woke up, it was dark outside. There was a lamp burning on the bedside table and the Tiffany-glass shade threw softly colored patterns on the ceiling. She sat up, bracing her hands against the silky quilt beneath her. Which meant she was on a bed. *Whose* bed?

Certainly not her own. She glanced down and sighed thankfully as she realized she was still wearing her white blouse and black skirt. Her scraped knees had been treated and her low-heeled black pumps were still on her feet.

Then her gaze shot around the room. It was big, beautiful and filled with shadows. Nerves jittering in the pit of her stomach, Shea pushed herself off the mattress, walked to the closest window and peered out into the darkness. Moonlight spilled onto the ocean, painting the crashing waves in an eerie, phosphorescent light. There was a balcony outside her window and when she opened the doors to step outside, she noticed the garden below. The roar of the waves slamming into the cliffs sounded like the heartbeat of a giant and set her own into a fast-paced rhythm.

"Where the hell *am* I and how did I get here?" She couldn't think. Couldn't recall what had happened to her. Then suddenly, in a rush, images poured into her mind and she remembered feeling the heat surround her. Flames jumping into the air, flashing across her skin. The strong arms around her middle. The deep voice ringing in her ears.

This was so much worse than she'd thought.

Whoever—whatever—had taken her from the parking lot was probably close by. Which meant what, exactly? Clearly she wasn't in jail or in one of the internment camps set up across the country. She'd heard enough whispers about those places to know they were hardly this luxurious. Clearly the MPs hadn't captured her. So who was it who had taken her? And to where?

The ocean told her nothing. It was a big coast, after all. She looked over the edge of the balcony and considered clambering out over the rail, hanging by her hands and dropping down. The bushes would break her fall. Probably. She could do it. It wasn't *that* far.

"You won't jump."

Shea jolted and spun around at the sound of the voice. A man stood in the middle of the room. Well over six feet tall, he looked tough, dangerous and too damn good. But it wasn't just the raw sexual energy shimmering off of him in thick waves that drew her attention. It was the sense of . . . familiarity she felt. As if she knew him. *Had* known him. His black hair hung to his shoulders, his broad chest was covered by a bloodred shirt and his faded black jeans clung to muscular thighs. His arms were folded across his chest and his pale gray eyes were fixed on her.

"It's you," she said, remembering now how the reflection of the flames engulfing her had danced in his eyes. That explained the familiarity, she told herself. "You were there. You got me away from that mob."

"I did."

"Why? Not that I'm not grateful, but why would you do that for a stranger?"

"You're not a stranger," he said, his deep voice rumbling through the room with all the power of the crashing waves below.

"But I don't know you."

He took a step toward her and Shea instinctively backed up until she felt the cold, damp balcony railing slam into the small of her back.

"You do," he insisted, never taking his mesmerizing eyes off her. "Your body recognizes mine even if your mind is still closed to me."

Shea was forced to admit that he was right about that much, anyway. The sense of recognition she felt toward him went deeper than just the incident from that afternoon. She couldn't understand it. She was sure she'd never seen him before, and yet there was ... something. The closer he came, the more her body practically hummed with anticipation. But she deliberately ignored it. Sex wasn't the first thing on her mind at the moment. Terror was superseding everything else.

Shea swallowed hard and asked, "Who are you?"

"Torin."

"That tells me nothing," she said. "Your name doesn't explain who you are or why and how I'm here."

"You know how. I brought you here."

"Yeah, you did," she said, remembering the flames surrounding her. "But why?"

He shoved his hands into the back pockets of his jeans and shrugged. "It was that or let the crowd kill you. Would you have preferred that?"

"No. No, I wouldn't." Shea inhaled slowly and then let the air slide from her lungs. She remembered the mob circling her—and he was right. They would have killed her—with the blessing of the MPs. After all, a dead witch meant no paperwork.

"You have nothing to fear from me," he said. "Surely you know that."

"How would I know that?" She shook her head and

concentrated on the chill dampness seeping into her body from the balcony railing. At least that was tangible. Real. Nothing else seemed that way at the moment. "One minute I'm about to get stoned to death or something and the next I'm standing in fire and you're . . ." She scrubbed her hands up and down her upper arms in a futile attempt to rid herself of the bone-deep cold that permeated her body. "Oh, God. You were *in* that fire."

"Yes."

"So was I! But you're not burned." She looked down at her hands as if to reassure herself again that her skin wasn't blistered and charred. "Neither am I. How is that possible?"

"Long story," he said. "But we'll have time for it all. Now that you're here—"

"Wherever 'here' is," she muttered.

"My home. You're in Malibu. You're safe."

"And I should take your word for that?"

"I saved you, didn't I?" His mouth tipped briefly to one side in a smile that lived and died in an instant. "I should get points for that."

"If a hungry tiger saved me from a bear, should I be relieved?" Shaking her head, she said, "No, I don't think so. And what happened to the man who grabbed me in the parking lot and—" Her memory dredged up the horrifying images. "I—I—"

"Set him on fire," he finished for her.

"Oh, God, I did . . ." She caught her breath, then locked her gaze with his. "Like Aunt Mairi. But I didn't mean to. Didn't even try to. How could I have known that would happen?"

"You've had the dreams," he said, moving closer still until she was no more than an arm's reach away. "You felt changes rippling through your body. I know you have because the Awakening is on you."

"Awakening?" She knew that word. But how? And was that really the most important consideration at the moment?

"The Awakening was foretold centuries ago. When the last great coven cast a spell of atonement."

Atonement. She shivered as he spoke, his words creating images in her mind. Images that were at once foreign and familiar.

"Each witch was to live without magic through many lifetimes until this year. This time."

"No," she whispered, though everything in her said *yes.*

"Each of you will awaken in turn," he continued. His voice was impossible to ignore; his pale eyes somehow swirled with power. "One every thirty days until the atonement is complete and your tasks fulfilled."

"Tasks?" Shea shook her head—this was crazy. All of it. *Then why,* something in her asked, *did it feel so right?*

"You are the first, Shea. You are the hope of the coven."

"You're wrong. This is a trick. The MPs are trying to make me look guilty and you're in it somehow."

His features went cold and hard and his voice dropped several notches. "I do not work with the Magic Police. You think I would hand over a woman to them?"

"Maybe," Shea argued, though something was telling her she was wrong about him. That she should trust him. Still, trusting people these days was a dangerous business.

And what he had told her couldn't be true. This had to be an elaborate plot. Machinations from the feds.

It was the Salem witch trials all over again. Only this time the hysteria had spread until it circled the globe. Every country in the world was actively pursuing women who "might" be witches. And God help the ones who actually *were.*

"None of this makes sense," she whispered, more to herself than to him. "I'm not a witch. I'm *not.*"

"Denial alters nothing. You are who you were always meant to be."

She threw her head back and glared at him. "And what's that?"

"Mine," he said.

Yes, her body answered. Her blood felt thick and hot in her veins and her heartbeat was jittering crazily in her chest. Staring up into those pale gray eyes unsettled her and she wondered if he knew that and played on it. How many other women had he brought here? How many others before her had he swept in and carried off?

"I'm not yours. I'm not anyone's," she argued as she eased to one side, trying to put some distance between them. It didn't matter what her body felt; her mind was in charge and that was how it was going to stay. "And I'm not a witch. I didn't set fire to that man."

"You did," he told her, his voice deep and even. "You're a hereditary witch, Shea Jameson. The power runs through your bloodline. Your aunt, your mother, you. Even now, I can feel your power emerging. Growing. You feel it, too."

"No," she said, shaking her head wildly and looking around her for an escape that simply wasn't there. "Look, ever since my aunt Mairi was . . . burned at the stake, people have been watching me. The MPs. The Bureau of Witchcraft. Right after she died, I even changed my name and hid for a while. But even BOW didn't seem interested in me anymore. It's been ten years since Mairi died and I've *never* shown any sign of power. And I don't feel a damn thing emerging."

"You're lying. To me. And to yourself." He braced his hands on the railing on either side of her, effectively trapping her and holding her in place. "I was at the school. I watched the man approach. I waited for your power to erupt. For your survival instincts to force you to remember who and what you are."

Shea glared up at him. "You watched? You saw that man attack me and you did nothing?"

"It was necessary for me to stand back while you unlocked your powers. You've been fighting against their emergence for too long."

"That man *died!*"

"He was nothing," Torin said with a barely concealed sneer. "A predator. A human who lived his life on the misery of others. If you had not stopped him, he would have brutalized more women as he had done to others before you."

"It doesn't matter," she argued, realizing that she was never going to be able to get the mental pictures of what she'd done to that man out of her head. "That doesn't give me the right to—"

"Survive?" He snapped the word at her and Shea shoved ineffectually at his broad chest. He didn't even budge. But the contact between them sent heat flashing through her, like a sudden fever, enough so that she had to take a breath before she felt steady enough to say, "I didn't mean to kill him."

"Then master your powers before it happens again."

"Master something I didn't know I had until today?" She laughed shortly and felt the sound scrape against her throat. "Of course. Why didn't I think of that?" She sighed, feeling the crushing weight of this oh, so miserable day fall down on top of her.

"You're not alone in this," he said softly, drawing her eyes up to his again. "As I've said, I am Torin. Your Eternal."

"My Eternal," she repeated tiredly. "What's that mean exactly?"

"It means you are right where you are supposed to be, Shea Jameson." He touched her cheek and she could have sworn she felt the heat of flames rising up in her again. "I will stand beside you in this."

God, it was tempting to believe. To trust. To think that she wouldn't have to stand alone against whatever would happen next. But she couldn't do that. Couldn't risk it. Though her body clamored for his, though her hands itched to reach out and touch him, she refused. She was forced to fight her own attraction to the man just to keep her mind straight.

"I'm just supposed to trust you?" She had gone from seriously deep trouble at the school to being in way over her head here. "I don't even know where you've taken me."

"We're not strangers," he said, each word tight with banked emotions. "Your soul knows me. As you will. Your memories will begin to return now as your power grows."

"Right. Memories." She bit down hard on her bottom lip, trying to convince herself she was dreaming. But the pain that stabbed her mouth was proof enough that this was all real.

Her skin was buzzing at his nearness, as if she were reacting to an electrical charge. The color of his eyes seemed to swirl like gray clouds in a high wind. His mouth was firm and full and fixed in a grim slash that told her he wasn't feeling much happier than she was.

"This is not a dream," he told her as if he knew exactly what she'd been thinking.

"Nightmare, then?"

"Ask yourself why you're not afraid of me."

"Who says I'm not?" She lifted her chin, daring him to contradict her.

"I do. It's not fear I feel coming from you, but arousal."

She wouldn't even respond to that.

"I look familiar to you, yes?" he asked, and took her upper arms in a firm grip.

His touch opened up something inside her. She felt the barest flicker of recognition from deep within. That sense of familiarity was back and she knew, deep in her soul, that he was telling her the truth. There was a connection between them. Maybe she would remember him, eventually. But the question was, *what* exactly would she recall? Was he to be trusted, as he said? Or would her memories tell her to stay as far away from the sexually powerful man as possible?

"No," she said softly, meeting that strange gray stare. "I don't know you. I don't want to know you. I just want to leave."

"And go where?" He slid his hands up her body until he was cupping her cheeks in his big palms. She felt the overwhelming rush of heat slicing from his body into hers and she nearly trembled at the force of it.

But she wasn't going to give in to something that made zero sense to her. This was all some sort of bizarre mind game. And he was the puppet master. In the years since witchcraft had been revealed to the world, the crazies had really come out of the closet. "That's none of your business."

"Everything about you is my business, Shea."

When she sucked in a gulp of air, the fear she tasted was dark and bitter. "What do you want from me?"

"Everything," he admitted, "and I will accept nothing less."

"Who the hell are you?"

"I'm the one who saved your very fine ass from that mob."

"Funny," she said softly, "I don't feel 'saved.' I feel trapped." She pulled free of his grip, though her body instantly missed his touch. Quickly, she moved to one side so he wouldn't reach out and grab her again. "And how did you do that fire thing without burning us both to a crisp?"

Frowning, he lifted both arms and fire danced across his skin. Snapping, hissing flames flashed over his body, wrapping him in a blanket of living fire.

"Oh, my God . . ." She swallowed hard and backed away until she once again slammed into the railing.

"I *am* the fire, Shea Jameson." The flames on his body winked out of existence, leaving his skin unmarked, untouched. Magic shimmered in the air between them. "Just as I *am* your other half."

She stared up at him as the moonlight shone on his features, giving him a shadowy, evil look that sent her heart plummeting to the soles of her feet. "You're crazy."

"No," he said, his voice clipped. "But I am out of patience. I have waited centuries for this day. And I will not wait any longer." He reached out, scooped her up into his arms, and before she could shout a protest, carried her back into the room and tossed her onto the bed. "There is no escape from your destiny, Shea. Tonight it begins."

She scrambled away from him, never daring to take her gaze from his. "What? What begins tonight?"

Torin walked across the room, opened the door and stepped through it. Before he closed it again, he sent her one long look and said simply, "The mating ritual."

Chapter 3

Torin left the bedroom with one last look at Shea. Everything in him burned. The flames that were a part of him seemed to lick at his insides as well, consuming him in a fire that could not be smothered. He closed the door firmly, then stalked down the long hall and stopped at the head of the stairs. The lighting was dim, shadows spilling from the corners. His housekeeper, an older woman named Anna, looked up at him.

"No one goes in there." He glanced back down the long hallway at the closed door. He wanted Shea to accept where she was and that she wouldn't be leaving. If he gave her an hour or two to herself, he had no doubt that she would come to realize that their joined path was now set in stone. That there would be no escape from the destiny they had both been chasing for centuries. Time to herself would make her that much more receptive when he returned to her.

Finally, he swung his head back around to meet the older woman's gaze and repeated, "No one goes in. I will take her food later."

"Understood," Anna said, sitting down in the nearby chair to keep watch.

Torin smiled briefly. He had every confidence in Anna's loyalties. This woman and her family had been with him for generations, traveling from one country to another as he followed his witch through her many incarnations. They were honorable and unquestioning and he trusted them as he did few others.

Leaving Anna on guard, Torin took the stairs to the main level of the house and walked directly to the library. Acres of books surrounded him. Floor-to-ceiling bookcases ringed the room, broken up only by the wide windows that offered views of the landscaped lawn. In this room, too, the lighting was dim, as if Torin preferred the shadows to the light. And perhaps that had been true for the last few hundred years. Now, though, he had changed, he told himself. Now there would be light. There would be *life*.

All Torin could think was that finally Shea was here. Where he wanted—needed—her to be. His body ached for hers. His mind reached for thoughts of her, like a balm to his fragmented soul. With the completion of the ritual, they would be one. Her body, her soul, would be laid open to him—and his to her. As it was always meant to be.

And what had once gone so terribly wrong would at last be righted.

Every inch of his body hummed with need and it cost him greatly to remain apart from her. But he called on his immense will and vowed to give her an hour or two alone. To settle into the situation. To realize that she had no choice. The Awakening was on her and it was long past time for them to begin the ritual.

Damned if he would wait even one more night to claim what was rightfully his.

His mind racing, he stopped in front of one of the windows and stared out at a yard drenched in darkness. There were no spotlights on his property. Torin didn't need them. His eyesight was as keen in the dark as it was in daylight. Incandescent lighting would have served only his enemies. Of which there were many.

And now that the Awakening had begun, those enemies would be gathering.

"Does she remember?"

He shook his head, barely sparing a glance for the man who stood in the shadows, watching him. Well over six feet five inches, Rune, too, was an Eternal. His long brown hair was tied at the back of his neck by a strip of rawhide. His features were sharp, his eyes swirling with power. He wore his standard uniform of black T-shirt and black jeans and the steel tips of his boots winked in the lamplight.

"No," Torin told him, disgusted. "She looks at me and sees only danger. Her memories are still blocked. But her body remembers," he assured himself, remembering how she felt curled up against him. "For now, that's enough."

Rune moved closer, the scowl on his face deepening. "With the Awakening, her mind should have opened as well. How are we to claim them if they don't remember?"

Torin turned his head to glare at his old friend. "We *make* them remember. Force their hand if we must. Remind them of everything that has gone before. We've waited centuries for this and for me, at least, the waiting is done."

Rune crossed his arms over his chest as he met his friend's glare with one of his own. "I know what is coming as well as any other Eternal. But your woman is the first to Awaken. It's up to you to set us on the path. If this doesn't work, we're all fucked."

Torin snorted. He didn't need to be told that their mutual goals were balanced atop a dangerous precipice. Every Eternal had been marking time through the centuries until the moment of Awakening arrived. If they failed now, all had been for nothing. Which was why he would not fail.

"I know exactly what's at stake here. Nothing will go wrong."

Accepting his friend's word, Rune nodded. "My witch is still unaware of what's coming. Until she Awakens, I'll stay here and help you."

Torin smiled, surprising even himself. How long had it been since there had been anything worth smiling at? How many centuries of agony had he survived, watching his woman and being unable to claim her? The constant burning of unquenchable want had been his companion through eons. Now, though, he sensed the end in sight. The time when all of the waiting would be rewarded.

"When have I ever needed help getting a woman into my bed?" But even as the words left his mouth, Torin knew that this woman was different. This was more than a few hours of pleasure. This was eternity. And unless Shea gave herself to him with that knowledge, with complete acceptance, nothing would change and their chance would be lost.

"How will you spark the memories?" Rune demanded.

"She's already having visions," Torin told him. He'd been keeping watch over her for years. He knew that her aunt's execution had opened a narrow path into the past for Shea. He'd seen her wake screaming from nightmares that she didn't realize were actually memories. He'd watched as she fought to maintain "normalcy." In secret he had given her his protection each time she ran from enemies both real and imagined.

And he'd hungered. Just as he did now.

Through lifetime after lifetime, Torin had burned for her and only her.

"She must recall the past. *That* life."

"She will." She had to. Torin turned his gaze back to the dark landscape as his thoughts drifted briefly to that long-ago age. To the moment when everything had changed for them. Images flew through his mind, clear and distinct. He felt the power rising. Felt the crash of failure, the terror and the raw grief of regret.

They'd given up much on that night.

All in a quest for too much power.

He pushed both hands through his hair and refocused his gaze on his own image in the glass. He was a man and not a man. A legend, yet more than that. He was, essentially, caught in a stream of time that had no definition.

Until now.

His gaze took in the man beside him. An Eternal. A brother. Less than human, yet more than mortal. There were others like them as well. Beings who had survived the centuries and who now had one chance for something more.

All that was required was for their witches to accept their destinies.

And *them*.

Chapter 4

She waited a few minutes after her gorgeous kid-napper left before she quietly opened the bedroom door. The long hallway was dark but for a few lamps set into the wall. The illumination they gave off was barely more than candlelight. There were at least six doors off the hall and at the end, near the head of the stairs, Shea spotted a woman with steel gray hair and a stick-straight spine sitting in a chair. The older woman was reading a book, but Shea wasn't fooled. The woman wasn't taking a break.

She was on guard duty.

Crap.

Closing the door with a soft *snick*, Shea looked fu-tilely for a lock, then silently admitted that even if there had been one, it wouldn't have kept out the man who had just left. She'd never seen a man more . . . power-fully *male*. It was more than his muscles, though they were plenty impressive. There was something else that fed into the indomitable male thing. A sort of aura that clung to him. One that spelled danger to anyone foolish enough to cross him.

Which she definitely planned to do.

Mating ritual?

She really didn't think so.

But even as that thought blasted through her mind,

her body was reacting in a completely different way. Desire pumped through her, making her skin feel heated and too tight. Her mind was shouting at her to run and her body was urging her to stay.

He'd saved her, after all.

Rescued her from a mob that would have killed her, given half a chance.

But he's not even human.

Hard to forget the way those flames leapt and danced across his skin. Hard to forget the flash of something dangerous in those pale gray eyes of his, too.

Shea blew out a breath, and tried to come to grips with what had happened to her life in the span of a few short hours. She knew only one thing for certain. She had to get away. From the man asking too much of her and from the enemies she knew would now be tracking her relentlessly.

She had to disappear.

Again.

She leaned back against the closed door as her gaze swept the plush room. She had to give her kidnapper credit. At least he'd brought her to a damn palace. But an elegantly appointed trap was still a trap.

"Where the hell am I, anyway?"

Malibu, she remembered suddenly, though knowing where she was didn't help her any. Long Beach, her home, her car, were about thirty miles away. He'd swept her out from under a murderous mob and taken her from everything familiar only to drop her into the middle of the unknown. *Fine,* she told herself with a nod of her head. She'd been in tough places before this one. She knew all too well how to deal with threats. She'd been handling her own safety for years now. It was *him* she didn't have a clue how to deal with.

Torin.

Just thinking his name sent ripples of awareness

spreading through her. She closed her eyes against the sensation of impending . . . *something*. It was something she couldn't name. The moment she did, though, images dredged up from some distant corner of her mind flashed across the backs of her eyes like a kaleidoscopic slide show. Faces, places, voices all presented themselves in a staggering flood that made absolutely no sense. It was as if they were someone else's memories rushing through her mind, but if that were true, why was *she* seeing them?

She saw fires burning, heard a scream that sounded as though it was pulled from the depths of a soul. She glimpsed a blossoming darkness that stretched and spread like a black flower rising from death's garden.

Instantly Shea opened her eyes, gasping for breath even as her stomach did a fast lurch. She clamped her mouth shut and swallowed convulsively against the sudden urge to retch. Things were bad enough without her being sick on top of everything else. She knew she couldn't afford to give in to whatever it was she was feeling. She had more important things to consider at the moment. Nerves jangling, mind still reeling, she pushed away from the door, crossed the room to the balcony and stepped outside.

Lifting her face to the cold wind driving at her, she hoped to let the images that were still fresh in her mind fade away. For months now she'd been having dreams filled with frightening shapes and sounds. She never could remember them on waking, but more than once she'd shot out of bed, desperate for a breath that wouldn't come. Now, though, those mental dream collages were stronger, clearer. She didn't know what was happening, but whatever it was, she was convinced it had something to do with Torin.

So the sooner she got away from him, the better.

The icy breeze off the ocean pushed at her as if trying

to keep her in the room. But Shea knew better than that. She couldn't stay here. Yes, he'd saved her from the mob, but he hadn't let her go. And she wasn't sticking around to see what else he had planned for her.

The only one she knew she could trust was herself.

Her gaze focused on the world beyond the fenced yard surrounding her. There were dangers out there, she knew. Hadn't she been running for the last ten years of her life? She knew that the MPs and BOW were somewhere watching. She also knew that civilians, like the ones at the school who had surrounded her with fear and hatred just that afternoon, could be even more dangerous than the feds.

And still, there was little choice. She had to take her chances.

She couldn't stay with her jailer. His presence was doing something to her. And she couldn't risk sticking around to find out what more might be coming. Not only that—there was another good reason to run.

"Mating ritual," she whispered, reminding herself that not every danger came with a threat to her life.

Heat instantly blossomed deep inside her and her body trembled at the thought of being under, over and around that incredible male. But she couldn't help how her hormones reacted. That was just nature. Chemistry.

She was more than that.

She had a brain and she was going to use it.

Looking down at the hydrangea bush beneath the balcony, Shea considered just how badly she might be hurt if she dropped herself into it. "Worst-case scenario, I break a leg and I'm trapped here," she murmured, as if hearing her own voice would infuse her with the courage she needed. "Best case, I'm out of here and on the run."

She didn't have the suitcase from her car trunk, but a quick check of her bra told her that she still had her stash of emergency money. She'd find the closest bus or train station, buy a ticket and disappear.

Not daring to waste any more time, Shea climbed over the edge of the balcony and sent one last look back to the lush, empty room she was leaving behind. Warmth and luxury weren't everything, though. Sometimes safety was the open road and a cold wind at your back. She took a breath, then turned her mind to the problem at hand. Carefully, she lowered herself until she caught the bottom of the railing, her hands gripping the base of the twisted iron tightly. Chill dampness leached into her bones and fed the dark cold already settling in the pit of her stomach.

She could only hope that her jailer wasn't currently in a room with a view of the hydrangea bush. Her legs swung free, her feet instinctively groping for a foothold that wasn't there. She hung in place for a slow count of five, then bit her lip, closed her eyes and let go.

A brief yet seemingly interminable amount of time passed and then she dropped into the bush. Heavy branches and bunches of lilac-colored flowers broke her fall, but the air rushed out of her lungs on impact. Wincing at the noise she'd made with her fall, she waited to see if there would be an outcry, if someone in the house had heard the commotion and was even now racing out to recapture her.

But there was nothing, so she took a breath and did a quick mental inventory. Nothing broken, thank God. Sore, bruised undoubtedly, but she was ready to run. She peered up and around the thick dark leaves and was relieved to see that the bush surrounding her backed against a wall of the house. No windows. So no way for Torin to have seen her fall.

Now all she had to do was escape before he discovered she was gone.

Scrambling, Shea fought her way free of the heavy

plant, then staggered to her feet. Instantly, she headed for the darkest shadows on the lawn. She knew there was a high wall around the property, but she'd already noticed the sturdy, ancient trees lining the perimeter. Surely one of them would be close enough to the wall that if she was lucky, she could use it to vault herself to freedom.

Freedom.

That one word was like a talisman. She had to stay free, not just of Torin but of the agencies chasing her. Free of the civilians who would no doubt be on guard for her. She had to find a way to hide deeply enough that the world would, eventually, forget about her.

Shea clung to the shadows, keeping low, half expecting to hear a shout at any moment. To feel strong arms covered in flames wrap around her. To look up into gray eyes that were as merciless as they were mesmerizing. She took a breath and ducked beneath a low-hanging branch of an oak that looked as though it had been standing in that spot for a century or more. Taking off her shoes, she tucked them into the waistband of her skirt. Bare feet would make climbing easier. A dense canopy of leaves hid her from sight as she hiked her skirt up to her thighs, grabbed hold of a heavy branch and pulled herself up. Her injured knees scraped against the bark and pain she didn't have time to acknowledge shot through her.

Shea tossed a quick glance through the leaves at the brightly lit house behind her.

No sign that anyone was after her. Yet. Clinging to a branch, she pulled her shoes free and then tossed them, one after the other, over the wall. Her bare feet walked up the heavy limbs of the oak until she was within reach of the top of the wall. Leaning out, she held tight to the tree with one hand and reached for the wall with the other.

Don't look down, she told herself, focusing solely on the top of the cinder-block wall. She bit back her fear, released the tree and clambered onto the wall, stretching out flat atop it. She threw a quick glance at the street below.

Torin's house was set back from the main road, where streetlights threw soft golden circles of light. Here by the wall, there was only more darkness. *Better,* she thought. Staying out of the light would help hide her. She swung over the edge, dug her toes into the wall, then carefully dropped to the ground. Blindly, she searched for her shoes, tugged them on, then hurried toward the road.

She hated having to be anywhere near the main street, since Torin would be following her soon. But what choice did she have? She wasn't even sure where she was.

Her heels tapped lightly on the asphalt and she cringed at even that slight sound. But better to risk the noise than to step on something and injure herself before she got a running start.

Her breath came in uneven gasps and her long red hair fell in tumbled curls around her shoulders. Her gaze continually swept her surroundings and she jolted at every brush of wind against a bush. Somewhere down the road a dog howled and Shea shivered.

Overhead, clouds raced across the sky. The ever-present wind tugged at her hair, her clothes, with icy fingers and through it all, the pulse beat of the ocean thrummed in the air.

At the corner, Shea pushed her hair back from her face and paused in the shadows, scanning the road in front of her. Not much traffic. Must have been later than she'd thought. The residents were all tucked in behind their privacy gates, secure in their elegant mansions. And with any luck, none of them would ever know she had been there.

She stepped into the street, avoiding the circles of light thrown from the old-fashioned streetlamps. Thankfully, this part of Malibu obviously preferred form over function. If they'd had the more modern lights here, she would have had a much harder time remaining unseen. As it was, she had to move quickly, walking on grass and gravel, trying to get as much distance between her and Torin as possible. Then she would be free to lose herself in a new identity.

The tightness around her chest loosened with every step. She would survive. She'd done it before. She could do it again. This time was no different.

But it was different.

The last time she'd disappeared, she hadn't been a murderer. Now she was. She'd killed that man who had attacked her. It didn't matter that she hadn't meant to. Mistake or premeditated, he was just as dead. She bit down on her bottom lip and told herself that it was an accident. She'd never hurt anyone in her life until today.

Shea swiped one hand across her eyes, wiping away the sting of tears with impatience. Being sorry wouldn't accomplish anything. Wouldn't change anything. What had happened, happened and there was just no going back.

So she would go forward.

And what about the *fire*? The pulse of energy that had jolted from her fingertips? What was she supposed to do about that? For ten years, she'd been denying that she was a witch to anyone who would listen. Now, though, that argument wouldn't work, even with herself. There was magic inside her, whether she wanted it or not. And she really didn't.

Even being suspected of witchcraft was dangerous.

To actually *be* a witch was usually a death sentence.

Frowning at her own scattershot thoughts, Shea told herself that she'd do what Torin had said and would learn to control it. Just because she apparently carried magic within her didn't mean she had to use it. She would stop the magic. She'd figure it all out. But she'd do it her way, on her time. She wasn't going to trust anyone. Certainly not a man who could manifest the very flames she was terrified of.

On her own, she'd be safe.

It was the only way.

She smiled to herself, ducked beneath the overhanging branches of a jacaranda tree, lacy leaves tickling her skin. The soft slide of her shoes on the grass was the only sound except the ocean. Even that lonely dog had stopped howling. Maybe that was a good sign, she thought.

She was free. The danger was behind her and safety lay within reach.

A deep voice erupted from behind her. "Gotcha!"

Chapter 5

"Gone?" Torin narrowed his gaze on the housekeeper. Anna was practically vibrating with agitation. Her eyes kept shifting to avoid looking directly into his and she had her hands fisted so tightly at her waist that her knuckles were white.

To save time, Torin started for the staircase, wanting to see for himself that Shea was indeed missing. He heard Anna and Rune right behind him, but didn't bother looking back. Instead, he merely growled, "What do you mean, she's gone?"

"Just what I said. I know you told me that no one was to go in her room," Anna said a little breathlessly as she hurried to keep up with him, "but I heard an odd noise and thought it best to check it out."

"And ..." He hit the top of the stairs, took a sharp left and stalked down the hall, gaze fixed on Shea's open door.

"And, nothing," the older woman said. "She wasn't there."

"Where in the name of the gods could she have gone?"

Rune's viciously muttered question reverberated in Torin's mind. Along with another one all his own. Why would she go? Foolish woman. She knew she was in danger. Hadn't he just saved her from a mob only hours ago? Why would she risk running?

Had he pushed her too hard, too fast? Had he expected too much too soon? No, he told himself firmly. It had been aeons! How patient was he to be, damn the witch!

With those questions and more running through his thoughts, Torin walked into Shea's room and opened up every sense he possessed. He closed his eyes, reaching out to her, trying to locate her as he had done through countless centuries. There was a bond between Eternal and Witch and no matter how tenuous those strings of attachment grew at times, they were never completely severed.

Unless . . .

He threw a look at Rune. "There's nothing. I can't feel her at all."

"Then she's been captured. They've probably got white gold on her to tamp down her power."

White gold inhibited magical abilities. For Eternal and Witch alike. It was like a dampening field where power was muffled and connections were nearly impossible to maintain. Torin couldn't use the very magic that bonded him and Shea to track her. Once that power was shut down, his link with her was if not shattered, then at least muted.

He walked to the balcony and stared out at the night and the world beyond his compound. Here he'd offered her safety. He'd offered her power and the mating that would usher them both from the dark past into a future unstained with old sins and bitter regrets.

And she'd fled from it.

"By the stars," he muttered, "what was she thinking? Does she really trust herself to the compassion of humans?"

Rune came up beside him and clapped one hand on Torin's shoulder in camaraderie. "You said yourself, she doesn't remember. Doesn't know yet who and what she is. Or what you are to her."

Torin turned on him, fury bubbling like a black brew. "And I'm to be *patient* for how long? For centuries, we've waited. Now that the time's come, I should have taken her the moment she entered this house. I thought to give her time to adjust. To accept that the mating would begin." He pushed away from the balcony rail and shook back his long fall of black hair. "No, patience has not served any of us. Now I will find her and we end this. Finally and at last, we end it."

Rune stared at him for a long moment before nodding agreement. Torin didn't care whether his fellow Eternal shared his sentiments or not. Nothing mattered now but Shea Jameson. And may the gods protect whoever was trying to keep her from him. Because Torin was devoid of mercy.

He set one hand on the railing and vaulted over the balcony. He landed softly, just beyond the bush that had obviously broken Shea's fall. Idiot woman, did she not realize what she risked by putting her own life in danger? Did she really believe that the humans of this world were more trustworthy than *her Eternal*?

Chapter 6

More scared than she'd ever been, Shea fought back as strong hands grabbed her and dragged her off her feet. Before she could take a breath to scream, a heavy hand dropped over her mouth. She tried to bite it, but failed.

"Lock her down!" A different voice, deeper, whispered the command. More than one man was circling her, touching her, wrestling her to the ground.

"Watch her hands!" someone else muttered viciously.

Her hands. The energy pulse. The fire. She didn't want to hurt anyone, but she wasn't going to allow them to hurt her, either. She lifted both palms, but dropped them again when she was slapped so viciously that her head snapped to one side and tears spurted from her eyes.

Still, she kicked out wildly, and in her blind attempt to free herself, connected with someone. She heard a grunt of pain. Then another man grabbed her ankles and held her still. Shea bucked in their grasp, writhing and struggling, but they were too strong and there were just too many of them.

Fear rose up fast and thick inside her. Her mind raced and her heart beat so frantically, she felt as though it would pop out of her chest. She'd been caught. Before she'd made it a mile from Torin's home, she'd been found and trapped. And if she didn't think fast, she was going to disappear at someone else's hands.

Something cold draped around her neck and even while she struggled, Shea sensed a weight dropping onto her soul. She felt heavy, leaden. Her body wasn't affected by whatever they'd done to her, but her soul was being crushed. She tried to lift her hands, but couldn't find the will. The spark of energy she'd felt that afternoon when she'd faced the mugger was blocked up inside her, struggling, as she was, to escape.

"Stupid witch," one of the men whispered, so close to her ear that she felt his hot breath on her skin, "you think we'll give you a chance to fry us the way you did that poor bastard today?"

Oh, God. "I didn't—"

Someone slapped her again, but she couldn't see who. It didn't matter. They were all against her. All of them working in concert to keep her from escaping. They might as well have been one entity. In the darkness the men surrounding her were merely darker shadows. Moving, constantly moving, as if they were being careful to not make themselves targets.

She couldn't hurt them—and they knew it, so their caution was simply born of their underlying fear. That she understood. Hadn't she been living with ripe, glorious fear for more than ten years herself? Hadn't she jolted at every knock on the door? Every ring of the phone? And what good had any of it done her?

She'd still ended up here, a captive lying in the dirt, with strangers' hands moving over her as she lay trapped. Whatever "power" she might have had was asleep. And she wished to hell it wasn't.

Yes, this afternoon she'd killed a man with magic and had been sorry for it. Now, she would give anything to have that power at her command. She had to get away. And there was no chance of escape now. That strong hand stayed cupped over her mouth while she was forced onto her stomach. Bits of dirt and gravel dug into her face. Her arms were wrenched behind her back and a plastic zip tie was fixed around her wrists, digging painfully into her skin.

She moaned and squirmed against the restraints until a new voice entered the fray and Shea stilled to listen.

"It's her, isn't it?" A woman's voice, excited, breathless. "I was right. I knew it, I told my husband when I saw her at that man's balcony, 'that's the woman from the news,' I said. The witch who killed that poor man today."

That was how they'd caught up to her, Shea thought with an inner groan. A civilian had spotted her and turned her in. But who did the woman call? Who were these men and what were they going to do to her now?

"Yeah, it's her, lady," a man said in a voice hoarse from too many cigarettes. "Now get on back to your house. We'll take care of this."

Take care of it how? Shea wondered frantically. Were they going to kill her? Torture and rape her first? Witches had no rights and she knew that a grateful public would no doubt pin a medal on anyone who could prove he'd killed one.

Suddenly Torin was looking much better to her. Now she wanted nothing more than to be back in that luxurious room with the tall, fierce-looking man standing between her and danger. If that made her a coward, she was willing to live with it. But since she was on her own, she had to try to reason with the men hulking around her.

How many were there? Three? Four?

Her heartbeat thundered in her ears and the taste of fear was sharp and bitter on her tongue. She squirmed ineffectually against the man holding her from behind, but managed to twist her face free of the other man's hand.

"Stop, please . . . I'm not what you think." Lies. She was exactly what they thought she was. What she'd denied being for ten long years. And the worst part? They all knew it.

"Hear that?" a man on her right said, then mocked in a falsetto tone, "Please."

"Don't listen to her," another one told him. "She might spell you."

If only she could.

Someone snorted, then ordered, "Go get the van."

Van?

They were taking her somewhere. And how would Torin ever find her?

She shook her head, desperate now to somehow reach these men. "I don't know any spells. Really. I'm not what you think. I'm a sixth-grade science teacher. That's all. This is a huge mistake."

Her only hope was to convince the men she was innocent. But, she reminded herself, mistakes happened all the time these days and women still disappeared.

"Gag her."

"No!" She was already bound—if they gagged her too, she didn't think she could stand it. Shea pulled in a deep, terrified breath. She was out of time, out of hope. No one was riding to her rescue. There was no cavalry and she'd just run from the one person who might have kept her safe.

She was falling into a hole of her own making and now she could do nothing to keep it from growing even deeper. She was flipped over onto her back and despite her pleas, one of the men leaned down to fix a gag to her mouth. And she got her first good look at her captors.

Black uniforms. Yellow armbands. Gold badges that winked in the indistinct light.

The Magic Police had finally caught up with her.

Chapter 7

Torin noted Rune jumping down after him, but he didn't wait for his old friend. Instead, he followed the fading scent of his woman and rushed across the yard to the wall. Through the blind rage and the pressing need to find her, a flicker of admiration rose up inside him.

She'd climbed the damn tree and scaled the wall to escape him. Shea Jameson was a woman of strength. A witch of great power. And one with a spine stiff enough to take risks she had no business considering. While he could stand to one side and respect her formidable will, he resented the fact that she had risked her life rather than trusting him to protect her.

When he found her, he would make sure he convinced her never to defy him again. She would trust him because it was by damn his due. Hadn't he been at her side when death had claimed her, lifetime after lifetime? Hadn't he been waiting for her soul to be reborn so that he could once again pick up the mantle of protector?

Would this not prove to the woman that he had earned his place at her side?

Once on the street, he followed her trail, running through the darkness, at home in the shadows as he was nowhere else. The roar of the ocean thundered in the background as waves crashed against the cliffs. Lights blazed in the houses he passed, but he paid them no mind. What did he care for civilians when his mind was focused solely on his witch?

Torin stopped dead when her scent abruptly disappeared. He caught no sign of her on the wind and even reaching with the deeper senses of an Eternal gained him nothing. Shea had disappeared as completely as if she'd stepped into a hole in the earth. Muttering darkly under his breath, he dropped to one knee to closely examine the ground.

There'd been a fight here. A struggle. She'd been forced to the ground by three—*four* men. And a woman. Torin frowned to himself as he recognized the scent of one of his neighbors. A nosy older woman forever spying on the world outside her own home. She must have seen Shea at the house and reported her. Which meant those who had taken Shea were no doubt official agents.

That was something, he told himself, even as a wild, frantic urge to find her swamped him. Officials, though cruel, rarely killed the women they captured outright. They would take her to a camp. Somewhere they could interrogate her. Lock her away. From *him*.

The rage already blistering Torin's insides flashed into a consuming inferno as he felt the lingering traces of Shea's fear and panic. He looked up, long hair lifting in the wind as his eyes narrowed on the dark road stretching out before him. Human males had grabbed his woman and if they had hurt her, he told himself, then they had best hope their God was looking out for them.

Rune ran up to join him as Torin stood. Cold, vicious fury burned within him, strangling every breath, flooding him with an iciness that was as black as the night surrounding them.

"Gone," he said, the one word ground from his throat like jagged glass. His body tensed, his huge hands curling into fists at his sides. He couldn't feel her. Couldn't sense her presence anywhere. And that meant only one thing.

Whoever had taken her had locked her powers down. "Where?"

Torin turned his head to glance briefly at his friend. "No telling. I can't sense her."

Rune cursed under his breath and then quieted, gathering his own strength for whatever came next.

Torin felt the warmth of solidarity begin to ease away the ice within him.

"We follow the scents of her captors as far as we can." He knew even the stench of humanity would dissipate with the wind and distance. But it was somewhere to start.

He lifted his arms and allowed the fire that was the essence of him to come. Flames danced and licked across his skin until every inch of his body hummed with the magical energy rushing through him. He felt his strength swell and build until finally it erupted, filling each of his cells with the power he had commanded for centuries.

He didn't care if the old woman or any of his other neighbors glanced out their windows and saw him. Torin wouldn't bother disguising himself or his true nature. The humans could do nothing to him and he had no time to camouflage himself simply to prevent them from having to admit the existence of even more magic.

Now he focused his mind on one thing.

Finding the men who had taken Shea from him.

Their scents were still clear to him, staining the very air with trace signatures. He easily picked up on the lingering sense of the men's fear and arousal. These men enjoyed their work, he realized grimly—capturing and tormenting women, whether witch or not. Soon, Torin thought, he would show them the error of their ways. But first he would use them as they used the women they captured to feed their own base instincts.

He would allow these men to guide him to the only woman in the world who mattered.

He looked again at Rune and saw that he, too, was enveloped in living flames, the immortal soul of each Eternal. With the strength of the fire coursing through them, they could travel short distances in the span of a breath. Their magic was less complicated than the witches to whom they were bound. But their physical strength and their prowess at battle more than made up the difference.

Magic flowed through the Eternals, yet as powerful as they were, they faced limits that could leave them vulnerable to an enemy. Flashing themselves across distances took a toll and would eventually drain the very powers they depended on.

When they took someone else along for the ride, their powers were taxed that much more quickly.

Even Eternals required rest or the magic of sex to restore their body's energies. But he couldn't afford to waste time worrying about whether he would be strong enough to free Shea once he found her. Instead, he would push himself to the very limits of his abilities. And if an enemy caught him at a weak moment? He would still find a way.

For Shea, there was nothing he wouldn't do.

Wouldn't risk.

"We go now," he ordered.

Rune nodded.

And in an instant the flames winked out and all that was left on the road were the ever-spreading shadows.

Chapter 8

"That wasn't so hard," one of the men said from the back of the van.

Shea lay at his feet, stretched out on a smelly gray carpet. There were no interior lights in what had to be a cargo van. A row of seats ran along each side of the vehicle while she lay like an offering on an altar in front of the men celebrating her capture. There were three of them back here with her, and one driving.

They'd sent four men to capture one witch.

She didn't know whether to be amused, flattered or even more scared. Clearly, the worldwide fear of magic was growing. They were taking no chances anymore.

The shadows were thick inside the van, but as they whizzed along the freeway, the outside lights flashed across the faces of her captors like a rhythmical, painfully bright strobe.

She wasn't comforted by what she saw.

These men looked hard and cold. Their features were taut and their eyes were bright with both fear and excitement. That didn't bode well for her. The older ones were watching her warily, while the one young recruit in the bunch had more than curiosity shining in his eyes. There was a raw hunger there, too. Shea inched a little farther away from him.

The men noticed her slight movement and a booted

foot came down on her middle. "You just lay there, witch. Don't try a damn thing. You hear me?"

She shivered, nodded and avoided meeting their gazes again, not wanting to give them any reason to get rougher with her than they had already. Magic Police. *Legal bullies,* she thought, trying to keep her features from betraying her thoughts.

The MPs were one of the first agencies that had sprung up after magic had been outed to the world. Headlines around the globe trumpeted the news that all of those sleazy tabloid papers had been right all along. Magic *did* exist. The public outcry for protection from so-called deviants had resulted in every nation pushing through legislation to somehow identify and then secure supposed witches. It had sounded reasonable even to Shea at the time, despite the fact that her own aunt Mairi had been the first witch to be captured in the United States.

Locating and securing women of power had seemed a logical response. Of course it would be safer for these women to be studied and kept from hurting anyone else. Her aunt hadn't meant to kill, any more than Shea herself had.

While the general population ranted about public safety, Congress and other bodies like it had kept cool heads, talking only about security.

But even laws written with the best of intentions sometimes became another entity entirely over time. Mairi's execution had heralded the first change. And during the last ten years, the agencies formed to keep witches secure had instead become jailers and executioners. All under the legal government stamp of approval.

People didn't care what happened to a witch—as long as she wasn't living in *their* neighborhood.

As with anything else, though, there were underground movements within movements. Just as BOW and the MPs had gained in authority and popular-

ity, there were other groups equally dedicated in their
own way to finding the witches. Religious zealots saw a
witch's power as an affront to God. The Seekers hunted
witches in the hopes of somehow stealing their powers
for themselves. The RFW, Rights for Witches, struggled
and fought through the court system, claiming that a
witch was entitled to basic human rights.

Everyone wanted something from the magic community, which was now so deeply in hiding that most of the
women captured by hunters were ordinary humans, with
no powers at all. Just as with the Salem witch trials so
long ago, all it took was innuendo, rumor or an enemy
with a grudge, and any woman could find herself locked
away with little hope of eventual release.

Shea still couldn't understand how any of this was
happening—not in general, but to *her* in particular.
Hard enough to accept that magic was alive and well.
But to acknowledge that *she* was a witch was an even
harder admission. She'd been denying the possibility for
years. Ever since her aunt Mairi's public execution.

Shea's mind whisked back to that last day with her
aunt, her only family. She'd been granted a "private"
visit with Mairi, in an openly bugged room, mainly because the MPs and BOW were hoping to catch Shea saying something incriminating about herself.

But they'd been disappointed. She and Mairi had
cried together, had tried to make sense of what had happened and then they'd prayed, futilely as it turned out,
for a presidential pardon.

There was no hope to be found. Not when there were
dozens of witnesses ready to testify that they had *seen*
fire leap from Mairi's hands to engulf the abusive ex-
husband trying to drag her off. Self-defense hadn't even
come into the trial. A *witch*, people said, had nothing to
fear and was instead herself a living, breathing weapon.

Mairi, stunned by what she'd done, unable to understand how it had happened, hadn't been able to explain a thing. She had been too traumatized to even attempt to save her own life.

The general public hadn't wanted an explanation anyway. What they wanted was blood. Eye for an eye. They quoted the Bible—*Thou shalt not suffer a witch to live.* Reporters followed Shea, as Mairi's only living relative, waiting for her to display the same kind of power. It was hereditary, pseudoscientists claimed on every nightly talk show. In the blood. If Mairi was a witch, then it stood to reason her niece would be, too.

And Shea had been all too worried that they were right.

When Mairi was tied to the very modern steel pole in the middle of a gas grid, Shea had stood there, keeping her gaze locked with her aunt's. Every instinct she had was yelling at her to run. To get as far from what was happening as possible. But she couldn't. She had to stay. For Mairi. So that her aunt could die knowing that not *everyone* in the room relished her suffering.

As the prison guard had flipped a single switch, gas rushed from pipes beneath Mairi's feet. Then another switch provided the spark that ignited a conflagration. In seconds, Mairi was in the middle of an inferno.

Her screams still echoed in Shea's dreams.

After that, Shea had disappeared. She'd left everything she had known. Walked away from her job, her apartment. She'd had no friends to lose, since they had slipped away as soon as Mairi was arrested. Shea cut her dark red hair, dyed it a nearly invisible shade of dark blond and became one of the people she used to give dollar bills to when she passed them on the street. For a while, she stayed in shelters, not trusting any city long enough to remain in one place for more than a night or two.

But after a year or so she took a job as a waitress,

working for cash, no questions asked. She rented a room from her boss and even briefly made a friend. For six months, she had lived like a regular person. Then a news program ran a "Whatever Happened To . . ." segment, starring her. They'd showed clips of Mairi's execution and shots of Shea tearfully defending her aunt to news media that couldn't have cared less.

She ran again that night.

And hid in one big city after another. She'd managed to stay under the radar, avoiding BOW and the MPs, always staying one step ahead of them even as she kept up a facade of normalcy. Finally, a year and a half ago, she'd retaken her own name and accepted a job doing what she loved. She'd thought at the time that the principal who hired her was broad-minded enough to overlook the fact that Shea's aunt had been executed as a witch. She had to wonder now if perhaps Ms. Talbot hadn't hired her as a favor to BOW so that they could keep an eye on her.

Whether it was true or not, all of that was over.

Now she knew she was what they had long suspected her to be. The accusations were true. They knew what she was capable of. And so did she.

"We're not there yet," a deep voice said. "Don't let down your guard until we've handed her over. No telling what a trapped witch will be able to do."

Trapped.

She really was. She was on her own.

Under different circumstances, she would have found the situation laughable, since that was the reason she'd *left* Torin's house—to be on her own, trusting no one but herself.

See how well that had gone.

"White gold stops their powers for real?"

Oh, God, that was what they'd put around her neck the moment they'd grabbed her. White gold. No wonder she felt as though there was a lead weight pressing on her soul.

Shea turned her head toward the speaker, the youngest, most excited one of the group. He leaned forward, bracing his forearms on his thighs, and watched her as if he expected her head to start spinning around. As if he were looking forward to watching it. He licked his lips in anticipation and she shivered again before turning her head away.

"Yeah," someone else said and Shea closed her eyes. "White gold shuts their power down flat. Don't really know why. Something about it being a conglomeration of an element of the earth or some damn thing." He snorted and Shea sighed. "Doc Fender figured it out about eight or nine years back and we've been using it ever since to trap these bitches and keep 'em compliant."

"Any of 'em ever get away?" the young one asked. "I mean, you know, do magic even with the white gold chain around their neck?"

Shea listened carefully, longing for a ray of hope. She was disappointed.

"Not a one. The white gold shuts 'em down, makes 'em as helpless as kittens." He drew a breath and released it. "Supposed to act like a sort of a blanket, covering up what they can do."

"Then why do we have her tied up and gagged?"

"Just cuz she can't use magic don't mean she can't scratch your eyes out or kick your nuts up into your throat. You want to risk it?"

Disgusted with herself for not doing exactly that back when they'd first captured her, Shea tried to ignore the conversation rolling around her. She didn't care what they had to say anymore. They were just the henchmen. The guys who did the dirty work for the Bureau of Witchcraft. It was BOW she was worried about.

The MPs were probably taking her to an internment

center. If she was lucky. If not, she would just vanish until her body was discovered in a culvert somewhere. But no, she thought, if they were going to kill her, they could have done that already.

She stared out the back window of the van and groaned as the wheels hit something in the road. Her body jostled and every square inch of her felt the ache. But pain wasn't important. What she wanted to know was where she was headed and what she could expect.

Was it only yesterday afternoon when she'd warned her student Amanda Hall to run because her mother wouldn't be leaving whatever camp she'd been taken to? Now . . . less than twenty-four hours later, Shea herself was in the same situation. Ironic? Or just punishment?

She *had* killed, after all. There was no denying it.

Outside the van, freeway lights flashed by and the roar of traffic sounded like a caged beast trying to get inside the van.

"Did she really kill a man today?" the young voice again. "She looks so . . . helpless."

"Helpless? Not likely," someone growled with a snort. "Bitch flipped that poor son of a bitch the bird and he went up like a tiki torch at a barbecue."

A couple of the men laughed and Shea closed her eyes on a wave of sorrow. She'd have to live with what she'd done—if she was allowed to live at all.

"Shut up, Dave." The strongest voice spoke up again. Then he leaned out over Shea so she could look up into his face.

He had dark eyes, short dark hair and a jaw that looked as though it could have been carved of granite. The name stitched into his uniform read L. HARPER. In another life she might have found him attractive, until she looked into his eyes long enough. His dark eyes were filled with hatred. There was nothing soft or merciful about him and as his gaze met hers she tried to cringe back from his hard stare.

"Don't you get fooled by how a witch looks, kid," he said, speaking to the other man as he stared into Shea's eyes. "They're all evil. Right down to the core. Kill you as soon as look at you and do whatever they have to, to escape."

Shea shook her head wildly, trying to silently argue with him, but he wasn't buying it.

"Don't try the big sad eyes on me, witch," he murmured, leaning in so that he could speak in a whisper. "I've seen what your kind can do. And I'm not going to rest until you're all locked up or burned at the stake. With any luck, you're going to end up just like your aunt did."

Tears fell from the corners of her eyes and streaked into her hair, but Shea couldn't stop them. Fear clawed at her chest, scraped at her throat. She looked up into those eyes and saw her own death written there.

And though it was far too late, she silently screamed for the one person she believed could have saved her.

Torin!

Chapter 9

Torin faced an ugly truth. He had no idea where Shea had been taken. She could be at any one of several internment camps—or she might have been killed outright.

But even as that thought registered, he rejected it. Though he couldn't sense her, he had no doubt that if she were dead, his body would feel her absence. It had been so in the past and he had no reason to suspect that it had changed. She lived. But where was she?

"Which do we try first?" Rune's voice, sounding as irritated as Torin felt, shattered his thoughts.

Scowling into the night, Torin considered their options. They had already followed the scent of Shea's captors as far as they could. But the trail had ended on the 405 freeway, close enough to a transition that the car carrying Shea away from him could have gone in either of two directions.

A decision must be made. Any action was preferable to a stalemate.

The challenge lay in forcing himself to think like a human. Their minds were convoluted; logic rarely reared its head. The mortals he'd known over the centuries were driven by fear—which led to mystifying choices that often left Torin wondering how they had managed to survive as a species. But now, to find his woman, he must find a way to guess what these particular humans would do next.

There were two internment camps within driving distance of Malibu. The first lay deep in the Angeles National Forest, surrounded by hundreds of acres of emptiness. Secluded, far from any city, it would be the more difficult of the two to infiltrate, since there was nothing but open space around the camp itself—leaving any who approached visible to the guards standing watch.

The other was on Terminal Island in Long Beach. Closer, but far easier to find a way in. With the city surrounding it and the busy traffic of a harbor, he and Rune would hardly be noticed. Once a prison, it had been turned into a detention camp when the first witches were discovered. The camps were all heavily guarded, he knew. And their fences were laced with white gold that would tax the Eternals' powers. His choice was which location to try first.

He was tempted to take the closer route, investigate the camp in Long Beach. But if Shea were not there, the authorities would be on alert from his visit and all of the camps would be strengthened, making the Angeles Forest camp that much harder to penetrate. The same would hold true once he and Rune invaded the old FEMA camp in the woods, but even on high alert Long Beach would be easier to breach.

"We go to Angeles Forest," he said finally. Decision made. But before he left he threw another long look at the freeway stretching out toward Long Beach.

He would find her. Wherever she was.

No one could keep her from him.

Chapter 10

The Terminal Island internment camp used to be a federal prison. It squatted on an artificial island between Los Angeles Harbor and Long Beach Harbor. Back when California was still a Spanish territory, the island was little more than a mudflat known to locals as Rattlesnake Island. But in the early twentieth century, the feds built a prison there and called it Terminal Island. The name had always had a sort of funereal feel to it, in Shea's mind. But she'd never really noticed it much unless she was driving over the Vincent Thomas Bridge to San Pedro.

Now, though, everything had changed. The island had been emptied of everyday criminals when witchcraft was exposed and now it housed hundreds of suspected witches. Turned out people were more afraid of magic-casting women than they were of common murderers.

"What that says about people, I don't know," Shea whispered to herself, carrying a set of sheets along with a flat pillow and a threadbare blanket in her arms. She marched behind a heavily armed female guard and two other prisoners. She wasn't the only witch to have been captured tonight.

Fluorescent lights cast an ugly glow over the sickly green walls and the faces of women peering through their barred cell doors. Shea felt dozens of stares fixed on her and she could only suppose that watching the arrival of new prisoners was the sole entertainment the women in here got.

She tipped her head back to look around and saw that above her there was another whole floor of cells. She wondered just how many women had been tucked away in this prison and forgotten. Her stomach churned and the heaviness on her soul felt worse than ever. The white gold chain around her neck continued to send icy threads of misery throughout her body as if reminding her that there was nothing she could do to free herself.

She took a deep breath and cast sidelong glances to the cells she passed on her walk. Women of all different ages and races stared back at her, hopelessness glistening in their eyes as they watched the latest arrivals.

Soon, Shea thought, she'd be one of them. Just another rat in a cage, locked away until someone, somewhere, decided what was to be done with her. And though the thought of being shut up behind bars terrified her, the noise in the prison was the worst part.

The incessant clang of steel bars slamming shut. The desperate sobbing, and under it all the softly pitched crackle of women's voices rising and falling to the rhythm of the sea just beyond the prison walls. A guard shouted, a woman cried out and somewhere close by another prisoner moaned as if she were dying.

Despair clung to the walls and tainted every breath Shea drew. Panic was clawing at her, closing her throat so she could barely breathe, filling her eyes with tears she refused to shed. She wouldn't give her jailers the satisfaction of seeing how scared she really was.

The female guard pushed the first woman in their line into a cell and slammed the door shut. The *clang* jolted Shea out of her thoughts and sent a cold ball of lead dropping into the pit of her stomach. Again they walked, continuing on past the rows of cells, their measured steps drowned in the cacophony of sound.

Shea's mind continued to turn to the fierce man who had rescued her less than a day ago. She'd run from him, thinking that he was too dangerous. Too connected to the visions that haunted her. Would she have been in deeper trouble if she had stayed with him? Right now, she couldn't imagine that.

The guard stopped and the prisoner in front of Shea stepped into a cell, the metal door sliding shut behind her with a finality that was soul shattering. Then it was only Shea, following the grim-faced guard.

An hour or so ago, the men who had captured her had reluctantly turned her over to the prison guards and Shea had been almost grateful. Yes, this was prison and God knew when—or if—she'd ever get out again. But at least, she'd told herself, she was away from the more imminent physical threat the men had presented.

Her arms tightened around her burden and the scent of bleach wafted up to her from the well-washed fabrics. She wore a pale blue jumpsuit and white sneakers with no laces. Her hair was loose and still damp from the supervised shower she'd been forced to take on arrival.

The tiny humiliations that had been heaped on her made all of this seem even more surreal. A bored prison guard had run her fingers through Shea's long, thick hair, looking for concealed weapons. Another guard had watched Shea strip and then searched her discarded clothing. She tried not to recall the degradation of the strip search. And thinking about the inoculation the nurse had made as painful as possible only made her want to cry, which was useless. Then there was the open shower area that almost reminded Shea of high school gym classes until the water came on and it was icy cold. Two female guards had kept watch while Shea bathed as quickly as she could and then dried herself with a scratchy white towel.

The only item she'd been allowed to hang on to was the white gold chain around her neck, lying like ice against her skin. The cold sensations sank deep into her spirit, blanketing whatever she was or might have been.

This was her life now, she thought, glancing into the cells as she passed, watching woman after woman meet her gaze, then look away. A few stood, chins lifted, quietly defiant, but they were in the minority. Most had been beaten, emotionally if not physically. They, like her, were trapped in a cage designed to hold them forever.

There was no presumption of innocence for a witch.

"In you go."

Shea looked at the guard in front of her and then turned her head toward the open cell door. Swallowing the bitter taste of fear and regret, Shea walked into the narrow, cheerless room. Pale green walls here too, in a cell no bigger than six feet by five feet. There was a slender bunk covered by a thin mattress, a bare toilet and a tiny sink with buttons rather than faucet handles. A single hard chair was the only other appointment in Shea's new home. Glancing around, a fathomless well of desolation rose up within her. She let out a long sigh and slowly turned to watch the guard close the cell door, shutting her in.

Smiling, the guard stepped close to the bars and Shea moved back two paces, driven away by the cold gleam in the guard's eyes.

"I heard about you," the woman said, her voice nearly lost in the surrounding swell of sound. "Killed a man today, didn't you? Enjoy it?"

"Of course not," Shea said, arms tightening around the bundle of bedsheets.

"Sure, I believe you." Sarcasm was thick in her voice and the woman's eyes flashed with something dangerous. "Everyone knows what happened. Word spreads fast in a place like this. You used magic to kill a man."

A swift, sharp stab of regret shot through her but she defended herself anyway. "He was attacking me."

"Found you out, didn't he?" the guard taunted. "Knew what you were and so you had to kill him. Shouldn't have done it in front of witnesses, though. That was stupid."

Shea took a deep breath. "That's not what happened."

No one would believe her. No one would ever hear her side of the story. New laws were being rushed through Congress every day. Laws that said dangerous witches weren't entitled to a trial by their peers—because their peers were in prison. No human jury would sit on a trial for a witch because they were too afraid of retribution.

So there were no trials anymore.

Witches were now immediately imprisoned and, if deemed warranted, executed.

"It's exactly what happened," the woman said. "You're no better than your aunt. And if you weren't wearing that chain around your neck, you'd kill me in a heartbeat to escape, so don't bother telling me any lies."

The slurs on her aunt stung. Mairi had been one of the kindest, most gentle people Shea had ever known. And in one horrifying instant, she'd become Public Enemy Number One.

Shea's gaze dropped to the name tag the guard wore. JACOBS. When she spoke again, it was in a calm, rational tone. If she could win this woman's understanding, maybe even make a friend here, there was a chance she could make her new life a little less hideous. "Officer Jacobs . . ."

"Don't say my name!" she shouted, cheeks paling even as she pulled a nightstick from her belt and slapped it hard against the white gold bars, making Shea jump back farther and drop the sheets and blankets to the cold, cracked linoleum floor at her feet.

The harsh *whack* stilled everyone nearby. The silence was almost as unnerving as the racket had been before.

"Don't ever say my name," the woman said, eyes wide, mouth twisted into a feral snarl. "You try and spell me, witch, and you won't live to see your legal execution. You'll die right here."

Shea's gaze locked with the guard's—and what she read in those dark brown eyes sent a chill racing through her. There was no safety anywhere now, she thought, realizing that the guards here had complete control over the inmates. And the "accidental" death of a witch wouldn't even raise an eyebrow.

"Don't you push me, Witch. Understand?"

Shea nodded, holding her breath, leery of even *thinking* about arguing, lest it show on her face. Slowly, the women around them came to life again and hushed voices once more whispered into the stale air. Seconds ticked past and the activity in the prison continued as if nothing out of the ordinary were happening—and that was probably true.

Threats and beatings were nothing new in the prison system, Shea realized. And not even the ACLU was willing to stand up and speak for a witch.

She was alone here.

Atonement, Torin had said. Was this part of it? Was she being punished now for something that had happened in another world, another life?

Alone, she shivered at her own thoughts and the empty dread filling her.

As the guard moved off with one last fulminating look, Shea slowly walked to the cell door to look out at her new home. The cold from the white gold did battle with a new kind of chill inside her.

Someone in the distance shouted, "Lights-out!"

One by one, the overhead lights blinked off as Shea looked across the dozens of women in nearby matching cells. Darkness crept along the cellblock and those women's faces receded into the shadows.

As the last light flickered out, Shea understood a horrible truth.

They were *all* alone.

Chapter 11

Two men wouldn't have stood a chance at breaking into the internment camp nestled deep in the forest.

Two Eternals, on the other hand, encountered little trouble.

Torin felt the drain to his powers from the proximity of the white gold that had been sprayed across the chain-link fence surrounding the camp. Though his magical abilities were weakened by the man-made element, his physical strength remained. He and his fellow Eternals had been created to be strong, nearly invincible. As if the demigod who was their creator had foreseen that one day man would find a way to abridge their magic, he had seen to it that Eternals would never be completely defenseless.

Torin and the others like him boasted superhuman strength and endurance. Their magic was not as extensive as that of the witches they protected, but their physical abilities were more than a match for the witches' enemies.

The guards at this prison wouldn't stop him from finding Shea.

Comfortable in the shadows as he would never be in the light, Torin moved with stealth, focused solely on the prisoners locked within the grim walls. There were armed guards patrolling the perimeter, and roving white lights swept the cleared area in front of the camp with clockwork precision.

Which worked in their favor.

It took only moments for Torin to realize the rhythm of the lights and understand how to avoid them. He shot a look at Rune, positioned off to his right, and nodded. As one, the two closed in on the enclosure, moving so quickly the human eye could barely track them.

The guards were oblivious and would remain so for as long as possible. Torin approached the wall, reached within himself for the power of the flames and instantly found himself inside the camp. As brightly lit as the outside was, here it was pitch-black. It was a calculated risk, drawing on his flames. A flicker of a flashlight beam sliced through the darkness on occasion as guards moved through the prison on their rounds.

I will find the cells. You locate the records room. See if there is mention of any new prisoners. Speaking telepathically to Rune, Torin parted ways with his friend a moment later. He had a more important mission to take care of.

The white gold layered throughout the prison dampened his powers but didn't shut them down completely. A witch, who was of the earth, was more directly affected. An Eternal was born of the sun. Created from the very fires of the star, the Eternals could more easily withstand the cloying pull of white gold. Though even they couldn't withstand its proximity for long.

Torin's well-honed senses were tuned toward Shea. To the particular hum of her mind, her emotions. Her never-changing soul. After centuries spent near her, he knew the vibration of her life's energies as well as he knew his own and so he was aware almost immediately that she wasn't there. Still, he had to make sure.

The cellblock wasn't hard to locate. A huge building in the center of a barren yard. There were bars on the high windows and a guard posted at the steel door. Not a problem, since he wouldn't be using the entrance.

Once again, flames erupted across his skin, and this time Torin knew he wouldn't go unnoticed. He was inside the prison proper. Guards would see the flash of brightness as his powers, dampened though they were, burst free, but they wouldn't have enough time to stop him.

Instantly, he disappeared and rematerialized inside the cellblock. Outside the building warning sirens wailed as word spread of his presence. He paid them no mind.

Women in the cells awoke at the noise and started calling out to each other. And to him. He listened for one voice in particular and wasn't surprised when he didn't hear it. The time for stealth was past, so he called out, "Shea Jameson! Are you here?"

"Get us out of here," a woman shouted back.

Other voices joined that refrain.

"Who are you?"

"*What* are you?"

"Help!"

His long legs ate up the vast hall separating two rows of cells. The white gold continued to affect him, but its presence wasn't strong enough to completely incapacitate him. He felt the drain on his powers but refused to surrender to it, calling on his own inner strength to keep going. Nothing in this world or the next would keep him from his woman.

"Is Shea Jameson here?" He suspected she wasn't and yet he called out anyway, determined to leave no stone unturned. His shout thundered over the women's softer cries and for a split second, silence followed.

"Don't know who she is." A woman in the last cell answered him, her voice confidently shattering the quiet. She stepped up to the bars, grabbed hold of them and gave them an impotent shake. "Can you get us out of here?"

He stopped to look into her pale blue eyes, reading the fear and frustration written there. She tore at him, this nameless prisoner. As they all did. If he could have, he would have freed all of them. He was an Eternal, created to protect and defend; it went against every instinct he possessed to stand by as any female—especially a witch—was harmed in any way.

Even with the white gold chain around her neck and the bars separating them, he could sense her power, brutally buried within her. Fury for those who would cage women such as her—such as Shea— swept through him. But he had a mission. One that didn't include playing hero.

"I cannot," he said. He didn't have the time to linger and had no way to get the woman to safety if he did help her escape. As it was, precious seconds were already gone. Rune was no doubt on his way to meet him and Torin hadn't found Shea. Or even a trace of her.

"Damn it," he whispered, as a sense of unease crept through him. He was wasting time while Shea was being held somewhere else, in a place too much like this one.

The witch stretched one arm through the bars for him, but couldn't quite reach. Her fingers closed helplessly into her palm. Blowing out a breath, she whispered, "You're an Eternal."

Shocked, Torin narrowed his gaze on her. The Eternals were legend among witches, he knew. Their existence wasn't a secret. But how had she recognized him as such? He felt no recognition for her. A buzz of warning slid through Torin's veins. "How do you know of us?"

She laughed shortly. "Word travels," she told him, running one hand through her short, spiky black hair. "When witches get together, we share information. I ran into a woman a year or so ago who told me about you guys."

"How do you know I am one of them?"

She shrugged. "Who else could have gotten in here?"

Accepting that, he stepped closer and caught her scent, an earthy aroma that reminded him of both forest and sea. It was a blend of scents that usually clung to women with magical abilities. As if the elements themselves, gathering in the woman's blood, were surfacing through her pores, allowing her to be one with nature and the very earth that would bolster her magic. There was something else here, too, he thought, trying to make sense of it.

"Who told you of us?" Was there another Awakened witch out there that they must find? He had thought Shea to be the first. And if there was another, where was her Eternal? Why hadn't he found her?

Though there were witches all across the globe, there were only a select few to whom Eternals were bound. They were the chosen ones. Members of the once mighty coven that had paid a deadly price for their arrogance eons ago.

Instantly, the witch behind the bars shook her head. Face pale, eyes blazing, she said, "I'll only tell you if you get me out."

Still the sirens blared, shattering the night. Women up and down the cellblock screamed and cried out for help. At the end of the long, dark hall, the steel door swung open and a wide swath of light slashed through the shadows. Guards shouted. A burst of gunfire chattered outside the walls and in response the caged women shrieked and moaned.

The dark-haired witch never broke eye contact with him. "I can tell you what you need to know," she said quickly. "But not unless you get me out. I don't need your help after that. I can teleport."

The abilities granted to witches were wide and varied. If this witch was a teleporter—one who had the ability to shift across distances, much like an Eternal—then

he could leave her to her own devices once she was free.
And he needed to know what she knew.

Torin bit off another curse and threw a look down
the hall at the group of guards rushing inside the prison.

"Get me out and I'm fine," she said, words tumbling
from her mouth in a desperate rush. "But I'm marked
for execution and unless you help me escape, the knowledge you need dies with me."

"Damn all of this straight to hell." He was caught. If
he wanted her information, he must free her. Besides,
he was wasting time standing there arguing with her.
"Stand back."

Reluctantly, she did.

Torin brought forth the flames, fighting the drag of
the white gold surrounding him. The fire burned for him
as always, although diminished slightly. He centered the
flames on his right hand. The living fire crackled and
spit as he reached toward the lock on the white gold
cell bars. He'd have only moments before direct contact
with the gold began to affect his powers. If this took too
long, he could find himself as trapped as the witch—and
forced to fight his way out. Though that wouldn't present a problem, it would take time he didn't have. He
had to risk it, though, for the information she offered.
He laid his burning fingertips to the locking mechanism
and instantly felt an icy draught push through the flames,
flooding into him. Torin held fast, his gaze fixed on the
lock, his powers centered on the task.

Flames fought with ice. The witch urged him to hurry.
The prisoners continued to shriek and scream.

"Stand down!" a guard shouted, running now, heavy
footsteps echoing through the hall, despite all the noise.

Torin paid him no attention, but the women in the
cells were doing all they could to slow the guards. Bits of
food, books, magazines flew through the bars, aimed at
the armed men. The prisoners were risking everything

to help one of their own escape. No doubt in the hope that one day it would be their turn.

Rune appeared in a flash of flame alongside him just as the lock gave way.

"What the hell?" he demanded, looking from Torin to the witch rushing out of the cell.

"Not now," Torin told him, reaching for the witch even as she threw herself into his grasp. He fought through the dampening effect of the white gold, called on the flames once more and let them engulf him and the witch as a deadly hail of bullets flew at them.

Chapter 12

Sounds echoed softly in the cavernous prison as the women settled in for the night. Sighs and sobs and whispered prayers were a constant murmur that sounded like the rush of wind through trees. The darkness was alive. With the fluorescent lights off, the only illumination came through each prisoner's narrow window. The glass was dirty and beyond the pane were heavy bars that Shea suspected were also coated in white gold. But at least she had one small slice of the outside world to cling to.

Alone in her cell, she did her best to shut out the murmuring, the despair. With her bed made, she lay on the hard mattress and stared out that window, wishing she were anywhere else.

Somewhere out there Torin was looking for her. She was convinced of that. No man who had promised a mating ritual with the seriousness he had would allow her to escape him. And now that she was praying he'd show up, the question was, would he be able to find her?

She closed her eyes and focused her thoughts on the tall man with the fierce gray eyes. He'd called himself an *Eternal. Her* Eternal. Why did that sound familiar? That one word seemed to resonate with her. She brought his face into her mind and concentrated with everything she was.

How odd, she noted absently, that only hours ago, *he*

had been the enemy. Now, he was hope. Before, she'd worried that he was somehow connected to the strange dreams and visions that had been haunting her. She no longer cared. She'd take the dreams. Whatever he had planned for her had to be better than this.

With his image firmly in her mind, she finally slept and the dream came.

She was at home, in a small cottage on the edge of a thick wood with a stream rushing nearby. A peat fire burned in the hearth and herbs hung from the ceiling rafters. There was a wide window overlooking a garden that looked lush even in the moonlight. Everything was in its place. Warm throws and pillows rested on the pair of chairs drawn up to the crackling fire. Pots and jugs lined shelves where several precious books were carefully stacked. The bed was wide and lumpy, covered with a quilt she'd pieced together herself.

In her dream, Shea recognized this place. She was herself and yet at the same time she was someone else. Someone in a different time. The woman who lived here. Worked here. *Loved* here.

She turned and caught her reflection in the shiny bottom of a copper pan. Familiar, yet strange. The green eyes she recognized, but the thick black hair was different. Her face was heart-shaped and her lips were red and full. She was . . . another.

In a dream that was so real, she smelled the peat smoke, tasted the warm, earthy scent on her tongue. Even in sleep, she felt flustered, as confusion spiraled through her mind. How could she be so at home in a place and time that wasn't hers? How could she know that there was a village just a mile or so away? And that the herbs hanging over her head were for medicinal uses?

She rubbed the forehead that wasn't really hers and yet was, and tried to make sense of things.

Then the door behind her crashed open, slamming into

the wall. Heart racing, Shea spun around to face the giant of a man filling the open doorway. His long black hair was braided at his temples. He wore a simple homespun shirt and brown leather pants tucked into heavy brown boots.

His gray eyes locked on her and her still-frantic heart leapt in her chest. She knew those eyes. Had known them, she now thought, through countless lifetimes. Something inside her loosened as even in the dream she felt pieces of a puzzle slide inexorably into place. Then she wasn't thinking at all. Every inch of her body burned with a hunger that she recognized. Embraced. An icy wind slid through the room to caress the flames and send them dancing and writhing, making twisting shadows on the rough-hewn walls.

"You weren't waiting in the village," he accused.

"Do I look like a woman to take orders?" she asked, but her voice was flirtatious.

"You look like my woman," he told her and slammed the door closed, shutting out the world.

Shea felt the thrill of that simple statement whip through her like a stray lightning bolt. Her gaze met his for a long minute; then she rushed to him, throwing herself against him.

His hard, strong arms came around her, lifting her off the floor. The scent of him filled her senses, as his heat seeped into her bones and kindled fires inside her that seemed on the brink of eruption. Carrying her, he stalked to the bed in the corner and dropped her to the mattress. She tossed her hair back out of her eyes, licked her bottom lip and tugged up the hem of her floor-length skirt, showing him her legs, loving the glitter in his eyes as he watched her.

"Is it a battle you're in the mood for, Torin?" she asked on a sigh. "Or is there not something else you would find more pleasurable?"

"There is at that," he said and tore his clothes off, tossing them to the floor.

Shea inhaled sharply, letting her gaze slide over his muscular, battle-scarred body. He was a warrior like no other. She couldn't imagine her world without him in it. She ached for him. For his touch. For the taste of him. Every time he came to her, it was as the first time.

Magic.

She shivered as that word danced through her mind with a surety that felt natural. As if that word were as much a part of her as her eyes, her breath. Not for the first time, she felt as though there was . . . something she should know. Remember. A flash of an image rushed through her mind and was gone in an instant. High cliffs. A cave. With a fire caged within.

Frowning, she tried to grasp the image. Instead, it niggled at the edges of her brain, teasing a memory that refused to be born.

"What is it?" he asked, reaching for her, pulling her up to sit beside him.

"Nothing. 'Tis nothing," she whispered, not wanting him to think her mad, and unwilling to waste cherished time with him on foolish ramblings. And yet . . . "'Tis only that I feel sometimes as though there's a part of me lost somewhere."

He stared at her for a long minute, then ran one hand over her breast in a slow caress. "Seems to me that all the parts are where they should be."

She sighed and arched into his touch, craving that sizzle of heat that slipped from his skin to hers. He had become as necessary to her as breathing and she wanted nothing more than to relish his hands on her body. Still, she said softly, "You laugh, but there's something amiss, Torin. Something I must—"

"Hush now, lass," he said, laying one finger across her mouth. "Don't fash yourself over this. When the time is right, you'll know. You'll have it all. That time is not now."

His pale gray eyes stared into hers and Shea could have

sworn she saw shadows moving there in those depths. Shadows of things that had been, things that would be. Her breath stilled while her heartbeat quickened.

She shook her head, embarrassed by her foolishness and wild imaginings. And when she looked again into his familiar eyes, she saw only her own reflection staring back at her. Smiling, she asked, "What do you know of it, you great beast?"

He grinned at her, one corner of his mouth lifting as he pulled her off the bed and onto his lap. Pushing her skirts out of the way, he had her straddle him, her bare thighs atop his.

"Beast, am I?" he asked, slipping one hand beneath the fall of her skirt to slide his fingers up the length of her leg and toward her hot, damp center. She shivered in his arms and sighed out his name.

"Beast is what you are," she said then, "if you don't give me what we both need."

"Then name me Torin," he said, lowering her onto his gloriously hard body. "For a beast I won't be."

He pushed himself home and she welcomed the invasion of his body into hers. She groaned and arched her back, swiveling her hips to take him higher, deeper. The thick fullness of him claimed her completely, as if he had been made to join his body with hers.

His fingers at her hips, he gripped tight and urged her to move on him and so she did, because it was all she wanted, needed. Her body sang under his touch, her blood burned and her soul shattered. Again and again, she took him deep, hard, rocking on him, setting a rhythm that he matched and controlled.

Their eyes locked and when the first of the pleasure ripples coursed through her, she looked into her beast's eyes and almost—almost—found what she was searching for.

Chapter 13

"They shot you." The witch pushed out of Torin's arms once they'd reached the nebulous safety of the treeline and stared at the bloodstains on his shirt.

"It's nothing."

He'd flashed from the prison just as the bullets went flying, but still a couple of them had caught him. The bullets had passed through, doing little enough damage that he would be healed by the morning. Torin was unconcerned about a few bullet holes in his flesh. Compared to a slice from a broadsword, they were barely more than insect bites. Instead, he focused on the situation.

Yes, they were free of the prison, but not free of the danger. The guards would soon pour out of the camp and begin searching the surrounding woods. They'd have to be long gone by then.

Before he could say anything else, Rune spoke up. "You want to tell me why you rescued her?"

"She knows of another Awakened witch."

Rune shot the woman a dismissive glance. "Impossible. She's lying. Yours is the first."

"Shows how much you know," the witch snapped. She shot a look over her shoulder at the camp as more lights burst into life until the whole compound blazed like a sun in the darkness.

Torin had no patience for arguments between Rune

and a witch. There was little time and all of it mattered. He couldn't bear thinking of Shea in a place like this. Surrounded by enemies with no one to turn to. He had to find her.

"You say you know who we are," he said. "Then you know Eternals can sense the Awakening. We feel the changing pulse in the weave of the universe as one of the chosen comes into her powers."

"Apparently," she countered, moonlight glinting in her eyes, "you're not as all-knowing as you would like to think."

"Then tell me of this witch," he said, demanding the answers she'd promised him in exchange for her rescue.

"Take this off of me first," the woman insisted, pointing at the white gold chain draped around her neck.

"You would bargain with me? Again?" He glared at her, but the witch held her ground.

She lifted her chin, met him stare for stare and said, "I would bargain with the devil himself to get as far away from here as possible. I can hardly draw an easy breath with this damn thing around my neck. You know I can't take it off myself. So if you want your answer, free me."

Rune snorted. "You've a hell of a nerve. We've already saved you. We can just as easily leave you here for the guards to find. With that chain on your neck, you won't go far."

Torin nodded, watching her to judge her reaction. He knew he wouldn't leave her to the mercies of the prison guards. As an Eternal it was his nature to protect all women—especially women of power. But she didn't have to know that.

"You're not going to leave me here. You can't," she argued simply. Her gaze shot from Torin to Rune and back again. Her short, spiky hair somehow made her look elfin, vulnerable. "You want the information I hold, so you'll do as I ask and take this weight from my neck."

When Rune would have continued the argument with the stubborn witch, Torin held up one hand for silence. Behind them, the compound was coming alive. The double doors swung open and a dozen or more armed guards spilled through. The searchlights were a brilliant white against the surrounding darkness and Torin knew they had only moments before they were found. He could grab the witch and flash away with her. But he didn't want to be hampered with the woman in his search for Shea.

The choice was a simple one. Get the information she held or not. Save her or let the guards reclaim her.

The answer was, there was no choice. He would do what he must—as he always had. Without a word, he gathered the fire, focused its strength and touched the tip of one finger to the center links on the white gold chain lying against her skin. The witch held perfectly still, her gaze locked with his.

The flames he called forth were the very essence of magic, so they didn't harm her skin, but a moment after he had channeled his power, the chain's links had melted. Then he simply flicked the offending antimagic device to the ground.

The witch smiled, inhaled deeply and stretched languidly as if she were a cat stepping from a confining cage. She sighed in relief before saying, "Thank you, Eternal."

Unmoved by her gratitude, Torin dismissed it. "Thank me by keeping your word. Tell me who is this Awakened witch and where is she?"

She slanted her sharp blue eyes on him. A smile curved her mouth as she said, "Her name is Kellyn. And she's standing in front of you, Eternal."

Then she swept out her arms, tipped her head back and whispered something that struck him as old and powerful. She laughed and was gone an instant later, in a shimmer of movement that seemed to ripple the very air.

"A teleporter," Rune muttered in disgust.

"As we are," Torin reminded him. He glanced out to where the prison guards were beginning a concerted sweep of the area. "I don't care that she's gone. But if she was telling the truth, something is very wrong. If Kellyn is Awakened, how is it we didn't sense her coming into her power? And where is her Eternal?"

Eternal and witch were closely bound by the link between them, one created by fates and the old gods. The Eternals, who were created to protect these few special women, instinctively felt when one member of the coven was Awakening. At that time a ripple of awareness moved through the Eternals and the sister witches of the coven. Like a pebble tossed into a lake, the effects of the Awakening echoed within them all.

So how could they have missed the Awakening of another witch?

"What do you mean *where* is he? *Who* is he?" Rune replied.

Over the centuries, the Eternals had drifted apart, each of them watching over the many incarnations of his witch. But being witness to a mate's life and death over and over again during the course of hundreds of years eventually took a toll on all of them. Some elected to disappear, to seek solitude and remain apart from their brothers until the time of the Awakening. Not the wisest course, Torin thought, but understandable.

Still, that left the remaining Eternals with the problem of locating those who had gone missing when they were needed. Now, with the Awakening at last upon them, those absent Eternals should be making themselves known again—if only to guard their own Awakened witches. So if Kellyn had been telling the truth, where, Torin wondered, was her Eternal?

"Should have caught the witch before she teleported out," Rune told him. "Forced her to talk. Tell us all she knew."

"We'll find her again," Torin said, letting the problem go for the moment. Nothing was as important to him as locating Shea. "Just as we'll discover who her Eternal is and why he isn't with her. But for now—"

Rune smiled grimly as the shouts of the prison guards sounded, closer now. "Right. First witch first."

Torin gave him a brief smile. "Exactly. We find Shea. We go to Long Beach—that's probably where they've taken her. The prison there will be on alert after tonight's business, so we'll have to map out a plan."

Rune smirked. "They can't keep us out."

"No, they can't."

"And if your witch isn't there?"

Torin scowled off into the night, taking in the brilliantly lit prison with the women trapped behind its walls. Carefully tempered rage bubbled within him at the thought of his woman at the hands of prison guards. If they hurt her in any way, he would not leave a stone of their prison standing. "Then we keep looking. Nothing will keep me from her."

They surrendered themselves to the magic in unison. Flames burst into life and they were gone an instant later. The guards saw nothing and the night held its secrets.

Chapter 14

Shea wandered the open area, grateful to be out of her cell even though there were walls topped with barbed wire surrounding her. She felt the heavy presence of white gold and knew there was plenty of that material placed around the edges of the prison as well. It seemed the chains around their necks were not nearly enough to assuage any fears the guards might have about their prisoners.

But at least, Shea thought, she could see the sky. She tipped her head back, watched seagulls wheeling and dipping in the wind above her and wished with all her heart she could join them.

The "exercise" yard was small, enclosed on all sides by yet more walls, with armed guards standing in turrets at each of the four corners. There were two guards at each post—one watching the prisoners and one scanning the open harbor. She shivered a little at the implication. They were all too prepared for any rescue attempts—not that people were lining up to help a bunch of accused witches.

She shifted her gaze away quickly, not wanting to be caught studying the guards. In the short time she'd been there, she had already learned to keep her head down. To stay under the radar. The nights were long and terrifying in this place. The guards wandered the darkened aisles, crashing their nightsticks against the bars just to watch the women in the cages jump.

Only that morning Officer Jacobs had shoved Shea's face into a wall for daring to look directly at her. Then she'd used her nightstick to deliver a couple of quick blows to Shea's side. The bruises had been horrific, but were already fading, thanks presumably to her new-found magic. The pain was spectacular, but more than anything it was the despair that continued to choke Shea. She couldn't see a way out. Couldn't think of a thing to help herself. And she had heard the stories of torture somewhere in the bowels of this place.

Sooner or later, she knew it would be her turn.

But it wasn't only the guards she had to worry about. There were feds everywhere. Since her arrival, Shea had learned more than she wanted to know about Terminal Island.

The island itself was crowded with federal agencies. There used to be cottages here, before World War II, to house Japanese fishermen and their families, who lived on the island. But then war with Japan had broken out and the Japanese had been forced to give up their land and property and move to detention centers inland. The village was razed. Ironic that now there was a new generation of so-called un-Americans who had been sent to Terminal Island. The prison itself took up a small portion of this island once used for off-loading cargo.

New cottages and apartment buildings had been hastily built for the use of the jailers and their superiors. The entire place was a fortified, secured center. To keep the women in and others out.

She watched her fellow prisoners. Women rambled around the enclosure in pairs and alone. Some sat and talked quietly while others walked aimlessly, around and around in circles. One or two simply sat on benches and cried. Nowhere to go, nowhere to run, but being able to move outside the tiny cell they spent most of their time in felt like a vacation.

In the two days she'd been there, Shea had already noticed that the two distinct groups of prisoners—the ordinary human women swept up in a tide of fear, and the women of power, women with witchcraft humming through their veins—acted as one outside the cells. Though they were all different, they were also all in the same boat. Amazing, really, that women who would have, in the outside world, been the first to spit on a witch . . . in here, were compatriots with them. Linked together against a common enemy.

Their captors.

For years, Shea had been running and hiding. Odd to finally find a fatalistic peace in the very prison she'd been trying to avoid.

"Ms. Jameson?"

Shea jolted at the sound of her name and whirled around, expecting a guard, and then laughed silently at her own stupidity. No guard here would be calling her "Ms."

A short blond woman with anxious blue eyes hurried up to her.

"It *is* you." The woman grabbed Shea's hand and held on, as if clinging to a life rope in a roiling sea. She took a shuddering breath, blew it out again and said, "I thought I recognized you, but I never expected to see you here. Although I never thought to find myself here, either."

Shea's mind scrambled to find the woman's identity. In the last day or so she'd been through so much, seen so much, she could hardly string two coherent thoughts together beyond the one all-consuming one: *Get Me. Out. Of. Here!* But as the woman continued to talk, it finally dawned on Shea where she knew her from.

School. This was the mother of Amanda Hall. The very girl Shea had been talking to when all of this madness had started.

"It's Terri, isn't it? Terri Hall?" Shea said when the woman wound down.

"Yes," She whipped her hair out of her eyes and looked around quickly, making sure no one was close by. "I met you at parent-teacher conference night last month. God, that seems like years ago now. Amazing how fast things can change. How long have you been here, Ms. Jameson?"

"Call me Shea. Just a day or two."

"Then you must have seen my Amanda since my arrest. Is she all right?"

All right but terrified, Shea thought but couldn't bring herself to say it. No more than she'd tell this poor woman that talking to her daughter had started the slippery slope and landed Shea in prison. Terri Hall was locked away from her daughter and Shea couldn't even imagine the terror the woman must be feeling. Especially since, unlike Shea, Terri hadn't done a damn thing to deserve this. Instinctively, she reached out to soothe and comfort.

"Amanda's fine," she said, squeezing Terri's hand. "I saw her at school and told her to stay with her grandmother and not to go back to school."

"Good, that's good," Terri muttered. "I still can't believe any of this is happening. I'm not a witch, for heaven's sake. One of my neighbors told the MPs that she saw me lighting candles and saying a spell." She laughed shortly and wrapped her arms around her middle as she lifted her gaze to the soaring sky above them. "I was saying a prayer for my husband. He died last year."

"I'm so sorry." It was all crazy and getting worse every day. Ten years after the existence of magic had been revealed, and people were still reacting out of fear.

Terri nodded and sighed. "Thanks. I'm just so worried about Amanda. And my mom. What if they're arrested next?"

Shea had no easy reassurances for her. She knew as well as Terri did that her family was now in even more danger. BOW and the MPs would be watching every move they made for who knew how long.

As for Terri ... women caught up in the mob mentality of the witch hunt were pretty much out of luck. Unless the RFW took up Terri's case, she had no chance of getting out of this camp.

And unless Torin found her, Shea was in the same boat.

"Why are you here?" Terri finally asked, then stopped and winced. "I'm sorry—shouldn't have said that. I mean, I know about your aunt and—"

"It's okay," Shea said, not wanting to get drawn into a conversation about it. Especially not here. In places like this the walls really did have ears. There was no telling how many people were listening in on conversations. They weren't even safe outside. A parabolic microphone or two could cover most of the yard.

As if Terri had remembered the same thing, she lowered her voice. "Are you ... like your aunt?"

A few days ago Shea would have said no. Now, she was living a new reality. Now, she was dealing with the knowledge that she'd killed a man and was, very possibly, in jail for the rest of her life—at least until her execution. But she looked into the other woman's eyes and saw compassion. Amazing just how good it felt to be offered understanding. Slowly, Shea nodded.

Terri smiled. "A month ago, that might have terrified me," she admitted quietly. "Now, though ..." She looked around the yard again. At the dozens of women, in a range of ages anywhere from eighty to teens, and she sighed. "There are other things more scary. There's being snatched from your home in the middle of the night and locked away without a chance of even speaking to your own child. There's fearing that you'll never get out."

"We really shouldn't be talking about this," Shea whispered, glancing up at the closest guard tower. The man wasn't looking in their direction, but that didn't mean a thing.

"They've already locked me up," Terri said firmly. "They're not going to *shut* me up, too. You know, before this happened, I was like anyone else, reading about magic and the witches and how BOW and the MPs were doing their duty to protect the people . . ."

Shea took Terri's elbow and started walking. She wasn't sure why, but somehow she had the feeling that it would be more difficult for their jailers to overhear them if they kept moving in and out of crowds. And she tried to subtly warn her student's mother that being outspoken in prison wasn't necessarily a good thing. "Terri . . ."

She walked and shook her head before giving Shea a half smile. "I know. I know they listen. I know they watch." Her gaze slid to the side, where two female guards stood together, watching over the prisoners. "But I'm still a citizen. I still have rights."

"Not really," Shea told her.

"There's a sad statement."

"You have to be careful," Shea said. "No one here is concerned about your 'rights.' To them, we're less than human. They'd like nothing better than a chance to take us all down. So if you want to see Amanda again—do what you can to stay unnoticed. Don't stand out in this crowd, Terri. Blend in. Don't make waves. You might drown in them."

She huffed out a breath. "Seeing Amanda. What're the chances of that, I wonder."

"Probably not good," Shea admitted, then added, "but you'll make it worse for yourself in here by not being careful."

"I know that, but underneath all of the fear, I am *furi-*

ous," she said softly and her voice toughened up as if to prove it. "I've met a few . . . *interesting* women here and the thing is, they're no different from me. Not at the bottom of it, you know? I mean, we're all just people. Some good, some bad."

Oh, Shea wished she had met Terri under other circumstances. They could have been friends. Instead, they were prison mates with definite dates of expiration. "Yeah, the problem is, that doesn't seem to matter."

"All I'm trying to say is if people would just *talk* to witches, they wouldn't be so afraid."

"You're right. But at the moment," Shea told her, keeping her voice low, "fear's in charge and logic didn't even get a seat at the table."

They walked through the yard, the breeze off the harbor carrying the smell of the sea and the illusion of freedom. Off in one corner, a lone woman sat with her knees drawn up, back against the wall, quietly crying to herself. Just seeing the emotionally beaten woman stiffened Shea's spine.

She wasn't going to be afraid. Not anymore. She was through being the helpless victim, racing through the dark, trying to avoid her enemies by disappearing into an uncaring crowd. Talking to Terri had helped, too. Terri had allowed her own sense of injustice to trump her fears and Shea could do no less.

Dropping one arm around the other woman's shoulder, Shea said, "We'll find a way out."

And she realized she believed it. She wasn't going to be locked away here forever. She'd find a way out even if Torin didn't come for her. Damned if she'd let these bastards win. She and Terri would get out. Somehow. She wouldn't be a statistic and simply disappear.

She wouldn't lie down and die without a whimper.

Chapter 15

Torin felt her presence the moment he and Rune flashed into the internment camp.

Standing in one of the guard towers, he let the body of the guard he had killed drop at his feet. Quick snaps of the neck and both men in the eastern tower were dead. He didn't spare a glance to where they lay sprawled across the floor. They didn't matter. They were predators. Kidnappers and worse.

Rune was even now dispatching those in the north tower, but Torin couldn't think beyond Shea. Through the foggy haze of the white gold dampening her powers, her spirit called to his and electrified the beast within him.

For two days he and Rune had worked out the logistics of getting her out of this prison. Now that the time was here, he knew there would be casualties he couldn't prevent. Deaths he couldn't stop. Yet he had no choice. This could be their only chance. The Awakening had come and there was nothing more important to him than securing Shea and together accomplishing their task.

He and Rune had mitigated the danger as much as they could, reducing the damage that would be done here today. Now, it was left to the fates. In late afternoon the yard was crowded with prisoners. Shadows pushed out from the walls, inching across the ground even as the first brilliant colors of sunset stained the sky. Torin focused his concentration on the women below, searching for the one witch who called to him.

His head snapped up as a burst of gunfire chattered from the south and west towers. The guards had seen them. But instead of firing at the Eternals in the towers, the guards concentrated their fire on the prisoners. As if to kill them all before any had a chance at escape. Bullets sprayed wildly across the open expanse of the yard below. Women shrieked and ran for cover. Some dropped where they stood, their blood running across the concrete in scarlet rivers. In their quest to stop Rune and Torin, the remaining guards cared nothing for how many women died in the attempt.

Torin cared.

He instantly flashed to the west tower. A guard hastily swung his gun around, but Torin was faster. The man died with a howl of protest as his partner pulled a knife and stabbed Torin in the back. Pain lanced through him but didn't stop him. He dropped into a crouch, came up fast and knocked the guard off his feet. Once the man was down, Torin pulled the knife from his body and returned it to the guard. Blade to the heart.

Eyes wide, mouth forming the word *no,* the second guard joined his partner in hell.

Below him, the women's screams scraped the air, but through the frantic shouts and pleas, he heard one voice calling him by name.

"Torin!"

He leapt to his feet, scanned the ground below him and spotted his witch on the far side of the yard. Her long red hair lifted like a flag in the wind and she waved both hands high over her head. He smiled to himself, noting that Shea Jameson wasn't cowering. She was standing tall and proud and his unbeating heart filled with admiration.

They hadn't broken her. Not yet. Not ever.

Chapter 16

Warning sirens screamed to life.

Torin knew they had little time to spare. The tower guards were dead, but there were more just like them throughout this prison. In seconds, reinforcements would rush into the prison proper.

His gaze swept the yard again, searching out the dangers, pinpointing where he would need to be to get his woman to safety. His knife wound was deep and painful, but nothing he hadn't experienced before in centuries of battle. He hadn't the time to spend healing himself. He would need all of his powers focused on the escape.

He flashed to Shea's side and she threw herself at him. Instantly, the world righted itself again. She was alive and in his arms, and the rest he would deal with.

"Torin!"

She held on tightly to him, her face buried in the curve of his neck. As if she knew she belonged there, accepted what they were and always had been to each other. This, he thought, would make the coming days easier. To have her acceptance, her cooperation in the task ahead would make all the difference.

But cooperation or not, he wouldn't be letting her out of his sight again.

With her body pressed to his, he felt the chill of the white gold chain around her neck seep into him, sending ice racing after the fire in his veins. She was stronger than she thought, he told himself. Even with the drain of the white gold at her slender throat, he felt her magic bubbling with her.

Despite the chill of the dampening element against him, his body responded immediately to her presence. Heedless of the danger, he was hard as iron and aching to begin the ritual. But his mind overruled his dick. This time.

"We have to go," he said, glancing over as Rune flashed in to stand beside him. The Eternal's gaze swept the crowded yard—the screaming women, the wounded prisoners stretched out across dirty asphalt, the remaining guards who were running for cover to wait until their cavalry arrived.

"I know," Shea said. "I'm ready." She released him, took a step back, then reached out and grabbed the hand of the blond woman standing beside her. "I mean, *we're* ready."

Of course this wouldn't go smoothly, Torin told himself with an inward groan of frustration. Never once in centuries had Shea stopped surprising him.

"Damn it!" Rune's curse was deep and vicious.

Shea shot him a dark look. "I wasn't talking to you." Then she shifted her gaze to Torin's and he felt the strength of that stare hit him hard. "This is my student's mother. She's not a witch. And if she doesn't get out of here, they'll kill her. They'll torture her for information she doesn't have."

"We don't have time for this," Rune told Torin.

"We don't have time to argue about it, either," he shot back, before turning his gaze back to his witch. "You insist on this?"

She met his gaze squarely. "I do."

Nodding, Torin looked at the other woman, who watched him through stunned yet resolute blue eyes.

He took her measure and noted that she hadn't shrunk back from him, though a man appearing from a tower of flames had to have shocked her. "Your name."

"Terri. Terri Hall," she said, words tumbling from her mouth as she reacted to the dangerous situation. "And I do need to get out of here. I have to get to my daughter."

"Torin," Rune interrupted, "there's no time to save another. We had a mission and we've been here too long already. More guards will be coming."

But Torin was looking not at Rune but at Shea. Her green eyes were locked with his and she was measuring him, seeing who and what he was. He sensed that her memories of their shared past hadn't cleared yet. And so the choice he made now would decide much for her. He knew this moment would brand him in her eyes for all time. Could she trust him and learn from him? Or would he be as uncaring as those who would see her dead?

The choice was a simple one.

"Take the woman," Torin told Rune flatly.

Shea smiled and Terri blew out a relieved breath. From somewhere in the distance more shouts lifted into the air. He didn't like leaving these other women to the less than tender mercies of the guards, but there was nothing he could do to help them. Not yet, anyway.

"You have to get her to safety," Shea insisted, spearing Rune with a commanding stare. "You can't just get her out of here and then dump her somewhere. She needs to be *safe*. And not only her. You'll need to take her daughter and mother, too."

Terri gasped in surprise.

Rune's mouth worked as if he longed to tell her no, but to his credit, he remained quiet until he muttered a curse and simply asked, "Anything else?"

Pride in his woman prompted Torin to smile at his friend's fury.

"Yes," Shea snapped, unamused. "They'll need money and I want to know where you're taking them."

"Money's not a problem," Torin replied. The Eternals' god, Belen, saw to it that his warriors had all they needed to survive in a human world. "As for safety, there are places. Sanctuaries."

Shea looked to Torin, demanding, "Where?"

He scanned the area again, knowing time was short and the guards would soon locate them.

"The closest one is in the Uinta Mountains of Utah," he said. "The camp is well hidden. Both witches and human women are welcome to hide there. It's far from civilization and the witches there have laid down wards and protective spells so that their camp is overlooked by those who would search for them."

She nodded and looked at her friend. "Terri? Is all of this okay with you?"

The blonde shot a wary look at Rune. She had little choice but to risk going with him. It was that or die, never seeing her child again. Torin wasn't surprised when she spoke.

"Sounds good. And thanks for getting my mom and Amanda out, too." Her gaze shifted around the prison enclosure, briefly taking in the bodies of the fallen women. She shivered and swallowed hard, lifting her chin in a show of defiance. "Always wanted to live in the mountains. Besides, the farther from here, the better."

"We go, then," Rune said. First, he reached out one hand toward the chain around her neck. "This must come off."

"If we don't get rid of the necklace, the white gold will drain Rune's powers slowly, making it harder for him to protect you and your family," Torin said.

"Do it." Terri tilted her head to one side and barely flinched when Rune's fingertip blazed into flames that touched her skin and didn't burn. The necklace dropped unheeded to the ground. She lifted one hand to rub her neck, then stared at Rune as if wondering if she was jumping from the frying pan into a living, breathing fire.

"Trust them," Shea said and those two words filled Torin with pride.

Rune held out one hand to Terri. "If we are going, woman, we must go now."

"Right." Terri linked her fingers with his and as the flames rose up to swallow them, Shea actually heard Terri laugh.

"Now are you ready?" Torin asked, reaching out his hand to free her of the draining white gold links at her throat.

Gunfire erupted in the distance. Shea took a breath and nodded. "God, yes. Let's go."

Flames raced from his body to the links against her neck. Seconds passed; then she sighed as the hated necklace dropped free of her body. "That feels much better."

Guards shouted, women screamed and yet more gunfire blasted the air. Wrapping her arms around Torin's neck, Shea held on tight and whispered, "Get us out of here."

With a whoosh of sound and a bright flash of flames, they vanished.

Chapter 17

"Madam President, the director of the Terminal Island detention center is on line two. He said you're expecting his call?"

Cora Sterling, first female president of the United States, looked up at her chief of staff. She gave him the warm, motherly smile that had gained her the trust of a nation and allowed her to be at the epicenter of a historic election. "Yes, thank you, Sam. I'll speak to him in a moment."

"Yes, ma'am." The tall, handsome man nodded and left the Oval Office.

Cora sat on one of the twin pale blue upholstered sofas placed opposite each other. A reading lamp burned softly on the nearby table and the latest sheaf of papers sent to her by the Senate was scattered across the cushions beside her. *I love this room,* she thought, as she stood up and crossed the navy blue rug with the presidential seal embroidered into it.

Being here, in the White House, was something she never took for granted. She'd worked hard to get here. To belong here. Though at times it all still felt surreal. A widow with a grown daughter, Cora had always been an ambitious woman—but this, she thought wryly, went well beyond her ambitions.

The sound of her heels was muffled as she walked

with a confident stride to stand at her desk and stare at the phone. The HOLD button flashed as if insisting that she pick up. But she took a moment to ground herself.

She was the president, after all.

She smiled to herself. Six months in office and she still wasn't used to it. Cora Sterling, middle-class girl from Sugar Land, Texas, first female president. Her election had made history. Her term in office, she told herself, would do the same. She had run on a campaign of reform and domestic safety.

With witchcraft alive in the world, the people were frightened. Frightened enough to vote for her when she had promised to protect them—and she would keep that promise. She had vowed to resolve the witch situation and to bring a halt to the fear that seemed to be the underlying thread of society these days.

If witchcraft existed, she insisted on the campaign trail, then it was time that the world accept the new reality and find a way to work with it. She solemnly swore that she would not allow this country or any other to revert to the hysteria of the Salem witch trials.

And that was just what she intended to do, Cora told herself firmly. Reaching out one hand, she lifted the phone. "Mr. Salinger?"

"Yes, Madam President." He paused and audibly swallowed. "I'm afraid I have bad news."

Her grip tightened on the receiver. Taking a slow, deep breath, she shifted her gaze to the south lawn of the White House. Outside were gardens, soft in the moonlight, being guarded by a full company of armed Marines. Beyond the lawn, the fence had been fortified, sprayed with white gold, and tourists were no longer allowed up close to the "people's house." No more photo ops in front of the nation's capital. Not when you had to worry about a witch getting too close to the president.

The witchcraft scare had driven every decision made

in D.C. for the last several years. And fear was a harsh taskmaster. The security was such that Cora even had a Secret Service escort with her at all times *inside* the White House. About the only place she could count on being alone was in the privacy of her own bedroom.

"I'm sorry to hear that, Mr. Salinger," she said in the soothing, calm tone people had so come to count on. "What's happened?"

"It's Shea Jameson."

"Yes, I assumed as much." Cora sighed. Only yesterday she'd spoken to this man to tell him in no uncertain terms just how important Ms. Jameson was to Cora's future plans. The young woman had become the face of a movement.

Her aunt the first witch to be executed, Shea herself hunted for years and now, finally, thanks to her power erupting, caught and jailed. She was young, pretty, a schoolteacher, for heaven's sake. And her records all indicated Shea was a thoughtful, ordinary woman—at least until her innate witchcraft had erupted. Hers was the face Cora needed to project as she tried to make the very changes she'd promised the voters.

"What's happened?"

"She's escaped. Well—" Salinger corrected himself quickly. "She was broken out. There were some deaths. My men—"

"How many of your prisoners died in this escape?"

He paused and Cora heard the rustle of papers as he did some quick checking. "Five women dead, four injured, one of those not expected to make it."

Rubbing her forehead against the burgeoning ache, Cora turned away from the French doors leading to the south lawn and stared instead at her desk. The Resolute, it had served Reagan, Clinton, the Bushes and Obama and now it was hers. Along with the responsibility that anyone sitting behind it must accept.

She ran her fingertips across the intricately carved English oak surface and reminded herself that she'd earned this position. She'd served first as governor in Texas and from there moved to the Senate. Two terms had solidified her reputation as a straight-talking, no-nonsense candidate. When her husband died fifteen years ago, Cora had taken her only child, Deidre, out on the campaign trail with her and the two of them had been an unbeatable team.

And she'd walked into this office, ready to take on the problems of not only her country but the world. Now was not the time to get fainthearted.

"And Ms. Jameson?" she asked, cutting into Salinger's excuses and apologies.

"Gone," he admitted. "I gave the orders you insisted on, Madam President. She wasn't bothered ... much. The guards mostly kept their distance, and simply watched. If they'd been closer to her when the men appeared ..."

She straightened, disregarding the man's insinuation that somehow all of this was *her* fault, and focused on the last word he'd said. "Appeared?"

"According to the surviving witnesses, yes," the man said, nearly babbling now with nerves. "Two men 'appeared out of nowhere,' killed the tower guards and showed up in the prison yard." He cleared his throat and added, "Witnesses swear the two men were covered in flames."

"Flames?"

He heaved a sigh. "Yes, ma'am, that's one thing everyone agrees on. The two men looked like pillars of fire."

"I see." She inhaled sharply, but kept her voice cool, despite the shock of this news. She remembered the reports from the first attempt to apprehend Shea Jameson. Supposedly a man made of fire had swept her away. Who was he? Where did he come from? And how in heaven could a man of fire be tracked?

Was there more than witches to be concerned about? she wondered. What other kinds of magic might there be, still waiting to be revealed?

"Very well," she said abruptly. "Do everything you can, use whatever resource you need, but I want Shea Jameson found, do you understand?"

"Yes, but—"

"And make no mistake, I want her unharmed." Cora wasn't interested in hearing more of his apologies or his whining. "I'll be notifying BOW. They'll be in contact with you. Give them everything they require, Mr. Salinger."

"Of course, Madam President, but I don't think they'll be able to find her. Not as long as this . . . *man* is with her."

"You'd be surprised what properly motivated people can do, Mr. Salinger. Keep me informed if anything changes."

"Yes, ma'am, I will—"

She hung up and let her fingers trail across the surface of the telephone. She shifted a look around the Oval Office she'd worked so hard to reach. She wouldn't allow Shea Jameson to disappear into the underground. She needed her. If they were going to make the necessary changes to society and the world at large, the two of them had to work together.

Whether they wanted to or not.

Chapter 18

Traveling by fire was disconcerting, to say the least.

Torin could travel only so many miles in brilliant bursts of flaming energy. So at the end of every jump, Shea looked around quickly to see where they were. Beach, jump. Freeway, jump. Parking lot, jump. Middle of an intersection—shriek and jump.

By the time they "landed," Shea was shaken and just a little bit nauseous. She let go of Torin, took a breath and bent at the waist, letting her head hang down as she fought to settle her stomach. Not easy since she thought sure she'd left her stomach behind two jumps ago.

"You all right?"

"I will be," she said, more steadily than she felt at the moment. "The important thing is I'm out of that prison."

"No," Torin corrected. "The important thing is to *keep* you out. We're not safe yet. We have to keep going."

Shea straightened up and whipped her hair back out of her eyes.

She really was inside a completely different world now, Shea thought. Traveling by fire. Sending a friend to a sanctuary. As she quickly considered her new reality, she also acknowledged that she had been relieved to hear about the sanctuaries. Witches were organizing to save themselves and others. They, like she, had decided not to lie down and die with a whimper—and knowing she wasn't alone in her fight made her feel stronger somehow.

Turning to look up at him, she said, "Just give me a second to get my stomach back where it belongs before you do that fire thing again, okay?"

He gave her a slow smile. "Didn't like it?"

"It was . . . amazing," she admitted, though her insides were still a little shaky. "But not looking forward to doing it again real soon."

He shook his head as he stood there like some fallen avenging angel, his gray eyes sweeping their surroundings, constantly vigilant. Finally, he looked at her. "No. From here, we'll drive."

"Thank God." At least a car she understood.

"We have to keep moving," he said. "BOW and the MPs will be looking for you. We have to get lost. Quickly."

Then he took her arm and dragged her behind him across a well-lit parking garage. He stopped in front of a sleek black sports car that looked so fast, so powerful, she half expected it to growl at her in greeting.

"Get in."

"Are we stealing somebody's car?" she asked, even as she headed for the passenger side. "Don't we have enough people chasing us?"

He shook his head. "It's *my* car. I have several I keep in different locations—just to ensure that I have one when I *need* one. So get in."

"Right." She got in, strapped the seat belt into place and instantly slumped against the black leather seat. She hadn't even been aware of just how much tension was trapped inside her body. Until it all released at once, leaving her feeling as wobbly and insubstantial as a wet noodle.

He fired up the engine and Shea smiled. The car *did*

growl. As he peeled out of the parking space, she asked, "Where are we going?"

"Safe house for tonight." The muscle-bound car streaked through the parking garage like a hungry cat chasing down prey. Its tires squealed against the concrete floor and its engine seemed to echo with a rumble throughout the structure.

She leaned her head against the seat back and barely noticed as parking lights flashed past like lightning bolts in a dark sky. As Shea's mind drifted, Torin drove on, steering the car onto the freeway and into the night. And as he drove, visions filled her mind and in those visions, lightning *did* crack against the heavens.

Voices rose out of the past, whispering, chanting. As the words formed in her mind, Shea shifted uneasily and the power within her howled.

> *Moon, our Goddess, we call to thee*
> *Your daughters call on your power*
> *Bless us now with your bounty*
> *Before us let our enemies cower.*

Over and over again, the voices rose and fell like waves on a churning sea. Shadows swirled through her mind and her heart as what she had been fought to exist once more.

Shea moaned and fell deeper into the past, into the images hidden in her own memories. As Torin steered the car through the night, Shea walked through mist, her sisters at her side.

She felt power churning in the air and smiled. Whips of lightning skittered through the clouds, illuminating them from behind. Wind tore at their clothing and hair and shrieked an accompaniment to the chanting of the gathered witches.

A pentacle lay etched into the dirt, candles at each

of its five points. Despite the fierce wind, the flames on the wicks of those candles burned tall and straight with hardly a flicker of movement. Shea followed the others and formed a circle around the great star on the ground.

She felt, more than saw, others there as well. They were on the fringes of the circle, lost in darkness, yet somehow she knew they were trying to reach the witches. Stop them.

But nothing could have stopped them.

As one, the witches dropped the white robes they wore and stood skyclad, all of them, their skin glowing in the pearly half-light of moon and the bolts of lightning. Long hair flew about their heads and in their eyes—reflected around the circle—was a hunger and a thirst that Shea recognized, while instinctively, a part of her pulled back from it.

But the past can't be rewritten and she was no more than a ghost in this scene—an unwilling observer, trapped in the body she used to occupy. And so she was caught, a fly in a web, forced to relive this moment, this terror.

Her mind fought against it, but the memories had been hidden too long. They came rushing from the darkest corners of her brain with an inevitability she couldn't turn from.

A full moon slid out from behind the clouds and jagged streaks of lightning still cracked and sizzled overhead. The storm was in the very air, charging each indrawn breath with power pulled from the elements of earth and sky.

The women of the circle lifted their arms and their voices came together to make their demands. The hushed whispers were lost in the wind, but the words had a power of their own and seemed to pulse in the night.

We await the knowledge and the power
We who gather are as one
We embrace the dark and spurn the light
We demand your strength and your might

"Oh, God!" Shea sat bolt upright in the car seat, breath heaving from her lungs as she looked at the Eternal beside her. "What did we *do*?"

Chapter 19

Landry Harper was pissed.

All that work capturing the witch, only to have the assholes in charge of the prison let her escape.

His hands tightened on the steering wheel as he drove through traffic near his home. He'd been called out, ordered to find the witch. Again. The GPS tracking signal put her somewhere in his territory and if she was there, he'd find her. It was what he did.

He hadn't always, he remembered. Once he'd been a teacher, like her. Once he'd faced classrooms filled with young faces etched with boredom and had tried to teach them history. Until his own world had shattered and then what had once happened in ancient Rome had become less important than what was happening *now*. History was being rewritten. The entire human race was under attack. And it was up to people like him to protect the innocent from the damned.

His gaze shifted to the photo attached to the dashboard of his jeep. A smiling woman looked out at him from the faded image and everything in him tightened with determination. Focus. She hadn't seen her attacker coming. Hadn't known that the neighbor she trusted would one day "lose control" of a power no one should possess.

The explosion had rocked the neighborhood.

His house had gone up like a torch and the wife and child he'd left sleeping when he went to work were dead in an instant.

The witch next door had escaped the blast, of course. Her power had saved her.

Until Landry had found her, six months later.

Just as he would find this one.

And when he did, she wouldn't be going back to detention.

Chapter 20

"You're remembering," Torin said, glancing at her. "That's good."

"Not from my point of view." She was shivering from a cold seeping through her body that was almost as debilitating as the ice she'd felt from the white gold. But this went deeper. Into her bones. Her soul.

Shaken, she tried to pin down that memory even as it slipped away, back into the mists from which it had come. A part of her was grateful.

"You have to remember, Shea," he said. "All of it."

"Do you? I mean, were you there?" She shook her head, closed her eyes briefly and swallowed a rise of nausea. "You were, weren't you? In the shadows. I couldn't see you. But I felt you. I knew you were there, trying to reach me."

"And *failing.*"

No, she thought wildly, he hadn't failed. She had. She and the others. He had tried to get to her but hadn't been able to fight through the wards her sisters and she had set in place to keep him and his brothers out. The memory came back again and this time she wasn't swept into the action, but could look at it objectively. As if it had happened to someone else.

And hadn't it?

Shea had always believed in reincarnation in the abstract. After all, it seemed unreasonable to assume that humans were allotted a measly eighty or so years only to wink off into oblivion. The universe was too intricately designed, too vast for her to accept that life was so brief. Besides, even in high school, she had accepted that past lives affected the way you lived this life. Why else could you instantly feel either affinity or enmity for a complete stranger when meeting for the first time?

So, yeah, reincarnation made sense to her. But accepting punishment for something she had done in another lifetime was a little hard to grasp. Could she really be held responsible for something done hundreds of years ago?

Shea fought to steady her heartbeat, ease her breathing, but it wasn't helping. Nothing was helping. The echoes of that memory still rippled through her system, making her shake with both fear and something all too like excitement.

Her stomach rolled and bile rushed her throat. She swallowed hard and lowered her window as they careened along the freeway, dodging in and out of traffic as if by . . . well, magic. Even the cold didn't stop her from wanting the slap of fresh air in her face. Her hair flew out into a tangle and she had to push it out of her eyes.

"In the memory," she managed to say, "I'm me, but . . . not."

"I know."

"In prison, I had a different dream. About—"

How to tell him that she'd dreamed of sex with him that was so hot she'd awakened sweating and so needy she'd had to touch herself just to ease the pain? No. Wouldn't be going there. Not yet. "You were there. And I was living in a cottage and it was hundreds of years ago, but I knew that place. That person that I was then. And I knew you."

"You always know me," he told her and she studied his profile in the flash of streetlights as they passed them. His jaw was strong and his straight nose and lips made her want to take a bite out of them. His hands were on the wheel and he was driving as if he was accustomed to doing ninety-plus miles an hour.

He was a modern man, obviously, but there was an old-world warrior feel to him, too. She heard it in his speech at times. A formality of sorts, from another time. As if he hadn't really left behind that man he'd been in her dream. As if he was the kind of man who didn't bow to whatever age he was living in. He forced it to bend to him.

"What do you mean I always knew you?"

"You know exactly what I mean," he said, steering the car across three lanes of freeway to take the connector ramp to another freeway. He hit the accelerator even harder. "We've been together through the centuries, Shea."

"That can't be," she whispered, though everything inside her yearned toward him. Every cell in her body already believed. Her heart, her soul, all felt the pull of him and if her mind wanted to argue, the rest of her really didn't want to hear about it.

Besides, she argued silently, how else could she explain any of this?

"You're a witch. I'm your Eternal. It's as it has been between us since the beginning."

She breathed deep, drawing in the fading scent of the ocean as they raced in the opposite direction, headed God knew where. It was too much. All of it. *Her Eternal. Centuries. Magic.* How was she supposed to make sense of this? How was she supposed to know what to do? If her memories were true, then she had made the wrong call before. What was to prevent her from doing it again?

A fresh wash of sickness rushed through her.

"Stop the car!"

"No."

Fury erupted inside her at the way he dismissed her need. She couldn't breathe. Couldn't think. She felt as if she were ready to burst. She needed out of that damn car. She needed to stand on her own two feet and try to remember who she was *now*. That was the woman she was interested in. Shea Jameson in the here and now. She couldn't change the past, but she could, by God, have a say in her present and her future.

Something rose up inside her as if she had called for it. Rising, burning, it nearly choked her in an effort to escape. She surrendered to that feeling, rode the wave of it as it crested within her and moments later, she literally *saw* sparks flying in the air between her and the huge man in the driver's seat.

Like flares lifting from a campfire, the sparks shone frantically, then went out, but ever more of them appeared, swirling like a swarm of fireflies. When she shouted "Stop!" a second time, a rush of power filled the word and the high-performance car sputtered and died.

"Damn it, I don't know whether to be proud or pissed." He cursed low and deep as he steered the coasting car to the side of the freeway.

They were near Irvine Ranch now and traffic blew past them as if they didn't exist. Shea hardly waited for the car to stop completely before she opened the door and bailed. She heard Torin swearing viciously again, but paid no attention as she waved one hand in front of her, shattering the fence that bordered wide-open hills and valleys spilling along the freeway.

The wind screamed at her and the roar of traffic sounded as if it were twenty miles instead of twenty feet behind her. She ran, her feet stumbling on the uneven ground, and then she was in the high grass, still running.

Above her, the first stars were bursting into the sky. The moon was a sliver, casting no light into the darkness, but she didn't care about that.

She ran because she had to.

Because the haunting memories overtaking her were too much to handle.

Not just of the last few days, when she'd found out what it was to be locked down and helpless . . . but the memories of the past—of lives she'd lived and died. Memories of dark magic and chanting voices. And Torin.

Always Torin.

He caught up to her in a matter of seconds. His big hand came down on her arm and he spun her around to look at him. "Running away?" he challenged. "This is what you've become? A coward?"

"I'm no coward," she shouted back, mortified to feel the sting of tears.

"Where would you go? Half the country will be looking for you by morning."

"I don't care," she cried, her power rushing through her, as if now that it had been unleashed it was too much to control. Fire tipped the ends of her fingers like the tiny flames on birthday candles. She looked at them, surprised and yet somehow comforted at the evidence of her power, too. It was that *other* her, she assured herself. The one who had stood in moonlight and called on shadows. The witch who had opened something dark and embraced it with welcoming arms.

That wasn't *her*.

"I just need to think," she shouted, willing the flames on her hands out and then staring at them as if she couldn't believe what was happening to her. "I need to figure out what it is I'm supposed to do."

"You're supposed to mate with me," he told her flatly, grabbing her other arm and pulling her to him.

Yes, her body shouted, arching toward him, her

breasts aching for his touch, his kiss. She could almost feel the warmth of his mouth around her nipple and she groaned with a need that was primal. All-consuming.

She wanted him. Needed him. But she'd had him in the past, she reminded herself, and nothing had changed. Nothing had stopped her from opening herself to the dark.

"According to my vision, we already tried that a few hundred years ago. Nothing happened." *Not true,* her mind whispered slyly, reminding her of what she had found in his arms. The glory. The pleasure. The soul-shaking orgasms.

Oh, God.

But she had *not* experienced a huge growth in her magical abilities.

"It's different now, damn it. Don't you see?"

She whipped her hair out of her eyes and fought back the hungry whispers in her mind. "How? How is now any different?"

"It's the Awakening, Shea," he said, his voice lost in the burst of something wild and fierce she felt at his words. "In all those other lives, we were working our way toward now. Toward this lifetime. The end of the spell cast so long ago. At last it's begun. The time of atonement is here and you're the first—we are the first . . ."

"What are you not telling me?" She could hear the unspoken words waiting to be acknowledged.

"Nothing." He let her go, took a step back and shoved one hand through his long, dark hair. "It's nothing. Another witch. When I was trying to find you. She said *she* was the first. Her name was Kellyn, but it can't be so."

"Does it matter who's first, for God's sake?" She laughed and didn't like the sound of hysteria she heard.

His gaze speared into hers. "No. It only matters that you're here. With me. And we have a chance to end what was started so long ago."

She scrambled backward a few steps. "I talked to some of the witches in prison. They told me that a chosen witch and her Eternal share power when they mate."

"Not a sharing, more of a merging. You will be stronger with the mating."

Stronger. That could be good. Or terrifying.

"And what do you get out of it?" she asked, though she already knew she would go through with the ritual. She had decided that while she was in the camp. She was never going to be helpless to defend herself again. Not if she could prevent it. She would learn. She would remember. And she would become powerful enough to protect herself and any others who needed her help.

"I get *you*, Shea." His gaze locked on hers and she felt the fire inside him burning all around him, like a halo of power and strength, wrapping him in its intensity until it had no choice but to burn outward, enveloping her as well.

"I've wanted you for lifetimes. Through all the years, through the centuries." He took a step closer to her and his gray eyes swirled as if lit from within. She saw shapes and colors and shadows playing out in their depths. Sensed that he was feeling as tightly wound as she was— that his hunger was more than a match for her own. Something inside her woke up and stretched its arms, eager to accept him, to ease this soul-deep need Shea had never known before.

"You're mine," he said. "You always have been. As I am yours."

They were alone on a darkened hillside, standing beneath a small slice of moon. and she could see him as clearly as if there were a spotlight shining down on them. Her body yearned and her heart ached and still her mind argued. She had to understand what was happening and how to control her powers. She had spent years taking care of herself and she needed to be in on what was happening in her life.

"In this merging, your powers grow, too?"

He inclined his head.

"What kind of growth? I mean, do you get super hearing or X-ray vision or something?"

One side of his mouth tilted into a smile. "No. My abilities will be strengthened. I'll be able to flash-travel for longer distances without resting. I'll be stronger physically, more able to protect you. And our minds will connect, allowing us to communicate without words."

"You'll be able to read my mind?"

He shrugged. "Not so much read as hear you when you reach for me. And you will be able to do the same."

"Would this happen for you with just any witch?"

"No." He swore it to her. "Only you, Shea. Only you are for me."

She *felt* the truth of that, as if the knowledge had been stamped on her heart and soul at the beginning of time. She'd only needed to hear it to recognize it. He was hers. As he had always been. And still, Shea needed to be an equal in whatever came next. In whatever the two of them faced.

"Torin, I've been taking care of myself for a long time."

"I know," he said, watching her. "But I have been close, Shea. Always."

She took a breath and let it out slowly. "Okay, but my point is, I'm not the kind of woman who just turns her own safety over to someone else. If we're going to be together, then you have to treat me like a partner—not a damsel in distress."

He gave her a quick, unexpected grin that left her nearly breathless at his sheer physical beauty. "I have never considered you weak, Shea. Or less than an equal. We are a unit and will act as one."

That was good, she thought. She didn't want to be in the dark about anything anymore.

"Where are you taking me, Torin?"

"Away."

"How far?"

"Tonight—to a safe house."

"Not what I meant," she said. "I have to be a part of this, Torin. You just said we were a unit. So tell me what you're planning." Shea wasn't about to let herself be kidnapped again, either, not even by her supposed destined lover.

"It depends on you," he told her, his hair flying about his face in the sharp wind. "Only you know where we have to be. I'm keeping nothing from you, Shea. The answers you seek are buried in your memories. Once you open yourself to them and your powers, you'll know where we need to go."

True again. And again, she felt a soul-deep recognition of something that would have seemed like fantasy only weeks ago. The Awakening was about *her*. Her memories. Her powers. She was going to need all the strength she could find. Just as, she thought, looking up into Torin's eyes, she was going to need *him* beside her.

The flutter of energy pulsing through her made Shea smile in spite of everything and gave her a sense of completion. All her life, she'd felt as though there had been something missing. Some piece of her lost. Now at last she was finding it.

"Okay, I think the power thing has started." God, a few days ago that statement would have terrified her. She had been ready to run not only from the authorities but from what she had sensed in herself. Now she welcomed that surge of something . . . extra.

She was a witch. Like her aunt before her. Like the thousands of women worldwide who were coming into unexpected skills and talents. Like the women already living with power and the fears that accompanied it. She was a member of a proud sisterhood that had survived throughout the centuries despite witch trials and persecution. It was past time for her to take pride in who she was and learn to use the gifts given her.

In fact, Shea's newfound sense of self believed the more strength and power the better. "How do I get my powers to open up completely?"

"Sex. With me. *Now.*"

Chapter 21

The tracker worked perfectly.

A tiny silver chip in the witch's gorgeous hide and they could find her anywhere she went. The GPS gave her location and no matter what she did to block it, that signal would continue, leading him right to her. Each witch had a coded signal, so each one could be identified by the frequency her transponder gave off. He had her. Just as he'd known he would.

Landry tracked witches. And when they escaped, he got them back. Dead or alive.

He knew his orders. The higher-ups wanted this witch alive. But, he told himself with a small smile, "Accidents happen."

He set the scope to his right eye, leaned his weight on his elbows and took a breath, letting half of it slide from his lungs. Then his finger tightened on the trigger and the high-powered rifle jumped in his arms.

The witch fell and the big man with her covered her with his body before Landry could get off another shot.

"But one's enough if you do it right," he assured himself and slipped down the hillside, losing himself in the high meadow grass.

Chapter 22

"Shea!" Torin threw himself on top of her even as his eyes scanned the hillsides, looking for the shooter. Blood poured from a wound high on her shoulder. He stanched the flow with his bare hand, but he knew it wouldn't be enough.

They couldn't risk staying here and they couldn't leave with her bleeding out. She wasn't immortal—not yet, anyway—and if she died, the Awakening was finished before it began.

That thought slammed into his mind and he shoved it right out again. "Screw the Awakening, Shea. I won't let you die. Do you hear me?"

"Torin?" Her voice was too soft, too fragile. He'd rather have her shouting at him than the sound of pain coloring her words. "What happened?"

"You were shot." Blood continued to seep from her shoulder, trickling through his fingers, running across his hand. In the darkness, the blood looked black, but he knew it was bright red. Knew that she couldn't stand to lose much more.

"Shea, you've got to trust me," he said, mouth close to her ear. "Can you do that?"

She tried to move and gasped at a sharp stab of pain.

"Don't move," he ordered. "Just talk. Can you trust me?"

"Yes, I trust you," she said, closing her eyes and biting down on her bottom lip. "I don't know why, but I do."

"That's good enough for now." He wouldn't think about the sting of his witch not knowing why she should trust him. Or about the centuries he'd spent at her side. Now it was all about stopping the bleeding so he could get her to safety. "Reach out and take my free hand with yours."

She barely moved her arm, whether from pain or fatigue or just plain shock, he didn't know. Didn't matter.

His fingers threaded through hers and he tried not to notice the chill in her skin. How much blood had she lost?

"Now center yourself, Shea."

"What?"

"Call on your magic."

"I can't." Her head rocked tiredly from side to side.

"You can," he insisted as her blood continued to pour across his hand and into the dirt. Panic like he'd never known before took a vicious bite of his very soul. "You shut down my Viper while we were doing ninety miles an hour. You can do this."

"Can't. Cold."

"You'll be warm soon enough," he muttered. "Now focus. Pull on your strength, your energy, feel it move into my hand, joining us."

He felt a slight sensation of her power, a small trickle of warmth when he needed a tide. Her pain washed over him, staggering him. His connection to her was growing, though, so he took as much of her pain as he could. He had to force her to ignore the rest.

"That's it, Shea. Do it. Damn it, forget the pain and focus. Feel my hand in yours, feel me reaching for your power."

The trickle increased, linking the two of them with wispy threads of heat. He felt it and nodded, ready now to try to heal her. "I'm going to call on the flames to seal your wound."

"Burn me?"

"It won't burn you. Remember? The flames are magic. But I can't heal you on my own." Even as he concentrated on the woman who meant more to him than his own existence, another part of Torin was aware of their surroundings. The dark, high grasses where any number of enemies might be hidden. The ridge from which the shot had come.

Was the hunter even now preparing to make another attempt on her life? Would she be taken from him at the very moment they had been destined to join? *No.* He refused to lose her. Not again. Not in this life.

Overhead, stars glittered and in the darkness he called on the fire that formed the core of him.

More of her power moved into him and his fire burned hotter, brighter. "Our energies must be blended, joined. Trust me, Shea. Don't fight it. Give me your magic and trust me."

She nodded, her face pale against the grass. Only yards away, cars flowed along the freeway like fish in a river. Never stopping, never noticing anything around them. But they couldn't have seen Shea and Torin even if they were looking for them. The magic soaring around them moved like fog, a thick gray mist to conceal and protect.

The flames rushing through Torin's body, racing to the hand he held to Shea's shoulder, were the brightest light in the shadowy world they inhabited.

"Do it, Torin," she whispered, eyes locked with his. "I trust you."

His heart swelled as his own magic burst forth in a rush. His hand erupted into flames and caressed her injured shoulder with a magical balm that made her sigh and squirm beneath him. Their hands linked, their powers as one, Shea breathed easier, and seemed to gather herself as her body healed.

The joining was strong, rich, and filled him with a sense of rightness that he'd waited several lifetimes for. This was the woman who was his other half. The heart and soul of him. He would never lose her again.

He watched as the wound closed and the angry red flesh paled and smoothed into unbroken skin beneath his hand. She took a breath and let it sigh from her lungs—and Torin could have sworn he felt her relief as his own.

At last Torin pulled his hand free, inspected the wound and smiled to himself. "It's done."

"It doesn't hurt anymore," she admitted and slowly sat up beside him.

She looked down at their joined hands and watched, bemused, as Torin's flames licked at their fingers in wavering bursts of bright orange and yellow.

Finally, she lifted her gaze to his. Lit by the starlight, she said, "You're amazing."

"Together," he corrected, "*we* are amazing."

She nodded. "I'm starting to get that. Now what?"

"Now we discover how these people are tracking you. But not here."

"Where, then?"

"I know a place." He wrapped his arms around her, called on the flames and in a breath of light and heat, flashed them both away.

Chapter 23

It took several jumps to reach their destination. By the time Torin led Shea into the small mountain cabin, he was feeling the drain of magical energy. He'd used too much both on the travel and on healing Shea without allowing his body to recharge. Rest would do it, he knew. But sex would do it quicker.

And he had no wish to rest.

His gaze dropped to the curve of Shea's behind as she walked into the cabin ahead of him. Even in the ugly prison uniform, her beauty couldn't be hidden. She was the woman who had held his heart for hundreds of years. Her energy, her spirit, her soul remained the same throughout her many incarnations. All that she was called to him on a cellular level.

He had watched her over the eons, seen her learn and change and been witness to the growth of her soul into the woman she was here. Now. In this lifetime, he had seen her resilience. Felt her determination and courage. Her warmth and humor. And he had loved her more than he ever would have thought possible.

"Where are we?"

"Somewhere above Palm Springs," he said and she turned to face him.

The cabin was cold and dark. Shea shivered and he waved one hand at the fireplace, where kindling and logs lay waiting. Instantly, flames erupted on the stacked wood, sending brilliant patterns of light dancing around the small room.

She sighed. "You do that so easily."

"As will you."

She walked toward the fire. "I don't know. I feel . . . as if something inside me is locked down and struggling to get out."

"Your power already escaped you once tonight."

"I don't know how, though." She laughed shortly and shook her head. "Seems like that's something that would come in handy."

"I can help."

She looked at him over her shoulder. "I hope so."

"Trust me."

"I guess I am." Scrubbing her hands up and down her arms, she said, "I've never been as scared as I was the last couple of days. I never want to be that scared again. Or that helpless."

"You won't be," he said, and internally he made a vow. "I'll keep you safe."

She gave him a tired smile. "I'm counting on that. But I want to learn how to keep myself safe, too. I won't be at the mercy of witch hunters again."

"Good," he said and walked to her. His steps were soundless, a big man moving with the stealth learned over centuries of life. "You're stronger than you know already, Shea. Getting stronger still is the one sure way to ensure your survival."

She nodded. "Who shot me? God, I can't believe I was shot."

He reached out one hand to touch the bloodstain at her shoulder. It still felt all too real to him. Hearing her soft cry. Watching her fall. Feeling her blood seep through his fingertips to soak into the earth. Fury roared within him and he fought to keep a tight rein on it. There was no target for his rage—and he couldn't risk frightening Shea further. One day, though, there would be payment made for what was done to her.

"I don't know who shot you. I don't know how they found you." That fact was a daunting one. If he didn't know how they had found her once, how could he prevent it from happening again? Staring into her eyes, he found the only explanation possible. "I can only think that you've been tagged."

"Tagged?" She frowned. "You mean like the microchips people put in their *pets*?"

"Something like that. I have to check you for it and get rid of it. Otherwise, they'll find us too easily again."

"Hell, yes," she blurted. "Find it. Burn it. Do whatever." She ran her hands over her body, scraping her palms across the cotton jumpsuit, digging into the collar and hems, but found nothing.

"Take it off," he said.

She lifted her head and stared at him. "Excuse me?"

"The uniform. Take it off."

She folded her arms over her chest. "Um, how about you just check it while I wear it?"

Torin sighed and shook his head. "This is no time for modesty between us, Shea. You can't wear the damn thing anyway. It's crusty with dried blood."

She blew out a breath, looked around the room and spotted a quilt tossed over a chair back. "Fine. Turn around."

"We are mates," he told her, irritated that she would cling to something so foolishly human as embarrassment. "I will know your body as you will know mine. Nothing will be hidden from us."

"Will be," she repeated, frowning. "We haven't done the mating thing yet and it's a little disconcerting to strip down in front of a—"

"I'm not a stranger."

"No, you're not," she agreed. "But you're also not my lover. Not yet, anyway. So turn the heck around."

Gritting his teeth, he did, but only because it was faster than arguing with her. He closed his eyes and listened to the fabric rustling, the zipper sliding down as she undid it hastily. His blood pumped thick and hot in response. His instincts roared as he fought for control.

In moments, she'd tossed the uniform at his feet. "There. Check."

He did, and couldn't find a thing. Which could mean only one thing. "They've implanted it somewhere on your body."

"No, they didn't."

He turned around and stared at her. She looked every inch a pagan goddess: her long, dark red hair hanging about her shoulders, her creamy skin glowing in the firelight and the faded quilt held to her body like a battle shield. His body stirred again and a burning ache settled in his dick. If he didn't have her soon, the agony of wanting her was going to kill him.

Shaking his head, he asked, "Did they examine you?"

She squirmed a little in memory. "They did everything to me. Even a strip search, which is just as much fun as it sounds."

He blew past that. "Did they give you a shot? An inoculation?"

"Yes," she said, thinking back, "they gave me some antibiotic. Said there was flu in the prison and it was to keep me from contracting it. Because they *cared* so much about their prisoners," she added with a sneer.

"Where did they give you this injection?"

"Oddly, in my neck. Hurt like a bitch, too." Her voice trailed off. "You think?"

"I do. Show me." He stepped closer and she lifted her hair out of his way. She leaned her head to one side and

Torin bent to examine the smooth skin at the base of her skull. He spotted it immediately.

"There's something there," he whispered, his mouth so close to her skin that he could almost taste her.

The scent of her drove him mad. That intriguing blend of earth and ocean that clung to the skin of a witch—while at the same time smelling different on each of them. Shea's scent was powerful and subtle. Like the witch herself.

"Well, get it out," she yelped, reaching around to drag her fingernails across the back of her neck.

"I will, but it's going to hurt."

"Fine. Whatever. I don't care. Just do it."

The pride he felt for her rose up and did battle with the lust that was damn near choking him. He wanted her and admired her and tonight, he was going to *have* her. He would feel her writhing beneath him. Feel her body take him inside, accepting him and their mating and all that it entailed. But first ...

Reaching to the sheath at his side, he pulled out a knife with a wicked silver blade. One edge was razor sharp, the other jagged with silver teeth designed to rip and tear.

"Holy crap," she murmured and backed away a step.

"Be still. This must come out or our enemies will be able to track us."

"Right. Enemies. Track." Her gaze was locked on the knife blade. Her eyes looked enormous and glittered with the shifting shadows of the fire.

"Trust me, Shea," he said, his voice compelling her to look up into his eyes.

She did, meeting his gaze squarely, with a courage that obviously cost her. "You keep saying that and I keep doing it, despite being terrified. Why is that?"

"Because we belong to each other." He looked deeply

into her eyes, willing her to believe. "Now turn and let me take care of this."

With a long, deep breath, she did.

"I'll take as much of your pain as I can."

"I'm fine. Just do it and be done, okay?"

He lifted her thick, silky hair and bunched it in one fist as he laid the tip of the knife to the tiny scar on her neck. At the base of her skull, nearly hidden by her hair, it was so small, he knew it had to be a microchip.

Silver, of course, so it wouldn't be a constant drain on her powers and thus tip her off to its existence. Silver for witches was a conduit to other elements. It focused their powers, channeled their energies—and the fact that their enemies had used that element against her fried his ass.

Torin edged the tip of the knife into her skin and winced as blood welled and trickled down her back. She jerked a little at the pain, but then held steady, the only sign of her distress her heavy, uneven breathing.

"Almost," he whispered, then dug the chip free of her body and caught it in his hand. "Hold on to me, Shea."

She automatically reached back and laid one hand on his side. He felt the fire of their joined energies and carefully fed them onto the bleeding cut on her neck. Instantly, the cut healed and he used his thumb to wipe away the blood.

"Did you get it?"

"Yes."

She turned and looked down at his palm. "It's so small."

"Microchips." He walked to the fireplace, set the chip on the mantel and slammed the knife handle down onto it. When it was splintered, he gathered the pieces and tossed them into the flames.

"Thank you."

He slanted a look at her. "You don't have to thank

me for caring for you," he said. "It is what I will always do."

"Why?"

"Because you are mine as I am yours."

Her voice was soft, her eyes flaring with a hunger they had shared over the centuries. "I don't even know you."

"You do. You just don't remember."

"Same thing."

"Stubborn witch," he said with a shake of his head. Digging into the pocket of his black jeans, he tugged out a cell phone and flipped it open.

Her eyes widened. "Seriously? A magical guy uses a cell phone?"

"Satellite phone. We can use technology, too. We live in the modern world, Shea, and fashion it to suit our purposes." He waited. Rune answered on the second ring.

"The woman's safe," Rune said with a tinge of disgust. "She and her mother and daughter are *packing*, for chrissakes. What is it with women? They're on the run, with crazies after them, and they want to take time to pack? What is that?"

Torin smiled at the image of three mortal females driving his friend insane. "Before you go to Sanctuary, check Terri's neck."

"Why?" Instantly Rune was serious.

Shea's gaze was locked on his as she realized that she might not be the only one tagged for recapture.

"Shea had a microchip embedded at the base of her skull."

"Shit."

"If Terri's got one too, you could lead BOW straight to Sanctuary."

"Bastards," Rune grumbled. "She's not even a witch."

"Just check."

"On it." He disconnected and Torin slipped his phone back into his pocket.

"Will Terri be all right?"

"Yes. Rune will see to it."

"Okay." She took a breath and looked up at him. "Now what?"

"We run."

She sighed and Torin could see how tired she was. But she was also strung tight enough to snap. Not a good combination in an Awakening witch. "Go take a shower. Rinse off the dried blood. You'll feel better."

"I don't have anything to wear," she reminded him.

"Make something."

When she just stared at him as if he'd lost his mind, he gritted his teeth against the rush of frustration. He had to keep reminding himself that she was only now realizing what she was. That she didn't know how to use the innate talents the universe and the goddess Danu had blessed her with. "You have the power. It's inside you. Draw on it."

"How'm I supposed to do that?"

"Close your eyes."

She did, then opened them again. "Is this a trick?"

"Close your eyes, woman." When she had, he said, "Now get a picture in your mind. Imagine the clothes you want to be wearing. Right down to the last detail. Every button, every zipper. Got it?"

She scowled, scrunching her eyes closed tightly in concentration; then she nodded.

"Good. Now keep that picture in your mind and draw on the power you used to stop my damn car."

A short, sharp laugh shot from her throat and Torin smiled in response. She made quite the picture. His witch with her wild hair and smooth skin, wrapped in a quilt, dazzled by firelight. Every cell in his body went into overdrive. His need for her was more than lust. Sex with her felt as necessary as air to him. He had to have her. Had to touch. Taste. Explore.

"Now what?"

Her question drew him out of his fantasies and forced him to focus on the moment. Soon enough, she would be with him where she belonged.

"Bring up the power in your mind. Feel the rush, the rising sweep of it. Keep that image of the clothes in your head and let the power loose."

A moment passed, then two. And suddenly, the flames in the fireplace leapt and snapped. A wind rose up in the cabin and lifted her hair into a tangle of red curls around her head. He saw her skin glow with the sweep of power and felt the air sizzle with the strength of it.

She smiled, a beautiful, full smile, and she gasped in surprise and dropped the quilt. She opened her eyes. Looking down at her blue jeans, white shirt and dark green sweater, she laughed in delight.

"Congratulations," he said. She was so damn pleased with the ability to conjure clothes, and all he wanted was to get her naked again. He pushed back his own need . . . *again.* "Go shower. We'll eat, then figure out what's next."

Her smile died fast and Torin almost felt guilty for ruining her pleasure. But better that than get her dead.

When she headed to the bathroom, he took his phone out and made another call.

Chapter 24

Kellyn reveled in the freedom to do and be whatever she wanted. Thank the moon she was out of that hideous internment camp. For a second, she thought about the look of stunned shock on the faces of the two Eternals. Then she smiled and dismissed them for the moment.

She waved a hand at the ATM machine and instantly it spat out hundreds of dollars. She smiled again and tucked the money away in the designer bag she'd helped herself to at the department store inside Union Station. A train station for most of its life, the Beaux Arts building was today something of a national treasure, Kellyn mused.

Once a center for train travel, now the building with the arched ceilings and intricately carved plasterwork and acres of marble flooring was home to an upscale shopping center. Which, Kellyn told herself, was exactly what she had been looking for. After too long in prison drab, she'd *needed* to see something stylish. A chance to get lost in a well-dressed crowd and entertain herself with the game of using her power to obfuscate herself when she wanted to.

Of course, she could have spelled herself any clothing and accessories she wanted. It was nothing to snap her fingers and materialize a Coach bag or a glorious pair of Prada shoes. But it was more fun to walk into a store and walk back out with whatever she desired, knowing no one would—or could—stop her.

"Really, humans are just so simple," she whispered, glancing around at the traffic streaming up and down Massachusetts Avenue. D.C. in late September was still hot and muggy, but she didn't care. With a chant and a burst of power, she regulated her own temperature so that she was perfectly comfortable.

She took a breath and caught the scent of banked power. There was another witch here somewhere, no doubt trying to hide amid the throngs. The Awakening witches weren't the only women of power on the earth. Witches had been here since the beginning of time. But they had kept their magic a secret until that first Awakened witch had made her former lover a tiki torch. Now, none of them was safe.

Her eyes narrowed as she slowly surveyed the people around her. Witches were plentiful, but those on the loose were a dying breed. Most were either in prison or in hiding. For one brief moment, Kellyn considered finding the witch, seeing if perhaps she might become useful. But there were so many people, each of them with mind whirling, that picking the one witch out of this crowd would take more work than she was willing to invest.

She wasn't here to collect stray witches. Leave that to the Eternals. Like the ones who had rescued *her*.

Bless the fools, she told herself with another smile. With that damn white gold around her neck, she might have ended her existence right there in the damn prison. And what a waste that would have been.

She stepped out onto the sidewalk, moving with the crowd, keeping the rhythm of the city under her feet so that she was just another pedestrian. A faceless person lost in the crowd.

At the corner, she stopped to wait for a green light

and noticed an old man wearing threadbare clothes, sitting on a curb beside a grocery cart towering with his possessions. He held a hand-lettered cardboard sign that read HOMELESS.

Well, duh, Kellyn thought. She watched as mortals walked past the old man, eyes averted. Going on about their busy lives, their oh, so important lives, they didn't even slow down as they hurried down the street. It was as if as long as they didn't notice him, he simply didn't exist.

And something inside her burned. Before she could think twice about it, she walked toward the old man, who stared up at the crowd through bleary eyes. Her gaze swept quickly over the laden cart, noting everything from papers and cans to be recycled to a dog collar and leash and several copies of *National Geographic* magazine. *His treasures,* she thought wryly, as she dipped one hand into her bag and pulled out a hundred-dollar bill.

Offering it, she said, "Take this. Get off the street for a night."

He saw the money and a delighted smile curved his mouth. He then turned those rheumy blue eyes to her, and his smile withered and died.

"No," he muttered, shaking his head as he staggered to his feet.

"What?" Kellyn watched, astonished, as he hurriedly pushed his sign into the mess inside the cart.

Someone bumped into her in their hurry to cross the street. She hardly noticed.

"No, no, won't see," he whined in a singsong voice, shaking his head until his long gray hair floated like snakes in water about his head.

"What are you talking about? I'm offering you help," she said, in case he'd missed the whole point of this exercise.

He actually flinched, hunching his shoulders until he

looked like an elderly turtle. "Won't see the dark inside her," he sang to himself. "Won't see it, not there."

What the hell?

Kellyn glanced around, to see if anyone was listening to the old man, but naturally, no one was. What was it he saw when he looked at her? From somewhere deep inside her mind, a voice cried out, demanding to be heard, but Kellyn shut it down. Just as she dismissed this one old man.

She crumpled the hundred-dollar bill in her fist and squeezed. Someone else crashed into her and this time Kellyn whipped her head around, prepared to fight.

"Jeez, sorry, lady," the kid in baggy jeans and a faded T-shirt said. "Power down, huh?"

Power down? Not likely. Her power was rising, filling her, nearly choking her with the urge to burst free and obliterate her surroundings. Even Kellyn was shaken and nearly breathless from the eagerness writhing inside her.

The kid stared at her until his skin paled and his eyes were wide and horrified. Kellyn saw his fear and drank it in as ambrosia. This was what she thrived on. Fear. Horror. The old man was no more than a blip. Everyone else looked at her and saw only what she wanted them to see. She smiled, and the teenager grabbed up his skateboard and darted into the crowd, dissolving into anonymity.

Kellyn stared after him, fighting for control, holding on to the reins of the power within her even as her skin tingled.

A whimper caught her attention and she swung back around to see the old man shuffling away from her as fast as he could. The broken wheel on his cart sounded out a quick *whappeta-whappeta* as he went, his shoulders hunched as if expecting a blow, and still he threw a look at her over his shoulder.

"Won't see," he chimed again, "pretty lady with the dark inside. Won't see it. Not there, not there at all."

People stepped away from him as if he were somehow contagious. The crowd pushed into the street as the light changed, and Kellyn was still standing, rooted to the spot, watching that crazy old man run from her.

It was as if he'd somehow sensed what was crouched inside her. Was he so much more attuned than the rest of these ignorant humans?

Interesting. She watched him go and thought about following. Killing him. Watching the light drain from his already ruined eyes. But what would be the point? Even if he tried to tell someone what he'd glimpsed of her true nature, who would believe him? Hell, who would *listen* to him? She'd bring more attention to him with his death than he would ever draw alive.

"No," she whispered. "Leave him to his misery."

Shaking her head, she dismissed the old goat and walked down the street, feeling a hot breeze ruffle her spiky hair. She had things to do and no time to waste on unimportant details.

Pausing at a newsstand, she let her gaze scan the headlines quickly.

ESCAPED WITCH! DOZENS DIE IN BOTCHED MAGIC PLOT. WITCH ON THE LOOSE.

She smiled to herself.

"More than one," she murmured.

Chapter 25

Torin heard the shower running and tried to pull his mind away from the image of a naked Shea standing beneath the hot, steaming water, soap bubbles clinging to her skin ...

"You said you called Odell," Rune prompted, shattering Torin's thoughts. "Did he know of this Kellyn?"

"He did," Torin said, stalking to the front window and staring out into the night. The mountain was quiet, the sky black with stardust spread across its width like pinpricks of light through a sheet of velvet. The wind rattled the window glass and whispered across the top of the chimney.

Satisfied that they were still alone in the dark, he focused again on his friend. Before calling Rune to check in, Torin had placed a call to Odell, an Eternal based near his witch in London.

Odell was still watching, waiting for his witch to enter the Awakening. Meanwhile, he was spending most of his time breaking witches out of internment camps in the English countryside. He was running his own private underground railroad, spiriting witches and hunted humans to safety.

"Odell says Kellyn's Eternal is Egan."

"Egan." Rune muttered something unintelligible and

then admitted, "I haven't seen him in a couple of hundred years. After his witch's last incarnation, he disappeared."

"It's not good to be too alone," Torin muttered, though he could appreciate why Egan had felt compelled to find solitude. Watching your witch live and die again and again took a toll on even the most stalwart Eternal. Unless, of course, like Odell, you found something else to keep you occupied.

But even if he were thousands of miles from Kellyn, Egan should have felt her Awakening. Maybe this Kellyn had been lying, he thought. But why? What would she gain?

And if she was an Awakened witch, why hadn't Egan been called to her?

"Alone is what we do best," Rune reminded him.

"That was true for too long. But not anymore," Torin said. "Find Egan."

"A little busy here. Getting these women to Sanctuary, remember?"

"Right. Yes." Torin turned to look toward the bathroom when he heard the shower turn to the massage head, water pounding in regular rhythm. He muffled a groan at the image that filled his mind. Shea, thighs spread beneath those pulsing jets of water, trembling, gasping, helpless to stop her own pleasure from crashing over her.

His body hardened like rock. His breath caught in his chest and the flames that made up his soul threatened to engulf him, burn him to ash.

"We could get Cort to look for him," Rune was saying. "They were friends back in the day."

Torin forced his mind to the task at hand. "Yes. Good. Call him, then." A moment passed. "Where are you and the women?"

Rune laughed shortly. "Vegas, of all places."

Torin bit back an oath. "Are you insane? With all those people—"

"What better way to get lost than in a crowd?" Rune interrupted. "We're halfway to Sanctuary. I'll have them there by tomorrow. But I spent most of my reserve energies flashing them all here. Didn't want to risk getting in a car down in the L.A. area. Too many people looking for us to be safe on a damn freeway."

Torin remembered the sound of a gunshot and Shea's body crumpling at his feet.

"Good point." Since he knew Rune couldn't have transported more than one of the females at a time, he realized that the Eternal had made dozens of trips. Ferrying first one, then the next of the women and their belongings along a long, dangerous trek. "Can you get a car easily enough?"

With word of the prison break hitting every news channel and paper, they both knew the authorities would be watching everyone more closely.

"I keep a car here in a garage. It's safe enough. I'll have the females to Sanctuary by tomorrow night."

"You got rid of the tracker on Terri?"

"Yeah," Rune said. "Trust me when I say she didn't like it much. That woman's got a hard right jab. But it's out and we should be clear. Meanwhile, I'll call Cort. Get him moving on the Egan situation."

"Good." Torin listened as the shower massage changed gears, the pulses coming faster. He took a breath and let it out slowly. "I'll stay in touch. Don't know where we'll be by tomorrow."

"As long as you get the job done. The clock's ticking, Torin, and we can't lose."

That statement didn't deserve an answer, so Torin didn't give him one. He flipped the phone closed and tossed it onto a nearby table.

Then he turned and headed to the bathroom as if he were being pulled by an invisible cord.

The shower was incredible. A walk-in, with no door or curtain separating it from the room, it was constructed of sandy-colored tiles that were smooth as glass on the walls and the wide, built in bench, yet felt rough beneath her feet. Four faucets jutted from the walls at different angles and the air was filled with steam.

Shea stood under the pulsing streams of hot water, turning her back to the jets, letting the rhythmic blasts of heat pound against her shoulders, her neck. She'd been running for years. From the feds. From herself. Her destiny.

Now, there was no more running. There was only this moment and the next and the next. She wasn't alone anymore, either. There was Torin. And though a part of her still held back from him, unwilling to trust, to share completely . . . another part of her welcomed him.

And that side of Shea wanted him desperately.

She burned for him. Her body turned to liquid heat with just the thought of him. Knowing he was in the next room made her yearn to call out to him, to draw him to her. Yet she resisted. Once she'd opened that door, there would be no going back. Ever. She would be fundamentally changed and that scared her. She felt the power inside her, bubbling, churning, frantic to be free.

But what happened when it was released?

Would she become what she'd seen in her vision? Would she once again be the woman who could call on the dark and damn everything and everyone else around her?

The door opened and her head snapped up. Her gaze met Torin's as he stepped into the bathroom. His long, dark hair was swept back from his face and his pale gray eyes swirled with banked emotions. His jaw was tight as he approached her.

Naked, Shea stood tall and straight, facing him. She trembled as his gaze moved over her in a quick, thorough sweep.

"I've waited for this," he said. "For *you*."

"I know."

"No more waiting."

"I know," she repeated and lifted her arms in welcome.

Chapter 26

In a flash of magic, his clothes were gone and she looked her fill of his tall, muscular body. His erection was thick and hard and everything in her wept to feel that strength inside her. She needed him to fill her as she needed her next breath.

He was on her in an instant.

Body to body, flesh to flesh. She inhaled sharply at the slide of his wet skin against hers. His hands moved over her, exploring, delving, finding every curve, every crevice. As if it was essential to him that he touch all of her.

And she wanted that. Everywhere his hands went, flames followed. The magic fire that lived inside him pulsed out and into her, filling her with a swamping heat that sent her blood boiling and her mind dissolving.

He kissed her, his mouth forcing hers open, his tongue sliding inside, tangling with hers until breathing became an issue. Then that moment passed and Shea didn't care if she never drew another full breath. As long as he kept touching her.

He reached down and lifted one of her legs, hooking it across his hip. She swayed into him. Her body was taut with expectation, with need. She held her breath and waited, knowing that his first intimate touch would send her over the edge. His hand cupped her core, his fingers dipped into her heat and stroked her body.

"Torin!" She rocked unsteadily on one foot, locking her other leg around him to keep her balance in a world gone suddenly crazed.

"Come for me now," he murmured, while he stroked, caressed, teased. His fingers dove higher inside her, demanding she give him just what he needed. "Come for me now, Shea. And again and again."

Her entire body was one raw nerve. She moaned his name, heard the desperation in her tone, but she didn't care. She trembled from head to foot. And through it all, the hot water continued to pulse, slapping at his back, pounding against hers. Steam filled her lungs and he filled everything else.

His thumb caressed the sensitive spot at the apex of her thighs until she splintered, shuddering in his arms, riding the cresting wave of a sensation like she'd never known before. Her body pulsed in time with the water jets and Torin held her steadily, safely as she went limp in his grasp.

When she could hear again, he set her on her feet and held on to her waist, his big hands nearly encircling her completely. She looked up at him through dazzled eyes and knew that when he was inside her, his body locked with hers, the orgasm would be even more earthshaking than the one she'd just experienced. She didn't know if she'd survive.

"And now the mating begins."

Shea laughed a little and rested her forehead against his chest. "You mean that wasn't the beginning?"

"No," he said softly, running his hands up and down her spine, cupping her behind, squeezing. "That was merely to ease your first need. The rest is so much more."

Her heartbeat was crashing in her chest and she quieted to listen to his, to see if their hearts were beating in tandem. But she heard . . . nothing.

Startled, she lifted her head to stare into his beautiful gray eyes. "You don't have—"

"A heartbeat? No."

"What? How?"

He turned her in his arms until she was pressed against him, her back to his front. She felt the thick length of him and she wiggled her hips to feel more even as she listened to what he was saying.

"I am an Eternal. Immortal. But I am not human."

That should stagger her, Shea thought, yet at the moment it didn't matter. All that mattered were his arms around her, his hands at her breasts, his fingers at her hard, sensitive nipples.

"Fire is my element. Eternals were created by the sun god, Belen. He tore the fire from the sun and molded it into our souls. Brought us to life from the eternal flames. It is what makes me," he was saying, dipping his head to lick at the side of her neck.

She shivered.

"The sun god? You're saying actual gods exist?"

"Belen is not *the* God, but he is one of many in the pantheon."

Her whole body trembled as he blew gently on her damp skin.

"Through the mating, you will become immortal and I will receive a heartbeat. We will be one, Shea." His fingers tugged and tweaked at her nipples until she felt the drawing sensation in the pit of her stomach. "As we were meant from the beginning. Two halves. One whole."

"I'll be immortal?" Her voice was breathless and who could blame her for it? The things he was telling her—and doing to her—were incredible. She widened her stance, allowing his thickness to slide between her legs, rubbing against already sensitized flesh until she had to fight to remain on her feet.

He chuckled, a soft, dark sound that was nearly lost

in the rush of the water surrounding them. "Eventually. Immortality isn't a gift—it is something to be earned."

"As you'll earn a heartbeat."

"Yes."

"Then why haven't we done this before?"

He reached down, grabbed her thighs and lifted her off her feet as easily as if she weighed nothing at all.

"Torin!" She snaked her arms backward, linking them around his neck to hold on even as her back arched.

"You resisted," he told her, turning her so that the closest water jet was aimed directly at her. "You didn't want the mating, only the sex."

"Sex is pretty good," she admitted and steeled herself for what was to come. She knew what he was going to do and wanted it as much as he did.

"The mating is better," he whispered and held her so that the water pumped and pounded directly on her exposed center.

Shea shrieked as the first of the jets hit her clitoris. An incredible, overpowering sensation roared through her like a runaway train. She couldn't think. Couldn't breathe. Couldn't move. She was held in place by his strong arms so that she couldn't even twist in his grasp. She was helpless to do anything but leave herself open to the pulsing, pounding, hot water jets. It took only seconds to have her body exploding once again, hips rocking helplessly as she rode one wave after another of a pleasure so deep, so shattering, she thought she just might not make it through.

And when, finally, he released her, allowed her body to slide away from the incessant pulses of water, she knew her legs were too weak to hold her.

He set her down onto the bench seat and through the steamy air she struggled for breath. Then she looked into his eyes and whispered, "You're trying to kill me, aren't you?"

A slow smile curved his mouth and something inside Shea shifted, becoming more than a deep-seated yearning, more personal. More intimate than sex or desire.

Memories stirred at the back of her brain and though she knew she had to remember all she could, at the moment she didn't want the distraction. Right now, all she wanted was him. Her gaze briefly dropped to his erection and before she could think twice about it, she reached out and wrapped her fingers around him.

He hissed in a breath, pushed himself into her hand, and Shea felt a surge of power that had nothing to do with magic course through her.

"Tell me about the mating," she whispered.

He took her hand from him and threaded his fingers through hers. Voice tight, eyes churning with shadows and light, he said, "The mating connects us. Our souls. Our hearts. Our bodies. We become stronger together than we are apart. We unite to do what must be done. Every time we come together, the bonds between us will strengthen. At the end of thirty days—should we complete our task—the mating will be complete."

"If we don't complete it?"

"The mating will end and our souls will die."

Shea frowned, but told herself there was no choice here. She needed Torin. So they *had* to succeed. "I don't remember what I have to do. What *we* have to do."

"You are remembering," he told her firmly. "And with the mating, your mind will open as well as your body. The knowledge will come. But you must accept it. And me."

She stood up, and glanced at their joined hands before lifting her gaze to his again. "Tell me what to do."

He waved one hand and the water shut off. The resulting silence was as thunderous as a roar. Shea would have sworn she heard her own heartbeat pounding as loud as a drum. Her throat tightened and her stomach rolled with a thick mix of nerves and anticipation.

"Come," he said, drawing her from the shower, walking with her back to the bedroom.

She followed willingly, anxiously. Her gaze dropped, taking in his muscular back and sculpted behind. Her senses skittered wildly as she hurried her steps to keep up with his much longer legs. In the bedroom, he stopped and turned to face her.

There was a fireplace here, too, she thought absently, with a blaze already burning in the hearth. Shadows jumped and danced across the walls and in his eyes. Shea felt the enormity of what they were about to do settle on her shoulders.

This wasn't about sex.

Or at least, not solely about sex.

This was about taking a step toward what she was meant to be. To do. This was about undoing what she had done so long ago.

And instantly, her mind dredged up the image of the vision she'd had hours ago. Of standing beneath bolts of lightning with her sisters, calling to the darkness. A chill rushed across her skin, pebbling her flesh with goose bumps. She remembered the taste of the fear she'd felt that long-ago night. Remembered the instant of shame, of regret that had pressed down on her. She remembered what Torin had said about atonement and how long they had all waited for this time to come. And she remembered, at last, that this man, this Eternal, was her only shot at long-sought redemption.

She took a breath and looked into his eyes. There was so much there, she thought. So much more than she'd seen in the first terrifying moments when he'd appeared out of nowhere to whisk her away from a dangerous mob. His hand on hers tightened, pressing their palms flat together.

"For a true mating to begin," he said, "you must accept both me and your destiny. In the past, you held yourself apart from me. Though we shared sex, you refused the mating."

"Why?"

He shrugged, though she suspected his feelings went deeper than he allowed himself to show. "At first, you wouldn't risk sharing power. You and your sister witches clung to each other and shut out those who would have been the other halves of your souls. Then, later, it wasn't time. The Awakening had to arrive before the mating was possible again."

"And now?"

"It's time. At last. Do you accept me?" he asked quietly, every word a benediction, a hope.

It cost this strong, brave man to ask her to accept him and she knew it. Sensed it. But she also knew that this was the tradition he'd waited lifetimes for. Was she ready? Did she have a choice?

If she refused him now, she risked returning to the dark place that still lived inside her. The vision she'd had earlier was still vivid in her mind. With danger. Fear. And terror. She couldn't face this alone—and her Eternal was waiting for her. As he had been for so long.

"Yes," she whispered, her tone as reverent as his. "I accept you."

"And our past?"

"Yes."

"And our future?"

"Yes," she said and his fingers locked more desperately with hers.

"Do you take me as your mate? To stand beside you? To fight with you and to make right what once went so wrong?"

She swallowed hard and felt the hugeness of the moment crashing down on her. Each of her answers to his questions had spurred heat to quicken inside her. Now those flames flashed and burned so brightly it was a wonder she wasn't glowing. This last question, she knew, was the key to it all. To taking him as her mate. To vowing to stand and fight beside him. To trust him.

And even as she opened her mouth to give him her answer, a part of her held back from that blind trust she knew would be so necessary. How could she completely trust him when she didn't entirely trust herself?

"Shea." His voice was a demand. An insistence that they had come this far and she couldn't back away now.

She lifted her chin, looked him in the eye and whispered, "Yes, Torin. I accept you. I accept the responsibility. I accept the danger."

Flames erupted over their joined hands.

Bright orange and yellow light danced and jumped across their skin, searing the two of them together. There was no heat. No burning, no charring of flesh. But the flames churned and flashed brighter, hotter, until at last they winked out just as Shea felt a jolt of that heat shoot through her palm. It snaked along her arm and settled in her chest in a tight knot of heat that flared with every beat of her heart.

She sucked in a gulp of air and looked at him, startled. "What?"

"We begin," he said and dipped his head to claim her mouth with his.

Hands still joined, their bodies came together and Shea arched into him. In the hearth, flames snapped and hissed as they consumed the wood stacked there. The only other sound was the wind, rattling the glass panes as if it were an entity demanding entrance.

But for her, there was only her Eternal.

Torin tipped her back onto the bed and she sprawled beneath him, hungry now, ravenous to have him in her, on her, under her. She wanted to feel every inch of his hard body. She scraped her hands up and down his back, along his butt, dragging her short nails across his skin. He buried his face in the curve of her neck, nibbling, kissing, tasting.

She arched again, parting her thighs, demanding that he take notice, that he give her what she craved.

He did. He shifted one hand to her center and thumbed her core until she was writhing and twisting beneath him. Tension radiated from her into him. She felt his sex pressing against her hip and she wanted it inside her. Wanted *him* locked deeply within her.

When he raised his head, she looked into his eyes and in those pale gray depths, she read more hunger than she'd ever seen before. She thought she might burn up from the heat of his gaze and knew she wouldn't care. As long as she could feel him sliding deep within her, she wouldn't care about anything else.

It was a fever now, a soul-deep ache that demanded to be fed.

"Now, Torin," she ordered, turning into him, trying to straddle him so that she could feel his hard thickness inside. "Take me now, damn it."

"Now," he agreed and shifted, rolling her onto her back again, moving to kneel between her parted thighs. Then he paused and looked his fill of her. His hands touched her, parted her tender flesh and stroked her until she grabbed fistsful of the quilt beneath her and hung on for dear life.

"Is torture a part of mating, you bastard?" she demanded, lifting her hips into his touch, nearly whimpering for what he was denying her.

"It's the hunger," he told her in a voice choked out of his throat. "The craving claws at you. At me. Once begun, the mating will only become more powerful. More all-consuming. We will need. Always."

"Then take me," she told him, rearing up off the mattress to link her arms around his neck and pull his mouth to hers for a brief, hard kiss. "Take me now and then again. But be inside me, Torin."

"Always," he promised and keeping his gaze locked with hers, entered her body in one long, swift stroke.

She screamed his name as his body claimed hers. She clung to his shoulders, his back, as he pulled her up to sit on his lap. She twisted, grinding her hips against him, taking him deeper, higher. She rubbed her breasts against his chest and felt flames quicken there as well.

That knot of heat inside her chest flared brightly for an instant and burned behind her left breast as she rode him. She didn't care about the brief jolt of pain. It was gone in an instant and all there was, was *him*.

Their gazes locked, Shea moved on him. His hands at her waist set the rhythm for her to follow. It was fast, it was hard and it was everything.

The first stirrings of her climax tingled into life and were enveloped in a firestorm of sensation. She let her head fall back on her neck as she held on to him and continued to move, rocking, writhing, twisting, taking him as high and as deep as possible. His thickness filled her, and still it wasn't enough. She would never have enough of him. Heart. Soul. Mind. She felt the connection between them flash into life and she knew that nothing she ever did would be as important as this moment.

"Shatter for me," he commanded.

She did, instantly. Her body rocked and she called his name as wave after wave carried her over and above anything she had ever known before.

And almost before the last ripple sighed through her system, Torin moved her, shifting her in his arms, setting her on the bed. Facedown, she braced her hands on the mattress, and knowing what he wanted, went up on her knees, lifting her hips to him.

His big hands held her in place as he stroked his thick body back and forth across her so-sensitive entrance.

Shea couldn't believe it herself, but she needed him again. Now. The climax she'd experienced was barely complete and a fresh hunger was erupting within her.

She moved, pushing at him, twisting her hips despite his firm grasp on her body and when she looked back over her shoulder at him, her heart nearly stopped. In the dancing firelight, he was every inch an ancient warrior. His body was golden and hard and looked as though it had been sculpted by a generous god.

And he was hers.

He met her gaze and pushed himself into her heat. Shea gasped and moved against him, taking him even deeper and higher than she had before. He rocked against her and she felt every stroking glide of his body light up her insides like fireworks in a black sky.

Again and again, he claimed her, his body entering and retreating in a fast and furious rhythm that stole her breath and shut down her mind. Another orgasm shot through her and she cried out with the force of it. Then there was still more and he touched her center, rubbing his thumb across that one sensitive spot until she cried his name again and again, body shaking, trembling with the force of the climax claiming her.

Over the roar of her own heartbeat, she heard his hoarse shout as he finally allowed himself to follow her into oblivion.

Chapter 27

Hours later, when hunger for actual *food* forced them out of bed, Shea staggered to the bathroom on wobbly legs. She had never been so completely worn out in her life. And she'd certainly never felt so damn good about it.

Every muscle ached, every square inch of her body had been licked and kissed and touched and explored. Her mind was awash with fresh memories of what she and Torin had done to each other over the last few hours and just remembering had her wanting to do it all over again.

When she stared at her reflection, she hardly recognized herself. Her green eyes were glittering. Her long red hair was snarled and tangled and looked as if it had grown two inches in length. How was that possible? She laughed and told herself, "Magic."

It bubbled inside her, the power—growing and erupting. She felt the changes happening within her and gave herself up to them. Whatever came next, she would be ready for it.

Torin came into the bathroom and stood behind her at the mirror. One of his tanned hands slid up and down the front of her body and she leaned back into him as new desire quickened. God, would she ever have enough? Would she ever reach a point where she would

be able to say, *No, thanks, I have a headache?* She didn't
think so. And did she want to reach that point?

No. She really didn't.

She met his gaze in the mirror and saw those gray
eyes swirling with passion and secrets. His mouth, that
delectable, delicious, talented mouth of his, curved a little at the corners as he watched her reflection. He lifted
his left hand to cup her breast and his thumb and forefinger tweaked her nipple.

"Seriously?" she said on a half groan, "I don't know
how we'll ever get anything done if you keep touching
me like that."

"It has been centuries, Shea," he whispered. "Hundreds of long, dark years while I've waited for this time
with you. For the true mating. My hunger will not be
quickly eased."

She felt his erection rubbing against her behind, thick
and hard and soft all at once, and her eyes slid closed
as she parted her thighs for him. Again. And again. She
would always open for him. Always welcome his touch,
his invasion.

"Hold on to the counter," he told her, "and open your
eyes."

She did, unable to help herself. She stared into the
wide glass and watched as he took her. He hitched her
hips higher to give him entrance and she leaned over the
counter to make it easier for him.

He thrust home and she gasped with the erotic sensations swimming through her. He took her quickly,
fiercely, one hand at her hip to steady her, one hand at
her left breast, continuing to pull and tweak her nipple.
Over and over, he pushed himself into her depths only
to retreat and push forward again. He took her higher,
faster than he had before and Shea watched it all happen in the mirror.

His features tight, his gaze locked on hers, he moved

his hand from her hip to her core and the moment he touched her, she shuddered. Her body clenched around his and the rippling of her muscles tightened over him, holding him to her, forcing him to join her in another staggering release.

When she was leaning over the counter, struggling for air, he smoothed her hair back over her shoulder, and lifted her chin so that she was staring into the mirror at him. "Look, Shea. Look at your body and mine. See what is happening."

She did and at first, couldn't see what it was he wanted her to. Their reflections were blurred through her passion-glazed eyes, but at last she was able to focus. She looked at his hand on her breast and narrowed her gaze as his long fingers moved over a dark spot above her nipple.

"What is that?" She leaned closer to the mirror. Just over the dark pink areola of her breast, there was a bloodred mark. Elongated, with a slightly teardrop shape, it was almost like an oddly shaped birthmark, but she knew it wasn't.

"The mating brand," Torin told her, a satisfied tone to his voice.

She shifted her gaze to his. "A brand?"

He shrugged. "A tattoo of sorts, then. Our bodies, when mated, create this mark. I have a matching one."

Shea turned around to face him and looked at his left nipple. The same dark red mark was there as well. Her fingertip stroked the edges of it. "What is it? It looks like a teardrop."

Shaking his head, he bent to place a kiss on the mark above her breast. "It is a flame. A single flame to mark the beginning of the mating. Over the next month, the brand will grow and expand, marking each of us as belonging to the other."

She belonged.

Finally, at last, she knew where she belonged. She'd spent her entire life trying to fit in. Trying not to be the square peg in the round hole and it had never worked. There was always something different about her. Even before her aunt had shown her that their family carried witchcraft in their bloodlines.

She took a breath and slowly released it.

"Over the next month?"

"Yes. The mating is slow, giving witch and Eternal time to enjoy each other and the changes that happen between us."

She stroked one finger across his warm, muscled chest and smiled when he hissed in a breath at her touch. "Changes?"

"We will gain strength from each other, Shea." His hands moved up and down her body as if he simply couldn't touch her enough. "The brand begins it, linking our bodies and souls. As the thirty days pass, the brand will spread across our bodies and with each new flame that appears, the bond between us will be that much stronger." He dipped his head to claim a quick, hard kiss. "When we touch, we will be able to combine our magic to increase our joined strength."

"And when the thirty days are up?"

"My heart will beat and if Belen is pleased with me, I will gain more power."

"What kind of power?" she asked, leaning into his hands.

"I don't know," Torin admitted. "The mating is something of a secret even to us. None of us knows what will be until it's finished."

"Your god didn't give you many details."

"What god does?" he asked, one corner of his luscious mouth curving upward. "The goddess Danu, *your* goddess, was no more generous with information."

"Danu?" Shea shook her head and tried to think. But it was so hard with his hands on her.

"The Mother goddess," he told her with a shrug. "She who created witchcraft and chose the women to wield it."

"There is so much I don't know," she whispered, leaning her forehead against his chest, listening to the silence where there should have been a heartbeat.

"I will share with you everything I know," he promised. "But for now, you must know we have only until the next full moon to complete our mission. To find what was once hidden and get it to safety."

"What is it?"

"Black silver," he said and those two words dropped like icy stones into the room.

Shea swayed unsteadily as images raced through her mind at his words. A dark element created by witches, she thought. Black silver was imbued with power that had grown quickly and completely out of control.

"The Artifact," she whispered, not sure where that word had come from.

"Yes," he said, stroking his fingertips along the side of her breast. "You remember?"

She shook her head, frowning as her mind turned away from the memory. "No. Not really. It's just that when you said 'black silver,' I got a flash of something— but it was gone too soon for me to grab it."

"You will," he said. "You must."

"Right." She nodded and looked down to where his fingers stroked lazily over her newly born tattoo. "You said there were others, like me. Awakening witches. Will we all have this tattoo?"

"Yes," he said, bending now to flick his tongue across the tip of her nipple. "And each branding will be unique to that witch and her Eternal. Each of you will be marked according to your karma."

"And what about you?" she asked, struggling to hold on to her thoughts despite the fact that Torin had taken her nipple into his mouth. "What do the Eternals get from this, besides a matching tattoo?"

He stopped what he was doing, pulled his head back and blew a gentle stream of air at her breast. The dampness from his tongue, followed by his soft breath, caused a shiver of chill delight on her skin. "We become one with the other halves of our souls. We stop merely *existing* and begin to *live.*"

His tongue stroked the tip of her nipple and Shea sighed. So much had changed in her life so fast that it was almost impossible for her to imagine that it *was* her life anymore. She looked down at his mouth on her breast and sighed again as another tiny red flame erupted from inside to appear just beside the first of the branding.

She was part of something now.

Permanently.

There was no going back. There was no altering her decision even if she wanted to.

Already, Shea could feel herself *changing*. It wasn't just the tattoo, burning itself into her skin. It was something more elemental. More basic.

As she accepted who and what she was, the woman she had tried so hard to be—the everyday, ordinary middle school science teacher—fell more to the wayside. She wasn't ordinary.

And she wasn't going to pretend she was, ever again. Not even to herself.

Chapter 28

Rune felt the wash of magic in the air.

Sanctuary was close.

Thank the gods. Eight hours in a car with a curious, frightened little girl and her mother and grandmother were almost more than an Eternal could take.

Amanda hadn't stopped talking since they left Vegas in the predawn hours. Her mother, Terri, was the opposite. Hardly spoke a word. But Terri's mother had kept up a near constant litany of rosaries and prayers all along their route.

Their emotions and fears were battering Rune's energies, eating at them like water on rock. He'd be glad to have this chore over and done with. Battling evil and searching out Awakened witches were beginning to sound like a damn vacation.

"Damn it." He stomped on the brake, sending the SUV into a skid that had it sliding sideways on the narrow mountain road.

"You're not supposed to cuss," Amanda told him from the backseat.

"What is it?" her grandmother asked, fear ratcheting up her voice until it sounded as squeaky as an old gate.

"A roadblock," Terri muttered from the front seat, sliding a quick look at Rune.

"That's what it looks like," Rune told her, then said, "Quiet. Everybody."

Even Amanda closed her mouth. Not really surprising, since the child's world had come tumbling down around her over the last week. She was probably ready for another crash to hit. And, he thought, it might have.

Boulders lay strewn across the road, blocking passage. At first glance, it looked as though it was just a rockfall from the mountainside. But Rune didn't trust it. Seemed bloody convenient for a landslide to hit just before the boundaries of Sanctuary.

"I'll check it out," he told them, his voice soft but determined. "You three stay in the car."

He reached for the gun on the seat beside him and pulled the slide back, sending a bullet into the chamber. Whoever was out there, they wouldn't be taking Terri and her family back. Not without a fight, anyway. He had magic as well as bullets to draw on and he wasn't above using either of them.

Before he could open the car door, though, women dropped from the trees. At least a dozen of them. Some simply jumped down to the road; others slid along ropes that snaked from higher branches like tentacles.

"What the . . ."

"Rune—" Terri shrank back in her seat and threw a guilt-filled glance at her daughter. "Whatever happens, save Amanda."

"*Nothing*'s going to happen to any of you," he muttered, keeping his gaze locked on the women stalking ever closer to his car.

Some of them held automatic weapons and looked way too comfortable with them. Others held their hands out, palms up, invoking magical powers and preparing to use them. He sensed the magic in all of them and knew he was dealing with witches.

The question was, were they reasonable or were they more apt to fire first and ask questions later?

"Who the hell are you?"

A tall woman with long, dark hair pulled back into a braid that hung to her waist shouted at them as her fellow soldiers moved into position around her. She wore faded blue jeans and a black sweater and held an assault rifle as if it were an extension of her arm.

To answer her question, he simply flashed into fire and appeared again outside the car. Weapons shifted to him and he felt the women's hard, suspicious gazes as if they were knives slicing into him.

"You're an Eternal." It wasn't a question. The dark-haired woman, clearly the leader, shifted to look at the car. "Who are they?"

"Humans," he said. "Who the hell are you?"

One corner of her mouth lifted into a half smile. "You're in no position to be asking questions, Eternal. There are at least a dozen guns on you—not to mention the magical weapons."

"Immortal," he reminded her, with a small smile of his own.

"But not immune to injury. I figure we can put you down if you make a wrong move, so don't tempt me." Her gaze narrowed on him, she said, "I'll ask one more time. Who are the women traveling with you?"

Rune was as disgusted as he was furious. Felt like a damn fool. He'd stepped into a well-laid trap and couldn't see an easy way out. He glanced at his surroundings, taking the measure of the situation. One side of the road was a steep, rocky face of the mountain. The other side was covered in trees so thick he couldn't see beyond them. Behind him stretched a road that led back to civilization and danger for those whose safety had been entrusted to him. And ahead lay Sanctuary . . . if he could get past the witch guard.

Thoughts and options raced through his mind, but as long as he had Terri and her family to protect, there was only one choice. Truth. "Like I said. They're human. One of them escaped from Terminal Island detention center a couple of days ago. The others are her mother and daughter."

The dark-haired woman lowered her weapon and gave a silent signal to the other Amazons lurking close by. As one, they eased into a posture of cautious watchfulness. At least, he thought wryly, the guns weren't aimed directly at him anymore.

"We saw the news coverage of that escape. Report is, two men made of fire broke in, killed some guards and stole two witches."

"One witch," he corrected. "One human suspected of witchcraft."

She smiled then and Rune took a second for pure male appreciation. Not only was she mean as a snake and comfortable with weapons, but she was a damn beauty, too. He liked that in a woman.

"Now you want to tell me who you people are?" he asked.

"I'm Selena, commander of the Guardian Witches," she said, then looked at the women surrounding her. "These are the Guardians."

"Impressive," he said, shifting his gaze from one to the other of the witches watching him with less than welcome expressions on their faces. "Now, how about you let me through so I can get these women to safety."

"Not so fast," Selena told him and called out, "Rachel!"

A woman dressed completely in black approached and handed off her weapon to Selena. Her dark eyes caught Rune's briefly, then shifted to the car and his passengers. "I'll take care of it," she said.

Rune moved to intercept her and she snarled at him. He didn't much care. "Take care of what?"

"Relax, Eternal," Selena said. "Rachel's going to check them for transmitters. Her magic will pick up anything that shouldn't be there."

"I already got the tracker out of Terri," he said.

"Might be more than one." Selena nodded at Rachel, who stepped around Rune as if he were a pile of shit and she didn't want to risk getting her boots dirty.

Then the witch approached the car and Rune saw that her features relaxed a bit. She smiled at Terri and the others. "Don't worry. This will only take a second or two."

He watched as Rachel laid both palms flat on the roof of the car and closed her eyes. What looked like campfire sparks shot up as a wind ruffled her bright red hair and buffeted the heavy sweater she wore. Magic sizzled in the air around her and dropped over the car like a golden blanket that shimmered and shifted as if it were alive.

Seconds ticked past.

"Tracer!" Rachel shouted the warning and instantly, the other Amazons surrounded the car, backs to the machine, gazes fixed on the trees, mountain and sky.

"No fucking way," Rune insisted, already starting for the redheaded witch. "I got the tracer out myself. Cut it out of her neck."

"There's one you missed, Eternal," Selena told him. "And until it's out, nobody goes any farther. As it is, if they're following her, they've come too close already." She glanced at the other witch. "Rachel, find it."

"Right."

"Just a damn minute," Rune shouted.

"It's okay," Terri called out, stepping from the car. She looked at all of the women standing ready to protect her and her family and then glanced at Rune. "If there's another one, I want it out, too." She looked at Rachel. "Just do what you have to do."

The witch called on her magic again and ran her hands up and down Terri's body. Sparks flew and power shuddered in the air. Intense focus etched lines into Rachel's expression until she stopped at last. "Found it. Here. Under her breast."

"Impossible." Rune shook his head. He'd checked Terri personally. No way would he have been able to miss a silver tracker.

"Rachel's never wrong," Selena told him flatly, then said, "Get it done, Rachel."

"Trust me," Rachel said, staring directly into Terri's eyes.

Once again, Rune was impressed with the human's strength of will. She only nodded and closed her eyes. He wouldn't look away, though. He watched every move the witch made, ready to jump in and protect Terri even if it meant every weapon in the place would be turned loose on him.

Rachel lifted Terri's shirt, bared her breast and then laid her palm beneath the full curve. "I can feel it. It's deep. I can get it but it's going to hurt like a bitch."

"More good news," Terri murmured. "Do it."

He could only watch and wait. Not things Rune was good at.

Rachel held her hand beneath Terri's breast, closed her eyes and drew on her magic again. This time, the sparks flew like fireworks. Her hair lifted in that magical wind again and she chanted beneath her breath as Terri moaned softly and bit into her bottom lip.

"Mommy!" Amanda's shocked cry burst from the car and one of the witches reached through a window to comfort the child with a touch.

Seconds became minutes and minutes stretched into an eternity. Rune never took his gaze off Rachel until at last, with a single harsh cry from Terri, the witch grinned and held up her hand. Blood covered her palm but in the center of that dark red fluid lay a flashing silver chip, smaller than the one he'd taken from the back of her neck. Rune was forced to admit he'd missed it.

But how?

"It's bespelled," Rachel said, answering his unspoken question.

"You mean another *witch* spelled the metal used to track her sisters?" Selena's voice was horrified.

"It's the only explanation," Rachel said and destroyed the chip under her bootheel. She then turned back to Terri, healed her wound and patted her shoulder. "You did great."

"That explains why you couldn't find the tracker," Selena told Rune. "If there's a ward on it protecting it from detection, you wouldn't have noticed it at all. You'd have to be looking for it specifically to feel the magical vibration."

"That's just great," he muttered and told himself to call Torin the moment he could. If Terri had been bugged twice, then most likely so had Shea. "So what about it?" he asked Selena as Terri climbed back into the car to comfort her daughter. "Are you going to help these women or not?"

Selena nodded, turned and lifted both hands toward the rockfall blocking the road. A rush of magic spilled from her and the road opened, displaying the landslide to be nothing more than a well-constructed illusion.

Dropping her hands, she looked at Rune and the women in the car. "Welcome to Sanctuary."

Chapter 29

With Torin out rounding up food, Shea took some time to try to get things straight in her head. So much had happened so quickly, she hardly knew what to think anymore.

But one thing was sure. Nothing was ever going to be the same for her again. Not since her Awakening. Not since Torin.

She stood in front of the bathroom mirror and slipped out of her shirt and bra. Staring at the two tiny flames, the beginning of the mating brand at the tip of her breast, she felt a swirl of magic rush through her. She inhaled sharply and let it come, relishing the sensations of her very soul opening up to new possibilities.

"Torin said the memories would come," she whispered to her reflection, and noted the frown on her own face. "But can I afford to just wait? If there's magic in me, shouldn't I be able to draw on it?"

Seemed reasonable enough, she thought, still frowning. The question was, how to do it?

"Maybe it's just a matter of concentrating," she said. Lifting both hands, she placed her palms on the cold mirror and stared into her own eyes. With her mind focused on the magic, on the secrets she needed to know, she concentrated as she never had before.

Seconds ticked past and the silence in the room

closed in around her. The world narrowed until all she could see was the reflection of her own green eyes staring back at her. And just when she thought nothing at all was going to happen, she noted the change in her mirror self's eyes.

The green filled with shadows, darkened and then fired with sparks. Then her vision blurred, became indistinct while at the same moment, she felt raw strength pulsing inside her. Power. Magic. It was there, within her. She drew on it, giving herself up to it, surrendering to whatever might come next.

In her reflected eyes, she saw ... something. A woman. Looking into a mirror, as she herself was. Shea watched, swaying under the onslaught of the vision, as the strange woman murmured a chant. And in the glass the woman held, figures appeared. An image of Shea, under attack by a crowd of people and Torin, fighting for his life. For *their* lives.

And the woman surrounded by darkness laughed.

Shea jolted back from the mirror, breaking the link and shivering as the sound of that evil laughter continued to spill out all around her.

"I know I hit her," Landry said. He stood at attention in front of his superior's desk. There was always a follow-up interview after a hit. The MPs, like the feds, had to keep their paperwork straight. "I shot, she fell, the man dropped on top of her."

His boss wasn't happy about the situation, seeing as the Do Not Kill order had gone out and Landry was claiming he hadn't heard it.

"You were told not to kill her."

Landry shrugged. "Reception was bad. Missed that part of the call."

"Sure you did."

Orders or not, Landry told himself, no one cared

about a dead witch, not really. Well, except maybe for whatever big shot had put out the order in the first place. But for those of them in the trenches, a dead witch was a safe witch.

"Never mind," the other man said with a resigned sigh. "Did you see bodies?"

"No," Landry admitted, remembering the thick mist that had swept into the area, hiding his targets from him, obliterating the scene. "A fog came up suddenly and hid them. Hell, it hid my car, too. Took me a half hour to find it."

His superior sat forward in his desk chair, picked up a pen and tapped it against a neatly stacked sheaf of papers. "We sent a team out a few hours later. They found the car was on the side of the road, but the witch and the man were both gone. We found blood, yes, but no bodies."

Landry gritted his teeth. She'd escaped. Gotten away once more. But he knew where his bullet had hit her. She couldn't have gone far. Not even magically. "Let me track them."

His boss sighed. "By now, they've realized that she was bugged and they've gotten rid of it. You have no way of knowing where she went."

Leaning both hands on the desktop, Landry stared into the other man's eyes. "I don't need GPS. I can find her. And when I do—"

"Forget it," the man said with a shake of his head. "We've got plenty of witches around here to worry about. BOW's taking this over. We're out."

"Out? I'm the one who caught her in the first place!"

"And according to the feds, we're the ones who let her escape."

"It's the MPs' fault that the internment camp is loaded with incompetent morons?"

"Forget it, Harper. As far as our organization is concerned, it's over." He gathered up the papers and began to flip through them. Pulling one free, he handed it over. "I've got a new assignment for you. This witch is hiding out in Sunset Beach. Got a tip. So forget about the one that got away and go retrieve this one."

Landry stared at the legal notice giving him the right to apprehend and thought about not taking it. He knew he could find that witch and her man. BOW didn't have the right to tell him to back off. His insides jumped with adrenaline and restrained fury as he fought with himself over just how to handle this.

He wanted that damn witch.

But as the seconds ticked past, he had to admit that he also wanted to keep his job. It was important to him. To be on the front lines, protecting humanity from this plague of witchcraft. So, if he had to back off of one witch . . . he'd simply ramp up his efforts on the others. And maybe, one day, he'd get another shot at Shea Jameson.

Snatching the paperwork from his boss's hands, he glanced at the witch's name and address and nodded. "I'll have her to Terminal Island by this evening."

"Good. Dismissed."

As he left, Landry told himself he was a lucky man to be able to do the work he loved.

Chapter 30

"Did you recognize the woman in the vision?" Torin asked.

"No," Shea told him. "I wouldn't know her if I saw her out on the street, either. She was pretty much just a shadow in the dark. But she was looking into a glass and seeing *us*."

"Scrying," Torin said. "It's a way witches have of seeing the future, the past—" He broke off and looked at her. "Somehow you managed to do some scrying of your own. Your magic's coming back fast. Still, you should have waited for me to return before trying a spell on your own."

"Please. It wasn't a spell," Shea said. "I was just trying to *see*. And I can't always wait for you, Torin. I have to find answers for myself."

"We are together in this, Shea," he reminded her.

"Yeah, we are." She laid one hand on his arm and looked up into his gray eyes. "But the truth is, I'm the witch with the evil past and I have to do what I can, when I can, to get to the bottom of this. So while we eat, why don't you explain what it is we're supposed to be looking for?"

He frowned as if he didn't like what she'd said, but he had to admit she was right.

"Black silver," Torin said, "is the element created by

the coven centuries ago. Formed with breath and fire and blood a thousand years before the birth of the one called Christ."

Shea had had no idea that the black silver was so ancient. "*Before* the birth of Christ?"

He smiled at the stunned expression on her face. "Long before, when the earth was young and magic was widely sought. The coven was powerful even then and they sought more knowledge and hoped that through the creation of the black silver they could add to the wonders of the world."

"But . . ." Shea prompted. "There has to be a *but,* because the memories I've seen aren't of shiny, happy bunnies. They're of death and darkness and terror. So what the hell happened?"

Torin frowned at her as he considered her question. His pale eyes locked on hers. "Are you ready for the whole truth?"

"Doesn't seem to matter if I am or not," she countered, frowning as her memories darted away again. "You said yourself we have one month. We really can't risk waiting."

"True," he agreed, handing her one of the sandwiches he'd slipped out to get a while ago. Setting his own meal down on the table, he leaned toward her, looking into her eyes.

Since leaving the safe house on the mountain outside Palm Springs, they'd talked about anything and everything. Torin had been giving her lessons in magic but even as she felt her powers growing, Shea knew she still had much to learn.

They had finally stopped for the night at a tiny motel in Flagstaff, Arizona. There was an American Indian feel to the place. Kitschy, she decided, rather than tacky. There were old paintings on the wall, tepee-shaped lampshades and an unusable kiva-shaped fireplace. The beds were lumpy, but the sheets were clean and they hadn't wanted to risk staying at a more well-known hotel. This one was tucked away in the trees, hopefully far enough off the beaten track that no one would notice an escaped witch and her Eternal.

She unwrapped her sandwich, took a bite and chewed, despite the fact that at the moment the sub tasted like sawdust.

"Tell me," she prompted.

"Silver is an earth element," he said quietly and even the room seemed to hold its breath, waiting for the rest. "The metal focuses, enhances, a witch's power—"

"Wait a minute." Shea looked at him in confusion. "Gold's an element, too. So why does it drain us?"

"White gold drains. It's not a natural element, Shea. It's an alloy, made by man. They take gold and taint it with other metals. Nickel and palladium usually. Separately, the metals are harmless enough." He frowned and shook his head. "Combined, there's something in the metallic makeup that acts in the direct opposite of silver."

Nodding, she asked, "Okay, and black silver was created by *us*, so it's even stronger than natural silver."

"Exactly. Back in the day, the coven decided that if silver focused their energies, channeling their power into it would increase its strength immeasurably."

"It worked, didn't it?"

He laughed shortly, passed her a soda and nodded. "Hell, yes, it worked. The element itself was more powerful than any had imagined it could be. Over time, black silver was incorporated into objects of power that came to be known by many names."

Shea took another bite of her sandwich, knowing she had to eat. But her gaze never left the Eternal sitting opposite her at the rickety table. "What do you mean?"

Opening his soda can, he took a long drink and set it down again. "It was impossible to contain," he said, lost in his memories of an ancient time. "Power sang through the pieces of silver and called to those with the will to wield it. Depending on the nature of the one holding it, the black silver became the epitome of evil or a force for good."

"Oh, God . . ." Shea's mind raced with possibilities. How many terrible things had been done under the flag of good intentions? she wondered. "Tell me," she said. "Give me some examples. Ones I would know."

Torin scraped one hand across his face and she watched as he silently argued with himself. He was a completely disciplined man. Some would probably think him cold, detached. But she had reason to know that the unapproachable mask he wore disguised a man— Eternal—of deep passions and unswerving loyalties.

She'd never felt more safe in her life than she did in his presence. Which, she thought, was fairly ironic considering that the first day he'd saved her, she had run from him, landing herself in prison, for God's sake. But since that night, she'd come to understand that she hadn't so much been running *from* him as she had been trying to escape the feelings she had *for* him.

"Tell me," she insisted.

He nodded. "Very well, then. A few that you will recognize. In 1776, a pen crafted of black silver was used to sign this country's Declaration of Independence."

Shea smiled. "Well, that's a good one."

"And in 1862, the land mine, also crafted of black silver, claimed its first victim of many."

"Oh, God." Her stomach lurched unsteadily and she set her sandwich aside, no longer able to bear even the smell of it.

"Twenty-one years later, black silver seeped into the crust of a dormant volcano. The magma within instantly flashed and the sound of Krakatoa exploding could be heard three thousand miles away."

"Volcanoes, land mines . . ."

"The Wright brothers' first flying machine. Then later," Torin added solemnly, "the *Titanic*. Hitler wore an Iron Cross made of black silver, and Albert Einstein's desk lamp was created from the element."

"How do you know all of this?"

"I have had many years to follow its trail."

Shea shook her head, as if simply denying the truth of what he was saying would make it so.

"Neil Armstrong's lunar module in 1969 carried black silver in its casing, and in 1994 the black silver machetes carried by the Hutus were used to massacre eight hundred thousand Tutsis in a few short weeks."

"Right and wrong," she murmured, "good and evil."

He reached across the table and folded his fingers over hers. Shea felt the heat of him slide through her system, chasing away the bone-deep chill enveloping her.

"The element itself was neither good nor bad," he whispered. "It simply *was*. It was man who made the choices in how to use it."

"And that makes it okay that the witches created it?" Shea asked, pulling her hand free and standing up. She walked to the front window, and with the tips of her fingers pulled back just enough of the drapes to look outside. The lights in the tiny parking lot were dim, since only two of the four were working.

Beyond the asphalt lot, trees stood tall and straight as soldiers on parade. And overhead, the moon continued its glide across the sky. Every night, the moon was a little closer to completing its monthly cycle. And every night, they were a little further from the success of a mission that Shea didn't even completely understand.

"Come away from the window, Shea."

"What did the coven do with the black silver, Torin? You said they created it, but what did they *do* with it?"

He stood up, his chair scraping against the scarred

wood floor. Crossing to her, he pulled her hand from the drapes and drew her away from the window. "It was decided that they would gather all of the black silver they could and create the Artifact."

More memories stirred inside her mind, tantalizing her, tormenting her with snippets, twinges of recognition.

"Some of the magical element was gone, escaped into the world—as I told you, it showed up in many different times and places. But the coven was able to gather most of it and together, they used their powers to fashion the Artifact."

She closed her eyes, trying to grab hold of a thread of memory. "Describe it."

"A black silver crest, crafted from a series of interlinking Celtic knots, as many of those in the coven had come from Eire originally."

She could almost see it, Shea thought, focusing her mind on the nebulous images drifting through her consciousness.

"When whole, the Artifact is a key to the dimensional portals of other worlds, other realities. The magic captured within was so powerful, so all-consuming, that simply touching it would drive a mere man mad," he said, his voice deep, soft, mesmerizing. "When the coven saw what it had created, even they trembled. And so it was women of immense power who protected it—and the world."

The image in her mind dissolved like sugar in water. She sighed, opened her eyes and looked up at Torin. "What went wrong? I saw that vision, remember? I saw me—not me, but me—and the others, calling on something dark. Terrifying."

His jaw tightened and his pale gray eyes flashed. "It was the year 1200. The last great coven of witches, reincarnations of those who had first created the Artifact, arrogantly thought to harness *all* power for themselves."

This she remembered as he spoke. This vision floated back to her on dark wings and settled in her mind like storm clouds. She saw it all again as Torin described it. More, she *felt* it all again.

"They set a circle," he said, "and channeled all of their energies into the Artifact, hoping to open the doors to other dimensions, other avenues of power. Instead, they opened the gateway to Hell."

"Oh, God . . ."

He held on to her shoulders as she swayed in reaction to his words, to the memory. More images appeared in her mind and she once again watched as Torin described the events of that long-ago night.

"Demons poured from the doorway until at last Lucifer himself stepped through into this world." He paused, took a breath and regretfully admitted, "The Eternals couldn't breach the circle of power to reach their witches. We were forced to remain on the outside, battling those demons that escaped. We couldn't help. Couldn't get to you."

His fingers tightened on her shoulders and Shea reached up to cover his hands with her own, linking them as they should have been linked on that awful night.

She saw it all in a blinding instant. The blood, the terror. Pain and light and noise erupted in her mind in a rush. Shea shrieked in response, held her head and crumpled to the floor at Torin's feet.

He reached for her and something crashed through the window, shattering glass into the room until it fell like clear, sharp rain.

A metal cylinder clattered to the floor not more than a foot from them.

"Damn." Torin wrapped his arms around her and flashed them out.

An instant later, the motel exploded in a fireball that lit up the night sky.

Chapter 31

Sanctuary stood alone, deep in the Uinta mountains of Utah, a safe zone for women—witch and human. Here they weren't hunted. Here they could simply live. Of course the threat of discovery hung over them all the time, but hidden as they were, that threat was far less than it could have been.

Rune was the only male in the camp and as he stalked across the compound, he noted that several little girls were trailing after him, giggling and pointing. As if he belonged in a zoo, he told himself. Wasn't it enough that he was stuck here until his mission was complete? Irritation spiked. Then he stopped, spun around and flashed into flames.

Rather than being scared off, the girls screamed in delight. One of them waved a hand in the air, making rain spill from a solitary cloud directly over his head.

That should teach him to tease a witch, he thought as his magical flames spat and sizzled in the wet. A witch of any age. He swiped rainwater from his face as the tiny cloud dissipated.

"Girls! Go to your classes, please." Karen Mackey clapped her hands together and the children scattered.

"I'm sorry about that," she said, giving him a tense smile. "They haven't seen a man in—well, a long time."

"It's all right. I'll be gone soon enough. Once I know Terri and her family are going to be all right . . ."

"They're being assigned housing now," she said. "Thank you, for bringing them to us."

Karen was about forty, with short, dark hair that curled around her heart-shaped face. She focused wise blue eyes on him. "It couldn't have been easy."

"Wasn't." He didn't even want to think about the last eight hours, trapped in a car with three human females. His powers and strength were just now regenerating. But it was worth it, he knew. They'd managed to save more innocents from the world at large and that was worth any price.

Throughout the years, witches had lived in peace and practiced their magic in secret. Belief in magic died out. The supernatural was dismissed as legend. Until that day ten years before when power had exploded into the public consciousness. Since then, no woman was safe. Witch or human.

The Sanctuary network had been born and until the world came to its senses again—if ever—these women would have to remain hidden.

"They'll be safe here," he said and looked out at the still-snowy peaks in the distance. Spirit Lake spread out in front of them, shining dark blue in the starlight. The lake provided plenty of fresh water for the witches and the rough terrain discouraged most people from the area. Here at ten thousand feet, the camp was secluded and hidden by both heavy stands of trees and magical protection wards. Should any hikers stray too close to camp, a feeling of dark dread would overcome them, convincing them to run from the area.

So far, the only other beings the witches had had to worry about were the mountain goats that inhabited the region. It was as close to a perfect hiding place as they could get.

The moon slipped out from behind a stream of clouds

and painted silver across the surface of the lake. Shadows crouched and a wind whispered through the trees.

"They'll be fine," Karen told him. "We have many human women and children here. You don't have to be a witch these days to need a safe place. Sanctuary's protected from both magical incursion and human."

"Magic?" he asked, sliding a glance at her.

Frowning, she nodded. "We've had to upgrade, so to speak, our protection wards lately. We heard about a few witches, broken during torture, who've switched sides. Dr. Fender is still at work somewhere," she added, with a shiver of unease.

Rune understood the sentiment. Dr. Henry Fender began experimenting on witches some years ago. He was the one who had told the world about the uses of white gold in blanketing a witch's power. The word was that any witch who found herself on his table died screaming.

"Apparently, the good doctor is now convincing some of his 'patients' to work for him."

Rune scowled. The doctor had become legendary in a very short space of time. He had spearheaded the early efforts to contain the witches, but soon his sadism had forced even the government to cut him loose. There were limits, apparently, to what BOW was willing to do. "But the feds stopped using Fender a few years back."

"Yes, but he's taken over a large action group," Karen told him, barely restrained fury coloring every word. "The Seekers find witches and hold them so that Fender can perform more experiments."

This was not good. No witch would be safe as long as Fender was allowed to continue his madness.

"To what end?" he demanded.

"He's looking for a way to drain our powers and use them for himself."

Rage filled Rune, cold and dark, forcing him to battle his own instincts in order to remain calm. It wasn't enough that witches were being hunted, jailed and executed. Now there were human monsters looking to exploit them for their own greed? They talked about shutting down the power when in reality, what they wanted was to steal magic any way they could.

And people thought witches were evil, he told himself wryly.

Torin and the other Eternals had to know about this. They would have to find Fender somehow and send him from this world before he could do more damage. Finding one human male on this overcrowded planet would be quite the task, though. Yet, even as he thought about it, Rune wondered if an Awakened witch couldn't cast a locator spell. Why not use the very magic the man hungered for against him?

He reached for the satellite phone in the pocket of his black jeans. Torin needed to hear this. Not only about Fender, but about the second tracker the witches had found on Terri. If Shea was still bugged, their escape was going to be short-lived.

"No reception here, remember?" Karen asked, smiling at his phone. "We enchant a TV so we can keep up with the news, but as for everything else . . ."

"Right." Ordinarily, his satellite phone would get reception pretty much anywhere on the planet. But in Sanctuary, their magical wards shut down any electronic device they didn't specifically protect. So as long as he was on this mountain he was out of contact. He eyed the witch beside him. "Don't suppose you'd consider cutting a hole through the ward so I could make a call?"

She shook her head. "Don't suppose I would."

He muttered something, but she cut him off quickly.

"We can't risk it, Eternal. Not even for you. All it would take is one stray signal picked up by the wrong person and Sanctuary would be in danger." She scrubbed her hands up and down her arms. "As it was, the tracker Terri was carrying came all too close to the entrance. We'll have to be on high alert for the next few weeks, just in case."

He hadn't considered that. Realizing that he may have brought trouble to this spot bothered him more than he cared to admit. "Do you need me to stay? I can leave the mountain, make a call and come back to help guard the place for a few weeks."

Her head tipped to one side as she studied him. "You would do that?"

He inclined his head. "We in the magical world have to help each other."

"True," she said, taking a deep breath. "But in this case, it's unnecessary. The Guardians will be able to handle whatever comes our way. And if need be, we will all fight. Human and witch."

He looked into her eyes and read the fierce determination written there. And still he had to ask, "What about the Wiccan Rede . . . *An it harm none, do what ye will*?"

The leader of the witches gave him a rueful smile. "Times change, Eternal. You know we risk great damage to ourselves in using our power against our enemies."

"Yes," he said solemnly, knowing that whatever harm a witch did would return on her threefold.

"And yet, what choice do we have?" She shook her head and looked out over the starlit lake. "We use human weapons when we can and resort to magics only when there is no other option. We, each of us, are prepared to accept the karma of what we do—to ensure that we are not wiped from the earth."

"You believe you can hold this camp against all intruders?"

She smiled. "It wasn't easy for you to get in, was it?"

"Hell, no." He grinned suddenly, remembering the warrior women who had dropped from trees to challenge him. "Still not easy to know who to trust, though."

"True enough." She looked back at the camp, tidy log cabins with lamplight falling through the windows to lie on the ground like gold dust. "But the turned witches—traitors—are still few and far between. We'll survive, as will the other Sanctuaries around the world."

"It's bad times," Rune said softly.

"True again," Karen agreed, then looked out over the mountainous view. "But we've lived through bad times before. We will this time, too. Now that the Awakening is here, everything will change."

He slid a glance to her. "How much do you know?"

She smiled. "More than you think, less than I'd like." Shrugging, she continued, "The story of the last great coven has been handed down from mother to daughter throughout the centuries. We all know about the chosen few. And the tasks they must complete to ensure the safety of this world. We don't know who they are, but we know the time is now."

Rune snorted a laugh. He and the other Eternals hadn't considered that the witches had kept a chain of information going throughout the centuries. But they should have. Witches were clever women. And it didn't pay to underestimate a clever woman.

"The Sanctuaries hold libraries of spell books. Shadow books," she was saying. "We've saved the ancient tomes and added to them over the years. If the chosen ones need help they've only to seek out a Sanctuary."

Intrigued, he stared at the short woman beside him. "You've been preparing for the Awakening all along?"

"Of course," she said. "We *all* need the Awakened ones to succeed. If they fail . . . everyone loses."

"Good point," Rune said. But they wouldn't fail, he told himself grimly. He and his fellow Eternals would do everything in their considerable power to ensure that their witches prevailed.

Karen laid one hand on his forearm. "Tell them, Eternal. Tell the chosen ones that the Sanctuary libraries can be accessed by a dimensional spell."

"Dimensional? Hell, that's what got us into trouble in the first place! Opening portals into other worlds is a bad idea."

"It is," she agreed, with a shake of her head. "But that's not what I mean. Sanctuaries have all been equipped with a dimensional hotspot, so to speak. A way for us to share information."

"You manipulate dimensions?" Rune asked, astonished at the level of power in the tiny witch before him.

"Combining our magic makes us stronger," she pointed out. "If the chosen ones need our help, they've only to be close to a Sanctuary to open the portal."

Rune stared down at her, admiration shining in his eyes. "You amaze me."

"We do what we can with what we have," she said with a nod. "But in the end, we are all prisoners here. In these safe spots around the world. Cut off from families, friends, *hope.* The question is, how long will we have to hide? How long, Eternal?"

"Wish I knew."

It all depended, Rune thought, on the Awakening. On the coven coming together again, to end what they'd begun so long ago.

If that happened, then they would have proof to show the world that witchcraft could be an ally. That witches themselves could be trusted to help when the world needed it most.

He shifted his gaze back to the shadow-filled valley. *No pressure,* he told himself.

Chapter 32

"What was that?"

The moment his magical flames winked out, Torin cursed viciously and pushed Shea to the ground, covering her with his own body. Her breath came fast and frantic from beneath him. He felt her fear and shared it. Not for himself. He'd been battling evil for eons. Spilling blood was nothing new to him. But seeing Shea terrified and knowing that there were humans somewhere near who wanted her dead filled him with a fear he'd never known before. It tainted every breath.

"A grenade," he muttered, keeping his voice low, though there was clearly no need for stealth. The sound of the fire at the motel below roared into the night like a caged, starving beast.

He looked down at her wide, frightened eyes and wanted to kill whoever had brought her to this. In the span of just a few days, she'd been captured, tortured, chased and shot. And now someone had blown up the room she was in.

"*Enough.*" He planted a hard, fast kiss on her mouth and then stared into her eyes. "Whoever launched the grenade into our room is probably still down there. I'm going to find them."

He lifted his head to peer over the rock behind which he had Shea hidden. Looking through the trees, he could see what was left of the motel. His blood turned to ice, then an instant later, began to boil.

The room he and Shea had been occupying was an inferno.

The rest of the place didn't look much better. There were screams and shouts as people ran for their lives. But Torin was looking for those who would be running *toward* the flames. Whoever had tried to kill them would no doubt want to check the scene, make sure he hadn't failed.

Which meant Torin was going hunting.

"Stay here," he ordered, rolling off Shea to come to his feet in a crouch. He stared down at her and saw shadows from the intense light of the fire race across her features. "Right here, do you understand?"

She pushed up, swept dirt and pebbles from her cheek and stared at him. "Why? I might be able to help."

"I need you safely here while I find those responsible."

"And do what? Kill him?"

"Not until we've had a *talk*." He wanted information. He'd removed the tracker from Shea's body, so how did the assassin find them? He had to know which agency was funding this hunt. And he needed to know how to stop it.

Shea looked at the conflagration, flames shooting high into the air, sparks lifting, flying in the wind toward the trees, which were already beginning to smolder. She grabbed Torin's arm and hung on. "Forget about finding him. There'll be others here soon. Firefighters. Police. Let's just go. Now. While they fight the fire."

"Go where? Shea, if we don't stop this here, whoever is behind it will only follow us."

"Who cares?" she shouted it, but her voice was lost in the surrounding clamor. "Everybody in the free world is already looking for me, Torin!"

He went down on one knee beside her and grabbed

her upper arms hard enough to leave an imprint of his fingertips on her skin. Just touching her grounded him in a way that nothing else ever had. Knowing she was his now gave him strength that even his god would tremble at. He looked into her green eyes and felt love wash through him. Love like he had never known before.

"You are my heart, Shea," he said, sliding his hands up to cup her face in his palms. "I will do whatever I must to see you safe."

She covered his hands with her own. "Do you think you're any less important to me? Don't go down there, Torin."

"I have no choice. No one will harm you. Ever." He leaned in and kissed her hard. "Do you believe me?"

A second, then two, ticked past as he waited, staring into the eyes of the woman he'd hungered for throughout time.

"Yes," she whispered, meeting his eyes. "But—"

"No." He released her and stood up. He had her belief. He knew her trust wasn't yet his, but that would come. Provided he could keep her alive long enough for her to become immortal. Thirty days until the mating ritual was complete. Thirty days to find what was lost and return it to safekeeping. Then they would have the coming centuries together and *no one,* he told himself, was going to rob them of that time together.

"Stay. Here." Then he flashed into flames and was gone.

"How the hell can we get in there to see the bodies?"

"We wait."

The first man snorted, then shot a look of pride at the roaring fire consuming the back end of the small motel. "Be like waiting for the fires of hell to burn out."

"They're dead," his friend said, assurance ringing in his tone. "No way they got out of that in time."

"You best be right. The boss won't like it if the witch escaped."

"And just who," Torin asked, flashing in behind the two men, "is the boss?"

One of the men turned instantly, brought up the shotgun he carried and pointed it at Torin's chest. Before he could fire, the Eternal had grabbed the barrel and shoved it up. It discharged harmlessly into the air. Torin wrested the gun from the man's grip tossed it aside, then reached out and broke the shooter's neck with a quick twist of his hand.

The assassin's friend looked as though he'd seen a ghost. And he had. The ghost of death coming for him. Torin had no patience for those who would lie in wait and kill from a distance. He had no sympathy for those who killed for money. When he looked at the remaining man and watched the light of the fire dance over his wide, terrified eyes, Torin felt nothing for him.

Only the sheer determination to get what he'd come for.

Around him, the night was alive with sound. The fire. Shouts. Screams. And in the distance, a siren called out, wailing mournfully.

Standing in the treeline behind the motel, they were well hidden. He grabbed the man by the neck, lifted him high off the ground and looked up into small, frightened eyes. "Who is it you work for? Who is after Shea Jameson?"

The man frantically pulled at Torin's hand, futilely trying to loosen his grip. Nails scraped and scratched but couldn't help him.

Torin's hand only tightened around the man's throat as he kicked his legs wildly, looking for purchase, desperately laboring for air that wouldn't come.

Torin shook him like a dog. "Who sent you here?"

Fury spat at him from the man's eyes. His face was

red, mottled. His hands continued to tear at Torin's grip, hoping to ease it. Torin easily turned and slammed the man into a wide tree trunk, rattling the man's head so hard his eyes jittered. "Talk to me, bastard, or die right here."

Wildly, the man nodded. Frantic eyes rolled back in his head, feet kicked against the tree.

Torin eased off on the pressure slightly to allow the faintest whisper of air to enter the man's starving lungs. "Talk."

"Orders," he said, still sounding strangled even as he hissed in one small breath of air after another. "Over the phone."

"From *who*?"

"Don't know," he insisted, slapping now at Torin's hand, locked firmly around his throat. "Didn't ask! Stop!"

That last word came out on a wheeze as Torin's hard fist squeezed more tightly again. All around him, the fire roared and humans scurried, trying to save something of the burning motel. The siren continued to wail, closer now, and he knew that in moments there would be even more humans cluttering up the scene. He had no time to waste with this scum.

"You take blind orders to kill a woman? No questions asked?" The black fury inside him was growing, spreading.

"Not ... woman ..." the man managed. *"Witch."* Hatred fueled that word and glittered in the man's dying eyes. There was no remorse. No regret. Only a determination that burned as fiercely in his soul as the flames that ate up the motel behind them.

"I cannot let you live," Torin told him flatly. "No woman is safe—witch or human—while men such as you walk free."

Worry darted across the man's eyes but a moment

later was replaced by resignation and a kind of fanatic pride. As Torin's grip eased, he spoke again in a hoarse voice. "Killing me stops nothing. She'll never be safe. Witches should die. They'll find her. They'll kill—"

Torin snapped the neck beneath his hand and let the man fall. If no one moved the body, it would be consumed by the spreading flames of the fire he had caused. There was justice in that.

Either way, the threat was gone for the moment and Torin shifted his gaze to the trees where his woman waited. He'd wasted enough time on this task.

He called on the flames and flashed to Shea's side.

Kellyn felt the stars beginning to align.

She even gave the desk clerk at the Renaissance Mayflower Hotel a coy smile as he tapped his fingers across the keyboard.

"I'm sorry, miss," he said finally, and to give him his due, he did seem disappointed, "but our Presidential Suite has been reserved in advance."

A quick whip of impatience sliced through her, but Kellyn smiled through it. Leaning across the marble counter, she took the young man's hand and squeezed gently. The sparks flying from her touch went unnoticed by anyone else. "Check again. I think you'll find the room is in *my* name."

He stared at her, his eyes blank, his mouth slack. Her spell countered his objections and as she waited for his response, she whispered, "Do for me what I will."

The young man blinked, took a shaky breath and nodded. "Yes," he said, his voice as robotic as his movements. "You're right, of course. The room is reserved for you. I don't know what I was thinking."

Kellyn smiled again, relishing the sweep of power she felt. How did humans manage to stumble through their lives without the electrifying pump of something magical inside them? What boring, tiny creatures they were. And yet, she told herself, oh, so helpful when properly motivated.

"See? I knew you'd find the mistake," she assured him graciously. "Now, I'd like champagne and strawberries delivered to my suite in an hour. Please be sure the champagne is very cold. I'd hate to be disappointed."

Again her power crackled against the young man's skin and he nodded quickly. "I'll see to it personally."

"Aren't you kind?" When he produced a sign-in sheet for her signature, she simply waved her free hand at it and it disappeared. He went through the motions of filing the nonexistent paper away and then handed her the key cards. "You've been very helpful"—she paused to read the name tag pinned to his suit jacket—"Michael."

"Thank you, miss. My pleasure."

"I'm sure it was," she said, releasing him at last. As she did, his free hand swept to the spell-charmed wrist she'd held and idly scratched at his own skin. He would feel the burn of her spell for a few hours, but would remember nothing else about this encounter.

And should the original party show up to claim his reserved Presidential Suite . . . well, she would deal with them in the same way.

Turning, she walked down the long marble lobby, enjoying the quiet click of her Ferragamos. Power. It was all about power, really.

At the elevator, she waved one hand at the closed doors and they opened instantly. She stepped inside, leaned languorously against the wall and smiled to herself as the doors swept shut.

"Good to be a witch," she whispered to no one.

She'd waited through lifetime after lifetime for this and now it was all within her grasp. It was all coming together so nicely. As if it were Destiny. Preordained. And she believed it was. How could it not be?

She had a plan. More, she had powerful backers. Yes, she was being forced to deal with humans, but when the stakes were this high, she was willing to put up with some aggravation.

They didn't understand, of course. How could they? The humans believed that they were in charge. That she was their willing accomplice.

She laughed a little as the elevator opened onto the Presidential Suite. Above her head a wide skylight offered a view of the night sky, shining with stars and the ever-increasing moon. The floor was a mosaic pattern of inlaid marble and the wall sconces threw small shafts of golden light.

She walked through the suite, admiring the elegant furnishings, acquainting herself with the luxury she would quickly become accustomed to. Then she walked to the closest terrace and opened the doors.

The night air was soft and cool against her skin and the hum of the city spread out below her. Everything was just as it should be.

The plan was in place. All she needed now was to wait for the signal that would begin the game.

"Soon," she whispered, glancing up at the night sky as the moon darted behind a swath of clouds as if hiding from her. "Soon it will all be mine and no one will be able to stand against me."

Alone on the terrace with the night as witness, Kellyn laughed as power shimmered out all around her.

Chapter 33

Shea was watching the fire consume the motel, and the nearby trees, when her own personal pillar of fire erupted alongside her. What did it say about her, she wondered, that she no longer jumped in surprise when Torin did the flaming-man thing?

"He's dead, isn't he?" she asked, not even glancing at him. "Whoever did this is dead. You killed him."

"Them," he corrected, taking her shoulder and turning her to face him. "There were two. They were directed to kill you, but they didn't know who was giving the orders."

"So nothing was solved," she pointed out quietly. She turned her head as the first fire engine arrived and the howling siren shut off abruptly. Men scattered, running for hoses, shouting instructions, all while the fire raged and hissed at them as if taunting their puny efforts to extinguish it.

"You're safe again," Torin said.

"For now."

"Now is all we have," he told her and drew her to him.

She tried to hold herself away, but her instincts worked against her. She might not like what was happening, but her mind insisted that she could hardly blame Torin for protecting her. There were people out there—even now—plotting her death. Shea closed her eyes and sighed as she wrapped her arms around Torin's middle.

Burrowing into his steadiness, his warmth, she worried not about the now but about tomorrow. And the day after that. How were they supposed to complete whatever their task was if she couldn't unlock the right memory? How was she supposed to defend herself if her powers were still wildly unpredictable?

His hands swept up and down her spine and despite the situation, her body responded. Desire for this man was always only a breath away. And apparently, even the threat of imminent death couldn't defeat it.

"We have to go," Torin said, pulling her back from him so that he could look into her eyes.

"How?" she asked on a short laugh that carried a tinge of near hysteria. Pointing down the hill, she said, "The explosion took out your car."

He didn't even glance at the blackened hulk of the sleek Viper. "We'll find another. But for now . . ."

He pulled her close again and she nodded, folding herself around him as tightly as possible. "We go by fire."

"Close your eyes."

If anyone had looked up into the stand of trees, they might have thought that the inferno was spreading. But in a heartbeat, the tall tower of flames was gone and darkness reigned supreme again.

Rune's phone call a few hours later explained how they had been tracked.

"It was under Terri's left breast," he said. "I don't know if it will be the same with Shea, but that seems a good place to start checking."

"I will." Torin looked across the room at Shea. She hadn't spoken again since he'd flashed her to a new motel. It had taken longer than he would have liked to cover the distance between Flagstaff, Arizona, and where they were now, in tiny El Rito, New Mexico. But he'd wanted as much distance between them and the last attack as possible.

Now he was glad of it. If there was another tracker on Shea's body somewhere, they had to find it before whoever was after them had time to catch up.

Shea paced the small motel room. Her nerves were so tight, her power was spiking and Torin felt it as he would have a fever. Tension was ripe in the air between them and damned if he knew how to break it. He had done what he would always do. What he *must* do. Protect her. He would protect them all. If she couldn't see that . . .

"Doc Fender is back in the mix, too," Rune was saying and Torin paid attention.

He went completely still at that piece of news. "Are you sure?"

"The witches of Sanctuary are sure," his friend said. "He's the head of the Seekers."

"I've heard of them." Nothing good, either. They were a rogue band of militia types, well armed and scared. Not a good combination. But Torin had had no idea that Henry Fender was a part of that group. The man was infamous for his cruelty and his fanaticism. Knowing that he was part of an organized group operating outside of federal rules and regulations told Torin that the stakes had just gone higher.

Fender couldn't be predicted. The man was mad and dedicated to what he saw as his God-given duty. To destroy witches. He hadn't been heard from recently and Torin had hoped he was dead.

"The witches claim that he's turning some of his victims," Rune told him. "Offering to stop the pain if they'll help capture others like them."

"Bastard."

"Exactly. So keep your eyes open. Seekers could be on your trail as well as everyone else."

"I will." His gaze touched Shea again. He couldn't help but look to her wherever she was. It was as if unless he was touching her, he was only half alive.

Then Rune started talking again and Torin was caught up in the possibilities offered by the Sanctuary libraries of spell books. "She can reach them anywhere?"

"According to Karen, yes. Though it's easier all around if you're at least close to a Sanctuary. Something about power bridges built by the witches." He blew out a breath. "The magics are stronger when you can draw on combined power."

"Right. We'll try it."

Shea turned to look at him, a question in her eyes. He nodded to let her know he would tell her everything. She smiled briefly and Torin felt a rush of pride in her swell within him. His woman had a core of steel.

"Have you heard anything about Egan?"

"No," Rune admitted. "But I'm going to check in with a few of the others. See if anyone's seen him." He paused. "You know how it is, Torin. After centuries of waiting, some can only deal with it by disappearing. Keeping to themselves."

"That time is past," Torin said. "The Awakening is begun and we must all stand by our witches. So you need to find Egan."

"I will. Watch your back."

Torin hung up and looked across the room at his woman. The strength of his gaze finally caught her attention and she looked at him. "What are we going to try?"

"The witches of Sanctuary have set up a library of ancient spell books and shadow tomes. They say you can access whatever you need through a dimensional portal."

She laughed shortly, but there was no humor in it. "Sure. Dimensional portals. No problem. I'll get right on it." Shaking her head, she admitted, "I have no idea how to do that, Torin."

"We'll figure it out, Shea. Together."

She studied him for a long minute. "There's something else. What is it?"

"You may have another tracker on your body somewhere."

She jolted and immediately slapped one hand to the back of her neck where they'd found the first chip.

"It won't be there," he said, moving across the room to her with long, purposeful strides.

"Then where?" She swept her own hands up and down her body as if just by looking for the damn thing she would find it.

"Rune says that Terri's second tracker was discovered under her left breast."

Shea's arms instinctively came up over her breasts in a protective gesture that was as futile as it was understandable. "But they didn't give me an injection there. I would have known . . ."

He hated seeing that look on her face. The expression that was both furious and filled with sorrow. If he could have, Torin would have returned to that prison where Shea had been held and torn it down brick by brick until there wasn't a single stone left standing.

"They could have knocked you out for the procedure."

"But I'd remember—"

"Not necessarily. If it's there, Shea, we have to find it."

Slowly, she lowered her arms, took a breath and bit down on her bottom lip. "I know. It's just—never mind."

He watched as different emotions raced across her face, each one appearing and disappearing so fast he could hardly identify them. But he felt her distress. Felt the tangle of fear and anger and grief knotting inside her. Torin didn't want to admit that he might be the cause of her misery. "Don't dismiss it. What's bothering you? The fact that I killed those men who attacked you?"

She looked up at him and shook her head. "No. No, Torin. I know why you did it. I just . . . hate all of this. I hate being hunted. I hate that I can't remember what I need to. I hate feeling so out of control."

Torin smiled. "I didn't hear you say you hate me. I think we're making progress."

Shea laughed a little. "I never hated you, Torin. You scared the crap out of me, but I never hated you. And now . . ."

"Now?"

"I don't know what I'd do without you."

"You'll never have to find out," he vowed. "I promise you. I will be with you through all of this. You can depend on me."

"I know," she said, forcing a smile that didn't reach her eyes.

"Shea, I have to find that tracker."

She nodded, waved one hand in front of herself and instantly her clothes disappeared.

Hunger roared through him at the sight of her and he was pleased she had finally dispensed with her sense of modesty before him. Then he smiled, both at the view of her luscious naked body and at the display of her burgeoning control of her powers. "You're getting better. Stronger."

"Practice makes perfect," she said on a choked-off laugh. "God, Torin, just find it."

He moved in close, his gaze dropping to her left breast, where the mating tattoo was inexorably growing. The tiny red flames now formed a circle around her areola and were sweeping down in a delicate curve, following the swell of her breast and snaking toward her back, where they would eventually curve up and over her shoulder.

Pride filled him. This was his mark. The mark they had made together. And the shadow of her brand now stained his skin in the same pattern, proclaiming them a unit. Two halves of the same whole. His cock stirred, ready to claim her again. To coax more of those burning flames into life on her skin. To feel the heat of her pulling at him.

His fingertips traced the flames and he lifted his gaze to hers. He read a matching passion stirring in her emerald eyes and in response, his cock went to stone.

She reached up and held his hand to her breast, pushing herself into his touch and sighing at the cool glide of skin against skin.

"Touch me first, Torin," she said, near breathless. "Then find the tracker. I need you. I need to feel you inside me. Wipe away the screams and the fire and the crazy people chasing us."

His thumb and forefinger squeezed her nipple until she groaned. "I want you," he whispered. "I always want you. I wake in a fever to touch you and sleep dreaming of you. You are the witch who holds my heart."

She snapped her fingers and he was naked, his aching body on proud display for her. Shea smiled and reached for him, folding her fingers around his heavy thickness. Torin hissed in a breath and let his eyes close on a wave of pure pleasure.

In the midst of madness, in the turmoil of danger, all he could think about was possessing her. Laying claim to her again and again. He needed to feel the heat of the brand erupting on his skin and watch his mark on her grow. He wanted to be pounding his body into hers, feeling her slick, wet heat accepting him, taking him deep.

Her thumb caressed the very tip of him, sliding the bead of moisture she found there in tight, quick circles. He groaned and knew he was lost. He had to have her. Were the Seekers to come crashing at the door this instant, he would still have to have her.

Torin bent his head and took her left nipple into his mouth. He tasted her scent, that elemental mixture of earth and ocean and pure Shea and the cool heat of her skin. The burn of the brand filled him and increased the need already climbing to staggering heights inside him.

Shea held his head to her breast and stroked her fingertips along his cheeks, encouraging him to taste more deeply, to suckle more fiercely. As he did, she groaned, the soft sigh sliding into his very heart.

He dropped one hand to her center and found her wet and hot for him. Delving deep with two fingers, he heard her groan and pushed his fingers higher, so that he could caress her body from the inside.

She rocked into his touch, riding his hand as if everything in the world depended on the next few minutes. They were as one. Breathing shattered, bodies straining.

His tongue and teeth worked her nipple as his hands worked her core. His thumb caressed that one small nub of sensation until she let her head fall back on her neck and his name sigh from her lips.

It wasn't enough, he thought wildly. He needed to be a part of her. Now. He tipped her back onto the bed and was only vaguely aware of the screams of the old bedsprings beneath them.

Shea continued to twist and writhe against his hand, her voice encouraging him in a hoarse whisper more compelling than a shout. "I'm so close, Torin, so close."

"Go over for me, Shea," he urged, breath hot against her skin as he lifted his gaze to hers.

"No, don't push me over the edge yet." She shook her head wildly from side to side, laughing and gasping all at once. "Need you. Need you inside me. We go together."

"Together," he repeated, staring into her eyes.

He covered her with his big body and pushed his hard length into her depths with one long thrust. Locked together, bodies taut with the unreleased tension claiming them both, they held perfectly still, simply relishing the soul-deep pleasure of the joining.

Then she lifted her legs to his hips, reached down to curl her fingers into his butt and smiled up at him. "Take me now, Torin. Hard and fast and deep. Don't hold anything back."

"Never," he promised and kept his gaze locked with hers as his hips pumped furiously against her. The rhythm they set was blinding. White-hot cracks of lightning shot back and forth between them as power met, collided and then blended.

Again and again, he pushed himself into the only woman who had ever mattered to him. He felt his unbeating heart jerk in his chest as he watched ecstasy steal across her features.

Torin felt a stinging burn on his chest. He looked down at the tattoo on her breast and watched as the flames darkened, then flared brightly as their mating quickened, encompassing them both with the force of magic.

The incredible slide of his body into hers hastened the need already taking him over. He was relentless, pushing her higher and higher. The friction between their bodies stoked the inner fires until they lived and breathed as much as the flames that made up Torin's being.

Everything he was, he gave her, everything she was, he took. He bent his head again, tasting her skin, licking her as a cat would a bowl of cream. He couldn't get enough of her. Over and over, she cried out, matching his body on every thrust, urging him on, shouting his name.

He took her nipple into his mouth again and suckled her long and deep as his body laid siege to hers. And finally, he felt her reach the end of her endurance. She gave herself up to the liquid swells of her release.

As her body tightened like warm velvet around his, Torin spilled all that he was into her depths.

Chapter 34

"If we kill each other, at least we'll die happy," Shea said when she was sure she could speak without her voice breaking.

Tiny, delicious little aftershocks still trembled throughout her body, making her sigh with the quiet pleasure. The burning sensation on her breast had passed, and she knew without looking that more flames had been branded into her skin. Torin lay beside her, one arm tossed across her middle, one leg thrown over hers.

He took up a lot of space, her Eternal, but it was more than his massive size that was carving out a spot for him in her heart. It was his fierce tenderness. The vulnerability she only occasionally caught a glimpse of. The protection he offered her so willingly and the quiet determination to do whatever was necessary to keep her safe.

Also, he was the most amazing lover she could ever have imagined.

"You won't die," he said, his face in the crook of her neck, his breath warm against her skin. "I won't allow it."

She ran her fingertips up and down his arm, loving the feel of his skin beneath hers. "I know you'll do everything you can, Torin."

"No." He pushed up on one elbow and met her gaze.

She stared up into his pale gray eyes and wondered how she could ever have been afraid of that unusual stare. When she saw his eyes now, she saw the past and the future and the ever-shifting present.

"Don't make promises you might not be able to keep," she said softly, as she lifted one hand to touch the corner of his mouth.

"This promise will be kept. At all costs. Have I not proven that to you yet?"

Her heart clenched in her chest. Yes, he had shown that he would do anything for her. To save her. The prison guards he'd killed to help her escape. The assassins he'd killed to try to prevent further attacks.

"You have. But even the most stalwart protector can't defend against every danger, Torin. You're just one man."

"Eternal."

She smiled and corrected herself. "Eternal. I know you'll do everything you possibly can, Torin. But just in case something happens—" God, she didn't want to think about the possibility of being torn from him. Of dying just as she was discovering how to live. But the threat had to be recognized for what it was. "—I want you to know, this time with you has been the best of my life."

He laughed shortly.

"What?" Offended, she pushed at his arm, but didn't budge it an inch.

"You've been kidnapped, implanted with electronic bugs, imprisoned, shot and nearly blown up all in the space of less than two weeks."

"True. But you know what else I've been?"

He shook his head.

"I've been with you," she said, dragging her fingers across the breadth of his chest, tracing the curve of the mating brand. "I've been part of a team. I've found out

who I am and have begun to learn how to use *what* I am.
I've been made love to by a damn expert—"

He gave her a smug, purely masculine smile.

"—and if it all ends tomorrow, I'll regret leaving you,
but I won't regret a moment of anything else."

His arm around her tightened and the smile on his
face disappeared. "Nothing will happen to you, Shea. I
finally have you and I won't let you go. No matter what.
I need you to believe that. Believe in me."

"I do," she said, clutching him to her, holding tight
and fast to the huge man who had so quickly become the
most important person in her world. "I really do, Torin."

"Good." He kissed her, fast and hard. "Now, lie back,
and let me find that damn tracker so we can get out of
here."

Shea did as he asked and rolled to her back. Lifting
her arms, she stretched them out behind her head, baring herself to his concentrated gaze. His fingers moved
over and under the curve of her left breast, following the
trail of her witch tattoo that became more defined, more
a part of her, every day.

"Can you feel it?"

"No," he said. "I'm going to call on the fire, use magic
to find it. Hold still."

She watched him, unable to tear her gaze from the
man. His long, dark hair fell to his shoulders, and his
pale eyes were narrowed and focused on his task.

Flames leapt into life on his fingertips. With his right
hand, he slowly traced the curve of her breast, pressing
the living fire into her skin.

She felt the heat, dizzying as it spread across her
chest, over her abdomen and then lower, settling in the
very center of her. The heat became an ache and despite
the situation she was in, Shea felt the stirrings of need
whip through her again.

Torin had explained that once the mating began, they

would feel a constant need. With every day that passed, their bond became stronger. The brand grew and spread across their skin. Their mental and physical link was defining itself anew at every moment.

It was as if they actually were two halves of a whole, finally coming together after an eternity apart.

All Shea knew was that she ached for him. Ached to feel his body pressing down onto hers. Until their thirty days were over, their mating would become more frenzied, more intimate, more vital. Though she couldn't imagine it getting any better than it already was.

Torin continued his exploration of the curve and mound of her breast, forcing the flames and the power they sprung from to dig deep within her. To go beneath the skin and into the very muscles of her body and finally, he found what he sought.

"It's there," he said, voice tight with an anger he refused to release. "Magic found it, but I'll have to cut it out as I did the last one. Rune told me one of the witches was a metal caller and pulled the tracker out of Terri's body. I don't have that magic."

Shea nodded, tightening her fists over the headboard behind her. "It's all right. I'm ready. Get it out of me, Torin."

He straightened, held up one hand and his knife appeared, lamplight glinting off the long, wicked blade. Looking down at her, he held Shea's gaze for a long moment.

"Do it, Torin."

"This will hurt, but I will take as much of your pain as possible."

She nodded and braced herself. The tip of his blade dug into her flesh at the base of her breast. She arched up off the bed and clenched her jaw tight at the sharp slap of pain. He was forced to dig for the tracker and before he was finished, Shea was whimpering. The muscles in her arms were locked in the death grip she had on the headboard. A single tear seeped from the corner of her eye and a relieved breath slid from her lungs as he held up the chip to show her.

"Is that it?" she asked. "Is that all of them?"

He stretched out his hand, laid the tracker on the bedside table and smashed it with the hilt of his knife. Frowning, he bent to her breast again and ordered, "Hold on to me so that I can seal your wound."

She pried one hand off the headboard and laid it over Torin's shoulder. An instant later, heat bloomed on her flesh as their combined powers linked to heal the slice beneath her breast.

When he was done, he bent his head and tenderly kissed the spot where his knife had cut her. His tongue traced the pattern of red flames branding her skin and followed the circular tattoo until he came to her nipple. Then he pulled it into his mouth and used his tongue and teeth to drive the last of the pain from her body and mind.

"Torin . . ."

He looked at her, lifted his head and whispered, "I will check your body myself. Every square inch, until we are sure you're free of their traps."

Shea lost herself in the passion between them. Pain was forgotten. Fear was quickly shelved for another time. She wanted, more than anything, to feel alive. Completely alive. And that was possible only when he was inside her.

"Maybe," she said, rolling over onto her stomach and looking back at him over her shoulder, "you should start checking me now. If you're going to be thorough, it could take a while."

He gave her a slow, satisfied smile. "Perhaps you're right," he said, sliding the flat of his hands up her thighs to the curve of her behind. "I should be thorough."

"Let me help," she offered, going up on her knees as she grabbed hold of the headboard again. She wiggled her behind and parted her legs in invitation. "I don't want you to miss anything, now do I?"

"I promise you," he said softly, "no matter how long it takes, nothing will be overlooked. I am a very patient man."

Torin came up behind her and ran his fingers through the dark red curls guarding her damp, hot flesh until her hips rocked and her breath came in short gasps. When neither of them could take the separation any longer, he mounted her and shoved himself into her depths.

The slap of flesh meeting flesh, the harsh, labored breathing and the whispered words of promises and pleas were the only sounds in the dimly lit room as once more, the witch and her Eternal made magic as old as time itself.

"The closest Sanctuary is only a day from here," Torin assured her. "We're near enough for you to try to make contact with the portal."

"Right." Naked, Shea sat cross-legged on the floor in front of the mirror Torin had ripped off the wall. She was about to attempt a portal opening spell and she knew that spellwork was more effective if done skyclad. Though it felt weird to be sitting naked in front of a mirror. They were in a roadside motel just outside Norman, Oklahoma. She glanced around at the oh, so familiar generic motel furniture and squelched a sigh.

Since going on the run, they had been in far too many of these motel rooms.

"If you have trouble with the spell you've written, we can go to Sanctuary in person tomorrow."

She nodded, glanced up at him and gave him a brief smile. "We've been focusing for days, channeling our powers together to be strong enough to enter the portal. I can do this."

"I have faith," he said. Holding the mirror upright for her, Torin watched as she lit a single yellow candle.

The wick caught and a wavering flame danced in the stillness. "Yellow for confidence, divination, to stimulate the conscious mind," she whispered.

"You remember," he said just as softly.

"Yes. More every day. But not quickly enough." Taking a deep breath, she closed her eyes, waved her hands over the candle flame three times and whispered the chant she had written only that morning.

> *Widen my eyes that I may see,*
> *the secrets of eternity.*
> *A spell to open up my powers*
> *Is what I need in this hour.*
> *My sisters wait upon my task*
> *A little help is all I ask.*

Torin grinned, but kept silent so he wouldn't interrupt her concentration. But damned if he wasn't enjoying watching his woman find her magical feet. She was proud and resilient and as stubborn as ever. But at the heart of her, she was pure female. And all his.

"I see the portal," she said, a half smile on her face. She opened her eyes, stared into the mirror and spoke without looking at Torin. "It's like a bubble. Shining with the light of a million suns. It's wavering, like a mirage in the desert."

"Can you reach in?" he asked quietly.

"I think so." She drew one long, deep breath and leaned forward, over the dancing candle flame toward the mirror.

Torin said nothing as she reached *into* the glass, her hand and arm disappearing from sight. Her features were twisted into a mask of concentration. "It's right there. I can touch it. Feel it. I just have to . . . *grab it*!"

As she said the last two words, she jerked back, pulling out of the mirror. The candle flame snuffed out as if an unseen breath had blown on it.

"I did it," she whispered, glancing up at him with a wide smile.

He looked at the worn leather book she held in both hands and felt an answering smile on his own face. "You found the book you wanted?"

"I found the book I cast the spell for," she said, caressing the cover. "Hopefully, it will give me what I have to know about casting more spells and gathering up the magic we're going to need."

A week later, Torin and Shea were holed up in yet another motel somewhere in Ohio. The last town she remembered going through was Brecksville, a suburb of Cleveland. Since she was geographically challenged in the best of times, she had no idea where that might be on a map. All she really cared about was that they were as lost to the world as they could be.

Although she knew all too well that nowhere was safe.

Not for Shea.

She and Torin had discovered that hard truth during their cross-country ride. Didn't matter if he'd removed all of the electronic trackers from her body. Their enemies would eventually find them anyway. Shea's face was on every news channel. Her eyes stared out at them from the covers of magazines and the grainy front pages of newspapers.

She'd hoped that as more time passed, her story would be forgotten—or at least be moved to the back of the line, behind more breaking news. But rather than the story dying down, it was ratcheting up as the whole country took an interest in the witch who had escaped Terminal Island.

So the two of them kept moving, driving when Torin's incredible stores of energies had been sapped. Cars were easy enough to come by. Magic allowed them to take what they needed, leaving behind no memory of their having been there. Being a car thief wasn't high on Shea's list of occupations, but then she preferred being a thief to being dead. Over the following days and nights, Shea saw more of the country than she ever had before and knew that if she hadn't currently been listed as Public Enemy Number One, she might have even enjoyed the trip.

As it was, all she felt was trapped. The motel was small and clean, but had been decorated sometime in the seventies. There were pink and orange shag throw rugs on the floor and wildly flowered bedspreads. The walls were painted a dark pink and boasted a wallpaper border of orange and pink daisies at the ceiling.

Under other circumstances she might even have been amused at the place—it was like stepping back in time. But for Shea, this room was yet one more box in a series of boxes where she'd been holed away, denied any freedom of movement. Wherever they were, that closed-in feeling rose up like solid white gold walls around her and Shea wondered if she'd ever really be free again.

Every night on television, the news channels displayed their Witch Alert Boards. Tiny colored pushpins dotted maps of the country and showed exactly where witches were being caught and imprisoned. There were talk show hosts who made jokes about flying witches and suggested to their audience that they study the night sky and lock up their broomsticks. There were children playing MP and witch on the streets.

And worse—for them anyway—there was a reward of fifty thousand dollars being offered for Shea's return.

That she didn't understand at all. She was a witch, just like so many others being herded into camps and prisons all over the world. Why was she being singled out?

"Stay inside," Torin said as he walked to the motel room door. "I'll get food and be back in a half hour. Stay away from the windows and don't open the door to anyone."

Irritated, Shea snapped, "I get it, okay? We've been doing this for days, Torin. I know the rules."

His jaw clenched, but he only nodded as he left.

The moment he was gone, she regretted tearing into him. After all, he was all she had. The Eternal had been by her side through all of this, had kept her safe, and she felt the connection between them growing every day. She didn't need to see the spreading tattoo on her skin, already circling around to her back and toward her spine, to know that the bonding between them was almost complete.

She felt it with every breath she drew.

Every time he touched her, she knew that she belonged with him and no other. Every time she thought about her past or her future, he was there. A part of it all. He was the only person in the world she could count on. And even he was still somewhat of a mystery.

He hadn't told her any more about the last great coven and what had happened after the portal into Hell had opened. He'd insisted that she remember the rest of it herself.

"You know enough now," he had said, holding her close, their bodies still locked together. "I've given you some of the knowledge, but the Awakening must come from within you. You must be able to draw on your memories as well as your power if we are to complete this task before the month is up."

"But the month is nearly half over," she whispered now to the empty room. "And I don't have the answers I need yet."

Oh, she was learning, remembering. Her dreams were filled with ancient images. Of Shea and Torin through the years. She saw him, unchanging, unflagging, always there, always near her. She saw herself, crafting spells, calling on magics—and those dreams had quickened her latent powers and given her a road map of sorts to spells and chants.

Yet, the most important information continued to elude her.

Shea scrubbed her hands up and down her arms and fought the tendrils of uneasiness that crept through her. Without Torin in the room with her, she felt vulnerable. Amazing how much *space* the man took up. And the aura of strength and fearlessness he gave off was usually enough to quiet her own anxieties.

She was so rarely alone now, every sound, every rattle of the windowpane made her jump. She half expected one of her former prison guards to leap at her from out of the shadows. To lock her down again and carry her away.

Away from Torin.

She could study the book she'd plucked from Sanctuary again, but she believed she had learned as much as she could from the ancient volume. Written in Old English, it hadn't been easy to read, but the spells and enchantments contained in it had fed the opening power within Shea.

She would return the book and take another as soon as they neared another Sanctuary. Until then, her subconscious continued to examine what she'd learned for ways to use it. Even as her power grew, she felt herself straining against the cage that enclosed her.

How could she complete her task if she was never to step out of the protective circle Torin had drawn around her?

With the walls feeling as though they were closing in on her, she moved to the window, and despite Torin's orders, carefully pulled back only the edge of the garishly flowered drapes. Instantly, she drew a relieved breath. Just looking at the outdoors was enough to calm the nerves pulsing inside her. But even as she admired the sweep of the world beyond the glass, she remembered that she had enemies and they could be closer than she'd like.

She quickly scanned her surroundings and idly noted that most roadside motels looked exactly alike. Low-slung buildings with mostly empty parking lots lying beneath lights that flickered until they winked out altogether. At least this one, she thought, offered a view of a stand of trees just across the street.

Lifting her gaze from the trees, Shea stared up at the waxing moon shining down from a star-swept sky. The crescent-shaped moon didn't throw much light, but its pearly glow mesmerized her. The longer she looked, the more she felt herself responding to an inexorable psychic pull. Whispers resonated in her mind and echoed in her soul. It was as if the universe itself was reaching for her. Her skin felt charged, as if there were small electrical pulses beating within her bones.

She took one long breath, then another. Power grew and bubbled within and she realized what she had to do. This magical pull on her soul was something she couldn't ignore. No matter what enemy might be waiting for her, no matter Torin's fury when he found out she'd disregarded his orders, the moon called and she must respond.

Chapter 35

For one second, Shea paused to consider the danger inherent in what she was about to do. Her instincts were important, though—hadn't Torin himself been telling her so? Insisting that she trust the Awakening? Besides, she told herself, when she had accepted the mating, she had also accepted the danger. So she really didn't have a choice, did she?

Carefully, quietly, she opened the door and stepped out into the still air. The late-September evening in Ohio still carried the humidity of summer. Cloying, nearly suffocating in its damp heat, the air wrapped itself around Shea like a blanket she couldn't toss off.

The scent of the trees filled her and she sensed that power quickening within her again. Witches were of the earth and the elements strengthened her with every breath.

Over the last few days, bits and pieces of magic lore and ritual had come to her. Reading the old spell book had opened the door in her mind just a little wider, to allow memories to creep in. Images, thoughts, just appeared in her mind as if they had always been there and she simply hadn't been open enough to recognize them for what they were.

She knew that a waxing moon was a good time for renewal spells. For starting over. For working toward goals.

And what better goal than staying alive and solving her own private mystery?

Heat pressed around her and a soft wind sighed past, bringing just a breath of coolness to her skin. She wore jeans, a T-shirt and boots that she had conjured magically. Starting across the parking lot, she kept to the shadows and practically tiptoed, to keep her steps as silent as possible. She paused every few seconds to listen, but all she heard was the sound of a dog barking in the distance and a few lonely crickets chirping wildly.

The motel office was around at the front of the building and the room she and Torin had taken was at the very back of the motel. Since the fire in Arizona, she hadn't been willing to put any innocents at risk, so she had insisted on staying as far from everyone else as possible.

There were only a few cars in the lot. She hurried past them, hoping no one glanced out their windows to see her. This was a risk and she knew it. Just as she knew that everything depended on her regaining her lost memories. Should she have remained in her motel room, safe but ignorant? Or was it better to trust her instincts and call down the moon while hoping for the revelation she needed?

She had no doubt what Torin's opinion would have been. But this was her choice. Her decision. She wasn't being reckless. She was being proactive.

Torin would be furious if he returned and found her outside, unprotected. And maybe it was foolish, she told herself. But at the same time, if she didn't find a way to unlock her past life, her past mistakes, how could she ever correct what had once gone wrong?

She kept her head down and hurried across the darkened parking lot. Across the street, there was a row of trees and beyond them, she knew, was a meadow. She'd seen it when they had arrived earlier that afternoon.

Shea sent furtive glances up and down the quiet road,

then darted for the treeline. She pushed past the low-hanging branches and inhaled the scent of pine. Fallen needles under her feet cushioned every step, as if even nature were helping her remain hidden.

She kept walking when she reached the meadow, wanting to get as far from the road as she could. There were no homes within sight and the silence was cathedral-like. The only sounds were the soft sigh of the wind through the knee-high grasses and the distant roar of an engine as it traveled along the road.

She didn't have much time and she knew it. Torin would be back soon. She wanted to be in their motel room waiting for him.

Alone beneath the moon, Shea glanced up at the wide night sky. A hazy light seemed to filter down from the heavens and as she drew the night into her lungs, she felt the power of nature slide through her veins. This was witchcraft at its best, she thought, not even sure where that insistent thought had sprung from. A witch and the night. This was where power was to be found and knowledge gathered. This was where the heart of her strength resided.

She'd always loved the night. Even as a child, she'd felt drawn to the darkness. To the sweep of stars overhead. To the phases of the moon. More comfortable in shadows than in bright light, Shea had never asked herself why she was so much more a night person than anything else. It just . . . *was*.

Now, at last, she understood.

Her body felt alive. The hot, damp air clung to her like a lover's hands. She ached for Torin's touch and knew that the pull of the moon combined with her connection to her Eternal was ramping up the desire she always felt for him.

But then, what better magic was there than sex well done?

Shea?

Jolting, Shea realized that Torin's voice was whispering into her mind.

Are you safe?

She focused her power on reaching out to him. Closing off the fact that she was outside and on her own, she simply assured him, *I'm fine. Just working on a spell.*

That was true enough anyway.

I will return shortly.

Which meant, she thought as she closed her mind to him, that she didn't have much time.

Smiling, she shook her hair back from her face and accepted that the time was right. But this was magic and she had learned from her dreams and memories that high magic was best done skyclad.

She glanced around her one more time, just to make sure she was alone; then she took a breath, snapped her fingers and the clothes she'd manifested that morning vanished. She stood naked and warm beneath a sliver of moon.

The wind kissed her skin and the cool white light of the moon seemed to seep into her body, filling her with a sense of peace that was welcome, soothing. As if the moon had been waiting for her, hoping to be discovered again.

"I'm here now," Shea whispered, surrendering to that peace washing over her. She tipped her head back to stare up into the heavens. Her long hair brushed the bare skin of her back. She lifted her hands, palms up, as if to catch the pale light drifting over her. Her eyes wide, she fixed her gaze on the milk white crescent, the center of who and what she was.

And as she stood in that soft light, words came to her. Words of power. Words of supplication.

"Goddess, hear me. I seek answers," she said, her

voice strong and even. "I seek truth. The life I led is long past, but its echoes remain. Help me find my way, Goddess. Fill my heart with strength and my mind with truth."

Her words sounded overly loud in the pervasive quiet. It was as if the very earth had taken a breath and held it. Shea felt as though she were balanced on a thin wire stretched between her past life and the present. As if one wrong step on either side would end her quest before it began.

And still, she stood beneath the moon, welcoming its light, its strength as its elemental power slid through her. The wind kicked up, caressing her with suddenly icy fingers. Goose bumps raced along her skin. Her heartbeat thundered in her ears. She waited, silently beseeching the moon to open the doors of her mind and give her access to all she had once laid claim to.

Her hands remained cupped, drawing down the power of the moon, pulling it within herself.

"Mother moon, hear me," she said in a whisper. "Grant me the knowing. Help me in the Awakening."

In the next moment, she swayed as if an invisible weight had been dropped on her. Her breath was strangled in her chest and her mind expanded as hundreds of images appeared in her thoughts as if someone had whisked away a concealing curtain.

Shea gasped at the rush of information, trying desperately to make sense of everything she was seeing, feeling. She invoked the moon again, whispering, "Show me. Teach me. Help me find the path."

Moments ticked past and she was lost in the magic of the moon. Light filled her, streaming through her body, along her arms, to the tips of her fingers. She felt the swell of rising power and gave herself over to it. Her body hummed with heat and life and strength. She felt the innate talents she had carried through centuries stir within her. She experienced the complete joy of knowing that this was what she had been meant for.

Shea smiled with satisfaction as the past came to life in her mind.

"Well, look what we have here."

Shocked, she came up out of the moon magic as a drowning woman breaching the water's surface. She struggled for air that felt too thick and hot to breathe. Her mind felt muddled with the onslaught of too much information absorbed too quickly. For a moment, she didn't even remember where she was.

Then she saw the man walking across the moonlit meadow toward her and she remembered everything.

"You're a witch, aren't you?" he asked, then answered his own question. "Sure you are, standing out here naked as the day you was born, looking up at the moon. You doing a spell, witch?"

"No," Shea said softly, realizing that no matter what she had gained with this spell, she'd risked her own safety by coming into the night alone. She should have waited for Torin, she told herself. But it was too late now for regrets.

She faced the man and watched him warily as he approached. About forty, with graying hair and a beer belly, he smiled, but it didn't touch his eyes. In one hand, he held a pistol, barrel pointed at the ground. With the other, he scrubbed at his whiskered jaw as if trying to decide what to do next. He let his gaze move over her with open admiration.

Shea shuddered with revulsion as his eyes washed over her like a mud slide.

"You're a pretty one," he mused, "I'll give you that. But you're still a witch." He lifted the gun and casually aimed it at her. "Seems to me, I could shoot you right here and nobody'd think nothing of it. Hell, they'd probably thank me."

And give him the reward. But he didn't know she was the witch everyone in the country was searching for. That, she thought, was at least one thing she had going for her.

Should she run? No. He'd only chase her down—or shoot her. Besides, Shea told herself, she'd be damned if she ran again. She was through hiding from what she was. Done apologizing for her existence to a society that was so blinded by its own fear it couldn't see the wonder of magic or the women who wielded it.

She wasn't the witch she had been only two weeks before. She wouldn't ever again allow herself to be captured or used. She wouldn't allow anyone to put their hands on her. Not ever again. Times had changed. *She* had changed. She'd learned far too much to ever go back to what she used to be.

This one man thought he would capture her. Terrorize her. She looked at him and he suddenly seemed small and far less frightening than he had only a moment ago.

He was in for a surprise.

"Yes," she said, "I am a witch."

His eyes widened as if he hadn't really expected her to admit it.

Shea snapped her fingers and instantly she was wearing the clothing she had zapped off herself only a short while ago. Maybe it had been a mistake to give this man proof that she was a witch, but damned if she'd stand there naked in front of him, letting him look at her as if she were the last steak at a barbecue.

"Got some power, do you?" he asked, raising the gun higher, taking aim at a spot right between her eyes. "Think that'll be enough?"

Not so very long ago, on that last day at the school when a man had jumped out at her, she had been terrified. She'd reacted instinctively—killing him without even meaning to. This time was different. This time, she wouldn't lose that hard-won sense of control.

He reached out and Shea let him grab hold of her. She needed him close. And the closer he was, the less likely he would be to shoot.

The power she felt beneath the moon washed over her in a lush, clean sweep of amazing magic. Through her fear, Shea felt her own strength rising.

"Not gonna fight me, huh?" He grinned as if he'd just been given a present. "Good for you."

She smiled, reached up and laid two fingers against his forehead. He dropped like a stone and was snoring before he hit the ground.

"Yes," Shea said softly. "Good for me."

Chapter 36

The moment Torin stepped into the motel room, he knew something was wrong.

Gaze narrowed, he swept the small room thoroughly with one quick glance. Shea wasn't there. He opened his senses to her, instantly dropped the bags of food he'd brought and flashed to her side in the middle of a moonlit meadow.

"God!" She slapped one hand to her chest and staggered backward. "You scared the *crap* out of me!"

He grabbed her and held her close, wrapping his arms around her and pressing her tight to his chest until the steady beat of her heart calmed the fury churning inside him.

"How do you think I felt when I returned to the room and you were gone?" If he had had a beating heart, it would have stopped the moment he realized she wasn't where she was supposed to be. Now that they had mated, the protective instincts he felt for her were more all-encompassing than ever before.

"I told you not to leave the room—" He stopped, looked down at the snoring man at her feet. "Who is that?"

She shrugged. "I don't know. He came up out of nowhere while I was drawing down the moon."

Torin gaped at her. "He *saw* you working a spell?"

"Yes."

"Woman, do you have no idea of the dangerous cloud we exist under?"

She pushed away from his grasp, folded her arms over her chest and said, "I know exactly what danger we're in. Just as I know that unless I remember what we need to know, we're not going to be able to complete this quest, or mission or whatever the hell it is."

"And you thought to regain that memory in public? Where anyone could see you?" *While he was gone?* When he thought of everything that might have happened to her without him at her side, it chilled him to the bone. "Do you trust me so little that you couldn't wait until I returned? So that I could be with you? To guard you?"

"If I didn't trust you, I wouldn't be with you." She blew out a breath and shook her head. "This wasn't about *you,* Torin. I felt the call of the moon and I went with it. I knew what I was doing. I knew the risks. I'm not some stupid heroine in a bad horror movie."

He pushed one hand through his long hair. "You took the same kind of chance those women invariably do."

"No, I didn't," she argued. "I'm not helpless. I can take care of myself." She pointed at the man curled up in the grass, sound asleep. "There's my proof."

Hating to admit she had a point, Torin was forced to acknowledge, at least privately, that she had managed to protect herself. Then he noticed the gun lying beside the sleeping man. "Did he threaten you?"

"Of course he did, but I handled it," she said, lifting her chin in a show of defiance.

So she had. A mixture of pride and impatience battled inside him. She was coming into her own, but at the same time, he worried that she would become too confident. Take one chance too many. If she had made a mistake and this man had shot her— She wasn't immortal yet. She could still die. And if the Awakening were stopped before it was complete, he would die with her. Soulless. Empty. There would be no eternity together. Not now. Not after finally experiencing a true union with her after so many centuries of solitude.

"You should have told me when our minds connected," he said.

"You would have stopped me," she answered.

"Probably."

"You should be proud of me, not angry," she said and he detected a slight quaver in her voice in spite of the brave front she was presenting. So the encounter with this nameless attacker had shaken her more than she wanted to admit. But even with her fear, she had maintained control of the situation. She had saved herself.

"I am pleased you are well, Shea. And that you were able to dispatch that human." He waved one hand at the snoring man in dismissal. "But striding into the unknown alone was a foolish choice."

She bristled, but better she be furious with him than dead.

"I survived."

"This time."

"Torin . . ." She went to him and laid both hands on his forearms. Her touch soothed him instantly. "I know we're in this together. I know you want to protect me. And I can promise I'll be careful. But that's all I can promise. If something needs doing, I'm going to do it. Okay?"

No, he thought. It wasn't okay with him that she put herself in danger. But he would find a way to protect her in spite of herself. Besides, the deed was done and now he needed to know what they could expect from the man once he woke up.

"I can hear you thinking, you know," she said softly. "You're not protecting your thoughts."

"It's just as well," he snapped. "You should know what it does to me when you're in danger."

She moved toward him and laid one hand on his broad chest. "I get it, Torin. But you have to know what it does to me to do nothing. To sit on the sidelines and let you take over."

"I'm not taking over. I'm protecting you."

"I need to know how to protect myself, too," she reminded him.

"You wouldn't if you would listen to me," he grumbled.

Shea actually laughed and he had to smile at the sound of it. She was not going to be caged, he thought. Not by her pursuers. Not by him.

Torin nodded at the man on the ground. "How long will he sleep?"

"I'm not sure. A day. Maybe two."

A short laugh shot from his throat. He could well imagine the man's consternation when he woke up. He would be confused and muddled and wondering when and how he had lost control of the situation. Torin knew that feeling himself. Trying to control Shea Jameson was an exercise in futility.

"Will he remember you?" he asked quietly, looking at the man and wishing he were awake so Torin could vent some of the banked anger choking him.

She frowned a bit. "Yes. I put him to sleep, but I didn't know how to alter his memories."

Nodding, he made up his mind. "We will eat and then leave. We can't risk him waking early. When he does rise, he'll no doubt contact the authorities. And if he realizes who you are . . ."

"I know," she whispered, lifting her face into the wind. "But, Torin, I had to do it." Her gaze met his, silently asking for understanding. His support. "I had to do what I could to find the answers we need."

He did understand. He didn't like it one damn bit,

but he understood the call of the moon to a witch. Knew that a woman like Shea would never be satisfied for long wandering in the darkness. She had a need to be in charge of her own life—and who was he to try to keep her from it?

"Did you discover what you were searching for, Shea?" he asked, pulling her closer, ignoring the insensible mortal at his feet. "Did you find the truth?"

"Yes," she said, moving into him, snaking her arms around his middle. "I did. My memories are awake now. At least, most of them are. They're just so jumbled together, I'll need time to sort them out."

He rested his chin on top of her head and cradled her to him in a gentle embrace. "We still have time, Shea."

"Not enough," she whispered. "Not enough."

The local chapter of Ohio Seekers met in the basement of a church.

The big room was mostly used for bingo, but tonight balloons and streamers decorated the paneled walls for the upcoming Father-Daughter Dance. Tables and chairs were scattered around the room and a stereo had been set up in the corner for the DJ. Long buffet tables stood decorated, but empty of the food that would soon be delivered.

The dance wouldn't start for another two hours, so the Seekers had plenty of time for their emergency meeting.

"I call this meeting to order!" The president, Martha Chapman, slapped her gavel against the dessert table for order.

She looked out over the crowd and smiled to herself. They weren't many, but they were proud. And determined. The handful of the righteous who showed up every week for the Seeker meeting were people she could count on. People she'd known most of her life.

Her pastor, the local hairdresser and the best mechanic in Ohio among them. There were a few teenagers who had seen the light and her daughter's pediatrician was attending his first meeting.

"Please, everyone!" she called out, smacking the gavel again. She loved it when they all came to order and turned smiling faces toward her. "The caterers will be arriving in a half hour to set up for tonight's big dance and there are a few things we have to go over before they get here."

The crowd subsided good-naturedly, eager to get on with the business of the evening.

"First, I want to thank so many of you for turning out on such short notice. Clearly, our phone tree is working well and a big thank-you to Shauna for being in charge of that for us." Martha applauded along with the crowd as her hairdresser took a bow.

Then, still smiling, Martha said, "We have good news. According to reports from our sister organizations, the escaped witch is somewhere in Ohio right this very minute."

Excited whispers rushed across the room like a sweeping wave.

"Do we know where exactly?" someone shouted out. "Ohio's pretty big, Martha!"

"Oh, Hank, hush now," she chided, wagging her finger as if the burly firefighter were a naughty six-year-old. "Would I come here and not have information to spread? Now, the word is, she and the man with her—"

"The guy made out of fire?"

"Yes, Tessie, him," Martha said, frowning at the interruption by the head cheerleader. "They were last seen in a motel just outside Brecksville."

"Why, that's no more than twenty miles from here!"

"Exactly!" Martha grinned, pleased that they were as anxious as she to prove themselves worthy of their

Seeker charter. "Now, what do you say? Why don't we go catch that witch and turn her over to Dr. Fender?"

"Isn't there a fat reward on her?" one of the teenagers wistfully asked.

"Yes, Christopher, there is," Martha said, her tone ringing with disappointment. "But only if you turn her in to the authorities and we don't want that, do we?"

Suitably chastened, Christopher shook his head. "No, ma'am."

"Remember now," she said, turning her attention to the whole crowd again. "We don't do this for the rewards, but for the satisfaction of doing God's work. What we do, we do for humanity. For society. For *God*."

Cheers erupted and Martha basked in the appreciation for a long minute. With the threat of witchcraft taking over the world, Martha had finally found her voice. Most of her life she'd felt a little *less* than she wanted to be. As a child, she'd planned to do great things, but somehow, getting married and having babies had stolen her life and her dreams away.

Now, at long last, she was getting the chance to effect real change in the world. She was making a difference. Standing up for the rights of ordinary people. She was doing what she could to make the world a safer place for her children and grandchildren. And the pride she felt swelled inside her until she thought she might bust.

"Now," Martha told them all, "Dr. Fender really wants this one particular witch. The scientific parts always confuse me no end, but he seems to think this witch is special. At any rate, she and the others like her may be the key to finally finding a way to drain *all* of their powers."

"And give them to us, right?" Tony, the owner of the Italian restaurant in town, asked.

"That's right, Tony." Martha beamed at him and imagined one day holding the power to defend her town and country. "Once we drain the witches, the righteous will be gifted with the powers taken from their dark souls."

"Isn't that, um, dangerous?" Tessie spoke up again. "I mean, if they're dark powers, wouldn't they turn us dark, too?"

Martha stepped down from the dais, walked to the teenager and cupped the girl's chin in her hand. Here was another soul she was influencing. Helping along the righteous path.

"Not at all, sweetie," she said. "Why, when those powers are torn from the Godless and given to True Believers ..." She paused and let the light of her zealous gaze sweep across the faces of her friends and neighbors. Let them see the glory of what they were doing. Feel the importance of the task they'd been assigned. This could be the most significant night of their lives. She smiled at each of them in turn, showing them all how proud she was to serve with them, how sure she was that they would be victorious. "Why, when this night's work is done, we will be true warriors of the Lord. We will be instruments of His peace."

"Amen," someone murmured and a smattering of applause broke out.

"And always remember, sweetheart," Martha said, looking down into Tessie's wide blue eyes. "You're on the side of right in this. Why, the Bible itself tells us, *You shall not suffer a witch to live.* Now, the Lord couldn't have been more clear in His instructions, could He?"

"I guess not," Tessie whispered.

Martha patted her on the shoulder and softly added, "We're doing God's work here, Tessie, each and every one of us—and don't you ever forget it."

"No, ma'am," the girl answered.

Caterers bustled in, carrying steam trays, sending the scent of barbecued chicken and potatoes and gravy into the air.

"My," Martha said, "that does smell good, doesn't it?" Then, clapping her hands, she smiled and added, "Now, I don't know about you all, but I've got a pot roast in the oven at home. So what do you say we go and get that witch so none of us is late for supper?"

Chapter 37

Shea sat at the foot of the bed and propped her face in her hands. She didn't like sensing Torin's frustration with her actions. His anger at being shut out of her decision. But they were both just going to have to live with it. She'd done what needed doing and she'd lived through it. Time to move on.

She listened to the sound of the shower and thought about joining Torin in the bathroom. But she discounted that idea a second or two later. They had to leave and if she went in there with him, it might be hours before they got moving again.

So instead she rifled through her newfound memories. As she'd told Torin, they were all so jumbled up together, centuries of them, it was going to take her some time to find the one they needed most. Shea knew he was waiting for her to tell him where they had to go. To have the vision. To awaken the memory that would give them direction. Speed them on the path toward straightening out this mess.

But so far she had nothing.

Shaking her head, she grabbed the TV remote and flicked it on, hoping for a mindless sitcom.

Naturally, the news popped on. Before she could change the channel, she was drawn into the report. On her.

"Shea Jameson has been missing now for two weeks." The camera shifted to show the yard at Terminal Island and the hundred or so women still trapped at the prison. The reporter did a voice-over the images. "An investigation into the escape is ongoing and BOW has been called in to assist. When questioned by this reporter, Warden Salinger insisted that this incident was a rarity and that his prison remains no threat to the general population."

Shea's stomach churned as she watched the prison guards in their towers pointing guns down at the women inmates as they walked aimlessly around the yard.

"Warden Salinger further states that magic was used to spirit away the missing witches and that he and his men were helpless to defend against it."

"Probably not a good idea to advertise that," Shea murmured, then stopped when her picture flashed on the screen. They were using her driver's license picture, so she looked hideous, but she was recognizable.

She watched the screen as the reporter gave her description to the audience. Nervously, she ran her fingers through her long red hair and winced. She had tried cutting off several inches and dying it dark brown—as she had done so long ago when she'd been alone and on the run. But it hadn't worked this time. By the following morning, her hair was down to the middle of her back again and the dark auburn color had replaced the indeterminate brown. It seemed that her Awakening powers were making it impossible to change her hair. Of course, once she got better with her powers, maybe she could try making a change magically.

Disgusted, she flicked the TV off, stood up and paced. If she added up all the steps she'd taken in aimless pacing over the last week or so, she probably could have walked around the world.

So instead she decided to channel her energies into a spell she had studied in the ancient Sanctuary book. If the whole world was looking for her, it was time she did a little searching herself.

She stretched out on the bed, stared up at the ceiling for long, quiet moments and let her mind go blank. She relaxed, counting each soft breath until her body was limp and her soul was lifting from her body. With astral projection, she focused on finding that woman she'd glimpsed once before in a scrying mirror.

Her spirit flew, unfettered, through a starry night, past homes with people tucked inside. She was a part of the night and yet separate. She searched for one woman in the masses. When she heard the the whispered chant, Shea turned, sweeping unerringly toward her goal.

Her mind searched while her body lay still on the bed, an empty shell. Bright lights pulled at her; the chanting voice became more distinct.

A woman sat alone in a dark room, features obscured by shadows thrown by the flames of a dozen white candles. *White,* Shea thought, *for purification and protection rituals.*

"I feel you," the woman said, head bent over the dancing flames. "You shouldn't have come."

"Why are you after me?" Shea asked, fighting to keep the connection with this woman. "It was you who sent those men who burned down the motel, wasn't it?"

"It was," she answered and though Shea couldn't see her expression, she knew the woman was smiling. "But don't worry. I don't want you dead."

"That fire was probably a mistake, then," she said, sensing the banked power inside the woman.

"A miscalculation. The fools were supposed to take out your Eternal and bring you to me."

"Why?"

"Because, Shea," the woman sighed, "separate, we are each powerful but limited. Together, we would be unstoppable."

"Who are you?"

"No more questions!" The woman waved one hand and Shea felt herself tumbling back the way she'd come, only to drop into her body, staring blindly up at the ceiling.

Breath heaving in and out of her lungs, Shea fought to steady herself. She'd heard the voice of her enemy. Felt the power surrounding her. And Shea knew the woman was far more powerful than she was.

She sat up slowly, her magic bubbling up inside her. Drawing down the moon had been dangerous, but worth it as well. She never could have attempted what she had just done without it. The renewal spell she'd worked had made her stronger. Just as mating with Torin was strengthening her powers. It eased her, knowing he was hers. Knowing that he would be beside her no matter what. Though she wasn't looking forward to telling him about the woman she had just seen and spoken to.

After all, she'd seen for herself what she and her sisters had done centuries ago. The call of the power had been so seductive, they'd only wanted more. And they'd surrendered to something dark and evil. She couldn't yet see it all. Couldn't find the mental key to that lock, but she felt the danger in her bones. And that worried her.

If she'd been tempted to evil before . . . what would keep history from repeating itself?

Maybe it was because she was already charged magically. Maybe her defenses were down after her encounter with the woman in the shadows. But whatever the reason, one memory suddenly rose to the surface of her mind, sweeping Shea into a past that was still alive with power.

The cold, dark night was lit only by the occasional whips of lightning darting across the sky. Clouds covered the moon, but its brilliance still managed to stain the edges of its covering with silver ribbons. Wind howled and the nearby sea crashed against the rocks on the shoreline.

Torin grabbed her arm as she walked up the hillside, her steps sure, her features set in an expression of grim determination. She stopped and glared at his hand on her arm.

"Don't do this," he said, his voice deep, urgent. "Can you not feel the darkness hovering close? The air itself screams."

"You worry too much," she said, with a shake of her head as she slipped past him on the path. "My sisters and I know what we're doing."

"No, you don't." He flashed into flames and blocked her way. "Your thirst for power is making you all blind to what is really happening."

"What do you know of power?" she demanded, gathering her cloak and pushing past him once more.

Overhead, clouds gathered and lightning crashed. The wind was cold and sharp and the sigh of the sea droned like the heartbeat of a restless god.

"As Eternals," she reminded him haughtily, "it is your duty to stand beside us. To defend. Protect. Not to mewl about danger when you lose faith."

His pale gray eyes flashed and swirled with explosions of magic as he reached out to take hold of her. He shook her hard, until the cowl of her cloak dropped away. The wind instantly lifted her long, dark red hair into a tangled halo around her head.

"My brothers and I stand as warriors. We are chosen to defend you all, even from your own arrogance."

"Arrogance?" She echoed the word with a wild laugh. "Is it arrogance to know who and what you are? What you are capable of? No, Eternal. It's you who are arrogant. To think you could stop us from what we know we must do."

"I am not the mewling weakling you think me, cower-

ing in the night," he told her, face grim, eyes still swirling dangerously. "I am the warrior who has never failed to be beside you in times of danger. Yet I'll not be silent when I see you walking blindly into disaster."

The icy wind tossed her hair across her eyes and she paused to pluck it free. Staring up at the giant of a man who was both lover and guardian, she forced a smile and fought for patience.

"Torin, do you not understand how much more we will be when this is completed? We have left the cloister of Haven to draw the magics through the Artifact for the good of all of us. Can you not see the lure of the knowledge we will gain?"

"At what cost?" he countered. "Do you barter your soul?"

She frowned, out of patience, out of time. "If it comes to that, it is my soul to do with as I will. Come with me or don't, Eternal. But do not think to stop me. I go to the stone dance to join my sisters."

"Shea?" Torin's hand on her shoulder drew her up out of the memory and she shivered as it faded.

"God, you tried to warn me, didn't you?"

"What?"

She was shaking. Trembling from head to toe in the aftermath of that memory. She could still feel the bite of the wind, hear the ocean, *see* the banked fury in Torin's eyes.

"Back then," she said. "Back in the Dark Ages or whatever, you tried to warn me. You tried to stop me—us—from opening that damn door. I wouldn't listen."

Still naked and damp from the shower, he drew her to the edge of the bed, sat down, then pulled her after him. She went willingly, curling up on his lap, burrowing her head into the curve of his shoulder. "And not much has changed over the centuries," he murmured.

She tipped her head back. "Do you really believe that?"

He met her gaze and gently smoothed her hair back from her face. "No. No, I do not. You're still stubborn, but there is no great thirst in you, Shea. You've learned there are limits to everything. You still won't listen to me, but . . ."

She slapped him. "I listen. When I want to."

"Ah. Yes, a fine distinction." He waved one hand and her clothing disappeared. Shea was grateful. She needed to feel the heat of his skin against hers. The solid strength of him.

"It's all I can promise, Torin." She looked up at him.

"As I suspected," he murmured. Then his hand stilled on her back. "We have to leave again, Shea."

"I know." She chewed at her bottom lip.

"What?" He glowered at her until Shea opened her mind to him and he saw for himself what she had done while he was showering.

"Damn it, Shea! You allowed an enemy into your thoughts."

"I was in hers as well," she reminded him.

"And what did you discover?"

"Not much."

"Was it the same woman you saw before? Who is she?"

"Yes—and I don't know," Shea admitted, scrubbing her hands up and down her arms. "All I know is she's powerful and she wants me."

"Well, she can't have you." He pulled her in close. "Leaving your body is a dangerous business, Shea. You shouldn't try it without an anchor."

Astral projection was a means of spiritual travel—to leave your own body behind and allow your mind, your very essence, to fly free. The only problem was, if you were cut off from your body, you might just end up stuck in the between world—not alive, not dead, just . . . *not*.

"Next time I'll have you with me, okay?"

"Agreed. Now that you've unlocked your memories, do you know where we have to go next?"

She mentally grabbed hold of the memory that had plagued her only moments before. "I don't know the exact spot yet, but I have sensed we have to go to England first."

"I thought we would eventually end up there."

She turned against him, pressing her breasts to his chest. "Of course you did. You remember where we were."

"No," he said softly, meeting her gaze. "None of the Eternals remembers that last night very well. I only know that the coven was based in Europe for a very long time."

"I remembered something else," she told him. "A name. Haven." She studied his reaction. "You know that name. Do you know where it is?"

"No, not precisely." He caressed her cheek. "The coven allowed no one into Haven. I know only that it was hidden from all but the coven. But after that?" He shrugged. "Back then, none of you risked sharing too much with us. None of you was willing to allow us too close for fear that you would lose some of the power you craved so desperately."

She laughed a little and the sound was filled with misery. "God, how did you stand any of us? I only remember pieces, but you've got all of the memories, don't you?" She looked up at him. "How do you see me now without seeing *her*?"

He cupped her face in his palms, his thumbs tracing over her cheekbones. His gaze locked with hers, he said simply, "I have always seen you, Shea. For who you are. Not for the hungers or needs that grip you as they do all of us. But the woman inside. The woman whose soul has finally found its way. Your time has finally come."

Shea dropped her head to his chest and just leaned

on him, feeling his strength. His permanence. This man had been with her through eternity. He'd watched over her even when she hadn't deserved his protection. And he was still here, supporting her even though he had every reason to mistrust her.

Funny, she thought. Since the moment she'd met him outside the school—and didn't that feel like a lifetime ago?—she'd wondered if he could be trusted. She'd held herself back, unsure of him or his loyalties.

Ironic to realize that through the centuries it had been *she* who was the one not to be trusted.

His big hand cupped the back of her head and held her close to him. "Trust yourself, Shea. Trust in the Awakening."

She nodded. "I'll figure it out, Torin. I'll get us to Haven."

"I know you will."

Shea took a deep breath and let it slide from her lungs. "Can you *flame* us over there?"

He smiled. "No. It's too far."

"I suppose it's not a good time to mention how much I hate flying then, huh?"

"We won't be flying, either," he told her, dipping his head for a quick, hard kiss. "With your magic Awakening, you could bring down the plane."

"Oh, God." Her mouth dropped open at the thought of crashing a jet with her powers. "Okay. No plane. Maybe not ever again."

He smiled, running his hands up and down her back until he created a wonderful friction that took her mind off the trouble at hand. "When your magic is stable, flying will be safe enough. Safer even, as you will be able to ensure that the plane comes to no harm."

"Uh-huh," she whispered, only half listening now as his hands swept to the front of her and caressed her breasts, her tender nipples. She wasn't interested in talking about planes anymore. Or witchcraft. All she wanted now was to make love to him once more before they left.

"So," he was saying, "we will take a boat."

"Okay . . ." She wriggled on his lap and felt his erection harden instantly. Then she smiled, bent her head to his chest and kissed the flaming tattoo that marked him as hers.

He hissed in a breath. "We will leave for New York immediately. The crossing will take several days."

She ran her tongue across the tattoo. "Okay, then. We'd better go."

"Not quite yet, I think," he murmured and lifted her off his lap just high enough to give him the room he needed to enter her body. He looked into her eyes. "I want you, Shea. Now and always."

At his words she slowly eased herself down onto his thick shaft. She took him in deeply and felt all the jagged pieces of herself slide into place. This was what she needed. This connection. This joining with Torin.

He moved within her, his gaze locked with hers and every stroke of his body made his eyes flare with more passion than she had ever known before. Her hands at his shoulders, she gave herself over to him and the real magic he created inside her.

Again and again, they moved together. She twisted her hips on him, sparking a delicious friction that sizzled along her nerve endings like live wires. Her heartbeat pounded, her blood pumped thick and hot in her veins. As she rode him, Torin dropped one hand to her center and used his thumb to caress her most sensitive spot.

More electricity arched between them. Brighter. Hotter. She let her head fall back and moved into him, over him. Shea felt his body tense and knew he was close to release. Just as she knew he would wait, contain his own passions until she had found hers. He would drag this moment on forever if it meant she had one more moment of pleasure. And knowing that, feeling that, she reached for the bliss and caught it.

Calling his name she shuddered in his grasp as her body erupted into a series of exquisite orgasms that left her quaking and limp. Only then did Torin claim what was his. Only then did he hold her body down on his and empty himself inside her, with a groan that was her name.

"Wow," she whispered, resting her forehead on his shoulder. "That just gets better and better."

He kissed the side of her neck. "And we will have eternity to improve on it even further."

She stiffened in his arms. "Torin. Something's wrong."

He lifted her off his lap and sprang to his feet. "What is it?"

"Darkness," she whispered. "It's coming."

Then the world exploded.

Chapter 38

The door crashed open.

Windows splintered in a shower of glass shards.

Shea screamed and tried to jump away from the glass, but her foot came down hard on a jagged fragment and the pain shot up her leg. Two big men grabbed her, each of them holding one of her arms, twisting them behind her back. Naked and terrified, shaken out of the cozy sexual haze she'd inhabited only a moment before, Shea looked to Torin as half a dozen strangers streamed into the room, shouting, waving clubs and guns.

Torin roared in fury and reached out for her, just as a middle-aged woman threw a knitted blanket at him. The soft folds draped over him and he sank to the floor under its weight.

"Torin!" Shea's scream rattled through the room. She twisted and pulled against the men's grips, but she couldn't budge them. What the hell was going on? What was in that blanket that it could take Torin down like that? "Who are you people?" she shouted. "What do you want?"

"That's enough of that, missy," the older woman said, shaking her head. "Keep your voice down. No point in shouting—no one's going to come to help a witch!"

Shea's stomach sank. *Oh, God.* They were here for her. To take her who knew where. Maybe there were prison guards waiting in the parking lot. Maybe . . . no. She deliberately stopped her imagination from racing ahead of the situation. The woman had said no one was coming to help her. Which probably meant that no one was coming, period. These people, whoever they were, were most likely doing this on their own.

"Just look at you." The older woman clucked her tongue in disgust. "Naked as a jaybird, and him no better!" She whirled around, faced a teenage girl and shouted, "Tessie Marie Grainger, you close your eyes this minute. I'm not going to have to explain to your mama that you saw a naked man while you were under my protection."

The blond girl in question stared at Torin a moment longer, then reluctantly closed her eyes. But the smile on her face said the memory was a satisfying one.

Shea squirmed and futilely twisted, trying to get free of the two men holding her arms behind her back. But their grip on her was so tight, so strong, she couldn't even snap her fingers to clothe herself. Instead, she was forced to stand naked in front of a room full of psychotic strangers. She felt their gazes on her like a caress from a dirty hand.

"Who are you?" she demanded, tossing her hair back and lifting her chin in helpless defiance.

"Watch your tone now, missy," said the woman who was clearly in charge as she reached down to toss the edge of her blanket across Torin's lower body. "Honestly. You magical people, not a sense of propriety among you. Both of you naked and it not six o'clock in the evening. No doubt you were having sex and it's barely dark out. Is it any wonder God-fearing Christians have to take matters into their own hands?"

Shea snorted at the woman's sanctimonious tone. "Don't make this about religion," she said. "It's not. This is just fear. You're afraid, so you're striking out."

Martha humphed. "Looks to me as if you're the one afraid here."

Torin groaned and struggled to sit up. He failed and his gray eyes flashed a warning that told everyone in the room they had better hope he didn't get free.

"Don't you waste your time there, mister," the woman told him. "I knitted that blanket myself. There's threads of white gold mixed in with the yarn, so it'll hold you."

Well, that explained why the blanket was having such an effect on Torin. It also cut short any hope of him escaping that blanket and getting them out of this. Shea's gaze swept the room, going from one face to the next. They all looked so . . . normal, she thought. Except for the fact that they were carrying clubs and guns and were holding her and Torin captive. Her gaze swung back to the older woman standing in front of her.

"You knitted a blanket with white gold threads?"

The woman turned to look at Shea, eyes wide. "Well, of course. How else could we control him while we take you? And let me tell you, missy, white gold thread yarn is pretty darned pricey."

Shea almost laughed. Almost. She was being held prisoner again, but this time, it wasn't prison guards. This time it looked like a local chapter of the PTA, for heaven's sake. "What is it you want from us?"

"Well, first things first, I think," the woman said. "My name's Martha Chapman. I'm the president of the local Seeker society."

Seekers. A hard ball of ice settled in Shea's stomach. She knew that organization. She knew about the experiments. About the tortures. About the deaths of too many women—witch and human alike—to count. She looked at the faces surrounding her through new eyes now and she didn't like what she was seeing. They didn't look crazy.

Just determined.

"Ah," Martha said, giving her a pleased smile. "I see you've heard of us. Isn't that nice?"

"You don't have to do this," Shea told her, frantically racking her newfound memories for a spell, a chant, anything that might come in handy at the moment. But her mind was drawing a blank when she most needed it. "We're leaving town. We would have been gone in another half hour."

"Well," Martha said, moving to the bed and dragging the floral bedspread off, "isn't it lucky we showed up when we did, then? Tony? Hank? You keep a good hold on her now, while I wrap this blanket over her."

"She's hard to hold, Martha," one of the men said. "We could use the cuffs."

"Of course. Don't know what I was thinking." Martha turned and looked at a young man. "Michael, go fetch the cuffs from the car." Then she turned back to wrapping the blanket around Shea's body. "For pity's sake, a woman tattooed. And on your breast, too! You would feed your babies with that awful ink covering what God gave you? You witches just have no shame at all, do you?"

It was clearly a rhetorical question. Shea tried to pull away from the woman. There was a fanatical light in those pale blue eyes that was damn unsettling. She was caught, she thought, shooting a quick look at Torin as he lay immobile on the floor. The blanket with white gold threads covered his body from the chest down and when he looked at her, she read helpless fury in his eyes.

"Her man there's got a matching tattoo, Martha," one of Shea's captors said.

"So he does." Martha turned around to look at him, flat on the floor. "Heaven only knows what that might mean. But, doesn't matter much to us, now, does it? It's not him we're here for, anyway."

"I don't like the look in his eye, Martha," one of the

men offered. "Think we should just shoot him now and be done with it."

Panic reached up and clutched at the base of Shea's throat. Torin was immortal, yes, but what if they shot him in the head? What would that do to him? Besides, she couldn't bear the thought of these maniacs shooting Torin at all.

Whatever she was going to do, she would have to do on her own. And fast. They had to get out of here. She couldn't be taken by the Seekers. God knew where she'd end up. And even though Torin was immortal, she knew all too well that he could be wounded badly enough to put him out of commission.

"You might have a point, Tony," Martha mused, as if trying to decide whether to have potatoes or rice with dinner.

"What are you going to do with me?" Shea spoke up into the charged silence, hoping that if she kept them talking, she could take their attention away from Torin and stall them somehow. Give herself time to come up with something.

"We'll be taking you to Dr. Fender, dear," Martha said, her tone as soothing as her eyes were mad. "He's moved his laboratory to upstate New York, so we have quite a long trip ahead of us."

Shaken, Shea drew a deep breath and swallowed hard. "You know who Fender is. Then you must know he's a monster. He tortures women. Kills them."

Martha slapped her. "Nonsense. He's never harmed a human woman. It's only witches he's interested in! Now, no more of your witch talk. Fender is a great man. He's at the vanguard of our movement. The light of knowledge in the darkness. Through him, we will be purged of your evil and take your powers unto ourselves for the glory of God."

Shea's gaze slid to Torin and she felt a surge of something hot and frantic pumping through her. She had to get them out. But how? These were not the kind of people she could reason with. And if she were to admit the truth, she didn't much want to reason with them anyway. What she really wanted to do was howl and scream and throw punches and spells.

Martha was in her face again, turning her chin until their gazes met. "Don't you get any ideas now, missy. Those cuffs we've got for you are white gold. You'll be quiet enough for our little trip, I'm thinking. Give you plenty of time to say your prayers to whoever it is your kind prays to." She paused and frowned. "What's taking Michael so long? Shauna, you go check on him now."

A woman standing at the back, her hungry gaze fixed on Torin, jolted into action and ran for the door. Apparently they all took their orders from Martha. Shea continued to search her memories. More desperately now, since she knew the moment the white gold cuffs were on her wrists, her magic would be dampened and she and Torin would be at the mercy of these . . . people.

From the corner of her eye, she caught movement. The young blond girl was edging closer to Torin. No one else seemed to notice. They were all too concerned with Shea, keeping her under control. But Shea kept one eye on the girl as she moved close enough to Torin to slip one foot beneath the blanket covering him.

What was she doing?

Slowly, the girl nudged the blanket aside, until Torin's lower abdomen and more were exposed. The girl's eyes widened in appreciation and to get an even better view, she accidentally pulled that blanket just a bit too far.

Instantly, Torin rolled out from under the weight of the white gold threads. The girl jumped back and shrieked. Martha whirled around, snarling, lifting the club she held in her left hand.

Torin threw a solid right punch into Martha's jaw and the older woman dropped like a stone.

In their surprise, the men holding Shea loosened their grip and she pulled free, reaching into her mind for the words she needed. Lifting both arms high, she found the spell and quickly chanted, *"Lock and key, from sea to sea, elements rise to free my lover and me."*

Instantly, the earth responded to her call. Wind howled through the room. Fire crackled at the base of the walls and a torrential rain pounded down hard enough to penetrate the old shake roof. Walls of water poured inside, drenching the would-be kidnappers. They screamed in fear and blind terror as Shea dropped the blanket, jumped at Torin and closed her eyes as he went to flames and flashed them to safety.

Chapter 39

Rune hadn't heard from Egan in more than a century. He hadn't thought anything of it, since he knew how hard the waiting was. He himself had vowed not to involve himself in his witch's life again until the Awakening came. Too many years of hungering for her and at the same time starving was too much even for an immortal.

So he could understand Egan disappearing. But if this Kellyn truly was an Awakened witch, then Egan should have been with her.

After leaving Sanctuary and contacting Torin, Rune was determined to discover what had happened to Egan. He contacted other Eternals, but no one knew any more than he did.

Which meant he would have to go back to England. Start where he'd last seen Egan and track him from there. Rune hopped a plane to Heathrow and thought about Torin and Shea being forced to take a ship. Six days at sea didn't sound like a great time to Rune. But he was guessing the mating sex was keeping them too busy to mind the delay in reaching their destination.

When the flight attendants came through announcing that they were beginning their descent, Rune stepped into the first-class bathroom. They were close enough now to England that he could flash out and not have to bother waiting for the jet to land. Besides, it amused him to think of the flight crew trying to figure out what had happened to one of their passengers once they discovered him missing.

They'd search the plane, check the manifest, and eventually convince themselves that the missing passenger never really existed. Or, he thought, they would simply realize that they had unknowingly been in the presence of magic.

With a quick grin at his own reflection, he went up in flames.

"Idiots!" Kellyn glared into her makeshift scrying mirror at the scene unfolding in the motel room in Ohio.

She should have spelled up a proper scrying tool. Then she would have had more detail. But after treating herself to a massage and a mani-pedi, she'd decided to simply enchant the mirror over the dressing table in her suite's bedroom.

Though if she'd had a proper scry glass, she might have been even more enraged. Standing before the mirror, watching the scene before her unfold in wavering, rippling images, she fought the urge to scream in frustration.

This should have been a simple operation. For pity's sake, she'd practically *handed* Shea and Torin to the Seekers. How could they have screwed it up so completely?

She knew the moment things were going to take a bad turn. As soon as that teenager stole a peek at the Eternal's dick, things were bound to go to hell. Although it was hard to blame the girl. Torin was, if nothing else, quite the specimen.

Surprising herself, Kellyn actually laughed aloud as she watched a middle-aged woman frantically trying to *swim* out of a motel room. Fool woman thought she could take her eyes off an Eternal for a split second?

Sheets of water poured through the shattered roof, spilling down on the Seekers even as Shea and Torin flashed away in a pillar of fire.

In an instant the Seekers were alone in a destroyed room, looking like nothing more than drowned rats.

Pitiful. Just pitiful.

Sighing, Kellyn told herself to end the spell, but she was caught. Like one of the idiot drivers who slowed down on a freeway to watch an accident, she couldn't seem to look away. Those morons in Ohio had not only blown the whole setup, they'd alerted the witch and her Eternal to the fact that Seekers were after them.

"That's what you get," she chastised herself. "Allowing someone else to set the Seekers on their trail. You should have done it yourself, as always. But really," she demanded, staring into the continuing mess of the failed operation in the mirror, "am I supposed to do *everything*?"

As she watched the magical rain, wind and fire stop and the beaten Seekers making their way home, she realized that this mess hadn't been a complete waste. At least she knew for sure that Shea was becoming more proficient with her powers. Calling down the elements had been a brilliant maneuver.

But then, the little witch had used astral projection to spy on Kellyn, hadn't she? Surprising, really. She hadn't thought Shea had that much backbone. But all the better knowing that she did. Kellyn had no use for a weak-willed woman, witch or not. She wanted women of strength at her side when she took from the coven what never should have been theirs in the first place.

She stared down into the scrying glass, waved her hand across it to close the spell, then looked closely at her reflection. Staring into her own eyes, she thought she caught a spark of something unfamiliar.

Laughing, she shook it off and tossed the mirror

aside. She reached for her glass and took a long sip of the cold gold-colored wine.

"It's not all bad," she said to the empty room. "Shea's powers grow, her Eternal's worried and now there's no place for them to go but back to the beginning."

"Concentrate."

"I *am*."

Shea shot Torin a dirty look, then refocused her concentration on the matter at hand. She'd been working on her magical abilities constantly for the last several days. Ever since they'd boarded the *Queen Mary 2* to sail to Southampton, England.

Waving her hand in a graceful gesture, Shea sent a tall crystal vase across the room to stand on the pedestal table at the foot of the curving staircase to the second floor of their duplex suite. She set the vase down gently, using only the power of her magic, and smiled to herself at the control she'd gained.

Now if only she could relax a little.

After escaping the Ohio Seekers, Torin hadn't bothered procuring a car. He'd simply drawn on his immense strength and flashed them, in a series of jumps, all the way to New York. They'd used magic to reserve a deluxe suite, then paid cash for the accommodations on the *Queen Mary 2*, leaving the very next day. Torin had sneaked Shea aboard without anyone seeing her.

England.

She used to dream about visiting Europe. About backpacking through the countryside. Seeing new things. Meeting new people. Now she was finally going to get there, but she'd be in hiding. Not to mention praying that Europe had enough of their own witches to worry about and wouldn't have her picture posted everywhere she went.

She wished she could enjoy this trip. She'd never

dreamed she would be traveling in such luxury. But as tense as she was, it hardly mattered. At any moment she half expected someone to burst through the cabin door, trying to kill her. Torin hadn't eased his battle-ready ways either. Whether he believed them to be momentarily safe or not, he was on constant alert. And though she appreciated it, Shea would have given anything for the two of them to really be able to forget about the world for a while and just be together.

Well, when he wasn't giving her orders, that is.

She glanced around at the amazing suite. Booking at the last minute and paying cash for their tickets, Torin had reserved the Balmoral Suite on the tenth of thirteen decks, at the very tail end of the enormous ship. They were secluded from everyone else, in their own little world. Exquisite paintings on the walls, comfortable chairs and couches. An incredible view out the wide windows to the sky and sea.

It was a duplex suite. Upstairs were the bedroom and a marble bath with a sea window and a Jacuzzi; downstairs featured a living room, dining room and a private terrace where you could sit in deck chairs high above the other passengers. The suite was almost twenty-three hundred square feet. Almost twice the size of her old apartment.

He'd been right about this, Shea thought. At first she'd insisted that he was making a mistake by booking the most expensive suite on the ship. She'd thought they should hunker down in a tiny cabin in the bowels of the boat. Incognito, sort of.

But Torin had insisted that the rich were rarely bothered. They had access to twenty-four-hour room service and could elect to stay locked away in their suite and never see another passenger or member of the crew if they wished. When the maids arrived every day, Shea and Torin merely stepped onto the wide private verandah until they were gone again. Safer all the way around.

And a luxury she wished she could enjoy more thoroughly.

Still, it was annoying that he seemed to be right so often.

"Again," Torin said from across the room.

She frowned at him. "Moving flowers from spot to spot isn't exactly honing my skills, you know."

"Controlling your power is the most important thing right now, Shea," he said, and pushed up from the comfortable sofa to walk toward her.

"Oh, I don't know," Shea said when he was only a step away. "I sort of think it's more important to remember where the hell we're going and *why*."

Torin grinned at the impatience in Shea's tone. And it suddenly struck him how very seldom he had smiled in the recent centuries. But these last days with Shea, despite the danger, despite the constant threat of attack, had changed him. The mating had touched something inside him that he wouldn't have believed existed.

Their matching tattoos were nearing completion and every time he saw his mark spreading over her shoulder and back from its beginning on her breast, Torin experienced a sense of rightness that he had hungered for all his long existence. His need for her increased by the day and he could barely manage to be in the same room with her without touching her. Tasting her. He wanted her safe. He wanted her happy. But mostly he simply wanted her.

Now she stared at him through narrowed eyes and he felt a flicker of pride rise up in him. These days on the cruise ship had been intense. For both of them.

They were hiding. True, in lush surroundings, but knowing that she was unable to so much as step out onto their terrace without first making sure she was alone was wearing on her. He could see it daily. Tension was ratcheting up inside her along with her powers and the mixture was difficult to bear. For both of them.

And yet, his witch stood tall and proud, refusing to surrender. Refusing to lie down and cry about her fate or what was expected of her. Her entire life had changed over the last couple of weeks, and yet she continued on, working toward the inevitable test that lay ahead of her.

Her powers were growing more quickly now. Since drawing down the moon and unlocking the door to her memories, she had triggered the release of her many gifts. Torin sensed her abilities developing at a staggering rate and knew that she fought daily for the control she needed. Her own need for knowledge was feeding her magical growth. And the mating sex was deepening those abilities, stirring to life old embers, echoes of past lives.

She would need every ounce of strength and will she possessed, he told himself solemnly. His mind raced ahead. To what they might face when they finally reached England's shores. There were still too many unknowns before them. They had to locate Haven. They had to find the Artifact. And, they were running out of time. There were so many things that could go wrong.

"You're worried," she said.

"Some."

Shea nodded, and walked to the windows that overlooked the sea, stretching out in front of them. At the horizon, sea and sky melded together into a seamless blue that seemed to slide into infinity.

"So am I." She glanced over her shoulder at him. "I still don't know everything that I should and we land in three days."

"It will come," he assured her. "Once we're in England, the sense memories will become thicker, more distinct."

"Maybe." She turned her back on the window to face him.

Backlit by the sun, she appeared to be gilded by a glowing golden light. Her dark red hair shone and though her green eyes were in shadow, he could have sworn he saw them flash with purpose.

"You need to tell me, Torin. What do you remember from that last night?"

Frowning, he started to argue, but she cut him off.

"We're running out of time. My magic is growing, I know. But I still feel like I'm in this blind. I need more information and I'm just not sorting through the opening memories as quickly as I'd like."

He pushed out of the chair and walked to her. "You're right," he admitted and caught the glint of surprise in her eyes. He smiled. "You thought I would argue with you."

Nodding, she said, "Well, you're the one who's been insisting all along that my memories had to come in their own time."

"True," he said, sliding one hand along her arm, hearing her breath quicken at his touch. How glorious it was to know that his woman felt everything he did when they came together. That the magic they created affected each of them with the same sense of eager anticipation for their next joining.

Taking a breath, he said, "But you managed to awaken your memories, Shea. Perhaps telling you now will help you sort through them at a faster pace."

He swept her up into his arms and carried her easily across the room toward the stairs.

"What're you doing?" she asked, linking her arms around his neck.

"I'm going to tell you all I know," he said, continuing on up the curving staircase to the luxurious bedroom on the second floor.

"And you have to tell me in the bedroom?"

He glanced at her and gave her a half smile. "It will take a while. You should be comfortable."

"Uh-huh. You're only thinking of *me.*"

"You are my mate, Shea," he said softly, meaningfully. "I always think of you."

Cora Sterling looked at her daughter and felt a surge of pride. Deidre Sterling was everything a mother could have hoped for. Brilliant, beautiful and strong-willed, she was, in essence, Cora told herself, a younger version of her mother.

Even a simple family dinner became an event at the White House. The Secret Service was always close at hand and the waitstaff from the kitchens tended to hover nearby, always ready to be of service.

But Cora didn't want any distractions when her daughter was there for dinner. As soon as she was able, she got rid of everyone so that she and Deidre could talk. Once the room was empty, she broached the subject that had been worrying her for days.

"The RFW has been in the papers a lot lately." She speared a bite of excellently prepared salmon.

"I know." Deidre pushed her chin-length blond hair behind her ears and smiled. "It's really exciting, Mother. Rights for Witches is growing faster than any of us had hoped."

Cora nodded and took a sip of cold white wine. "But there was trouble yesterday on the Mall."

A protest march at the National Mall had been scheduled for months. At most, people guessed there would be several thousand attendees. But more than fifty thousand people had shown up to march on the capital. The D.C. police were still sorting out all of the arrests they'd made. Even the most peaceful of protests somehow tended to engender violence of some kind.

All it took was one wrong word at the precisely wrong time and fireworks exploded, turning a demonstration into—in this case, at least—a near riot.

"The morning news was filled with coverage," Cora said. "People climbing on the Lincoln monument, fighting, for heaven's sake, in the Reflecting Pool. It was a disgrace."

Deidre sighed and leaned back in her chair. "It was disappointing, I know, but every movement has its share of hotheads, right? I mean, the important thing here is just how many people showed up. It was incredible." Her eyes shone and her smile flashed. "We never expected so many!"

"Yes," Cora said wryly, "I know."

Deidre winced a little at her tone. "I'm not trying to make things difficult for you, Mother. But this is important to me. I hate seeing how witches are being treated— rounded up and bundled off to internment camps? It's practically prehistoric!"

Cora chuckled. "Not nearly so dramatic, honey. You know that I've been working to solve this problem . . ."

"Oh, I do," Deidre told her, sliding a glance around the dining room in the president's private quarters as if to make sure no one was left to overhear them. "And it's great, really. But unless *everyone* steps up to protest what's happening, nothing will really change."

"It's dangerous, Dee," Cora told her daughter. "You could have been killed in that mob scene yesterday. If the Secret Service hadn't been there to pull you out . . ."

"But they pulled only me out," Deidre complained. "My friends were left to fend for themselves."

Dropping her fork onto the Reagan china with a clatter, Cora said, "You can't expect the agents to save everyone, Dee. You are my daughter. It's their duty to keep you from harm."

"Protect me but fry the witches. Is that it?"

"Watch your tone."

Instantly, Deidre got hold of herself. "Sorry. Look, I'm doing what I have to do. I don't expect you to approve, Mother, but you can't stop me from this."

"That's where you're wrong, Dee," Cora told her, reaching across the table to squeeze her daughter's hand. "I can do whatever I like. Not only am I your mother, but I'm the president. If I think you're in danger, don't for one minute believe that I'm not going to act."

Deidre looked into her mother's eyes and what she read there must have convinced her because her attitude shifted and she said, "I'm sorry I worried you. I'll try not to let it happen again. But I can't promise to stop my work with the RFW. It's too important. To me. To the *world.*"

Cora patted her hand and nodded. "I understand completely. But you must understand that I will do whatever I think necessary to ensure that you stay well."

"Of course," Deidre said and squeezed her mother's hand. "So, let's talk about something else. Did I tell you I found a condo I might want to buy?"

Cora sat back and watched her daughter, smiling at all the appropriate times, while she silently made plans to talk to the agents assigned to Deidre. Yesterday, her daughter's safety had been compromised. She might have died.

Cora would not allow that to happen.

Chapter 40

I always think of you.

Torin's words were simple, Shea reflected, but so profound. He was everything to her. She never would have thought that any two people could bond so completely in such a short time.

But these last few days had been the most amazing of her life. It was as if the magic itself was a living entity, separate from her, yet a part of her at the same time.

She was even dreaming about spells and enchantments. She woke up knowing the lore of crystals. She could create a talisman or craft a love spell. She could now list medicinal herbs and how they should be used. Her mind was filled to overflowing with the knowledge of the many lifetimes she'd lived. She remembered more every day. It was all there, in her mind, her heart. She had only to uncover the last of her own deeply buried secrets.

Torin carried her into their bedroom. She squinted against the bright afternoon light glancing off the water with a knife's edge. Automatically, she dimmed the light, but kept the brilliance of it. Because she wanted the curtains open to the light. Wanted the terrace doors open to the wind.

She drew strength and energy from the elements of nature and felt the sunlight and wind and sea filling her cells, becoming a part of her.

It was cold, but that was easily remedied. A wave of their hands and they felt only the kiss of the wind, not its bite. Torin laid her down on the bed and stretched out alongside her. Shea snuggled in, pillowing her head on his chest, listening to the silence within, still puzzled by the fact that a man so richly, thoroughly alive could have no heartbeat. She kissed the spot where beneath his shirt, the mating tattoo coiled.

"If you begin doing that," he warned quietly, "there will be no talking."

"Right," she said, feeling the sparks within her ignite. Being close to him only made the magnetic pull between them that much stronger. Shea ached to feel his warm skin against hers, feel his hard, thick body pumping into hers. Her core tingled and her breathing became fast and shallow as she fought to resist the lure of the mating. "Okay," she said after a long minute. "Talk first. Then sex."

"I agree," he said, his arm tightening around her. "So, that night. I've told you most of it already, but you're now remembering it for yourself, aren't you?"

"Yes." Everything Torin had already told her still resonated inside her. And as her memories had risen to the surface of her mind, she had seen it all so clearly, as if a part of her were trapped on that long-ago night and she was doomed to relive it over and over again in some twisted sort of loop. Like a mental journal, the pages of her life flipped past, showering her with the long-dead echoes of horrific sounds and scents and colors.

Yet, despite everything, there was a small, very secret part of her that was . . . excited by the memory. There was a dark place within her that relished every scream, every jolt of terror, every moment of danger that clung to the ancient images.

In the deepest part of her heart, Shea worried not about Torin's trustworthiness but about her own. She couldn't tell him what she was feeling. What she was dreading. But the truth was, Shea was terrified that along with her newfound powers the woman she had once been was being awakened.

That witch had been willing to lose everything that mattered to her in her quest for knowledge and power. What if she hadn't evolved as much as Torin thought she had? What if the darkness was still there inside her, simply locked away behind a door of secrets?

"You and your sisters would listen to no one," he said, his voice soft, low with memory and regret. "You were set on a dark path but couldn't—or wouldn't—see it. There was hunger for knowledge, yes. But more, there was the promise of power. Power such as no one had ever known before."

The afternoon sunlight, the luxurious ship, the tumult of her present life all faded away as Shea closed her eyes and let the lost images inside her rise. She saw it all, experienced it all, as his voice continued.

"The coven drew down the moon, gathered their energies and pushed their combined strength through the Artifact."

She saw it, as she had that long-ago night. Lightning whips of white light, brilliant in the dark. Jagged, scorching, the air sizzling as bolt after bolt jumped from witch to witch, the light itself growing, becoming something else.

"The black silver glowed and hummed with the accumulation of power. Lightning was everywhere, like a living beast." He paused, lost in his memories. Shea shuddered as her own mind continued playing out the scene.

"There was a blinding light," he said in a whisper. "Brighter than the sun at midday. And in an instant, everything changed. The Artifact opened a portal."

"The Hell gate," Shea said, feeling the sudden rush of a twisted sort of excitement along with a growing sense of dread.

"Yes," Torin whispered. "Demons poured from the

opening in numbers too many to count. Lucifer himself appeared and laughed at our feeble attempts to contain his minions. To restrain him. But we had no choice. We could not stand by and watch this legion descend on an earth unable to defend itself.

"We Eternals fought them, killing some, tossing more back through the gateway to their hell. But as the battle raged, we tried to get to you. The coven. Our witches. The strength of your circle kept us out, unable to reach you. Unable to help you. All we could do was fight the creatures your spell had released."

Shea heard the hiss of the candle flames, battling the sharp wind. Heard the shrieks of the demons and the shouts of the Eternals. She heard her own voice, rising with those of her sisters as they realized at last what their greed and arrogance had brought them to. They chanted then, despite the fear, despite the battles raging around them, and the voices, once lost in time, resonated once again in her mind.

"The coven," Torin went on, "seeing at last what they had done, joined the battle. Banding together, they worked as one. As they had joined their powers to open the portal, they directed their energies at closing the very door they had pried open."

She remembered. More, she lived the memory. Her heart, her soul, sang with the growth of the shadows. She felt the seduction of the dark calling to her as she fought with her sisters.

Lucifer, the fallen angel himself, with his dark eyes and magnificent features, had met Shea's gaze deliberately. And she had realized, even through the tumult happening around her, that he knew her most secret yearnings. He knew that even as she fought him, she wanted to join him. When he gave her a sly smile and encouragement that whispered in her mind, Shea had reached for what will she possessed and spurned his invitation.

Yet, even then, when she did all she could to undo the damage caused . . . there was a corner of her heart still yearning for the darkness.

Now, she had to wonder. What did that make her? Was she truly as evil as Martha and her Seekers believed? Would she turn on Torin and the world? Would she surrender to the shadows she'd railed against so long ago?

"Shea?"

"Yes, sorry," she said softly. "My mind wandered." *Into places best left alone,* she added silently. "Finish, Torin. Tell me what happened next."

He sighed, and slipped one hand beneath her shirt, sliding his palm over her skin, soothing each of them with the intimate caress. "The coven fought back. Somehow, their linked abilities were strong enough to push Lucifer back through the gateway, most of his demons with him. The portal sealed shut moments later."

"That wasn't the end."

"No," he told her. "The portal was closed, but not permanently. The beast lurked behind a magical barrier, all too close to a defenseless world. And so the last great coven charmed a spell of atonement. Sentencing themselves to eight hundred and ten years of life without their powers. Without the memories of who and what they had once been."

Everything in Shea went still as his voice brought to the surface the memories of that one moment that had sealed the fates of the witches for centuries to come.

"Incarnation after incarnation," he said, "each of you lived a life that was devoid of magic. All in the hopes that when the time ran out, you would have evolved enough to turn your backs on the greed and arrogance that had governed you. That you would finally be able to destroy the Artifact, thus permanently closing the gateway to Hell."

She remembered. And as she did, tears rained down her cheeks. For the mistakes made. For the atonement still incomplete.

"When the spell was spoken, the witches broke apart the Artifact that had stood in the center of their coven for thousands of years."

The physical pain of that action sliced through Shea again as it had on the long-ago night. The powerful black silver Artifact was shattered by the very magic that had created it in the first place. They had betrayed all that they were. They had turned their backs not just on each other but on their ancestors, the founders of the very coven they had destroyed. At the moment the Artifact was shattered, each of the witches who had been entrusted with it felt that same splintering of her soul.

"A shard of the Artifact was entrusted to each of the witches. The coven disbanded and the women of power drifted apart, with each of them hiding their piece of the Artifact in secret." Torin eased himself up on one elbow and looked down at her. "The waiting time began, with centuries crawling past, one after the other, until now. The Awakening is your time, Shea. The broken shards of the Artifact must be brought back together and finally destroyed. Or the world will never be safe."

With his words, her mind and soul opened to the call of the Artifact.

She felt the ancient stirrings and trembled.

Chapter 41

Rune found Odell in Sussex.

Tall even for an Eternal, Odell stood nearly six feet seven. His broad shoulders and square jaw only added to the image of a man best left alone. His dark brown hair hung past his shoulders and was usually held in place by a leather thong at the nape of his neck. He wore black leather, always, and the suspicious gleam in his pale gray eyes was as ever present as his legendary temper.

Not the man you would have guessed would be at the head of an underground safety network for witches and accused human females. But he was probably the best man for the job, Rune told himself. Odell had little patience and no sympathy with the mortal world's attempt at stamping out all practitioners of magic.

Sitting in Odell's country estate just outside Brighton, Rune drank the glass of Paddy's Irish Whiskey he'd been handed, then held it out for a refill.

Odell obliged with a grin. "I didn't expect to see you, Rune. With the Awakening upon us, I thought you'd be out after your witch."

He shrugged. "She hasn't awakened to her powers yet."

"Neither has mine," Odell admitted, stretching out his long legs in front of him. "When last I checked in on her, she was burying herself in research books, looking, if you can believe it, for a 'cure' to witchcraft." He shook his head solemnly. "Riona's a bloody scientist in this lifetime. Don't know how I'll put up with her when it's our time."

Rune laughed. He knew Odell was as anxious for his witch to call to him as Rune himself was. After centuries of waiting, of torment, the end was in sight. These last few weeks of waiting were going to be a trial.

He studied the amber liquid in the Waterford crystal tumbler, took a sip of the smooth, rich whiskey and said, "I can beat that. My witch gives guided tours of the Mexican desert."

Odell's eyebrows lifted. "A desert, you say? Better you than me. All that sand? No cold winds? No soft rains? No. It's all I can do to live here, in England, rather than in Ireland where me and my witch belong."

With ties to ancient Eire, Odell and his witch, as if by design, had yet to return to Ireland. In all her incarnations, Riona had never returned to the land of her birth—as if her spirit were deliberately punishing her. Taking the atonement one step further by keeping her from the country she loved.

Rune couldn't seem to relax, despite the comfort of Odell's home. He'd sought Egan and had come up empty. More, there had been no trail of him. No hint of where he might have gone or who might have seen him last.

"I don't understand it," he muttered, staring at his whiskey as if looking for the answer to his question in the bottom of his glass. "There was no trace of Egan in Scotland. Anywhere."

Odell laughed shortly and shook his head. "Did you expect to find him standing on his doorstep, waiting for you?"

Rune scowled at his old friend. "No, but I expected there to be some sign of him. Some clue to where he might be."

"He's not a child," Odell snapped, then took a breath and leashed his temper. "You said yourself that the waiting is an agony, Rune. Is it any wonder that some of us disappear from time to time? Centuries we've been kept waiting, dangling on the end of the witches' leashes. We're Eternals, man, not tame dogs to be told when to come and when to go."

"I didn't say that," Rune argued, realizing that he'd said the very same things all too recently to Torin. "But with the Awakening on us now, we should all be aware of where our witch is and what's happening to her."

"What makes you think he isn't?" Odell leapt up from his chair, stalked to the liquor cabinet and poured himself another splash of Irish. He kicked it back, then slammed the tumbler onto the closest table. "He owes no one an explanation of where he goes and what he does, Rune. He's no doubt keeping an eye on this Kellyn from afar. Waiting for her powers to awaken, just like the rest of us damn fools."

Rune stood up too, facing down the man he'd called friend for thousands of years. "Her powers *are* awakening. She's a teleporter, and a damn strong one, from what I saw. So if it's all kicking into place, where the hell is Egan?"

Odell scowled at him, fierceness carved into his features. "How am I to know? You come to my home and start fuming at me over another Eternal's problems? What sense is that, man?"

"I didn't start fuming until you started shouting, dumb shit."

Instantly, the fury on Odell's face drifted into an expression of amusement. "Well, you have me there. All right, then. Since you can't find your stray Eternal and you've clearly nothing better to do with your time than drink my whiskey . . ."

Wary, Rune watched his friend. "What?"

Odell slapped his palms together and scrubbed them briskly. "I thought I might convince you to come along with me on an adventure of sorts."

He'd been on an adventure with Odell once before, in 1014. He'd ended up a part of the battle against the Ulstermen and was witness to the death of the last hereditary high king of Ireland, Brian Boru. The war had been a glorious one, though, as Rune remembered it.

"What sort of 'adventure' is it this time, old friend?"

Odell winked and grinned. "I've a raid planned on an internment camp just outside Crawley."

"A raid?"

"Aye," Odell told him. "The camp's not far from Gatwick. Authorities fly the women in from all over England and Scotland, then trundle them off to the Crawley camp. I'm going in tonight to spirit away those sentenced to death." His features went hard and cold. His Eternal gray eyes were as icy as winter fog. "There are six slated to be put to the fire in the next week. I'm getting them out. And if you're not too busy, I might be able to use your help."

Rune smiled. He couldn't find Egan. Had no idea where to look next. So. Until he came up with a better plan, he'd do what he could here, with Odell. A raging battle with mortal prison guards sounded good to him at the moment. "I'm in."

Odell grinned and slapped him on the back hard enough to send a lesser man through a wall. "Excellent. We'll go now."

"Where do we take them once we've got them free?"

Odell laughed and the sound boomed in the otherwise still room. "That's the best part. The closest Sanctuary is in Ashdown Forest. One of the biggest tourist draws around these parts."

"Are you crazy?" Rune demanded.

"Not at all," Odell told him, already calling on the fire

and becoming a giant pillar of flame. "Hide in plain sight and those who chase you never find you."

"If he's not crazy," Rune said as his friend flashed out of the room, "then I certainly am."

An instant later, he followed Odell into the heart of the enemy.

The sea air was cold.

The ever-waxing moon tossed pale light onto the surface of the churned-up waves, highlighting them with an otherworldly green phosphorescence. There was music drifting into the air from the Queen's Room ballroom on the third deck. Shea stepped through the open terrace doors to the private verandah off their suite. She followed the music as if she could see the notes hanging in the air.

The song playing was an old one. If she'd had to make a guess at its age, she would have put it somewhere in the forties. It was slow and sad and bluesy, with a wailing saxophone that touched something inside her deeply enough to bring tears to her eyes.

"You cry?"

She didn't even jump when Torin came up behind her. What did that say? she wondered. Was she getting so used to him now? Or was she on such a high alert at all times it was simply impossible to startle her anymore?

"Shea," he said, wrapping his arms around her, pulling her back to his front. Resting his chin on top of her head, he asked, "Tell me why you're crying."

"It's silly," she said, staring out at the moon-dropped diamonds of light on the surface of the ocean. "I'm not even sure why. It's the music, I guess. It sounds . . . lonely."

"There's more to your tears than music."

She tipped her head back to look up at him. "Of course there's more, Torin. We're almost to England. Two more days and then what?"

"Then we do what we must to end this. Or at least, our share of it."

"Easier said than done," she whispered, turning her gaze back to the sea and sky. "I don't know where I hid my piece of the Artifact. I don't even know where Haven is."

"You *will.*"

"You sound so sure," she said and heard the envy in her own voice. "I wish I was."

Tiny white lights rimmed the edges of the ship's decks. It looked like a fairyland at night, Shea thought. Hundreds of people were on the decks below, but here, on the verandah, she and Torin were the only two people in the world. No one could see them here. They were alone with each other and the night.

"Your confidence is growing, Shea. I can sense it in you."

"Not quickly enough," she said.

He chuckled, a rare sound coming from him. "You always were impatient."

Being reminded of her past self did nothing to heighten Shea's self-confidence. Yes, she had been impatient. And greedy. And reckless. Did she still have those traits inside her? Were they strong enough to resurface? And if they did, could she stop herself from making the same mistake she'd made so long ago?

"Call the fire."

Her thoughts splintered. "What?"

"Call on your fire, Shea," Torin told her. "As you did on the day we met, when you stopped the attacker."

"When I killed him, you mean."

"Shea—"

Shaking her head, she pulled free of Torin's grip and ignored the iciness crawling through her without his touch to ground her.

"I don't need that power, Torin," she said firmly. "I

don't want it. I don't ever want to risk losing control again."

"If you fear losing control," he said quietly, "then there's a reason for that fear. It means only that you don't trust yourself."

"Damn straight I don't," she countered. "I *killed* that guy, Torin." She shuddered and wrapped her arms around her middle to offset the shivers racking her body. "God, sometimes in my dreams, I can still hear him screaming."

He huffed out an impatient breath. "The man was not worth one moment of your guilt or misery. He would have killed you, Shea."

"Instead I killed him." She looked at him. "I don't want to use the fire, Torin. I don't want to open that door again."

God, she thought with a wincing inner laugh. Opening doors. Wasn't that what had gotten her into trouble centuries ago? The coven had opened doors and nearly ended the world.

"Pretending it doesn't exist doesn't tame the ability. You can't claim *some* of your power and not the rest, Shea. This gift is yours. The magic is in you. *You* decide how and when to use it."

She stabbed her index finger at him. "Exactly. And I choose not to use it."

She tried to walk away from him, but he snaked out a hand and held her fast. Whipping her head around, she glared at him, but his grip only tightened.

"And if you need that power to defend yourself or an innocent?"

Good question. She didn't know.

"Shea," he said, his voice dipping so low she nearly didn't hear it over the hum of the great ship's engines and the slap of the waves against her hull. "You must trust me. I can show you how to use the fire. To contain it. Your fear, your inexperience, drove you before when that man attacked you. It wouldn't be the same now."

Was he right? Shea wanted him to be. She never wanted to lose control of her powers again. She had come a long way in a few short weeks, mastering abilities, channeling her energies. She'd learned so much, but there was still so much she didn't know.

And there wasn't much time left to cram for her upcoming test. Only another thousand or so years of things to study up on.

Could she really afford *not* to learn?

"All right," she said softly, before she could change her mind. "Show me, Torin."

He smiled then and something inside her fisted. Those rare, beautiful smiles of his never failed to stir her. But then, he had been right when he told her that once the mating had begun, the feelings between them would only intensify.

Her body burned for his constantly. Her soul cried out for him. He really *was* the other half of her soul. But still, there was something holding her back, keeping her from admitting even to herself how much she loved him, and she couldn't confess to him what it was.

She was afraid.

Not of Torin.

Of herself.

A seed of doubt lingered inside her. The worry that she wouldn't be strong enough to vanquish the darkness. That she would instead get sucked into it all over again. That the power raging through her would overwhelm who she was and turn her into something she didn't even want to think about.

But Torin couldn't hear her thoughts, thank God, so he didn't know about those night terrors that brought her up out of sleep, shaking. He didn't hear the sly whispers in her mind, reminding her of what she had once been—what she could be again.

He stood there, holding her, smiling at her, and Shea wanted to tell him what she was feeling, thinking, dreading. But she didn't want to risk seeing disgust on his features. Didn't want to see him turn from her, or stop believing in her.

She wasn't at all sure that she would be able to go on if she didn't have her Eternal at her side.

"We'll do this now, then," he said and released her.

The night was all around them, the moon drifting in a star-splashed sky. At the rear of the ship, with only the sweep of sky and sea surrounding them, they were as isolated as it was possible to be.

"Call the fire, Shea."

"How?"

"Feel it rise inside you. Hold your hands out in front of you and will the flames into existence."

She swallowed hard and did as he asked, making sure that her hands weren't pointed at him. How odd to have to treat your own hands like loaded guns.

Nodding to herself in silent encouragement, she concentrated on her hands. In her mind, she saw the fire and a rush of power pushed through her. She surrendered to it, allowing it to grow and burst free. Instantly, flames erupted at her fingertips and she jumped in response.

"Easy," he soothed.

The flames were wild, whipping in the wind, shooting from the tips of her fingers into the dark like tiny roman candles.

"Call it back," he said, from right beside her. "Tame each flame with your mind. Bend them to your will."

She tipped her head to one side, studied the fire and focused as she never had before. One by one, the flames obeyed, shrinking, then growing as she wished it. They danced across her skin, flared with brilliant color, then dimmed until they were hardly more than match flames, struggling in the wind.

Smiling now, Shea stretched her arms over her head, waved her hands and looked up so she could watch the lights she had created through her abilities and the strength of her own will.

"You are the most beautiful thing I have ever seen," Torin said.

Her heartbeat leapt and the flames on her hands magnified in response. Quickly, she gathered herself, quieted the flames and watched as they winked out, leaving her hands unharmed. Only then did she turn to Torin and look into his eyes.

"Beautiful," he repeated. "In lifetime after lifetime, the essence of you was unchanged. Your eyes, always this brilliant green. Your soul, always calling to mine. And always, I have loved you."

She swayed unsteadily, hearing those words and knowing just how deeply he meant them. She wanted to give them back to him. Needed to, as if her very life depended on it. Yet they stuck in her throat and died unuttered. How could she love him when she didn't trust herself?

"But now, in this lifetime, Shea, you are more beautiful than you have ever been." He moved closer and cupped her face in his palms. "Your magic drives you, but your heart guides you."

"Torin . . ."

"No more words, Shea," he said. "For what we both want, there is no need for words."

Torin waved one hand and her clothing disappeared. In the glow of the moonlight, her skin looked like porcelain. His unbeating heart swelled with the emotions crowding inside him. Torin had never, in all the years of his existence, felt what he did now, for this woman. This witch. *His.* Always and forever, *his.*

He dispensed with his own clothing an instant later and reached for her, pulling her body to align with his. The slide of her skin on his inflamed him. His flesh warmed, his body went to stone. Weeks now, they had been together. They had given themselves up to the mating sex and the fire they produced between them was searing. But they hadn't shared tenderness. And tonight, that was what he wanted-for himself.

For her.

Her arms linked around his neck and she went up on her toes to kiss him, parting his lips with her tongue, sliding inside his mouth to quicken the heat building between them.

He took as well as he gave, delving deep into her warmth, tasting all she was, all she would be. His mind raced with raw emotions and sensations that he had hardly had time to appreciate. On the run, chased from one supposedly safe spot to the next, running for their lives and on a quest, they had yet to be able to stand still long enough to thoroughly enjoy what they had found together.

Until now.

Breaking the kiss, he locked his gaze with hers as he waved his hand at the deck of the verandah. Instantly, there appeared a mattress of the softest down. Covered in snowy white linen with mounds of pillows at one end, it shone like a jewel in the darkness.

"Torin . . ."

"We take tonight, Shea," he whispered. "No training, no practicing, no worries for what will come. Tonight there is only us."

"Yes," she said on a sigh and allowed him to lay her down gently on the mattress beneath the stars.

Gently, lovingly, he traced the outline of her mating tattoo with the tips of his fingers. Starting at her nipple, he followed the line of flames around and back to her shoulder, her spine. Each tiny flame burst into color, life, as he touched them. her body instinctively responding to the call of his.

He felt his own branding burn on his skin and he relished the feel, because it marked them as one. It joined them as nothing else ever could.

Bending his head to her breast, Torin let his tongue trace the same trail his fingers had moments before. She sighed at the contact and held his head to her breast, hungry for more.

He gave her what she craved. What they both craved.

"Torin," she whispered, "you make me feel so much."

His hands moved over her skin, tracing every line, every curve and he felt his heart swell in his chest. She was everything and more to him. She had no idea what he would do for her. What he would sacrifice for her.

To save this witch, he would surrender the world if he had to. Because without her, he was nothing. Without her, there was only the loneliness of centuries past. The misery of knowing what he had found only to lose it.

Her hands slid up and down his back, then his chest, stroking the branding tattoo until the lines of each flame burned with a fiery red light and he felt the heat of every one of those flames licking at him.

She stroked him, reaching down between their bodies to wrap her fingers around his hard thickness. Sliding her hand gently up and down, stroking the tip of him until he was forced to hiss in breath after breath in a gritty determination to hold on. To not claim the release she was bent on giving him.

At last, though, he couldn't take her touch without the risk of exploding, so he pulled her hand free of him and smiled down into her emerald green eyes. "Not yet, Shea. There is much I wish to do to you. For you."

"You give to me all the time, Torin," she said, arching

off the bed toward him, needing the feel of his skin on hers as badly as he did.

"And it will continue," he vowed. "I will always put you first above all others. Your happiness means more to me than anything."

She stilled and looked deeply into his eyes. "You do make me happy, Torin. Happier than I ever thought I would be. After Aunt Mairi died, I was so alone and so scared. I never imagined I could feel like this. That I would find purpose again. That I would find *you.*"

He kissed her then, long and deep and hard. Dragging that moment on for a small eternity because the taste of her was staggering to him. But there was more he wanted, needed, to taste.

Sliding along her body, he caressed her skin, kissed every inch of her as he worked his way down, past her breasts, her abdomen, to the very heart of her. He parted her thighs with the touch of his hand. She opened for him eagerly, willingly. He dipped first one finger, then two, into her hot depths and watched her face as she lifted her hips into his hand. The mating tattoo burned a dark, bright red around her breast and an answering fire sizzled on his own skin.

He felt the mark chasing down along his spine and knew that Shea was experiencing the same. The brand was nearing completion and now it would burn fiercely whenever they came together. A reminder, he thought, of what they had earned. What they had become.

Moving now, Torin knelt between her thighs and watched her smile as she lifted her hips to welcome his body. But he wanted something more from her first. Wanted to take and give and feel her shatter.

Scooping his hands under her behind, he lifted her off the bed and held her, suspended. "Drape your legs over my shoulders, Shea."

"Torin . . ." She bit her lip and did as he asked.

He kept his gaze locked with hers as he lowered his head to taste her most intimate flesh. At the first swipe of his tongue, Shea groaned aloud and took a sharp, quick breath. That soft sigh of sound fed the desire pumping through him.

Torin licked and tasted and nibbled at her core until she was breathing in ragged gasps and twisting in his hold. She rocked her hips wildly, desperate for the release he kept pushing her toward. She fisted her fingers in his hair and held his mouth to her when the first ripples of sensation coursed through her and Torin felt every jolting surge of pleasure as it shook her to the bone.

Only when the last one had dissolved, leaving her body trembling with release, did he ease her back onto the mattress. He buried his body within hers in a long, hard stroke, laying claim to all she was. She urged him on with tiny, barely heard cries of ecstasy.

He felt lightning-like whips of energy snapping between the two of them. They moved together in a tender symphony of rhythm. Her body tightened around his, liquid heat, clenching down, pulling him deeper, deeper, until Torin was sure he would never completely be apart from her again. The fires between them burned and flared. He reached for her hand and twined their fingers together.

The mating fire erupted, burning brightly over their joined hands as their bodies shattered together, each of them jolting into a climax that was all the stronger for the sharing.

In the darkness, two decks above, the tip of a cigarette glowed in the darkness like the eye of a demon.

The watcher smiled.

Chapter 42

"It's time." Kellyn spoke into her phone and idly plucked a stray thread from her plum-colored silk shirt. "According to my contact, Shea and Torin are very close now. They should be right where I expect them sometime in the next twenty-four hours. I'll need to have everything in place well before so we're ready to go at a moment's notice. I'll handle all of the arrangements."

"Kellyn," the voice on the phone said patiently, "we've discussed this before. You've given me the coordinates for this confrontation and I've already made the arrangements. When we hang up, I'll notify them to set up immediately."

Rage swarmed like dragonflies in the pit of her belly, but Kellyn bit back her frustration and kept her voice cool and disaffected. She'd come too far to lose her temper now. She still needed this connection. So she took a breath and said, "I'm sure you remember how badly the Seeker operation ended."

"Yes, but my instructions weren't followed," the caller insisted. "And those who made the mistakes have been dealt with. This time it will be different. My own people are taking care of things rather than subcontracting it out. There won't be any blunders this time—I won't stand for it."

Neither would Kellyn. Which was why she wanted to

be in charge. However, there were still reasons for maintaining this relationship, so she would give it another try.

"Now, if the coordinates you gave me haven't changed . . ." the voice continued.

"They haven't." Kellyn knew exactly where the witch and her Eternal were headed. It might take Shea a bit longer to recall everything, but Kellyn's memories had returned some time ago. The past was wide-open to her and the future, if maneuvered correctly, shone with promise.

"All right, then," the voice said with confidence. "I'll make the call. Everything will be set up and waiting within the hour."

"Fine." Kellyn forced a smile and looked down on the street traffic in front of her hotel. Yes, the view had changed, but any view that could be seen from the very best suite in a luxury hotel was a good one. She laughed to think of Shea and her Eternal, darting across the countryside, staying in tacky motels and abandoned homes. All to avoid detection, she thought—for all the good it had done them.

Between the trackers implanted in Shea's body and the scrying Kellyn had been doing, the witch and the Eternal had been chased from one edge of the country to the next. She had enjoyed her magical meetings with Shea and was looking forward to the next time they met. Kellyn would talk Shea into turning her back on the coven and joining forces with her. Then the two of them would hunt down the other Awakened witches, each in turn. And in the end, the Artifact and the power would be theirs.

Smiling, she realized she was in a much better mood as she told her partner, "I'll go directly to the coordinates and make sure your people are set up correctly."

"That's a good idea. I'll contact them, let them know you're coming and that they should do as you order."

"Excellent." Nothing she liked better than men snapping to attention.

"Fine then," the caller said easily. "And Kellyn, see that nothing goes wrong this time. I don't want the witch dead. She's no good to either of us unless she's alive."

"I know that even better than you." Kellyn hung up and tossed the phone onto a nearby chair.

She didn't need to be reminded about anything. Especially not by one who had only recently joined in the hunt.

Kellyn had been waiting for this for centuries.

"Soon," she whispered, chuckling as a pedestrian rushed into the street and was smacked by a taxi. "Soon, I won't need anyone. Shea and I will take charge of the Awakening and nothing will ever be the same."

Shea and Torin were the first to leave the ship.

Actually, they left before the ship landed in Southampton. The moment they were close enough to shore, Torin flashed them out, leaving behind the luxurious interlude.

But time was passing and she had no room for regrets or looking backward. Torin had been right, of course. The moment she had set foot on British soil, she had known exactly where they had to go. Was it a sense memory? Was it a clue left behind in her subconscious when her memories were unlocked, allowing her to recall her past lives?

"Shea?"

"I know where to go," she said. "Pembrokeshire, Wales. But just get us close. I want to do a spell before we go to Haven. Make sure we're not walking into a trap."

"Good idea."

They were on the final leg of their journey. In ten days, the moon would be full and their time would be up.

As Torin's flames enveloped her, Shea silently prayed that nothing would go wrong.

Deep in the heart of the Sussex Sanctuary, Odell and Rune relaxed beside a campfire. Flames leapt and jumped into the night sky. Swirls of sparks flew briefly and winked out like dying fireflies. All around them, the community of women worked to integrate the newcomers, freed by the raid on the internment camp.

"That went well," Rune said, lifting his glass of beer in a salute to his friend.

"It did," Odell agreed. "Only three guards dead and six women freed." He grinned. "Was a good night's work."

"And they'll be safe here?" Rune looked around. They were in a long-forgotten cavern beneath Ashdown Forest. In ancient times these carved rock walls and rooms had no doubt hidden away others, looking for peace from their pursuers. Today, it was alive again with the sound of desperate voices.

"Safer than they were, for damn sure," Odell told him flatly. When he spoke again, he smiled. "It's ten square miles of 'protected' land. There are the tourists, of course, but Ashdown was the 'home' of Winnie the Pooh," he added with a snort of laughter. "There are deer and all other manner of wildlife running all over the bloody place, so there are conservation people rabid about protecting it." He looked up at the rock ceiling above their heads. "And these caverns were forgotten long ago. No one knows of their existence and they've been magically warded so they won't be found."

"Sounds good," Rune told him. "But they can't stay here forever." From down a long corridor came the sound of a woman softly weeping and his unbeating heart ached for the females caught in a web of treachery.

"No, they can't," Odell allowed. "But it's a good spot for now. There are other Sanctuaries posted around Britain and we'll move some of the witches soon, make it less crowded down here."

Nodding, Rune said thoughtfully, "You know, the last time I entered a Sanctuary, I wasn't exactly welcomed with open arms."

"Perhaps," Odell told him with a grin and a wink. "But you come to this one as a friend of mine, so you're trusted." His smile faded and he shook his head solemnly. "These women have been pursued and tortured and terrified. Is it any wonder they're willing to turn on the first male they see?"

"No. It's not." Rune stared into the fire and said softly, "If the Awakening goes as planned, this will change. There won't be a need for witch hunters. Witchcraft can take its rightful place in the world."

"Aye," his friend said, a rueful note in his voice. "If it goes as planned. And how many plans my friend, have we seen blow up in our faces over the centuries?"

"Yeah," Rune agreed somberly. "There is that."

Torin risked the magic, using his powers, his energies, to flash them, in a series of jumps, to Wales. Their minds linked, thanks to the ever-increasing strength of the mating, he took them to a high, grassy knoll above the crashing sea.

A cold, sharp wind swept in from the ocean, rushing past them to race across the countryside, sending villagers searching for their hearths. In the distance, heavy dark clouds gathered as if amassing their forces for an invasion.

Torin was oblivious to everything but Shea. His focus was locked on her, his sharp eyes watching every inflection of expression cross her face. She looked both pleased and worried about being where they were and he could see the glint of recognition shining in her brilliant green eyes.

As he watched, she walked closer to a burial mound that had been perched on the high cliff above Manorbier Bay for eons. A heavy, long capstone sat balanced atop two short, thick side stones. Centuries of wind and rain had pitted the stones deeply, but magic sang in the air around the mound.

"King's Quoit," Shea whispered, resting the tips of her fingers against the damp, heavy stone. She closed her eyes and he could almost *see* magic pouring from the stones into her small, fragile hand.

"You remember," he said, his words nearly lost in the rush of the wind. He could see her not only as she was now, tall and proud, yet still hesitating over her own powers—but as she had been then, on that long-ago night. The coven had gathered here, at the edge of the cliff. Here, where the capstone sang with ancient power.

There were other, more well-known standing stones. Circles of power, of magic, that stretched across the countryside. Today, they drew tourists and would-be scientists, looking to explain the unexplainable. But here, on this quiet cliff in an almost forgotten slice of Wales, stood one of the most powerful of all the stones.

"I do remember," she said, lifting her gaze to his. She turned her face into the wind, staring out at the sea, opening her arms wide, to welcome the gale that seemed to rush toward her. "My blood recognizes this place," she said, as if she could hardly believe what she was saying. "This was where we came to call down the moon. This is where we stood to open the door, the night we doomed ourselves. The night we broke faith with everything we were."

"Yes."

She glanced down at the capstone, and reached out to touch it again. "The magic here is thick, and ancient."

"It is," he said, moving around King's Quoit to take her in his arms. "But it is not Haven."

"No."

"Can you find it?"

She swallowed hard. His witch was worried, Torin reminded himself. Even if he hadn't been able to see her expression, he would have *felt* her distress. She was wound up, her emotions tangled together into a knot of expectation, dread and excitement. The anxieties of the last few weeks were taking their toll.

"I know where it is," she said and lifted one arm to point. "It's there. At Manorbier castle."

He frowned. "The castle itself?"

"Yes."

He looked off in the direction of the twelfth-century castle. The Welsh countryside spilled out in front of them like a dark green quilt, dotted with sheep and hedges and the bright blues and pinks and whites of late-blooming wildflowers. Torin's soul embraced being back in the land where all of this had started. Yet at the same time, he worried, not only for his witch but for the other witches and Eternals awaiting their turn at this journey.

The Norman castle Manorbier had once been the center of their lives. There had been livestock roaming free in the land surrounding the castle and within the outer and inner yards a veritable village had thrived. Now, he knew, it all lay quiet but for the echoes of the past and the ghosts and shades that clung to the brown, bracken-covered stones.

"I need to look at the castle, Torin," she told him and he turned. "There's a darkness down there."

"What do you sense?" His eyes were hard and his expression grim.

"I'm not sure. I can feel something. I'm going to use the magic in King's Quoit to help me with some astral projection and I could use an anchor."

"You have one," he assured her.

She clambered up onto the capstone and sighed heavily as the magic trapped within the stone seeped into her bones. "God, it feels good to be here. To feel this and know what it means to me."

Torin smiled, took her hand in his and held it tightly. "I'm here to guard your body as your spirit flies. Do what you must."

Shea stilled her mind, kept her breathing slow and measured and when she was ready, sent her soul on a search for hidden dangers. The earth fell away from her as she soared through sky and wind. A rush of freedom filled her and she knew that was the real danger of astral travel. You could become so lost in the sensations that you didn't want to crawl back into a body that would feel leaden on your return.

But she was on a mission and as she sailed over Manorbier castle, no more than a thought on the wind, she reached with her mind for whatever was waiting for them.

She felt it first. A smudge of evil like a dirty fingerprint on a white door. She swooped in closer, trusting that her disembodied spirit wouldn't be sensed or noticed.

Men and guns.

Gathered, hidden behind the walls and tumbled stones of the castle. Waiting for them. But how did they know she and Torin were coming? Shea returned quickly to her body. It didn't matter how their enemies knew about them. All that mattered was that the trap they had set wouldn't work now.

She came back with a jolt and looked up into Torin's swirling gray eyes. "It's a trap. There are men with guns down there and they're just waiting for us to show up. They're mostly around the inner yard—which, naturally, is exactly where we have to go."

He helped her off the capstone. "Then we won't disappoint them."

"Right." She nodded and looked from him to the castle far below. "Weird, isn't it? Our past was filled with betrayals and pain—now the present is looking pretty much the same."

"Yes, but we are not the same as we once were, Shea," he told her and pulled her close, holding on to her at the top of the world. "Nothing can defeat us if we stand together."

"We will, Torin," she said, tipping her head back to look up at him. "We do this together."

She was still staring into his eyes as his fire wrapped itself around them both and whisked them to their past.

Chapter 43

The stone walls of Manorbier castle were studded with bracken and the snaking, climbing tendrils of dark green ivy. Long unused arrow slits, like empty eyes, looked down on the modern world, and walls that had once rung with shouts and laughter lay quiet in the afternoon gloom.

Shea took a breath and let the scene sink into her soul. She was *home*, she thought and wondered how she could feel so sure about a place where she'd never been. But the answer was in her heart, her mind. Her very soul recognized this place as her spiritual home. As the land where she had been happiest—until the night everything had changed so drastically, so completely.

She felt the spirits clinging to this place, their energies stamped for all time on the castle that had been home and safety. Shea almost expected to hear the clang of swords as warriors trained in the outer yard. She turned her head to look at the sweeping staircase leading from the buttery to the great hall and imagined servants scurrying to and fro, carrying meals hot from the ovens. She remembered parties in the great hall and the respect granted to her and her sister members of the coven.

Before they turned from their legacy, life had been good here. At this castle, witchcraft was treated with deference. Shea and her sisters had been sought after for potions and healing, to attend births and deathbeds. They were seen as guides to the next world and the coven had protected those within these walls in thanks for the refuge granted them.

"If only we hadn't—" She broke off, looking up at the walls with the ivy creeping along the stones. Taking a breath, she sighed and admitted, "I can't help wondering how things might have been different if we hadn't turned our backs on who we were. On the Eternals."

"Shea . . ."

"No," she said, cutting him off by laying the tips of her fingers across his mouth. Shaking her head, she fought back a sheen of tears that clouded her vision. "I have to think of these things, Torin. I have to realize what I lost. What we all lost while chasing momentary glory, for God's sake. We turned away from everything important to us, thinking that we knew best. That we could control the uncontrollable. We should have mated long ago, Torin. We should have joined. And I'm sorry I held myself back from you."

He caught her hand in his and kissed her fingertips, stroking her skin with his tongue. "The past is gone, Shea. All we have now is the present. And our future if we can claim it."

Staring into those pale gray eyes, she felt his belief in her and clung to it. "We will."

They crossed the wooden bridge and stepped through a short tunnel, stopping just before entering the inner yard. On the left was a "modern" caretaker's cottage that looked to have been built more than a century ago. It was empty, thank heaven, Shea thought, reaching out with her power to scan for intruders. But there weren't any tourists around, for which she was grateful. Because she felt those who waited for them. Felt their tension. Their eagerness to kill.

Staying to the shadows, she whispered, "We have to

pass through the inner yard. Haven is through the great
hall and into the chapel."

"The *chapel?*"

She grinned. "*Through* the chapel."

Torin nodded and said, "Wait here. I'm going to flash
into the yard to draw our enemies' fire so I can pinpoint
their locations."

Shea took a breath and blew it out. Grabbing hold
of his shirt, she said soberly, "Be careful. If you get shot,
I'm going to be seriously pissed."

It was his turn to grin. "I'll remember."

He was gone in a brilliant explosion of flames. An instant later, as if from a distance, she heard a shout, then a
gunshot that shattered the air and wiped away all traces
of the past.

"Stop!" Kellyn shouted at the idiot who had disregarded
her orders and fired his weapon early. In a raging fury,
she reached out to him, fisted her hand and watched as
his eyes bulged and his throat closed. Without air, he
dropped, lifeless, and his weapon clattered to the stones
below. She scowled briefly at the dead fool, then glared
at the chaos in the castle yard. Bullets were flying from
every direction now that the one man had shattered the
silence.

The men sent to do her bidding were scattered all
along the ivy-covered stone walls, each of them with a
clean line of sight into the yard below. Before setting
up this ambush, they had cleared out the caretakers and
chased off the damn tourists.

It should have been simple.

If she had been doing this *her* way, it would have been
over and done.

The men her partner had sent had left their black
SUVs behind the castle on Kellyn's orders, rather than
blocking the old portcullis with them. For God's sake,

they'd done everything but blow bugles to announce their presence. If she hadn't been here to rearrange things, Shea and Torin would never have even approached Haven.

As it was, they'd been alerted to the danger now. There was no hope to salvage the situation. Kellyn looked below and saw that Torin was already moving to fight their attackers. Shea was standing half hidden in the shadow of a stone staircase, lifting her arms, calling on the elements to protect them.

Disgusted at the failure of yet another plan, Kellyn did the only thing that was left to her. Speaking into the radio in her hand, she ordered, "Concentrate your fire on the man. No one hurts the witch."

Bullets chewed up the lavishly tended lawn and spat chunks of stone from the surrounding walls. Rain dropped from the heavens and Kellyn cursed, knowing the storm had been called by Shea.

This was all going to hell too fast.

Shea watched her Eternal flash with dizzying speed from one corner of the yard to another, drawing their fire, never slowing. They couldn't hit him; bullets smacked into stone walls and chewed up the tidy lawn. Finally, he came back to her side with a smile. "We've made our point. They know now we won't be so easy to surprise again."

Reaching for Torin's hand, Shea said, "Bring the fire."

Fingers linked, palms touching, they stood against their enemies, a united front. Shea waved her free hand and murmured a chant.

> *From those who attack us in this field*
> *Moon, my Goddess, fuel my will*
> *Help me create a protective shield*
> *To honor you, no blood will we spill*

An invisible, magically created cloak lifted from the earth, reaching toward heaven, encircling Torin and Shea, protecting them both from the bullets flying around the inner ward of the castle.

As the shield grew in intensity, Torin drew on their combined strength, called up his fire and sent it rushing out in a wall of flame that swept across the yard and into every nook and cranny of the walls. Men shrieked in terror and dove for cover and still the fire roared, flames churning, swimming, seeking the enemy.

The men forgot about their assault in their haste to save their own lives. Bullets stopped. Guns fell to the ground. Rain pummeled the inner ward of the castle, coming down in such thick sheets that Shea and Torin were hidden from sight.

They raced to the great hall and from there, Shea drew Torin to the chapel. As they ran down the passageways beneath deeply carved rock ceilings, their footsteps sounded hollow and like the beat of drums. The walls around them hummed with ancient energies and the swell of power seemed to rush at them from all sides.

At last, though, they came to the far end of the chapel and faced a solid stone wall. Paintings done centuries ago still clung to the walls, faint images of their long-lost glories.

"This is it."

Torin looked at her, then turned for another glance down the long passageway behind them. They were still alone. But for how long, he couldn't guess. "Do what you must, then."

Nodding, Shea held his hand tightly, laid her free hand on the wall before them and whispered, *"Haven."*

An opening appeared before them. Dimly lit darkness was thick in the cavernous space beyond the wall, but there were flaming torches set into silver brackets that sent dancing flame shadows around the room.

Torin stepped in front of Shea, protecting her from whatever they might find beyond the entrance. Walking through the aperture, they stopped when the wall behind them closed again, sealing them into the secret chamber of the last great coven.

"Now what?" Shea whispered.

"Now it begins," a soft, familiar voice called out. "Welcome to Haven. We've been waiting for you."

Chapter 44

Frustrated, Kellyn kicked the body of the man she had killed with a thought, then flipped her phone open. She hit REDIAL and waited. It rang only once before it was answered on the other side of the world.

"Is it over?"

"No, it's not over," Kellyn snapped. She glared across the inner ward at the stone walls of the castle. The Eternal's fire had gone out, but the walls were blackened. "Your men screwed it up. Again."

"Now just one minute . . ."

"No!" Kellyn was so furious sparks of power arced off her body in a shower of dark red lights. "No, you listen to me. This is twice now. I went along because you could draw on certain influential channels that I needed. But we both know that I'm the one who holds the cards here."

"You need me."

"Not as much as you need me—a fact of which you're completely aware," Kellyn countered, finished with being amenable. She had tried playing by others' rules and so far it had gotten her squat. "From here on out, I make the decisions. If and when I need your help, I'll let you know."

"Just one damn minute," her erstwhile partner argued. "We're in this together. I have plans for Shea Jameson."

"I know that." Kellyn stepped out from under the

massive stone wall into the drenching rain. She looked around at the devastation wrought by this little battle and amused herself wondering how the humans would explain away all of the damage.

"So our alliance still holds."

"It does," Kellyn said tightly. She wished she could do without this partner, but she knew that in the modern world, not all power was strictly magical. "But if you send me another moron who won't follow orders, but instead shoots his weapon when he's nervous . . ."

The speaker ignored that and asked, "How many casualties?"

"I don't know." She opened herself up to her surroundings, touching on the trace energies of the men who had set up this clusterfuck of an ambush. "Three," she said a moment later, not bothering to tell her silent partner that one of the dead had been killed by her hand.

"Out of fifteen."

"And we're lucky there were so few." Kellyn shot her gaze again to the main hall of the castle and the chapel beyond it. Shea and Torin were beyond her reach. For the moment. She knew exactly where they had gone and would have followed if she could have. She knew precisely where Haven was.

She just couldn't get in.

Yet.

"What will you do now?"

"Whatever it is, it will be done *my* way," Kellyn snapped and closed the phone, severing the connection. Fury riding her, she stood in the driving rain, closed her eyes and vanished.

"Aunt Mairi?"

A tall, lovely woman with waist-length flame red hair smiled at her. Firelight from the wall sconces flared across her features in light and shadow that made her look ethereal. A ghost. Which was all she could be, Shea told herself. Anything else was impossible. A trick. Or maybe even a trap.

Shea shook her head and threaded her fingers through Torin's. "No," she whispered. "It's impossible. You died. I *saw* you die. I was there. They burned you at the stake and—"

Mairi Jameson smiled and hurried forward. "Oh, honey, don't be scared. It's really me. I didn't die that day. Damyn—" She turned and held one hand out to the man standing behind her, drawing him to her side. "My Eternal saved me. He flashed me out of the fire and brought me here."

"Your . . ." Shea looked up at Torin, who was grinning at the other Eternal. "You know him?"

"I do," Torin said, stretching out one hand to the other man. They clasped forearms and smiled at each other. "I haven't seen him in centuries. Not since—"

"Better we discuss that another time," Damyn interrupted, moving to drape one arm around Mairi's shoulders.

"It's really you," Shea said, still reeling from shock and wonder.

"It's me, sweetie. Really."

"I don't believe this. You're alive." Shea released Torin's hand and rushed to her aunt, gathering her up in a tight, hard hug. "Why didn't you *tell* me?" she demanded, torn between hysterical laugher and tears.

"I couldn't," Mairi explained, pulling back to really look at Shea. "Damyn explained that we had to wait until your powers Awakened and then wait for you to find your way here."

Of course he had, Shea thought. Hadn't Torin waited until she was actually attacked before rescuing her? So he could make sure her powers had Awakened?

"I can't believe you're alive and . . ." Shea took a good

look at her aunt and for the first time noticed just how she was dressed. She wore a one-shouldered white toga-like garment. Gathered at the waist, it fell in a straight column to pool on the floor, dusting the tops of her bare feet. But the most startling thing about the dress was that Mairi's left breast was bare. A mating tattoo of dark red roses encircled her nipple and swirled around behind her back to curl against her spine. Her Eternal's broad bare chest bore a matching brand.

The look was both sensual and powerful. Although Shea didn't know if she could bare her breast like her aunt dared. "You're mated."

"Of course," Mairi said, "and I wear the traditional dress to show both my pride in my mate and in the joining. To let all know that we are one." A frown creased Mairi's features and she reached out to take Shea's hand in a firm grip. "You have mated as well, haven't you?"

"Yes, well, nearly," Shea replied. "It hasn't been a full month yet."

Smiling her relief and pleasure, Mairi said, "Yes, I know." Her gaze touched both Shea and Torin. "Time is running out, Shea, and there are forces lining up against you. Working actively to keep you from completing your quest."

"We know," Torin said shortly. "We were ambushed in the inner ward of the castle."

Mairi glanced at Damyn. He nodded, called the fire and flashed out.

"Damyn will check to see that the intruders are gone. Do you have any idea who they were?"

"They could be anyone. We've been tracked ever since leaving California."

Mairi's eyes looked worried. "I'm afraid our enemies are more powerful than we fully know yet."

"What do you mean? Do you know who was behind this attack?"

"No," she admitted, frowning a bit. "I've scryed, looked into the future and the past, but the enemy masks himself—or herself—too well."

"It doesn't matter," Torin said quietly. "They will not be allowed to stop us."

Mairi gave him a brilliant smile. "You're right, of course, Eternal. Thank you for reminding me. Now, you both must be tired. Why don't you rest and—"

"I don't want to rest, Mairi," Shea told her aunt. "I want some answers. I want to know what's going on and exactly what I have to do."

Mairi's grass green eyes met hers and slowly she nodded. "Very well. We'll talk. Then you'll rest. Come. Let me reacquaint you with Haven."

Shea followed her aunt, keeping her fingers entwined with Torin's. As Mairi talked, Shea felt her own memories thicken like syrup and spill through her mind. She remembered this place. Remembered ancient times, when the walls rang with laughter, when she and her sisters worked spells and gathered knowledge.

She remembered her chambers here. She remembered leaving Haven to meet Torin for sex—just as she recalled withholding herself from the mating. Being unwilling to share her power, even for the chance at immortality. Even with the promise of her own powers growing with the joining.

Her long-ago self had wanted to master her powers on her own. She hadn't wanted to join permanently with her Eternal for fear of losing any part of herself to the joint whole.

And that obstinacy and arrogance had cost her much.

"Don't do that, Shea," Mairi said, sending Torin a quick look, silently asking for some privacy.

Torin looked at Shea, bowed his head and flashed out, leaving the two women alone.

"Do what?" Shea countered, her footsteps echoing

on the stone floor. "Remember? Isn't that what I'm supposed to be doing?"

"Don't look back with anger—it does no good and only splinters your energies just when you'll need them most."

"What about the anger I feel at you, Mairi?" Shea asked, stopping suddenly to whirl around and face the aunt she loved. "Can I remember that?"

"Shea . . ." Mairi's features were concerned, her green eyes filled with regret and sorrow.

"Ten years," Shea said, refusing to be swayed by the intense emotion radiating from her aunt. "Ten years I spent alone. Hunted. Afraid. You were all the family I had left. You're the one who raised me when I lost my parents. I watched you die and I was all alone. I had *no one*, Mairi. I mourned you. I cried for you. And all that time"—she threw her hands up high and looked around at the stone walls shot through with veins of silver—"you were here. With your Eternal. *Safe.* How can I not be angry about that?"

"I don't know," Mairi said, moving in close to take Shea's hands in hers. "I know it's asking a lot of you. I only know you have to find a way to release that anger or it will carve an opening in your soul for the darkness to creep in."

Shea shivered.

"I can't blame you for being furious with me," Mairi said. "But I didn't have a choice, Shea. Just as you now don't have a choice. We are what we were meant to be. We are the chosen. We are the remnants of the last coven. We owe a debt. To nature. To the world. And we must pay it."

Scrubbing her hands up and down her arms, Shea looked around the cavernous main hall. Images dotted the walls—carved from rock and embedded with silver, the magical charms hummed with power.

There were pentagrams, of course, and simple circles as well. Signifying the sacred ring, the circle was the ancient and universal symbol of unity and female power. Then there were circles with a single dot inside at the center, the Bindu, symbolizing the circle as woman and the dot as man, joined as one. There were circles quartered in equal lines of silver, the Medicine Wheel, symbolizing nature and the four elements. There was a carving of a snake, devouring its own tail, meaning life, rebirth.

And there was the spiral. It dotted each wall, over and over again. The silver spiral, Shea knew, was a symbol known all over the world since time began. It represented the female and the birth, growth, death and rebirth of the soul.

All magical. All powerful. The symbols were powerful enough on their own, but defined by the silver of the ancients, they generated a field of such magnitude even drawing a simple breath in their presence seemed to fill the body with strength and courage.

All of which Shea desperately needed.

In the torchlight, the silver winked and glistened as if alive. As if the heartbeats of long-dead witches had been caught in these walls and now they were silent witness to their descendants' actions.

She felt another shiver course along her spine, twisting her with cold, with an icy fear that lingered in the pit of her stomach. All of this power triggered not only her memories of unity and strength but other, darker memories as well. Her mind and soul remembered how she had once been drawn from the light to embrace the dark.

And that small part of her that longed to do it all again grew stronger.

"Shea!"

Mairi's voice brought her up out of her thoughts, but

some of them must have lingered in her eyes because her aunt's features instantly filled with concern. "What is it? What are you remembering?"

"Too much," Shea admitted, as a powerful tendril of fear snaked through her system.

Chapter 45

Cora Sterling paced the Oval Office, her thoughts moving too quickly to allow her to sit behind her desk. "What do you think, Parker?" she asked, sending a quick look at her chief of staff.

Parker Stevens was an old hand at Washington politics. He knew the ins and outs better than anyone else. Who to trust. Who to buy. Who to bury. Cora couldn't imagine doing without his advice.

Or his skills in the bedroom.

"Madam President," he said, "I think it's time you called the prime minister and told him that our escaped witch is in Britain."

She stopped and looked at him from across the room. Impeccably groomed, Parker had steel gray hair, piercing blue eyes and a hard jaw that was, at the moment, locked into an expression of distaste.

"You can't be serious," she said.

"I am. We want Shea Jameson back home, where she can be the figurehead for your reforms." He walked toward her with measured steps. "Our informants tell us she's in England somewhere and unless we get the help of their government, we're going to be hard-pressed to find her."

Cora didn't like that one bit. Turning, she stared out the wide window at the lawn and gardens, looking chill and dank on a late-September day. Summer was finally over and autumn was sneaking in, heralding the coming of winter. Cora felt a like sense of cold creeping over her.

"I don't want to owe Graham any favors," she muttered. "The last time he was here, he put up such a fuss about international internment camps, the press had a field day."

"I know," Parker said, coming up behind her and, showing her a rare touch of affection outside her bedroom, laid both hands on her shoulders. "But we need him. We'll find a way to leverage his help without bowing to the international internment camps."

"You think so?" She looked up at him, unsure until she met his steady gaze.

"I know it. Make the call, Cora. You'll still be in charge. I'll see to it personally."

For one brief moment, Cora allowed herself to react like a woman, and not the president. Leaning into her lover's embrace, she lifted her face for his kiss and then gave herself up to the sensual treats he was so damn good at.

When she finally broke free again, she tugged at the hem of her gray silk shirt and smoothed her hair back. "Parker," she said with a smile, "I don't know what I'd do without you."

He chucked her chin, then took both a figurative and a literal step back, once more becoming her most trusted aide. "Madam President, you'll never have to find out."

"Shea, I know you're feeling overwhelmed—"

"You could say that," she said, cutting her aunt off as she turned to stare at her. "First, Torin told me I was the first Awakened witch. But how can that be if you've been here ten years?"

Mairi smiled, hooked her arm through Shea's and led

her across the great hall. As they walked, she said, "I'm the High Priestess—or I was, long ago. The keeper of the flames. The watcher. A guardian of sorts, of our coven. Of our sisters and traditions."

"High Priestess?" Shea echoed.

"Sounds lofty, doesn't it?" Mairi asked with a small chuckle. "But all it means is that I was once responsible for our coven. It was my duty to see that we learned and grew, and that our coven served its purpose by serving the goddess Danu." She stopped and tears filled her eyes. "I failed. Not only myself, but all of you as well. I surrendered to the same greed and arrogance that the rest of you embraced. It was my responsibility to see that our sisters were given guidance. Helped along the path. I turned my back on all that we were."

"Mairi—" Shea heard the pain in her aunt's voice and all of her own fears and resentments faded away in her need to offer comfort.

"No, I should have filled my sisters' hearts with my love and spiritual guidance. Instead, I left them open to the darkness and then I joined them there." She sighed and a solitary tear spilled down her cheek. "I have much to atone for. As do we all."

"Isn't that why we're here?" Shea asked quietly, patting her aunt's hand in a gesture of love and solidarity.

"Yes, you're right," Mairi answered, smiling through her tears. "I can't tell you how much I've missed you, Shea. To have you here now is a gift beyond measure. And imagine," she added with a grin, "you're the first to come home."

Shea laid one hand on her aunt's arm. "There's another witch who claims to be one of us."

"What?" Confusion was etched on Mairi's features.

"Her name is Kellyn. Torin and Rune broke her out of an internment camp in California when they were looking for me. She says she's an Awakened witch."

"Kellyn's Awakening has begun? But that shouldn't be possible," Mairi murmured. "You were the first, Shea. Kellyn wasn't to come along until later."

"Well, somebody should have told her that," Shea snapped, then instantly regretted it. "I'm sorry. I'm just tired. And scared and worried."

"I know you are, honey," Mairi said, "and I'll do all I can to find out about Kellyn. But until then, come with me. I want to show you something important."

On the far side of the hall, they stopped again and Shea could only stare openmouthed. There was an arched niche carved into the stones and in that arch rested three cages—shaped like old-fashioned bird-cages, but they were made of fire. Living flames, shifting colors from green to red to yellow and blue, danced with abandon across the silver wires that made up the cages.

A memory flickered in the back of her mind and Shea grabbed hold of it. "These are for the Artifact."

"Yes," Mairi said, visibly pleased that her memories were coming back so completely. "Each shard that is returned to Haven will be stored here for safety. Until all of the pieces have been gathered. Then we'll rebuild the Artifact and destroy it magically."

Shea stared at the living flames and felt the enormity of the task ahead of them all. The shards of the Artifact had been hidden all over the world. Each witch was going to have to complete her own quest to retrieve that mystical slice of black silver. And as Shea had already discovered, that wouldn't be easy.

"Do you know where your hiding place is?"

"No," Shea admitted, wondering why that piece of the puzzle was still hidden from her. Why her mind hadn't provided the one link she needed above all others.

"It will come," Mairi assured her, pulling her into a hard, fierce hug. "Here at Haven you'll rest. Gather your strength and your memories will arise."

"I hope you're right," Shea said softly. "Like you said before, we're almost out of time."

In their chamber, Torin stretched out on the bed and watched as his witch stood naked before a mirror. Blood rushed to his groin and desire pumped through him, hot and fresh. He would never have enough of this woman, this witch, he thought. Eternity wouldn't be enough time to sate himself with her.

Her every breath was a seduction. Her touch was fire and passion to the point of madness. Her power shone around her, glistening in a pale yellow aura that throbbed with the beat of her heart.

Soon, he thought, his own heart would finally beat in tune with hers. Soon, they would be linked forever. Joined as they were meant to be joined.

Shea ran her fingers lightly across the mating tattoo on her breast and Torin hissed in a breath, feeling her touch on his own skin. She smiled into the mirror and waved one hand in front of her. In a flash of movement, she was dressed in the traditional garb of a mated witch.

Her left breast was bare, his brand on her skin glowing with a fiery red light. She looked like a princess of old, both demure and erotic, and Torin's body hungered for her.

"I didn't think I'd be able to wear this robe," she said thoughtfully, first watching her own reflection and then meeting his gaze in the glass. "But now, it seems right, somehow. To be here, to be wearing this. To have you with me. It's all . . . right."

"Come to me, Shea," he said, lifting one hand and stretching it out to her. He dissolved his clothing with a thought and nearly groaned aloud at the relief his body felt, being freed from its tight confines.

She turned and walked around the bed to sit on the mattress beside him. Torin lifted one hand to cup her bare breast and she closed her eyes on a sigh as his thumb stroked across the tattoo and her hardened nipple.

"You are magnificent," he whispered, rising up to claim that nipple with his mouth. His tongue and teeth toyed with her sensitive skin, hitching her breath, making her shiver with need, with an all-consuming desire.

He suckled her and she held his head to her breast. Her fingers slid through his hair and he felt each of her fingertips as he would have a match flame against his skin. Burning into him, searing him with the fires they created together. He drew and pulled at her nipple until he felt her body quiver in his grasp. Only then did he release her long enough to grab her at the waist and swing her atop him.

She tugged at the hem of her long white skirt until it was up past her thighs. She wore nothing beneath the traditional robe and Torin reached to stroke her center. Rubbing his thumb across her core in a circular motion, he watched as she knelt over him, rocking her hips in a rhythm he set.

"Take me inside you, Shea," he ordered, his voice thick with the need pressing down on him, strangling him.

Smiling down at him, she did just that, lowering herself, inch by tantalizing inch, to sheathe him inside her body. Damp heat surrounded him and his mind blanked out. All he could do was feel the sensations she aroused in him. Lightning arced between them, sizzling in the air, charging them both with magic, as rich and pure as anything he had ever felt before.

Making love here in Haven, where centuries of magic had lived and thrived, seemed to magnify what lay between them. As they joined, power sang in the air. He looked up at Shea, her branded breast bare, her head thrown back, her long, silky hair lifting in the rush of magic. Her arms swung wide as if accepting a gift being handed to her.

She rode him, rocking her hips to his, engulfing him, taking all that he was inside her—and when her first release crashed down on her, he experienced that torrent of sensation right along with her. Her sheath fisted around him, holding him tight, squeezing him until at last Torin gave himself over to the undeniable force of the last stages of the mating ritual.

The next few days passed in a blur of awakened memories and gathering magics. Shea worked with her aunt, practicing the ancient rituals, reacquainting herself with the witch she had once been. But it was more than magic and the ability to wield it. She fought to become a warrior witch, training with both Torin and Damyn. Her aunt's Eternal was strong and patient and between him and Torin, they managed to give Shea the rudiments of self-defense in an extremely short amount of time.

And through it all, Shea grew and expanded. Her mind, her heart, her soul, all responded to being within Haven's walls again. It was as if she was reconnecting, not only with her former self but with her sister witches. The women who had gone on before her.

Etched into the passageway walls that snaked throughout Haven in a dizzying maze of corridors and rooms were images of long-dead witches. Their features carved into stone and outlined in silver, they seemed to look out on the present from the mists of the past. Their gazes were fixed and compassionate. When she recognized her own features from past incarnations carved into the wall, Shea felt a sense of continuity. She had been here before and now she had returned. This time, she thought as she looked into those faces of the past, the coven would redeem itself. This time, the memories they made would be of pride and fulfillment.

There was safety here in Haven, she thought, sitting near the fire in the chamber she shared with her lover—her mate. Tradition. There was a peace that called to Shea even as she prepared to leave to complete her quest. And there was Torin.

Above and beyond all else she was feeling, there was her connection to her Eternal. This man for whom she would risk anything. This man from whom she was hiding her darkest fears.

"Shea," Torin whispered in the firelit darkness, "you should be sleeping."

"My dreams woke me up," she said, not adding that it was the dark thrill that had called to her soul, had shot her from a dream-filled sleep into a guilt-induced terror.

He left the bed, came to her and knelt at her side. "A dream? Tell me."

Shea reached for his hand and clung to the hard, solid strength of him. Her fears ratcheted in her chest until drawing a simple breath became a fierce act of will.

"You know," he said, firelight playing across his features. "You know where we must go."

"Yes," she said, meeting his gaze and hoping he couldn't see the dark edge of hunger shining in her eyes. "I know where I hid the Artifact."

"Then we go. First thing in the morning." He stood, drawing her to her feet, to lead her back to bed.

"Torin, wait." She leaned into him, wrapped her arms around his middle and burrowed in close. "Just hold on to me for a minute, will you?"

"For eternity," he pledged, his arms closing around her.

She hoped so, Shea thought, closing her eyes, only to see again the dark images that had awakened her.

Shea saw herself holding her shard of the Artifact high, moonlight glinting off its dark surface. She felt the push of the black silver as it crept along her skin, sinking into her heart, her very bones. She watched helplessly as her eyes and hair turned black.

As her mouth curved into a smile and her hand reached out to strike Torin down.

Chapter 46

The blackened ruins of a long-dead castle stood on a cliff overlooking an angry sea.

Torin had drawn on the magic and in a long series of jumps had flashed them all the way to southeastern Scotland. The trip had taken two days, since they'd rested to ensure that both of their energies weren't overly drained. It would have been too risky to be close to the black silver in a weakened condition—not to mention the fact that they had no idea if their pursuers would once more ambush them.

Shea had worked spells and used astral projection, but she hadn't seen any trouble coming. Only long days and one long night spent in Torin's embrace. The mating sex was richer, deeper now, as if each of their souls had claimed a slice of the other, bonding them so completely that there was no Shea without Torin. No Torin without Shea. As it was meant to be. Their minds were attuned. They didn't need to speak their thoughts to be heard. And still the mating connection continued, incomplete yet overwhelming.

The wind moaned as it ran through the knee-high grasses and across the rocks. A sudden slash of sunlight spilled out from behind a cloud and the baaing of sheep in the fields made the scene seem like a painting come to life.

Only ten miles from St. Andrews and the tourists who streamed through Scotland, this cliffside ruin might as well have been on another planet.

Shea stepped out of Torin's arms and took a deep breath of the cold Scottish air. The scent was familiar, teasing a series of vignettes to spring to life in her mind. A blazing forge with a blacksmith bent over the fire. A maid hurrying down long hallways with fresh linen. A kitchen boy stealing a cookie and dodging a slap from the cook. Tiny things all, taken separately, were no more than a blink's worth of time. Taken together, they were, simply, a lifetime.

"It's still here," she whispered, her gaze taking in both the castle and the cliffs beyond. "I was worried that maybe erosion would have sent the castle sliding into the sea."

Torin stepped up behind her, laid one hand on her shoulder and asked, "The shard is here?"

"Yes," she said, speaking quietly enough that she wouldn't disturb the ghosts still going about their daily business. Even though she couldn't see them, she felt them. Spirits who either couldn't or wouldn't move on, but instead clung tenaciously to the familiar. "It's on the chapel wall."

"A *church*?" Torin turned her in his arms and looked into her eyes. "You put a shard of the Artifact that Lucifer himself was after in a *chapel*?"

She smiled and lifted one hand to cup his cheek. "Hate to use a cliché, but as I recall, it seemed like a good idea at the time." Shea turned to look at the castle again. "I was scared, Torin. After that battle with the demons, we'd literally had the hell scared out of us. We each knew how potent the black silver was and how important it was to hide it where it would be safely kept for eight hundred years."

"And you chose this place." His gaze lifted to sweep

the surrounding area, searching, as always, for a potential threat. "Why?"

Shea looked up at him. "Now it's you who doesn't remember."

He frowned and shook his head. "Remember what?"

"This castle." She swung one hand out to encompass the hulking skeleton of a once-fortified, lovely place. "The Mackay built it for one of his daughters, Nessa. We came to her wedding here one spring. And it was here we first—"

A slow smile curved his mouth as he ran one hand up and down her arm. "I remember now. It was the first time you came to my bed."

"Yes, but it was more than that, Torin—it was the first time I felt completely safe. In your arms, I didn't think about witchcraft or power or knowledge. There was only you."

"If that were true, love, none of this might have happened," he said quietly.

Shaking her head, Shea reached up to hold his face between her palms. This she wanted him to know. To understand, before they set out on the last leg of this quest that would eventually unite them forever.

"It was true, Torin. With you, there was peace and passion and laughter." Her hands dropped and she bowed her head as if subconsciously apologizing for the woman she had once been. "But when I was with my sisters, I forgot everything I had with you. I listened to the demands of my own greed and let what was really important to me slide away."

Turning around, she leaned back against him and stared at the castle where she had found love and then lost it again so long ago. "So when I had to hide the Artifact—keep it safe—I brought it to the one place where I had known safety. However briefly."

"Shea, you had only to reach for me," he said, wrapping his muscular arms around her. "Then or now, I will be here for you. Always."

"I know that," she told him and took a quick, sharp breath, deliberately releasing memories that were as dust now. Time had moved on and she couldn't, no matter how much she wished it, reclaim what had been lost. But if she completed this task, finished atoning for what her earlier self had been a part of, she could perhaps find what she had not cherished nearly enough in the past.

With her Eternal at her side, Shea felt strong. Capable. The threads of their mating were rapidly tying them together and that bond continued to strengthen every day.

Still, she felt something else. Something she had yet to confess to Torin. The dark pulse of the Artifact called to her, as it had so long ago. She felt its pull, like an insistent song repeating over and over again in her mind and heart. It was there, just beneath the surface, tempting, teasing, reminding her what she had felt in that moment of supreme power, just before her ancient world had crashed down around her.

And a part of her wanted it.

Shea swallowed hard and fought the feeling. Fought the instinct that had her clamoring to go into the castle ruin herself to retrieve the Artifact shard. She wanted to be alone with that darkness. To feel the sweet sweep of power rushing through her. And so she kept her secret to herself, hoping that if she ignored it, nothing would happen. Nothing would go cataclysmically wrong.

Taking her hand in his, Torin said, "Let's go and get it. The sooner we're back at Haven, with that thing stored away, the better off we'll all be."

"Right." She nodded, took another deep breath and walked with him across the field and back into her past.

The interior of the ruin looked less picturesque.

Fallen stones tumbled on top of each other and

bracken and ivy were slowly covering everything, like a rich green cloak, dotted with autumn wildflowers. Torin could have simply flashed them to the chapel wall, but there was something about this place, about this task, that had them both preferring to walk.

It was hard going and perhaps that was as it should be, Shea thought. She clambered over huge stones, and with Torin's help, scaled a short wall that looked about to topple. The chapel was at the back of Nessa's castle. Shea remembered the girl's wedding day, when there were flowers gathered and hung from trailing ribbons along the castle walls. Musicians had played, voices lifted in song and whiskey had flowed like water.

Now, only the wind sang through the stones.

"There it is," Shea said, pointing to a wall with chunks as big as her fist missing. "The chapel's through there."

"I remember."

She looked around, worrying at her bottom lip. "It looks as though the doorway's been blocked forever. There are so many stones and vines, we'll never get through there."

"For this," he told her, gathering her close, "we'll call the fire."

She clung to him and when the flames rose up around them, they flashed from outside the walls to within the enclosure. Shea let go of Torin and stepped across the broken flagstone floor. A flutter of noise swept past her and she shrieked in surprise, ducking and covering her head.

"Just a bird," Torin said, looking around. "Doves have built nests in here."

She laughed a little at her own edginess and continued across what had once been a tiny, beautiful chapel. Grass and heather sprouted up from between the stones beneath her feet and the roof was gone, the sky stretching wide overhead.

"Sad," she whispered, remembering it all as it had once been.

"It is," he agreed in a hushed voice as low as her own.

Letting go of memory and the inevitable march of time, Shea turned to the west wall of the chapel. Her gaze landed instantly on a torch bracket. Hanging at a tilted angle because of the shifting of the stones, the black silver she had magically twisted into the shape of a simple tool, still hung where she had left it so long ago.

"That's it, isn't it?" Torin asked the question but didn't wait for an answer. He stalked forward and reached out one hand to grab it.

"Stop!"

He did, turning his head to give her a quizzical look. "What is it?"

How to explain, she wondered frantically. How could she tell him that every beat of her heart, every inch of her skin was compelling her to take that shard of mystical metal. To hold it once more. To feel that heavy darkness draping over her in a wild, sensuous pump of energy and power.

She couldn't even explain it to herself.

All she knew was that she *needed* to touch the black silver. *She* had to be the one to take it from the wall.

"Let me," she said, moving past him to reach up for the bracket she'd forged and hidden so many centuries ago. The burn of power from the Artifact reached for her, as if the metal itself recognized her and welcomed her back.

Shea's fingers closed around it and with a twist of magic she pulled it from the wall, holding it close to her. She felt it then. A burst of black energy that swept through her entire system in the blink of an eye. In the space of a heartbeat, she tipped her head back, clasped the Artifact to her breast and smiled widely at the churning sky overhead. Dark clouds gathered in an instant and thunder rumbled like the call of angry gods shouting down warnings.

But Shea heard none of that.

She was wrapped in the silky strands of a power so immense it stole the breath away. How could she ever have given this up? How was she able to walk away from the pulsing strength slipping into every cell of her body?

How would she ever let it go again? God, the swell of power inside her was unimaginable. She hadn't realized, hadn't known. Her mind raced with possibilities and she smiled.

"Give it to me, Shea," Torin said, his voice harsh and strained.

"One minute," she said, sighing as if to a lover as the black threads unspooled through her veins.

"Shea!"

He grabbed hold of her, giving her a hard shake that brought her up out of the darkness. "What? What is it? We have it. Everything's good," she said.

"No, it's not," he told her, glaring down into her eyes. "You changed. The second you touched that damn thing, you changed."

She twisted free of his grasp, still clutching the Artifact to her with greedy fingers. "What change? I'm still me."

"No. Your hair, your eyes, even your clothes are turning black, Shea! It's taking you over and you're letting it. You *must* resist its call."

No. She shook her head and stumbled back from him. But she risked a glance down and saw that he was right. Her blue jeans were now black. Her dark green sweater was also black and as she shook her head, she saw that her long auburn hair was now as black as night.

"Oh, God . . ." Fear rose up inside her, as thick and rich as the power she felt simmering inside the black silver. This was what she'd known so long ago, she thought.

This battle between herself and the hunger that could corrupt a soul and twist it beyond imaginings. Her heartbeat thudded heavily in her chest as she realized that she was becoming what she once was and couldn't stop it. Couldn't end it. Couldn't seem to pry her fingers off the Artifact.

"History's repeating itself, Shea," Torin said, his voice sharp as a blade, his pale eyes locked on her face.

Shea looked into his gaze and saw her own reflection staring back at her. But this was the face of a long-dead witch. One who'd gambled and lost. One who had so endangered her soul, she'd set herself on an eight-hundred-year journey of atonement. And for what? So that she could make the same mistakes over and over again?

A battle rose up within her. A battle for supremacy.

The witch against the power of the Artifact.

Against her own hunger.

Chapter 47

Shea's terrified gaze fixed on his. "Torin, it's much stronger than it was in the old days. It's as if it's been gathering power through the centuries and the longer it was here, unused, untapped, the stronger it became."

"You must fight it, Shea," he told her, coming toward her, one slow step at a time, as if sneaking up on the magical metal she held so closely. "If our mating bond is shattered before completion, if you pull away from me now, both of our souls will die."

She hadn't known that, but she instinctively recognized it as truth. A truth she couldn't allow to happen. She shuddered, a great, wrenching, full-body shudder that snapped her teeth together and locked her bones in a painful grip.

Lightning slashed the sky in jagged bolts. Thunder shook the ruin. Even the ground beneath their feet seemed to roll and quake with the gathering power.

"Take it," she ground out. "Take it from me, Torin."

He looked into her eyes and shook his head. "You have to give it to me freely, Shea. You have to willingly give away that power."

She knew he was right. Her mind was shrieking at her to do it. To uncurl her tight fingers from the black silver. Hand it to Torin and reclaim her own soul from the darkness. But it was so hard to fight her body's demands. Hard to fight against that rush of magic spilling into her.

Shea locked her gaze on Torin's. She gathered herself and concentrated solely on the Eternal in front of her. In his pale gray eyes, she saw love. Acceptance. Loyalty. She clung to the strength of those emotions. She thought of her own journey. All she'd been through in the last month. Her soul felt divided, one half leaning toward the light, the other toward the dark. She was torn, literally, between two desires, each of them as strong as the other.

And there was Torin. Still standing in front of her. Steadfastly watching her with love, with trust. She nodded, reached for her own strength deep within herself and slowly she forced herself to stretch out her cupped hands to him. To painfully open her cramped fingers from around the black silver, which had shifted shape in her grasp, becoming once more a slice of an ancient Celtic knot.

She looked down at the metal lying in the center of her palms, felt herself *yearn*, then deliberately released it.

Torin caught the Artifact, then reached out to grab her as she dropped in a dead faint.

Shea woke up, drew a deep breath and was relieved to feel that she was her true self again. She picked up a long hank of her hair, glanced at it and sighed to see the familiar dark red. "Torin?"

She sat up, looked around the ruined chapel and finally spotted her Eternal in the shadows. "Torin? Are you okay?"

"It is . . . difficult." His voice sounded hollow, different.

Scrambling to her feet, Shea rushed to him, drawing him from the darkness, only to see that the changes that had overtaken her were now affecting him. His familiar gray eyes were black as pitch. His hair was even darker than before and his clothing too was night black. "Oh, God."

Had he saved her only to lose himself?

He kept one hand fisted around the Artifact and she knew the burn of power he was experiencing. She reached for him and wasn't dissuaded when he lurched backward, away from her touch. Insistently, she laid one hand on his broad chest and let the connection between the two of them strengthen him.

"You have to drop that thing, Torin," she told him, her gaze searching the black pits of his eyes, looking for a flicker of recognition there. "Let it go. Now."

"One of us must carry it back to Haven," he insisted, lines of strain etching themselves into his features. "Better me than you. We've already seen it affects you far more deeply than it does me. I can survive it."

He was fooling himself. The changes sweeping through him might be happening more slowly than they had with her, but they were just as damaging. Just as dangerous.

It was as if he were far away from her already and Shea knew she didn't have much more time to reach him. She needed to get him to listen to her, as he had her. Sliding her hand up to cup his cheek in her palm, she shook her head and whispered, "We'll find a way, Torin. But we can't hold it. Neither of us can."

He closed his eyes and she felt the battle raging within him. He was drawing not only on his own formidable strength but their combined essences to fight his way back from the dark.

"Look at me, Torin," she said softly, waiting until his eyes opened and fixed on her. The blank, empty stare was unsettling, but she refused to be cowed. He had saved her; she could do nothing less for him. "You have to drop the Artifact. We'll solve this. But I need you with me."

He hissed in a breath and held it, caught in his lungs. She watched as emotions flashed across his face so quickly that it was hard to identify one from the other. All she knew was that she needed him. Wanted him. *Loved* him.

She hadn't once said that word. Not to him. Not to herself. She'd hidden from it, like a coward. She'd become his mate, become his partner and still had withheld that word. Why? To maintain that one last link to the self-sufficient person she had once been? Was it fear? Was it cowardice? God, she hoped not. Just as she hoped that confessing to him now would be enough to release him from the grip of dark magic.

"I love you, Torin," she said, her eyes shining with promise. "Do you hear me? I *love* you. Come back to me now."

The Artifact hit the stone-littered ground with a hard thump and Torin swayed unsteadily as the black power drained from him as quickly as it had stolen over him.

He gave a harsh, short laugh and scraped one hand over his face. Then his eyes shifted to hers and Shea released a pent-up breath when she saw the swirl of gray that she knew and loved.

"The bloody thing's a trap," he said, reaching for her, pulling her into him so tightly she could hardly breathe. "Carrying it back to Haven's going to be a challenge."

"Can we shift it, magically? Maybe use a spell to transport it back separately?"

"God, no," he said, burying his face in the curve of her neck. "I don't trust the damn thing one bit. Who knows how it might react to a spell? It's so powerful, Shea. I had no idea."

"You beat it, though," she murmured, nestling against him.

"Because of you." He captured her face between his

palms and turned her eyes up to his. "Because of what you gave me."

His gaze moved over her features like a caress. She felt the tenderness welling up inside him and everything in her responded.

"I felt your love," he said, "and that was enough to draw me back from the edge. Without you . . ." He shook his head and shifted to glance at the shard of black silver lying at their feet. The green grass around the Artifact was now brown and dead. As if just the touch of that dark magic was enough to suck the life from the ground. "I understand now, I think. What you and the coven felt so long ago."

"It's seductive," she whispered, her gaze, too, fixed on the knot of black silver. Even knowing what she knew, she had to fight to keep from reaching for it. From fondling it. From feeling the black rush of energy swimming through her veins again.

"More than anything I've ever known before." He tucked her in close to him again and wrapped his arms around her, seeking comfort, or offering it. "In the past, we, the Eternals, couldn't comprehend how you could all turn your backs on what was right and just, for the sake of the promise of more power. But now . . ." His arms tightened like steel bands around her.

"I know. And a part of me still yearns for it," she admitted at last. "I haven't wanted to say anything to you about this, Torin. But ever since we arrived in England, I've felt it so strongly. The Artifact calling to me. Whispering to me. And something inside me is listening."

His fingers threaded through her hair and held her head to his chest, as if by the strength of his will, he could keep her safe. Deny the very words she was confessing.

"But you didn't listen, Shea. You let it go. That counts as well."

"I hope it's enough," she said. "Because this thing is like nothing else on earth."

"It devours your soul, one nibble at a time. It's as if it's happening so fast and yet so slowly, you can't even see what it's doing to you until it's too late."

She heard the wariness in his voice and she shared it.

"How are we ever going to carry the damn thing back to Haven safely?"

He took a breath and let it out again in a rush. "I have an idea about that. But it will still be dangerous."

Shea squeezed him tightly, burrowing in close, as if trying to crawl inside his body completely. "It's not like we have a choice, Torin."

"True enough." He gave her one last, hard hug, then released her. "Let me tell you what I'm thinking. Then we'll go."

Kellyn was waiting.

She hated Wales.

Hated the cold. The wet. The wind.

Frustration and fury bubbled together inside her, creating a stew of dark emotions that rose up and threatened to choke her. But her strength of purpose, her will, conquered those more intransigent emotions and beat them into submission.

She wasn't about to let her own eagerness ruin a well-thought-out plan. This time it was her plan, done her way.

If she failed—which she deemed impossible—she would have no one to blame but herself. And better that way than having to deal with incompetent morons, no matter how well motivated.

Rain suddenly poured from a leaden sky, drenching her in seconds. Irritated and now soaked, Kellyn waved her hand and created an opulent cave in the side of the mountain. God knew it wasn't a five-star hotel, but she couldn't afford to leave the proximity of Haven. Her scrying mirror told her Shea and Torin were on their way back. If she missed them . . .

She shook her head, provided clean, dry clothes for herself, then created a fire. Easing down onto a make-shift bed of silk pillows and warm blankets, she watched the flames, losing herself in the mystic call of fire and darkness.

Chapter 48

The fire cage Torin constructed to contain the Artifact was a huge drain on his energies.

Especially since he had not only to cage the black silver but also to flash himself and Shea back to Haven. Their return trip was taking much longer. Even his strengthened powers were no match for the black silver. The jumps were shorter and the breaks to rejuvenate themselves were longer.

He glanced at his witch, read the fatigue in her green eyes and knew that her powers as well were being drained. They were linked so closely now, it was their combined energies being used to safely transport the Artifact to Wales. And the journey was taking its toll on both of them.

He hated knowing what this was doing to her and hated more the fact that he could do nothing to change it. Without their working together, the Artifact would never get back to Haven. He turned his gaze on the damn thing, resting on a now blackened rock beneath one of a pair of yew trees. They no longer set it on the ground, not knowing if the magic spilled into the earth or just blackened the patch of grass it rested on. Instead, they set it on rocks or suspended it from tree limbs with rope they fashioned magically.

Anything to keep from actually touching it. The effect it had on them was too severe to risk exposure to it again. Even with their combined magics, they might not be strong enough to resist its lure.

"We're nearly there," Torin said quietly, his voice barely carrying over the hiss and spit of the campfire between them.

They hadn't risked staying in a hotel or a B and B. Not only were they in constant danger of being pursued or attacked, but carrying the Artifact was an invitation to disaster. So instead they had camped alongside a river just inside the border of Wales. By morning they would be at Haven. Despite their flagging magical strength, Torin was tempted to continue on, get this business done. But he didn't dare chance it.

If Shea needed him, he must have his full powers to draw on.

"I know," she said, deliberately avoiding looking at the Artifact.

Torin understood. He too felt the pull of the dark reaching for him and she must feel it even more so. Shea was a direct descendant of its creators. A single link in a long chain. It reacted to her presence like a living thing and maybe, he thought, that was exactly what it was. Created from the breath and magic of the original coven, it was brought to life by the powers of the universe. Was it so hard to imagine that over time, it would grow stronger?

Become something else?

That thought was more disturbing than he liked.

Shea's gaze moved over open fields and a lake where the reflection of the nearly full moon shone like a spotlight from the heavens. Then she lifted her eyes to the sky and the moon itself, high overhead. "It's almost full now. Tomorrow, our month is gone."

"And we've succeeded."

"Have we?" She flicked an uneasy glance at the Artifact and worry glittered in her green eyes. Rubbing her hands up and down her arms as if to fight off a soul-deep chill, she reminded him, "That thing is still here. Its temptation is still buzzing around us. We haven't gotten it to Haven yet. Anything could happen. For all we know, there's another ambush aimed at us right this minute."

"We're safe here, Shea."

She looked at him. "How do you know?"

He moved around the fire to sit beside her, then drew her onto his lap, wrapping his arms around her. Leaning back against the gnarled trunk of one of the centuries-old yew trees, he said, "We set up wards, remember? No one can see us. No one will find us. Between both of our magics, we're safe."

"But that thing," she argued, refusing to look toward the Artifact again, "it doesn't want to be locked up, Torin. I can feel it."

"Whatever it is, it won't beat us," he said, tipping her chin up to look directly into her eyes. "Not if we stand together."

"How can you even trust me?" she asked. "I touched it and changed."

"As did I," he reminded her.

"Yes, but you didn't *want* the change. That's the difference—I did," she admitted. "At least, a part of me did. The same part that still wants to grab that thing and use it as it was meant to be used."

He shook his head and slid one hand beneath the hem of her shirt. His fingers unerringly found the tattoo encircling her breast. She shivered as he stroked each individual flame and teased her nipple until she wanted to squirm in need.

"How can I *not* trust you?" he countered. "You felt the pull of it. Your body and heart changed beneath its magics and still you resisted. You turned your back on what it promised. You *chose* atonement. You chose to do the right thing and you always will."

"I wish I were that sure," she admitted.

"You should be," he insisted. "You're not the witch you were so long ago. You've grown through the centuries. Your soul has been tested time and again and always you have met the challenges you faced with your head high and your honor intact."

She smiled and leaned her head on his shoulder while his fingers continued to caress her branding tattoo. "If I remember those past lives correctly, it was pretty close a time or two. I didn't always want to do the right thing."

"True," he acknowledged. "But you *did*, whether you wanted to or not. I was there, remember. Even when we weren't physically together, I was there, watching over you. And I saw your growth. I saw you fight to become the soul you are today. I have no doubts about your heart, Shea. How can I?"

She sighed softly and felt just a tiny bit of the weight on her shoulders slide free. "You make me feel as if it's all going to work out. As if I really am who you believe me to be."

"Trust me in this, Shea. You are a part of me." He nudged her face up so that he could look into her eyes and she could read the truth of his words shining out at her. "You are the best part of me. We are one and nothing will ever divide us again."

He bent his head to claim a kiss and Shea met his passion with a rising one of her own. It wasn't just desire pushing her, though; it was a need for tenderness. For the feel of his love wrapping itself around her, blanketing her in the warmth of the strongest magic of all. She linked her arms around his neck and leaned into him, feeling the burn of the branding tattoo on her breast and along her spine.

She accepted his need and offered him hers.

Sighs and whispered promises filled the air. And when their bodies as well as their spirits joined beneath the soft, pearly light of the moon, it was as if the goddess herself blessed them.

Yet still the Artifact shone darkly, its menacing promise alive in the night.

It was time.

Kellyn set down the scrying mirror, uninterested in watching Shea couple with her Eternal. She had seen what she needed to see. The first shard of the Artifact was free of its prison and on its way to *her*.

The very weave of the universe trembled at the possibilities spreading out before her. Even from a long distance, Kellyn felt the lush, dark call of the black silver.

She smiled to herself, hugging the nearly erotic sensation of power to her as she would have a lover. The magical metal created by the coven and lusted after by demons would soon be hers—and her hands literally itched to hold it.

Dousing the fire in her shelter, she leaned over and bathed herself in the coiling, shifting, thick black smoke, allowing it to seep into her pores. It filled her soul, not with the brightness of the light but with the absence of it. With the power of extinguishment. This was where the real power lay.

In the blackness.

In the shadows.

Night crept closer, now that the fire held nothing at bay, and Kellyn welcomed it.

The stain on her soul spread and she rejoiced in the inky crawl of it. She'd waited long enough. It was time to begin her own quest.

And the first order of business was to enlist Shea Jameson. She had no intention of turning the Awakened witch over to her partner or the Seekers or anyone else.

She'd only used them to get what she wanted and what she wanted was Shea. And then the rest of the Awakened witches. To help her claim what the coven had given up so long ago.

To finish at long last what had begun centuries past.

To accept the dark, open the Hell gate and welcome a new lord and master.

Manorbier castle stood silent and empty in the hush of dawn. Over the sea, the sunrise spilled slowly across the sky in dazzling color that brightened with each passing moment.

Torin and Shea stood together in the inner ward, surrounded by the heavy stones of their joined past. The castle was testament not only to the passage of time, but to the enduring legacy of man. And here Shea and Torin would add their efforts to that legacy. They would, at last, set the past right and claim eternity.

Shea held the fire cage in an uneasy grip. She wouldn't be able to relax until the black silver was inside Haven where it could do no more damage.

"We made it," Torin told her, as if sensing her trepidation.

Another voice, unexpected, spoke up. "Took you long enough."

Chapter 49

Shea whipped around at the sound of that impatient feminine voice. A woman stepped out from beneath the still-elegant curve of stone stairs sweeping up to the chapel. She was dressed in silk and denim and her short black hair was spiky, making her look almost elfin.

Until you looked into her eyes.

"It's you," Shea said, clutching the Artifact, still secure in the fire cage Torin had forged in Scotland. This was the woman she had seen studying them in a scrying glass. This was the woman who had done everything she could to trap them. To stop them. "You've been watching us all along."

Beside her, Torin stiffened. "I should have left you in that prison."

"Yes," she said amiably, "you should." Then she turned her gaze on Shea. "My name is Kellyn. But why not ask your Eternal who I am? He knows me."

"Kellyn?" This was the witch who awakened when she wasn't supposed to? Shea spared Torin a quick glance, somehow uncomfortable at taking her gaze away from the woman.

He stepped in front of Shea, moving to put himself between her and any possible danger. The dark-haired witch chuckled at the action.

"What are you doing here?" Torin demanded.

Shea sensed the tension in him. Every muscle in his body tightened, coiled, as if he were preparing to spring into attack. Shea stared at their adversary and had to admit she didn't *look* dangerous. But there was an air of darkness surrounding her that sent warning bells ringing in Shea's mind.

Torin kept his gaze fixed on the other woman. "What do you want here?"

Kellyn laughed dismissively and one eyebrow winged up.

Shea watched her. "Mairi told me that you weren't supposed to have come into the Awakening yet."

"Not everything moves to the schedule of the grand dear High Priestess," Kellyn mused, her eyes sliding toward the stone staircase behind her that led to the chapel.

Shea followed the woman's gaze, half expecting to see her aunt Mairi step through the open doorway. The last time Shea and Torin were here at the castle, they'd had to avoid the ambushers and race through the great hall to the back wall of the chapel to gain entrance. Had Kellyn arranged that trap? Probably. She had been working against them from the beginning, Shea realized.

"No men with guns today?" she asked.

"I don't need guns." Kellyn sneered and shook her head. "That ambush was not my doing."

"And we're to believe you?" Torin taunted.

Shea touched him briefly and felt his anger pumping through him. "What do you want, Kellyn? Why are you here? Now?"

"What do I want? Where should I begin?" She laughed, then changed the subject entirely. "How is Mairi?" she asked, her tone clearly indicating that she didn't give a damn. "Still pontificating? Still warning all and sundry about the evils of too much power? Don't suppose she bothers to recall that she too gave in?" Kellyn laughed again. "Remember, Shea? How she sent all of us out into the world, hiding shards of the Artifact?"

"Of course I—"

"But not her," Kellyn mused, moving closer. "Not the great High Priestess. She didn't have to go tromping off on an adventure. No, she just sat back and gave orders." Her features tightened and her pale blue eyes flashed with temper. "Well, I don't take orders anymore and neither should you."

Shea's mind tumbled with broken bits and pieces of the past. The days after that last battle with the demons had been filled with pain and torment and regrets. When together, they broke the Artifact, they had decided, all of them, to cast the spell of atonement and go out into the world, hiding the shards of black silver. Mairi hadn't given any orders. Not that Shea remembered anyway.

"You're not here to talk about the past, Kellyn," Shea said. "So why not get down to what's really brought you here?"

"You've no business here," Torin thundered, gaze fixed on the woman. "Leave now and there'll be no trouble."

"I'm here to talk, Eternal," she said smiling, lifting both hands as if in surrender.

Shea shouted a warning, convinced the dark-haired witch was going to use magic against them. "Torin!"

"Oh, relax!"

Torin didn't move. He was a pillar of strength. Coiled power. "What are you doing, Kellyn? If you think to harm Shea, know that I will kill you, Awakening be damned."

Shea's heart swelled with pride in him. Strong, relentless, and more powerful than ever thanks to the mating, Torin would be a much more formidable opponent than Kellyn realized.

Shea rested one hand on his back, covering the

branding tattoo so that he would feel the burn of her magic sliding into him.

"If I wanted her dead, Eternal," Kellyn said with a shrug, "she'd be writhing on the ground at your feet."

The easy, casual way she said it did more to convince Shea than any demonstration of power would have. There was something evil about this witch. Something deadly. Dangerous. Magic flared in her eyes and shimmered around her in a dark red haze as if it were all too much for her body to contain.

Torin speared the woman with a hard glare and spoke quietly. "Shea. Go to Haven. Take the Artifact to safety."

"That would be a mistake," Kellyn said.

"And why's that?"

"I'm sorry." Kellyn glared at Torin. "Did you assume I was talking to you?"

"Fine, then," Shea said, stepping out from behind her lover before he had a chance to let his anger explode. "Talk to me."

"Shea—"

"No, Torin. It's fine," she assured him, keeping her gaze fixed on Kellyn. "She won't hurt me."

"You know this how?" he demanded.

"Because she needs something from me," Shea told him, tipping her head to one side to study the woman looking at her.

"Aren't you the perceptive one?" Kellyn's mouth curved as she folded her arms across her chest.

"Not really," Shea said, keeping her grip tight on the Artifact within the fire cage, since she half expected the witch to make a grab for it. "You're not exactly subtle, Kellyn. You've been scrying on us for weeks. If you didn't want something from me, you would have killed me already. Or at least you would have *tried*."

"You know," the other witch said, "I always liked you, Shea. Back in the day, we were friends."

Somehow, Shea doubted that. This woman didn't have friends. Only people she used.

"That was then, this is now. So what do you want?"

"To make you an offer."

"Not interested."

"Too scared to hear me out?" Kellyn laughed, delighted. "So, eight hundred years pass and you're still the tentative one."

"Nothing tentative about the word 'no.' You don't know me," Shea said, taking a step farther away from Torin. "Eight hundred years is a long time. I'm not that woman—that witch—anymore."

She distanced herself physically from Torin so that she and the other witch were on more common ground. She didn't know what else was coming, but she had the distinct impression that it would be decided between the two of them. No Eternal was going to be able to help her now.

This was magic to magic, witch to witch.

And Shea knew, with a sinking sensation that dropped into the pit of her stomach like a ball of ice, that her powers were no match for Kellyn's. Even with the mating, she didn't have the strength Kellyn did. And that thought worried her. If Kellyn wasn't Awakened, how did she have so much magic churning inside her? Power rippled off the other witch in thick waves that were hard to miss. If Shea didn't do something to alter the balance between them, Kellyn would win.

She glanced at Torin. *Please. Just be still and let me deal with her.*

No. She's too dangerous.

This is for me to handle, Torin. Shea sent that last thought firmly, then shut her mind to him. She needed to focus on Kellyn. To prepare for whatever might come next.

"Talk him into butting out, did you?" Kellyn asked. "Good."

Shea knew the risks in this. If Kellyn killed her with the mating incomplete . . . hadn't Torin told her that their souls would die? Trepidation rose up inside her, but she pushed it down and steeled herself for what was about to happen. Too much was riding on her success to take any chances at failure. And there was only one sure way to give herself the edge she needed.

The morning air sparkled with promise. The sea crashed into the cliffs below, sounding like the heartbeat of the world—thunderous, impossible to ignore. Here, they had once traded the world's safety for their own greed.

Now, a time for the choice was here again.

And Shea would make the only choice she could.

"Shea, don't do this," Torin said, his voice low and compelling.

"I have to," she answered and snapped her fingers.

Instantly, the fire cage disappeared and the Artifact shard lay in Shea's palm. She swayed with the fierce release of its dark power into her system. It swelled inside her, erupting with the force of a long-dormant volcano at last allowed to show the world what it was made of.

Every cell in Shea's body eagerly drank in the energies pumping through her. As if from a distance, she heard Torin's shout and Kellyn's delight. But they didn't matter. Nothing but the rich, intoxicating buzz of something *more* inside her mattered.

"By the moon, I envy you," Kellyn whispered, stepping closer. "I've waited so long to touch it again. To feel that rush again. Let me just . . ."

Shea shot her a look of contempt and held up one hand to keep her at bay. "Stay where you are."

Kellyn's eyes narrowed thoughtfully. "Greedy, huh?" She shrugged. "Well, who can blame you? I wouldn't want to share it either."

Her now black hair flying in the wind, Shea fought

to hold on to who she was in the face of who she had once been. "It's not yours to share. It's not mine, either. It goes back to Haven. Where it belongs."

"Don't be stupid," Kellyn snapped. "Do you know what you're holding? Do you remember what it was like to command such dark forces?"

"I remember what it was like to lose control of it," Shea told her, trembling with the battle to hold on to her soul. Her heart.

The wind kicked up, howling, swirling around the three people in the inner ward of the castle. Cold dripped from the stone walls surrounding them like the spread of frost.

Shea's fingers tightened around the black silver and the element took a stronger grip on her as well. It whispered through her mind of glories to come. Of battles to be won. Of victory and more power than any witch had ever before claimed.

She heard it all and fought anew to retain knowledge of who and what she was.

"Think about it Shea," Kellyn said, her voice as musical and compelling as a chant. "Think of how the world has changed in eight hundred years. Think how much more we could have now. Think of the dynasty we could build. Together. The black silver craves us as we need it. We are blood-bonded, the coven and the Artifact. Each of the other, we are pieces in a puzzle, incomplete unless joined."

"She's lying to you, Shea."

Shea heard Torin, but her soul listened to Kellyn.

"We can be gods, Shea," the witch said, moving closer still until they were only an arm's reach apart. "Danu created the witches. Belen created the Eternals. We can be bigger than either of them. Mortals don't understand real power. But they will. Don't you see? We can harvest the darkness for ourselves. We can be what we always were meant to be . . ."

Shea swayed and locked her knees to keep from toppling beneath the onslaught of images racing through her mind. Dark, terrible, glorious images of witches running the world. Leaders of nations. No longer hunted, but the hunters. No longer held beneath the thumb of humans who couldn't possibly understand what the witches really were.

"And our souls?" Shea finally managed to ask, fixing her gaze on the witch in front of her.

Kellyn's eyes glittered with victory, excitement. She felt Shea weakening and was rejoicing in it. "With enough power, we can enchant a spell of immortality and live forever. Who cares about a *soul*? I'm offering you everything. All you have to do is reach out and take it."

Shea shifted a look at Torin and read his expression. His complete trust in her. How, she wondered. How did he trust her when she couldn't trust herself? Couldn't he hear the irresistible lure of Kellyn's words? Couldn't he feel the pull of the dark power? He'd held the Artifact. Didn't he realize what that black silver was doing to her, even now?

But his pale gray eyes remained steady on her, filled with his unshakeable belief in her.

"Stop thinking about him!" Kellyn shouted, as she clapped her hands together and a man-size cage with white gold bars appeared on the bullet-shredded lawn. The cage bars glinted in the early-morning sunlight.

"What're you doing?" Shea looked from Kellyn to Torin and back again.

"I'm taking care of your problem as I took care of my own," Kellyn told her. "The power's in you, Shea. Force your Eternal into the cage."

Torin tensed as if ready to flash out. But Shea knew he wouldn't do it, not without her. And she wasn't within reach. He wouldn't leave her, no matter the cost. She glanced at him, but kept her hand tight around the black silver still pumping dark energy into her body. The sweet rush of temptation pooled within her and she took short, shallow breaths, relishing all of the dark sensations.

"Do it, Shea," Kellyn demanded. "Then we'll finish our talk."

Chapter 50

Fingers and thumb caressing the smooth, glassy surface of the black silver, Shea whipped her head around, lifted her free hand and aimed her power at Torin.

"Close your mind to her, Shea," he shouted even as he was swept into the cage. Instantly, the white gold barred door slammed shut on him. His eyes flared with fury, but the anger was directed at Kellyn, not Shea. His hands fisted around the white gold briefly, but he let go a moment later, no doubt feeling the drain of his powers. "Damn it, Shea, let me out before it's too late!"

His voice sounded far away, muffled, and Shea knew it was because she was losing herself in the dark magics. She felt as if she were trapped in a slow spiral, traveling ever downward, becoming a part of the darkness itself. And a part of her loved it. Craved it.

Her gaze locked with her Eternal, though, and she somehow managed to gain a tenuous grip on her own inner strength. She looked at Torin, but asked Kellyn, "What happens now? What happens to him if I go along with you?"

He became a pillar of fire within the white gold cage, but the flames were a pale echo of what they usually were. And she knew he would never be free of that cage unless *she* freed him.

"Nothing," Kellyn said, strolling toward the trapped Eternal with a smile on her face. "Absolutely nothing will happen to him. *Ever.*" She tapped her fingernail against the white gold bars and made a face at the instant yet tiny drain on her power. "I did the same to my Eternal. Trust me when I say it works like a charm."

"Where is he?" Shea asked, still fighting the lure of the darkness. "Your Eternal. What did you do with him?"

Kellyn whirled around to face her, a wide grin on her face. "I dropped him into the ocean," she said and chuckled a little at the memory. "Right now, the oh, so pious Egan is enjoying the view at the bottom of the sea."

Shea shot a look at Torin and she saw his eyes fill with pain and fury.

"Remember," Kellyn was saying, "they are of the fire. Water will restrict and dampen their powers and the white gold bars are a continual drain. They can't drown, because they're unfortunately immortal"—she looked disappointed—"but they can be contained. Eternally— no pun intended, of course. You are the only one who can dispose of *your* Eternal, Shea. I'd do it for you, but some things are simply out of my control."

Shea heard the madness in the witch's voice and knew that if she continued to listen to the dark magics taking her over, she would soon be no better.

"You'll see," Kellyn assured her. "Besides, it's not as if we're *killing* the Eternals. We're just putting them where they won't be able to interfere in our business again. And with the mating ritual unfinished, his soul will die and he'll never be a threat again. It's all very easy, Shea," she whispered. "All you have to do is say 'yes.' "

The word echoed in her mind. She tasted it, tasted the aftereffects and looked into her own soul to see if that was who she really was. Her gaze shot to the curve of the stairwell leading to the chapel and Haven beyond. But no one was coming to help them.

This was her test, Shea thought. This was the moment her soul had spent eight hundred years preparing for. The moment when she would discover if she had grown, evolved—or if she was no better than she had been on that long-ago night.

She shifted her gaze to Torin, trapped in a cage, his immense strength and courage locked away by a crazy witch with delusions of grandeur. His eyes shone at her. The emotions he directed at her were clear in his gaze. Faith. Love. Beacons in the darkness where she battled for control of her own destiny.

I love you.

His voice rippled through her mind and she felt the power of him within her. The branding tattoo on her skin burned with a fire that reminded her of who she was. How far she had come and how far she still had to go.

Her fingers played across the glossy black surface of the silver she held and she smiled at the Eternal who had so completed her. With his help, she could resist the call of the darkness.

She would not bow down to greed again. She would not play the puppet to dark powers. Would not give up all that mattered in a quest to find the ephemeral. Would not succumb to temptations of the past that would destroy the future she wanted so badly.

"Catch!" she shouted and tossed the black sliver to him. Instantly, he shoved his arms between the bars of white gold, called the fire and captured the Artifact in the flames.

"What are you *doing*?" Kellyn's shriek of fury pierced the air.

"What I have to!" Shea answered, whirling around to lift both hands and push her powers at the black-haired witch. Fire flashed from her raised palms as it had on that first day so long ago. Only this time she was in control.

With a howl of rage, Kellyn disappeared.

Shaking from head to foot, Shea dismissed the witch and raced to Torin. She focused her powers on the locking mechanism and when it sprang free, Torin stepped out of the cage and she threw her arms around him, holding tight.

He held her with one arm while he balanced the Artifact in a ball of flame in his free hand.

"You had me worried for a moment or two," he said finally.

"I had me worried, too," she admitted, kissing his throat, his jaw, then going up on her toes to plant a hurried kiss on his mouth. She could trust him with her whole truth. He had seen her face her demons and win. She grinned up at him, feeling the sweet rush of peace race through her. "But I did it. I'm okay."

"More than okay," he told her, pride shining in his eyes. "Where'd you send Kellyn?"

She looked over her shoulder at the empty inner yard of the castle. "I'm not sure," she said. "My powers aren't cohesive enough to tell yet."

Torin frowned and grabbed her hand. "She's a teleporter. So wherever she is, it won't take her long to get back. We'd better finish this."

Inside Haven, Torin felt his breath leave him as he stared at his witch. She was transformed into something more beautiful than he could ever have imagined. Here, in the sacred halls of Haven, the Artifact was neutralized and the witch who had reclaimed it had become, at long last, what she was meant to be.

Shea wore the traditional robe, baring her left breast proudly as she moved with the regal dignity of a queen. She was the living, breathing epitome of pure, untainted magic. Her hair, skin, clothing were white and glowed with a brightness equaled only by the sun. On her bare breast her branding tattoo dazzled with a flaring, inner light.

She was literally the essence of magic, the power of creation and life. She was *female* in all her power and glory. Her green eyes shone with a strength of purpose he'd never seen there before and his pride in her knew no bounds.

Under the watchful eyes of Mairi, Damyn and Torin, Shea walked slowly across the great hall, lit by the wall torches. Shadows and light flickered wildly around the room, dancing over Shea as she carried the black silver in her cupped hands.

There was no danger now.

She had passed her test.

She had reached Haven.

Without hesitation, she lifted her hands to the first of three fire cages, set the shard of the Artifact into the flames and stepped back. Bowing her head, crossing her hands over her heart, she began to chant.

> *The past is gone*
> *Yet still lives*
> *My test is won*
> *This Artifact I give*
> *I am home where I was meant to be*
> *My debt is paid through eternity.*

The earth shook, sparks erupted from the flames and the bright light that had encompassed Shea slid from her to the cage surrounding the black silver. The flames, enriched by pure magic, burned even more fiercely and the dangerous shard was locked away.

The empty fire cages beside hers flashed with dancing flames and Shea knew that there were more cages behind these first three. All were flashing with fire, all awaiting the Artifacts that would be returned to Haven.

As the light left her, Shea was once again herself and yet so much more. She felt changed, but in a way that made her proud. She'd accomplished what she had set out to do. She'd righted a wrong, found the love of her life and won immortality to boot.

The test had been hard, but the rewards were tremendous.

And she couldn't have done any of it without Torin. Without the other half of her soul. Without the mate who made her life worth living.

She smiled at Mairi and Damyn, inclined her head in a gesture of respect to the once and future High Priestess of her reborn coven, then walked slowly, deliberately, to Torin.

He'd had faith in her even when her own faith had crumbled. He'd remained steadfast and loyal even when she had had no right to ask it of him. He had loved her through the eons and had waited for her to become what he had known she could be.

Outside, the full moon shone down on the castle where all of this had begun so many centuries ago. And in Haven, there was a sense of fulfillment as the first debt was paid.

Shea felt as if she and Torin were the only two people in the world. She wrapped her arms around her mate's waist and held on to him. The warmth of him felt so right. The heat of her bare breast pressed to his naked chest burned through her and she welcomed the mating burn as the tattoo completed itself. With her task finished, the thirty days at an end, the mating was fulfilled.

Closing her eyes, she let the moment register so that she would always be able to draw it up in memory and recall the instant she and Torin had at last become one forever.

She had come so close to losing him that she couldn't bear the thought of being apart from him. Not even for a moment.

"It's done, Shea. Your promise has been kept and you are the most amazing woman I have ever known."

"*Our* promise was kept, Torin. And I am the woman who loves you more than life. More than eternity."

The branding tattoos on their skin suddenly erupted into a flash of fire and heat, scorching them each with an inner blaze of eternal warmth as the images were seared into their skin for all time. Their mating was complete at last.

They each held on to the other and when that blast of heat ended, leaving them shaken but still linked together, Shea rested her head on Torin's broad chest. Smiling, she whispered, "Your heart's beating."

He took her face in his hands and kissed her with the promise of forever between them. "It beats only for you, Shea. And now we have an eternity together."

"It won't be nearly enough," she said, smiling through the sheen of tears blinding her.

"Never enough," he agreed.

Mairi sighed, reached for Damyn's hand and smiled at Shea and her mate.

"Can you feel it?" she asked, her eyes shining with expectation. "The very air shivers. The second sister is Awakening."

Read on for a sneak preview of the
next novel
in the Awakening series,

VISIONS OF SKYFIRE

Coming from Signet Eclipse in
October 2011.

Teresa Santiago opened her arms to the sky as if welcoming a lover. The storm raged overhead, and its energy and power filled her like long-dammed water rushing onto a floodplain. She felt it all and gloried in it. The sweep of sensation, the pulse of strength.

Lightning flashed and its charge slammed into the ground at the feet of the tall woman who stood amid the white-hot bolts like a pagan god.

Snaking across her eyes, whipping around her throat, her long black hair flew out around her in the charged atmosphere. Her fingertips practically vibrated with power as lightning danced to her whims.

Electrified white bolts cracked across the black sky, then forked into the desert floor. Sand geysers erupted all around her as energy sizzled and burned. Thunder roared. Clouds roiled. Juniper and manzanita dipped and swayed with the wind. Behind her, the ocotillo plants waved their skeletal limbs, scraping at her back like a demon demanding attention.

But she ignored every distraction—including her own apprehension. Exhilarating as it was to command nature in such a way, a part of Teresa cringed, horrified at what she was now able to do. The lightning danced, plowing into the earth at her feet, again and again. Every cell in her body sizzled from the near contact. She felt as if she too were electrified, and that small horrified part of her wanted to run and hide from all of this.

But she held her ground. She couldn't turn her back on the very legacy for which she had been in training most of her life. Now that it was here, magic opening up inside her, she would simply have to find a way to master it.

Four days ago, she had had the first dream. A terror-filled nightmare in which flames chewed at her skin while demons howled and crowds cheered. She'd jolted from sleep in a sharp panic, her own hair wrapped around her throat like a noose as she gasped for air that wouldn't come. She had known then that her *abuela*'s prophecies were coming true.

Then the magic appeared. Small things at first. Sparking a match without striking it against something. Approaching the television and it coming to life. Lightbulbs shattering at her touch. Streetlights blinking out when she brushed against the pole.

And today . . . she had followed her instincts, somehow *knowing* that the lightning was calling to her. At the first sight of a storm on the horizon, a deep well of power had opened up inside Teresa, as if it had been waiting for nature's fury to completely awaken. She had driven into the desert outside Sedona, Arizona, to meet that storm head-on. To walk into the maelstrom and somehow master it.

For more than an hour now, she had worked, pulling down the lightning, trying to direct it to specific targets—because what was the point of having the power if she couldn't control it? And in this time, when witches—and even those *suspected* of witchcraft—were being locked away or worse, she needed that control. Her new power would make her a magnet for disaster. She had to be able to draw on her own strengths to protect herself and those she loved.

"Come *on*," she whispered. "Focus, Teresa. Make it work."

Red sandstone rock formations surrounded her. With sunlight slanting across them, the rocks had always seemed to glow a brilliant orange and red. Now, under a forbidding gray sky, they were filled with shadows, their wind-carved surfaces taking on shapes of faces that seemed to watch her.

She was just outside Red Rock State Park and hoping that both the weather and the harsh terrain would keep tourists at bay.

October in Arizona meant cooler temperatures and an influx of the visitors who came to Sedona not only for the natural beauty but to gather at the many vortexes in and around the city. The vortexes were sites of spiritual ceremonies; they drew the mystical and the curious every year. Teresa had gone to a few ceremonies herself over the years, knowing as she did that there was far more to the spiritual plane than most people suspected.

Now, though, she drew on the spirituality of this place to open the heart of her magic. She waved one hand, directing the lightning toward a tower of red sandstone rocks. The jagged bolt of pure power slammed into the ground twenty feet away from the target, and she knew that wasn't nearly good enough. If she were attacked, "close" wouldn't save her life.

Teresa fought to hone her magic. To perfect the power that had begun to quicken inside her only days ago. She had known what was coming all her life. What she was destined for. But the mystery had been *when* her magic would appear. The world wasn't a good place for witches these days, but magic ran in her blood, stretching back through her family's maternal line for generations. She should have been able to draw on that legacy, but in the face of this new and overwhelming power, she was lost.

She stood tall, her cowboy boots planted far apart, to

give her a sense of stability she was sorely lacking. Gritting her teeth, she concentrated and swung her hand out again to direct another whip of lightning across the desert. Instantly, a jagged bolt flew—in the wrong direction.

"No!"

Teresa shrieked as her black truck exploded into a fireball. Flames jumped into the air, plumes of smoke twisted in the wind and flaming tires shot off the body of the truck like Frisbees from hell. As thunder rattled the sky and the wind howled, Teresa stared at the smoking hulk of her truck.

"Son of a bitch." She kicked the sand and thought not only of the incredibly long walk back home she had to look forward to, but also about her now burned-to-a-crisp cell phone. She couldn't even call someone to help her. She was stuck in the desert—no water, no food, no way home.

She'd grown up here, so she wasn't a stranger to the desert. But the thought of a long walk back to town through the rain with the storm chasing her sent her stomach to her knees. Add that to the fact that she couldn't quite shake the feeling that she was being watched . . .

Steeling her spine, she pushed thoughts of unseen watchers to the back of her mind. If they were out there, somewhere, there was nothing she could do about it. The important thing now, she told herself as she stared at the fire, black smoke billowing, was control. Just how in the hell was she supposed to protect herself from the dangers coming if she couldn't manage her own powers?

What good is it to be a witch, she demanded silently, *if you can't freaking control the magic?* Disgusted, she muttered, "Could this day get any worse?"

As if the gods were answering, Teresa heard a distant pulsing beat, like the heartbeat of a giant. The thrumming sound seemed to jolt up from the desert floor to her feet and into her chest, where it pounded along with her own suddenly galloping heart. Stunned, she just stood there, trying to assimilate it when she realized something else.

The sound was getting closer.

She whirled around, her gaze searching, straining to see past her surroundings to whatever was coming. Her own heartbeat was pounding in time to that otherworldly sound. She scanned the dark skies in all directions. The shadows of the craggy mountains jutted up from the desert, scratching at a sky still churning with ragged bolts of lightning.

Thunder boomed, but just beneath that awesome noise and power, there was something else. Something low-pitched and dangerous, like a tight-throated growl from a predator. Fear tightened into a hard knot in her belly. She trembled, swallowed hard and felt her breath catch in her lungs as she found the source of that growl. Against the lowering gray clouds, there was a darker spot.

A blot of black that was headed right for her. An instant later, Teresa identified the heavy, beating sound. The *whup-whup-whup* of helicopter blades churning through the air. Heart sinking, she looked around at the emptiness surrounding her and knew she was in deep shit.

She'd come into the desert to be alone with her burgeoning magic. But being alone also meant that there was no one to help her. Though, if that helicopter was what she thought it was, no one could have helped her anyway.

As the chopper closed in on her, she saw the bright yellow slash across its belly. Black and yellow. The MP's colors. Magic Police. They'd found her. Somehow, they'd found her, and she knew that if they got their hands on her, she might as well be dead.

A captured witch had little hope of escape and every expectation of execution. Though not until after torture and imprisonment, of course. Fear nearly choked her. She wasn't ready for this confrontation. She'd had no time to prepare. To conquer her magic and make it work for her.

The power she had been relishing only moments ago now felt like an anvil tied around her neck. She was about to be captured, and there wasn't a damn thing she could do about it. She couldn't even hop into her truck and make a run for it.

She had no weapon and the helicopter was even closer now.

Weapon.

She didn't need a weapon; she was a weapon.

"Now's the time, Teresa," she muttered, instantly lifting both hands high over her head. All around her, lightning danced, pulsed. The air was scorched from thousands of volts. Her hair lifted in the wind; her eyes narrowed on the helicopter. She stabbed one hand toward it, and a lightning bolt sizzled past the black beast, barely missing it. The chopper dodged, dropping several feet in an instant and turning slightly to allow someone to stand in the open doorway.

Someone with a gun.

"Damn it!" Teresa dove for the ground as the first crack of bullets chattering from the automatic weapon enveloped her. Still too far away, she thought wildly, but not for long. She ran toward an outcropping of sandstone rocks. *Yes, there might be snakes in there,* she thought, *but out here, there are bigger dangers.* She crouched behind a sand-encrusted boulder and jabbed her hand at the chopper again. And once more, lightning split the sky, racing to do her bidding. But it still missed the damn target.

"Teresa Santiago!" a voice shouted over a bullhorn. "Surrender now or we will kill you."

The thunder crashed, and the helicopter blades

sounded like the heartbeat of a hungry beast. Closer now, those same blades were churning up the sand, throwing it at her, stinging her skin and her eyes. She couldn't even risk turning her back to the flying sand since that would mean turning her back on her enemies. Every second that passed brought them ever nearer, and Teresa knew she had run out of time. There was no escape. She glanced around at the wild emptiness surrounding her and saw no options.

"Die here," she murmured frantically, "or die in prison. Not much of a choice."

So she did the only thing she could do. She stood her ground and threw yet more lightning at the men who had somehow followed her into the desert. Bolt after bolt shot toward the helicopter headed directly at her, yet none of them hit. Desperation fueled her movements, and she knew that her aim was only getting wilder but she couldn't do anything about that now.

How had they found her? How did they even *know* about her?

Fury laced her fear and somehow tangled in the threads of her power. She felt something new . . . something *old* that pulsed within her. Then it strengthened. Staring hard at the incoming helicopter, she sent one more bolt of lightning at her enemies, and this time she scored a hit. A small jagged bolt slapped the tail rotor of the chopper, sending the machine into a wild spin. Torn between elation and fear, Teresa watched as the pilot struggled for control. She didn't *want* to kill anyone, but damned if she'd stand still to be shot, either.

The pilot recovered, the chopper continued on and the gunman took up position again. Teresa braced herself for the inevitable.

She looked up into the face of death—the incoming chopper—and she lived.

A wall of fire appeared in front of her, and the bullets flying at her embedded themselves into the flames instead. Teresa staggered back in surprise, looked up and met the pale gray eyes of a warrior. Fire surrounded his body, enveloping him in a living wall of flame. His features were drawn in concentration, and his muscled body swayed with the impact of more bullets, but still he stood between her and danger.

"Hold on to me," the stranger ordered.

Teresa didn't even think about it. She jumped into the fire that covered the man, hooked her arms around his neck and shouted, "Go, go, go!"

And in another bright flash of flames, they were gone.

ABOUT THE AUTHOR

Regan Hastings is the pseudonym of a *USA Today* best-selling author of more than a hundred romance novels. She lives with her family in California and is already hard at work on the next installment of the Awakening series.